TRUST ME,
I'M DEAD

TRUST ME, I'M DEAD

SHERRYL CLARK

VERVE BOOKS

First published in 2019
by VERVE BOOKS
an imprint of
The Crime & Mystery Club Ltd
Harpenden, UK

vervebooks.co.uk

ISBNs
978-0-85730-805-4 (epub)
978-0-85730-804-7 (print)

Printed and bound in Great Britain by Clays Ltd, Elcograf S.p.A.

For my mum

1

Potatoes hate the light when they're growing. They prefer mounds of rich dirt, piles of compost, a hiding place deep beneath the surface. Potatoes were my favourites, and I liked to give them exactly what they craved.

The early autumn air was crisp, and I could smell windfall apples rotting sweetly under the trees. I knelt by the rosemary bush, tore off a sprig and rubbed the thick little leaves between my fingers, inhaling the tangy smell. My week had been filled with the remnants of summer, pulling out the last tomatoes and getting ready for beetroot and silver beet. I fetched my spade and fork from the shed and started work.

Digging the rich brown earth, forking in manure, pulling out weeds were all things I regularly submerged myself in, and gradually the sticky strands of my life dropped away until all that was left was the ache in my hip. The doctors said it would never mend completely after my 'fall' down the cellar stairs, and they were right. But this little town I'd found was the perfect place to become a recluse and, at forty-three, that had become my life's purpose. I wasn't happy, but I wasn't depressed and sad and angry anymore. That's what I tried to convince myself, anyway.

I stopped briefly for a cup of hot tea, and kept working. I sharpened the spade with a file and dug deep into my compost heap, readying the potato patch like a nurse making a bed, so focused on the neat row of piled dirt that I never heard Connor's approach.

When he tapped me on the arm, I swung around with the spade and sprayed his creased blue police trousers and sturdy shoes with compost.

'Shit, thanks, Judi,' he said, staring down at a large worm that sat on the toe of his shoe.

I bent and picked it off, placing it gently where it belonged.

'Sorry. But you shouldn't creep up on people like that.'

'I called your name three times.'

'I didn't hear you.' I stared up at his round, usually cheery face and didn't like what I saw. Furrow between his eyes, downturned mouth, curly hair too neatly combed. 'What's the matter? Boss changed your shifts again? We can do the movie thing another night.'

Senior Constable Connor Byrne was the one friend I allowed myself in Candlebark. We had a standing arrangement for movie marathons on Friday nights when he wasn't working. I put up with Arnie and Bruce Willis, although I liked Bruce better now he was bald, and Connor put up with what he called my 'arty farty stuff'. We had some fun arguments about things like who would make the best female version of Arnie.

'Nah, my shifts are fine,' he said. 'It's about... I have a bit of news for you.'

I rammed the spade into the earth and rubbed my hands down my jeans. 'Bad news by the look of it. Who's complained about my long grass?'

'Nobody.'

He looked around as if desperately trying to find something mundane to comment on. I didn't like Connor behaving oddly. It unsettled me. 'Do you want a coffee?'

His face brightened a little. 'Yeah, that'd be great. Have you still got some of that dark brew?'

'Sure. You could buy some for yourself, you know, instead of living on that powdered no-brand rubbish.' I took the spade over to the shed and brushed the dirt off it before standing it next to the fork, carefully avoiding Connor's eyes. 'You want a pumpkin? I've still got a couple here.'

'Um, I'll get one later.' He was at my back door vigorously clean-ing his shoes on my thick-bristled mat like one speck of mud would be the end of the world. I slipped my boots off and padded across the dark slate floor in my socks, shivering at the chill that soaked through me. Might be time to set a fire in the bluestone hearth and acknowledge winter was on the way.

Connor stood by the window, poking at my herb pots and dribbling water on to a couple of them while I made the coffee. I'd never known him to be so fidgety. Usually he sat at the table and chatted to me while I cooked. My hand shook on the pot and I scolded myself. *Get a grip, Judi. It's probably a local drama of some kind.* But my gut knew it wasn't, and I had an overpowering urge to tell him to go away and not come back.

Instead, I put two yellow mugs on the table and poured the coffee, wiping up the splashes and rinsing the cloth.

'You going to sit down any time soon?' he asked.

'When you stop nagging,' I said, but sat across from him and stirred my coffee half a dozen times, even though there was no sugar in it. 'Come on, spit it out. It's Andy, isn't it?'

He shifted on his chair, and it creaked. 'Yeah, it is. I'm sorry.'

My stomach lurched, and I swallowed hard. 'What was it? An overdose?' Connor knew all about my drug addict brother, the problems I'd had with him over the years. I thought I'd got used to the roller coaster dive when I heard any news of Andy, but it still confounded me.

'No, not exactly. Well, not at all...'

'The ultimate irony then. A car accident.'

'No. Look, I...'

'Is he dead or not?' The voice that came out of me was hard, dry, cold. Like I didn't give a shit about my own brother. Like I'd written him off, just like Dad did. Did I sound like Dad? I shuddered, hating myself. I hadn't written Andy off, I'd given up in despair first, and then I'd tried that thing called Hard Love. What a joke. I'd been packing up for my escape to Candlebark, he'd come begging for money and I'd said no. His druggie girlfriend gazing out at me with black-ringed eyes from the rusted, bald-tyred car in my driveway hadn't helped. He'd had no hope with someone like her.

'Yes.' Connor swallowed some coffee and the gulp echoed. 'He was murdered, Judi. In Footscray. I'm sorry.'

Murdered. It was as if a scalpel had sliced across all the connections to my nerves. I felt numb, unable to think straight. Then *Andy is dead.* Pain suddenly roared through me in a fiery blast and I couldn't stay there, couldn't bear Connor's sympathetic eyes. I shoved back my chair and walked through the house, wanting something, anything that might hold me together, but I had no idea what. My brain and heart thudded like duelling drums. My feet slowed in the tiny lounge room, and I stopped in front of a framed photo on the wall.

Andy and me at Luna Park, him about ten, me fourteen with enough makeup on to cover five clowns. He stood on a bench, laughing, mouth wide open, his arm lassoed around my neck, trying to distract me while I stood stiffly, upright, wanting to look like a model or at least a sophisticated eighteen-year-old. I'd been determined not to smile, to look aloof and mature, but at the last second before the camera shutter opened, he'd made me grin in spite of myself.

Afterwards I'd punched him, but secretly I'd loved the photo and claimed it for myself, hiding it from Mum and Dad. We were supposed to be at school that day, and had revelled in the delinquency. My knees buckled and I leant against the wall. 'What happened to you, mate?' I whispered, and tears trickled down my face.

'Judi?' Connor stood in the doorway, arms dangling at his sides. 'You OK?'

I brushed the tears away roughly. 'Yep, fine.'

He came and stood next to me, inspecting the photo. 'He was a happy kid, wasn't he?'

'Mostly.' A sob rose in my throat and I swallowed hard. 'Until the old bastard decided he needed taking in hand. Couldn't bear that either of his kids might turn out to be *hooligans*.' Connor remained silent and the words spurted out of me. 'Dad loved his leather strap. I used to dream about shoving it down his throat and choking him with it.'

'What did Andy dream about?'

'Getting out from under. When Dad died ten years ago, we both spat on his grave.'

'Andy never really got away, did he?'

I felt like it was me who was choking. 'All those years he spent, early on, trying to beat Dad at his own game, earn more money, have a bigger car. Why the hell men have to have their father's approval, when their father is a total prick, is beyond me.'

Connor put his arm around me, and I stiffened, but I managed not to shrug him off. He was trying to help, but he was overdoing it, getting too close. He said, 'Didn't the old man's death make a difference?'

'No. Andy blew the hundred grand Dad left him on partying and drugs. Told me he'd gone through the lot, like he was proud of it. All that did was make him into a full-blown addict.' I moved away from Connor, ostensibly to blow my nose, and walked back to the kitchen. The coffee was strong and bitter, but I really wanted a gin. I sucked in a breath, straightened my back, felt the wooden chair support me.

Connor sat down again and tried to hold my hand. I extracted my fingers and smiled. 'Quit the undertaker thing, will you? I'm really sad about Andy, but I'm not going to fall apart on you. I want to know what happened.'

Connor was used to my abruptness. 'He was shot. The detective in Melbourne said they thought it was a drug deal, but they have a suspect. A Vietnamese guy that he was seen in a restaurant with, someone he was mates with.'

I jerked back, knocking my spoon across the table. 'Mates? Some mate!'

'It happened down by the river. They found Andy's car parked in a side street. It's factories around there, so no one to see or hear anything.' Connor took out his trusty notebook and flipped through the pages. 'He wasn't found until the next morning. A couple of joggers on the river path saw his body – no attempt to hide it or anything.'

A steel band tightened around my skull and I tried to shake it loose, along with the picture of my brother lying alone and bleeding among rubbish and dead weeds. I was as useless to him now as I'd always been.

'Did they say anything about a funeral?'

Connor pursed his lips. 'The police can't find his partner, Leigh. She's not at the house, and not at her job.'

A small spike of shock ran through me. 'Leigh? His druggie girl-friend? I didn't think they'd still be together.'

'Yes. She's listed as his de facto.'

Given how she'd looked when I last saw her, I'd expected Leigh to be long dead. 'She'll turn up sooner or later, I suppose.'

'That's the thing. This detective down there says you'll have to claim the body and organise everything. He wants you to go to Melbourne, says he needs to talk to you.'

Go back to the city? No way. 'What the hell for? I haven't seen Andy for more than three years. I know nothing about what he was up to.' I sat back, crossing my arms.

'Well, the funeral... you know.'

'I could do that by phone.' I hated being dragged into it like this. 'Why can't they get Mum to do it? Surely they've contacted her?'

'He didn't mention your mother at all. He insisted it be you. He wants you to ring him on this number.' He pushed a piece of paper across the table at me.

'But?'

Connor shrugged. 'He sounds like a bit of a wanker, that's all. I shouldn't say it, being another police officer, but he's one of those hotshots. Pushy. Wants to solve the crime single-handed and add another notch on his belt.'

I laughed. 'And that's not your kind of cop, is it?'

'No need to be a smartarse,' he said, grinning. 'My job up here is all about the community, getting on with people to get the job done. I don't need to be a gung-ho master of the universe.' His pink face belied his words. He was a damn good cop for a small country town.

'Yeah, I know. You'd never have solved who tried to burn down the school if you hadn't had your ear to the ground.'

The truth of Andy dead washed over me again in an icy, drenching wave and my skin goose-pimpled. How could this have happened? Not his murder, but his whole life. It was as if it'd been leading him to that moment, that bullet.

He could've been anything, my little brother. He was smart and funny, and everyone loved him. Everyone except our parents, who'd done everything they could to force him into Dad's mould. Sober, respectable, rich. Do it their way or get the strap.

Dad tried to teach Andy how to box once. I'd watched for a few minutes, thinking I might learn something, but I soon saw that it was an excuse for Dad to give Andy a belting and make it look legit. Andy knew it, too. His eyes pleaded with me to help him, but I didn't know how. Was every memory of my brother so clouded with guilt?

It was way too late to help him now.

'I think you need to go,' Connor said.

I heard all the connotations of *need* in his voice, and my hand went to my stomach, as if I could somehow cover the gaping hole there. This would be the last thing I ever did for my brother. The thought made me want to curl up into a blubbering mess. Instead, I nodded sharply.

'OK. I'd better take the car.' I grimaced. 'Then I can come home sooner.'

'You should try starting it first.' He swallowed the last of his coffee, straightened his tie and stood. 'Got the keys?'

'Somewhere.' I scrabbled around in the kitchen drawer where I kept odds and ends and found the keys, covered in grime and bits of fluff. 'Can't remember the last time I drove it.'

It was a vintage pale blue Mercedes Benz, one owner, my father. The old prick had only put ten thousand kilometres on the clock. The only reason I'd accepted it as part of the bequests in the will was because it still smelled like a new car, instead of like him and his pu-trid, skinny cigars. I kept the Benz in my old barn, and Connor was horrified when he saw it covered in bird poo and dust.

I got in, pumped the accelerator a couple of times and turned the key. It started first go, motor humming nicely. 'Drive it out into the yard,' Connor said. 'I'll clean the windscreen for you.' He frowned at the bonnet and roof. 'On second thoughts, can you spare some tank water? I need to wash it. I can't stand to see a classic in a state like this.'

'It only has to get me from A to B. But I suppose I'd better not drift into the big smoke like a hayseed.' I rinsed as Connor washed, and then we tipped the leftover water on to the peas. No sense wasting any of it.

I waved Connor off in his white and blue police 4WD and went back to my garden. The compost had to be dug in, there was weeding and pruning to do, and I needed a spade in my hands. The earth wouldn't fight back; it would give.

As for Detective Hotshot, I'd call him after dinner. Whatever he wanted from me couldn't possibly be that urgent.

2

The plains around Melbourne are so flat that the city skyscrapers are visible from way out on the Calder Highway. As they came into view, I grimaced and turned the music off. What had been a nice drive in the country was now a journey into hell. That's what it felt like anyway, as I concentrated on driving and forced a mix of bad memories back behind the wall.

When I'd rung Detective Hotshot the night before, he'd sounded like he was in a pub. There was a lot of background chatter and the droning voice of a horse or greyhound race caller. He'd turned grumpy when I said I couldn't get to South Melbourne until 11am, but I wasn't getting up at dawn for anyone, least of all a bad-tempered cop. We'd agreed to meet at the mortuary in Kavanagh Street.

I managed to get lost somewhere around the back of Crown Casino, driving into a dead-end street that turned out to be a pedestrian area. I cursed and thumped the steering wheel and felt my heart bang against my ribs. *Calm down*. Cruising slowly, I avoided strolling office workers, circled around at the end and headed back to where I thought Kavanagh Street and the mortuary and Coroners' Court was. A large wall with silver lettering on it informed me I was finally in the right place. I'd been expecting a gothic red-brick building but this glass and coloured concrete place looked like an office block.

I found a parking spot on the street right outside and sighed with relief. Southbank had changed a lot – it was full of high-rise apartments jammed in between the river and the tunnels, and I guessed the ugly red funnel that jutted up above the streets was an air vent for all those exhaust fumes. I levered myself out of the car and stretched, flexing my bad hip while I looked around.

A group of people wearing ID badges on lanyards hung around out the front under the trees, smoking and laughing. None of them looked like cops. I slung my large black holdall over my shoulder, locked the Benz, fed the meter and set off for the entrance.

I had no idea where to go and followed the signs for reception, ignoring the one that said *Identifications*. Surely that couldn't be where I had to meet him? They knew who he was already.

A man in a stylish grey suit stood near the entrance, snarling into a mobile phone, running his hand through his dark hair like he wanted to pull it out, roots and all. His face was what the romance novels called 'chiselled', and I sneaked a second look as I edged past. *Nice*. I walked through the doors into a reception area, past the security guards, steeling myself for a sombre atmosphere. Instead, it was as businesslike as outside.

'Can I help you?' the receptionist said.

'I'm supposed to meet a police detective here,' I said. 'Is he around?'

'Do you know his name?'

'Um...' For a moment my mind went blank and I nearly said Hotshot.

'You looking for me?'

I turned and found the dark-haired mobile phone snarler gazing at me with an impatient expression. 'Possibly. You are?'

'Detective Sergeant Ben Heath.' He thrust out his hand.

I shook it firmly. 'Judi Westerholme.'

'I'm sorry for your loss.'

That's what the cops on TV say.

A laugh erupted from me that sounded more like a strangled cough. This guy was unreal. And he didn't sound at all sorry. 'Let's get this over with, shall we? You said you had some questions.'

'That's right.' He hesitated, as if checking me over and mentally reassessing me. 'Come this way.' He took me outside again and down the side path; sure enough, we were following the *Identifications* signage.

'Why are we here? Don't you already know it's my brother?'

He flushed. 'Yes, we identified him through fingerprints. But you're senior next of kin and... they do actually require a proper identification.' He strode on through the doors and I trailed in his wake.

I wasn't sure I did want to see my dead brother. The skin tightened on my face and I bit my lip. I wasn't being given much choice. He glanced back, annoyance on his face, and I hurried to catch him up. 'Bloody little Hitler,' I muttered.

'Sorry?' He stopped and I cannoned into his back. 'Is there a problem?'

Only you. I shook my head and trailed after him as he rang a bell and then we headed down a corridor. We ended up in a small area with a large internal window. A staff member, who was apparently there to support me, spoke on a phone and a few seconds later, lights in the room next door flickered into life, the curtain opened and a man in green scrubs came and stood next to a covered shape.

Oh shit. That was Andy. I didn't want to look, and I couldn't look away. Hotshot stood like a statue beside me, his face impassive, but a tic flickered at the side of his eye. The sudden tension in the room was electric and I had to break the circuit somehow. 'You always do it like this, behind glass?' I said.

'It's... simpler.' He nodded to the guy on the other side, who pulled back the sheet.

My brain screeched: *It's one of those horrible reality shows. Where are the cameras?* Then I focused on Andy's face and everything went silent. His blond hair was neatly cut, shorter than mine for a change, but he was missing the small diamond ear stud I'd given him for his twenty-first birthday.

He didn't look like he was asleep at all. He looked dead. Gone. Like a marble sculpture with no soul inside.

The silence grew until it was beating at my ears like bass drums, then sound came back to me in a rush. Hotshot clearing his throat beside me, the clock ticking, air conditioning whooshing. I took a deep, shuddering breath. That was it then. All those years of shared nightmares, backing each other up, talking about silly dreams of how we'd conquer the world and get rid of our parents. I'd lost the one person who truly understood who I was and why. It burned through my guts like white-hot steel.

Now I knew why they stuck the family behind a glass wall. That way you couldn't fall all over the body, begging them to come back, only to find how cold and dead they were. I wanted to get out of the place, pronto. My gaze zig-zagged to the door then back to Andy again. He was still dead.

Hotshot was talking to me but I couldn't understand him at first. 'What?'

'They need you to verbally confirm. Is this your brother, Andrew Westerholme?'

'Of course it bloody is.'

He heaved a sigh, as if I was being difficult for no reason. I wanted to hit him, like I used to belt Andy when he teased me about my ratty hair or nerdy boyfriends. I swallowed the rock in my throat and walked out of the room.

Outside, the air was hazy and warm, and I breathed in diesel fumes and pollution but it was better than the air-conditioned nothingness inside. As I waited for a car to pass so I could cross the street, I dug into my bag for my car keys, wanting to get the hell out of there and go home, though I couldn't help feeling I was deserting Andy yet again. The keys rattled in my hand.

'Where are you headed now?' Heath asked behind me.

I jumped and turned. 'No idea,' I said. 'Why?'

'You look like you're in a hurry to go, and I need to ask you some questions.'

He was assessing me again, his eyes sympathetic. That was the last thing I needed. 'What's the matter?' I asked. 'Aren't I what you expected? I suppose a druggie's sister is supposed to be all scungy and desperate.'

'Not at all.' He was trying to be diplomatic but it wasn't in him. He smoothed down his dark grey tie. 'How long was he an addict?'

'Years. More years than I care to remember.'

'But not recently.'

'I don't know! Like I told you last night, I hadn't seen him for more than three years, so I assumed...'

'The autopsy showed he was clean. Had been for quite a long while.'

'He got killed over a deal, didn't he? That tells me he got the urge again.'

Heath shrugged. 'Maybe. How come you hadn't seen him for so long?'

'He wanted money and I said no. Not while he was attached to his druggie girlfriend. He didn't bother to contact me again.'

'Not exactly the loving older sister, are you?'

A red haze rose up in front of my eyes and my hand clenched so hard on the keys that I felt the skin break. 'Oh for Christ's sake, get over yourself.' I walked to my car and fumbled with the door key, try-ing to get it in the lock, cursing under my breath. He was right behind me still, following like a bad smell, but I ignored him.

He whistled. 'Nice car. Is it yours?'

'No, I stole it because I couldn't afford a train ticket.'

I finally got the door open, threw my bag on to the passenger seat and started to get in.

He touched my shoulder, his hand warm. 'Hey, I'm sorry. It's been one of those days and I was rude. I apologise.'

'Yes, so?'

'Look – there's things about your brother's murder that don't make sense. It should be open and shut, but little bits don't add up and it's bothering the hell out of me.'

I paused, sagged against the door frame. 'Like what?'

'He hadn't used for several years. He had a partner, a kid and a house. A mortgage even. A decent job. All signs that he was doing OK. No reason to go back on to drugs, no reason for anyone to kill him. A deal gone wrong just doesn't hang right.'

'What did you say?' He'd been gabbling on but I'd only heard one word – it vibrated inside my head like a struck gong. 'Did you say he had a *kid*?'

'Yeah, a little girl, about two years old.' He raised his eyebrows. 'You didn't know?'

'Would I be asking if I did? Leigh is the mother?' I could still see her haggard face as she stared at me.

'Yes, but –'

I remembered what Connor had told me. 'She's still missing.'

'Leigh left her daughter in the care of a family friend. The woman is a foster mum. After a couple of days, when she saw your brother's death in the papers, she got worried and rang us. We've had an alert out for Leigh, but nothing so far.' He frowned. 'That's the other thing I needed to talk to you about. Apart from your mother, you're currently the *kid's* only relative.'

Something crawled over me like a giant millipede with claws. 'You mean you've contacted my mother? How come she didn't claim Andy's body?'

'She said she would, then she didn't come, and when two officers went to see her, they said she wasn't capable.'

'I'll bet.' She was never capable of being a mother. *Mum.* The word was an acid spray from the past. I'd been hoping she was dead when no one had mentioned her. The autumn sun burned down on the top of my head like a miniature furnace, matching the anger boiling up inside me, and sweat broke out on the back of my neck.

'So he's been lying in there all this time, for a whole week, and she hasn't bothered –' I took a couple of breaths, closing my eyes, repeating my personal mantra, blocking Heath out. *Peace and calm, peace and calm*. It helped a bit but not much.

'... go and see her.'

I caught his last words. 'I wouldn't go and see my mother if you paid me a million dollars.'

'No, not her, the child.'

'What for?' My stomach lurched up and down again. A roller coaster, like always. Out of my control. 'She's better off staying where she is.' Besides, she didn't need to see me – I was a complete stranger. I was nothing to her. I'd probably make her scream her head off. The local kids in Candlebark steered clear of me and Connor said that was because he'd told them I was a witch. Ha ha, very funny, I'd said.

'The friend can't keep her indefinitely. And she is your niece.' Hotshot rubbed the back of his neck. He had a nice range of unconscious hand movements going – I wondered if he'd scratch his balls next. 'Look, if you don't want to, that's your business,' he said. 'God knows I've seen enough family crap over the years to know it's unfathomable. But I still need to talk to you about your brother.'

My breath came out in a frustrated rush. 'I can't see the point. I don't know anything.'

'I don't think that's so. Look, how about we go for a coffee, or –' he checked his watch '– lunch, if you're hungry.' He pointed to a café across the nearby intersection. 'Just a few minutes of your time and then you're free to go wherever you like.'

Free to go. If only that were true.

He pulled a large, lumpy envelope out of his jacket pocket. 'I have some things of your brother's to give you, too.'

He was using them as a bribe; I wanted to grab the envelope and tell him to get stuffed, but suddenly I was too tired and miserable to argue. 'All right. As long as you keep me updated after this. About the investigation.'

'I will, I promise. We always liaise with the families.'

'You'd better.'

This time he pulled at his shirt collar like I was strangling him. 'OK. So... shall we go?'

I collected my bag, paid for another parking voucher for the Benz, locked it up and followed him down the street, feeling like I'd made a pact with the devil.

3

In every street in Southbank, there was construction and cranes and beeping trucks. It all looked like apartment buildings with shiny glass fronts, and I wondered who on earth was going to live in all those fancy shoeboxes.

Hotshot walked slightly in front of me, checking his phone and jabbing at the screen, presumably sending text messages. A few times I heard him mutter and curse, but I was too busy watching where I was walking, dodging building rubble and piles of autumn leaves covered in concrete dust. I rubbed my hip again, surreptitiously. It knew it was back in Melbourne and it was aching more than it had in months, damn it.

At the café entrance, he stopped and grimaced at me. 'Sorry about that. There's a lot going on at the moment.' He ushered me inside, and I passed groups of chattering office workers to a quieter table. Our feet clattered on the fake wood and the laughter and kitchen noises echoed against the high ceilings. Most of the customers were dressed in suits or business clothes, and I was glad I'd worn my one decent pair of black trousers and a silk shirt. We sat and Hotshot placed his phone screen-down on the table. I guessed that was the definition of politeness in Melbourne now.

'I'll order,' he said. 'What'll you have?'

'Just a double shot latte, thanks.'

He ordered at the counter, smiling at the young woman who beamed back and flicked her hair a few times, and our coffees arrived within a couple of minutes, so I guessed his good looks had some use. I drank a mouthful of my latte, savouring its flavour, and then another. I had to admit I missed Melbourne coffee, about the only thing I did miss.

I could feel Heath's eyes on me but I didn't care. I was desperate to take some painkillers for my hip, but no way would I do it in front of him. I didn't want him to add *prescription junkie* to the list of our family failings.

He laid the envelope on the table in front of me like it was the Holy Grail. 'Normally this would go to the funeral home but I kept it for you.'

'What's in there that's so important?' I said.

He tipped it up and a small pile of items skidded out across the polished tabletop. A gold watch with a worn brown leather band stopped against the side of my hand and I jerked back, pulling my hand away, holding it against my chest. Shit. Dad's old watch. What was Andy doing with that? Once upon a time he would've smashed it to bits with a hammer.

'Something wrong?' Hotshot asked.

'Nothing relevant to you,' I said, staring at the watch like it was a venomous snake. A picture reared up in my head: Dad carefully taking off that watch before he picked up the leather strap to give one of us a 'well-deserved punishment'. Always where the marks wouldn't be seen.

'These were all found on his... person. Do you recognise this?' Hotshot pushed a key towards me; it hung off a brass fob with the number 20 stamped on it.

I shook my head. 'Never seen it before, sorry.'

'No idea what the 20 is?'

'House number?'

'No.'

I leaned forward and inspected the other items. A set of keys that included a car key, one with the electronic locking button on the side. The diamond earring, thank goodness. A small red USB. A brown leather wallet that was soft and worn around the corners. I touched it gently, then flipped it open. Two credit cards, a Medicare card, some business cards, about a hundred dollars in notes.

A pink dummy sat by itself near the white ceramic salt shaker. I ignored it.

'What's on the USB?'

'Just photos,' he said. 'Mostly of his daughter. Er...'

'Yes?'

He rubbed his neck again. 'I suppose you don't know her name.'

I swallowed another fast mouthful of latte and it burned all the way down my throat. 'No, I don't,' I said at last.

'Mia.'

'Uh huh.' So now she had a name. Like naming your chooks or your sheep. Caused problems when they were headed for the chopping block. I wanted to slap myself, stop the horrible thoughts. Instead I focused on the keys.

'Are they the keys to his car? Where is it?'

'With us. It'd been broken into, so we had to fingerprint it, the whole forensics thing, and then tow it in. You'll need to get the window fixed.'

'Leigh will, you mean. It's her car now.'

'Don't suppose you'd have any idea where Leigh is?' he said.

'Nup. Don't even know her last name. I only met her once.' I could still see her pale face though, skin all blotchy and spotted with some kind of rash. And the way her legs buckled when she tried to get out of the car. I couldn't imagine her with a real, live, healthy child.

'There's a hundred dollars in the wallet,' I said. 'I thought you said he was going down to the river to make a big drug deal. Where's that money? Was he robbed? Why didn't the guy take his wallet?'

'Good questions.'

'Have you caught the guy yet?'

'No. Got a good idea who it is, a guy called Tran Duc, but he's disappeared. Plenty of family to hide him. One informant said he'd heard it was an accident. Andy attacked Tran first.'

'Oh yeah, right.' Across the café, three construction workers in fluoro shirts were all happily tucking into steaming meat pies. I wanted to pick up my latte glass and throw it at the nearest wall. 'Andy doesn't – didn't – attack people. He was too gutless. Couldn't even defend himself.'

'How long since you've seen him?' His tone was disbelieving.

I glared at him. 'Doesn't matter. That's the kind of thing that never changes. If he'd been a physical fighter, he'd have belted our father years ago.'

'That's family stuff. It's different. People do stuff in families that they wouldn't do outside – and vice versa.'

'True.' If anyone was going to kill Dad, it would've been me. My guts were churning like a washing machine. I picked up the envelope and put the watch into it so I wouldn't have to look at it anymore. 'I presume I can take all of this now.' I added the other items, tempted to leave the dummy on the table.

'I'd like to know what that key's for, if you find out.'

'Of course.' But I knew I wouldn't tell him anything if I didn't absolutely have to.

'What about Andy's body?'

'The funeral home can pick it up as soon as you like.'

'Him. Not it.'

'Sorry. *Andy*. I don't usually...'

In the silence that followed, I finished my coffee and Heath checked his mobile, thumbing the screen for messages. Once he grunted at what he was reading, then shook his head. The pigeons near the café entrance were dodging people's feet and, as usual, there was one bird with a dangling leg struggling to keep up.

Heath was slipping his mobile into his pocket when it rang, a bizarre cacophony of notes that sounded like the *1812 Overture*. When he pressed the green Answer, the voice on the other end was so loud I could hear it clearly.

'Heath, where are you, mate?'

'Southbank.'

'What are ya doing there? You were supposed to be back here by twelve.'

'I'll be on my way shortly.'

'Burns is not happy. You'd better make it soon as.'

'Yeah, yeah. Burns can wait.'

'Not about him – we've found Tran.'

My head snapped up but he was frowning at his watch.

'See you in thirty.' Hotshot disconnected and looked at me. 'Gotta go. Sorry.'

'Was that about the guy who killed Andy?'

'Could be.' He stood up. 'I'll walk you back to your car.'

I tried to pin him down with a glare. 'Are you going to let me know what's going on?'

'Yeah, of course. Give me your mobile number.'

'I don't have one.' I'd never had one in Candlebark, where reception was hopeless, and I hadn't planned on staying around. Now I was floundering.

'Really? I can call you at your brother's house then. That's the easiest.'

'Except I don't know the number there,' I said. 'In fact, I don't even know where his house is. How stupid is that?'

All the anger and frustration I'd been feeling was suddenly sucked down into the gaping hole in my guts. It seemed I knew nothing about my brother anymore, nothing beyond those early shared years and the few times I'd seen him off his face on drugs. Despite all the crap in my own life, I couldn't escape the knowledge that the vacuum of the past six years was mostly my fault. How much had I missed? I'd missed a child, for a start. *My niece*.

Hotshot scribbled an address in his notebook and ripped out the page, handing it to me after I'd struggled to my feet. 'I've got the phone number. The house is in Ascot Vale, off Union Road. Just Google Map it... um, have you got a Melways?'

I nodded, shoving the paper in my pocket. There was an old street directory in the back of the Benz somewhere. 'I'll find it.'

I followed him out the door, trying to keep up with his hurried steps, and stumbled over the sill, wrenching my leg, but I barely felt it. In the past two hours I'd been catapulted from one horrible moment to the next, and my body had reacted first, my brain slow to catch up. But by the time Hotshot left me at my car, one thought had emerged with shining clarity.

All the effort I'd put into walling myself off for the past six years – the move to the country, shedding all my so-called friends, blocking out all the emotions that threatened my peace of mind – had just been blown out of the water.

4

I sat in the Benz alone for a few minutes, trying to pull myself together. Really, I was desperately attempting to pull the shutters down again, rebuild the wall – whatever it took to get back to an even, unfeeling state. It wasn't working. I started the car and drove towards Ascot Vale, recognising familiar streets and shops, shaking my head at bland new units. This was where our grandmother used to live and, unconsciously, I found my way to her street and parked outside her old house.

It was a little 1920s-style weatherboard, and the doors and trims looked freshly painted by the current owner. Memories of visits to Nana – hot chocolate while we watched her beloved Hawthorn play on the telly, puzzle books she'd bought especially, her home-made cakes and biscuits – flooded in on me. She'd even shared her mangy dog, Woofer, with us because Dad wouldn't let us have pets. I blinked back tears and sighed. That was all long gone, as was dear old Nana.

I found the Melways directory and pulled Hotshot's notepaper out of my pocket, ready to look Andy's address up. The scrawled writing blurred in front of me and I shook my head. What the hell was this? The address on the paper was where I was right now – Nana's house! I screwed the paper up and threw it on the floor, glared at it, then bent and picked it up again, smoothing it out.

It still said the same thing. *28 Beronia Street, Ascot Vale.* I fumbled in the envelope and found the bunch of keys, then hauled myself out of the Benz and stood at the front gate; my brain said *No way*, but my skin prickled with a mix of suspicion and something strangely like hope.

Somehow Andy had ended up in Nana's house. Surely it was a weird coincidence. Nana had been dead for more than twenty years, and probably died of neglect since Dad and Mum scarcely went near her. When Andy and I were still at primary school, they used to drop us off at Nana's when they had some big function to go to, or a football game. Dad fancied himself as a sponsor of his local VFL team and loved the sucking-up everyone did when he gave them money.

They'd treated Nana as a free babysitter but she never complained. Instead, she'd spoiled us rotten, making the most of our times together. Cakes and biscuits cooling on the bench, little presents she'd bought and put away for the next time she saw us. She even bought a colour telly, she said, just for us, because we weren't allowed to watch it at home.

Then we just stopped going there. Dad bought the big flash house in Brighton, we had a paid babysitter until I was old enough to be trusted to look after Andy, and even though we begged, Dad wouldn't take us again. We were on the other side of town and it wasn't convenient. Sometimes, on a Saturday, we'd sneak off and catch public transport to visit her. She was always so ecstatically happy to see us that it made me cry, and I'd vow to visit more often but it was hard to get away without Dad becoming suspicious.

One day, Dad said, 'The old girl's dropped off the perch.' I didn't believe him. I thought he was making it up so we wouldn't want to visit her anymore. I wagged school the next day and went over to Nana's house. It was already stripped bare of all of her stuff, most of which was in the rubbish skip out the front, and a For Sale sign was on the front fence. Dad had her house on the market already. I climbed into the skip and ferreted around, but the neighbours had already beaten me to it. The only things left worth taking were an old photo album with half the photos missing, and her favourite Hawthorn footy club mug. Worthless to anyone but me. I took them home and hid them, hate for my father burning ever brighter in my heart.

Andy had been devastated. He refused to speak to Dad for weeks afterwards. He found a real estate ad for Nana's house with a photo on it, cut it out and wrote *Traitor* across the front of it, then framed it and hung it in his room. It lasted two days and then Dad ripped it down and smashed it to pieces.

How had Andy bought this house? Maybe he'd waited and waited until it came on the market, or seen it for sale and bought it on impulse. Either one implied planning and saving, something I hadn't thought he was capable of as an addict.

I pushed open the wooden front gate, which swung silently on oiled hinges, and stepped on to the paved red and cream path. I remembered a stretch of cracked concrete. The picket fence had been recently painted a rich cream to match the front door and window frames. The garden was lined with diosma and neat daisy bushes, instead of Nana's climbing roses over an arch. It all looked like some-thing out of *Better Homes and Gardens*, for God's sake.

Maybe I'd read Heath's handwriting wrong, but I checked again, and I was pretty sure this was the number. If the keys in my hand fitted the front door lock, that would confirm it.

I made it to the front porch, taking deep breaths, remembering Nana, how she'd open the door and immediately there'd be this huge smile on her face. The key slid in and turned easily. I unlocked the door and nudged it open, holding my breath, wondering what I'd see. The old floral carpet and long hallway were gone. Someone had renovated, ripping out half of the internal walls so I could see all the way through to French doors at the back. The original golden wood floors had been sanded and lacquered and the walls painted a light cream. Even the party wall with next door had been replastered and painted.

I liked the airy lightness, and I thought Nana would've too. I closed the front door and stood, listening, remembering, but all traces of Nana were gone. Was Leigh hiding in the house some-where? I shivered. No, it felt empty, silent, as if no one had ever lived there. I began wandering through the house, looking for signs of

Andy, but caught myself checking for drug paraphernalia, smudges of coke on the coffee table, roach ends in the ashtrays. I couldn't have been more wrong. This was a family house, with toys on the floor, a soft throw rug on the couch and some empty food jars on the bench.

The police search had made a mess, and somebody had tried to restore order, without much success. As I wandered, I tidied up, replacing and straightening, examining objects for clues to their lives. And stopping at each of my brother's favourite things – his guitar propped in a corner of the lounge room, his Bulldogs footy scarf over the doorknob, a few of his ancient classic cassettes in a neat row above newer CD versions. I couldn't help it – I hugged his scarf and breathed in his scent, but it was only some brand of spicy aftershave.

A studio portrait of a woman and child hung on the lounge room wall, drawing me like a fishing lure. The woman's dark hair was nicely styled, her makeup light over glowing skin. I sucked in a sharp breath. It was Leigh. She'd lost the black-ringed eyes and blotchy face, looked almost normal, a faint smile on her face. Nothing like the staggering wreck who'd screamed abuse at me that day. But it was her.

Which meant the child was Mia.

I took a good long look at her and felt dizzy. She was the spitting image of Andy when he was little. Big blue eyes, wispy blonde hair, slightly sticking-out ears and a grin that suggested mischief. I wanted to stare and stare, but I forced myself to step away, teeth grinding together – *nothing to do with me* – and kept searching for more clues to my brother and who he'd become.

In the main bedroom, I poked through drawers of underwear, cringing as I turned over satin boxers and tatty lace. I had no idea what I was even looking for. I sat down on the bed, suddenly drained.

Instant coffee was revolting but I needed something to keep me going. A large cup of strong coffee would help, and I found the milk in the fridge was still usable. A shopping list stuck to the door with an egg magnet caught my eye. That was Andy's handwriting. A week ago, he'd been thinking about buying onions and laundry powder. My grip tightened convulsively on the mug and I made myself loosen it before I snapped the handle off.

What exactly was I after? Perhaps evidence of Andy's new life, that he'd really managed to stay clean all that time. He'd had a child; he could have been planning on marrying Leigh one day. He might have gone ahead and married her and not told me. What kind of job did he have? Once upon a time, before the drugs, he'd been a successful young real estate agent, until he'd trashed that life forever.

Somehow he'd got his shit together and moved forward, created a normal life for himself again. I couldn't fathom how the hell he'd done it. I'd never really succeeded. I rubbed my temples. Maybe there was no big secret to it, but I couldn't stop looking. It was like an agonising itch I had to scratch.

My initial cursory search of their wardrobe niggled at me. I'd skimmed it because it felt weird, but now I returned to it, trying to see them through their clothes. Andy owned two suits, and a fair few business shirts and pants, and some stylish ties. Even his casual shirts were on hangers, and his shoes were all clean and lined up neatly.

The other side of the wardrobe – Leigh's – was noticeably empty, one dress sliding half-off its hanger, a red shirt on the floor. A sign she'd left in a hurry. The clothes that were left were all party-type apparel, and some stilettos and summer gear. She'd taken practical stuff, and she'd taken most of it, which implied she didn't think she'd be back for a while. I picked up the shirt – it was low-cut with a hotel logo on the chest and, instead of putting it on a hanger, I threw it back in the corner.

Andy had supposedly been buying drugs, maybe for her. She'd worked in a pub, not the most helpful place if you were an ex-addict, and just because he'd kicked it, that didn't mean she had. It wouldn't surprise me, but maybe I was being too hard on her. She did look pretty healthy in the photo. I let those thoughts sit in the back of my head while I continued on to the other bedroom.

Mia had more soft toys in her room than a shooting gallery stand at the Melbourne Show. They were piled in the corner mostly, with some battered favourites leaning against her pillow. A brown teddy with one eye missing and a grubby red waistcoat stared suspiciously at me, and I made this search fast and cursory. I couldn't tell if Mia's clothes were missing – no big gaps in drawers or the cupboard. Leigh might have wanted her friend to think she was coming back soon, so Mia's bag of clothes had been small.

In the lounge room I scanned the cassettes and their faded covers as I lined them up on the shelf. The Benz was too old to have a CD player and I hated listening to inane DJs on the radio. I ran my finger along the plastic cases, reading the titles – mostly old rock and roll, a few copied albums and mix tapes Andy had done himself. I recognised his faded handwriting on the labels.

My name jumped out at me as if it was in neon, and I reeled back, dropping the cassette. *Songs for Judi-Dude*. That's what he'd called me when we were teenagers. It flung me back twenty-five years in a second and icy fingers crawled up my spine. God, what had he put on that tape? How old was it?

I picked it up and checked the back cover, then smiled. A bunch of the old favourites – AC/DC, Jimmy Barnes, even INXS. We'd seen all of them play live when we could afford tickets. I wondered if he'd planned to give it to me one day. Typical that he'd guess I wasn't downloading music or watching YouTube. The handwriting looked fresh. I might have been asked to visit. To show me he was happy, that he'd made it without me. 'You were doing good, little brother,' I whispered and put the tape in my bag, planning to play it later in the car. If I listened now, I'd burst into tears.

I looked around. Everything I'd found confirmed what Mr Hotshot Detective had told me. Andy had been clean, living a normal suburban life with a partner and child. Exactly the opposite of what I'd expected after he'd driven away from me that day. He'd been grubby, skinny, hands shaking, hair long and greasy, and Leigh had looked worse.

The house reassured me somehow, as if it told me that Andy had never been a lost cause, that he'd always had it in him to find peace and happiness. God, how the hell *had* he done it? There was no answer here. My mind moved on.

The funeral. I had no idea how to organise it. I'd look in the phone book. Would Andy have wanted a church service? Cremation? Yes, he'd want to be fire and ashes, not down with the worms like Dad. I didn't know if I should wait for Leigh to turn up.

Where the hell *was* Leigh? Anger simmered inside me again. She was probably hiding out with her mates somewhere, getting high. She had no kid with her to worry about, to hold her back.

Stop it – she could be dead, too.

I wanted to be more charitable but the bottom line was, she'd bolted, leaving the kid parked with someone else. I'd bet money she knew Andy was dead – that'd explain the hasty departure, and the fact no one knew where she was. Maybe she thought they'd go after her, but I couldn't really see why.

So I'd have to make all the decisions. Maybe Andy had a will that gave those kinds of instructions. It was worth a look through his accounts and papers, if he kept any. To my surprise, I discovered them all in a cabinet drawer in the lounge, with a filing frame inside it holding suspension files and colour-coded folders, all neatly labelled and alphabetical, all in Andy's neat handwriting.

I shook my head. Time to get over this 'Andy was a hopeless, no-future loser' shit I had imprinted on my brain. If nothing else, it made me sound like Dad, and that sent a shiver through me. I sat on the floor next to the drawer and riffled through the files, reading the labels – Bank, Mortgage, Superannuation, Tax. It was the same everyday stuff that most people had when they were managing a mortgage, a job and a family. Mia's birth certificate showed she'd turned two a month ago. Other papers said Andy had been selling second-hand cars in Footscray, a job I couldn't imagine him doing in a million years. I flipped through the folder of his bank statements; they showed he was good at it, the fortnightly pays a healthy amount. He'd be on commission for sure so the salary indicated he sold his share. Leigh apparently worked part-time as a barmaid at a local pub. That was to be expected; she probably wasn't qualified for anything more.

There in the last blue folder was a large envelope with *Last Will and Testament of Andrew James Westerholme* on the front of it, and a solicitor's name and address in one corner.

I stared at it, unable to reach out and touch it. Its pure whiteness and official logo was like a slap in the face, a stab in the ribs. Nobody made a will before they hit forty. But none of the other papers I'd seen gelled for me either. A house, a mortgage, a steady job – I glanced through the superannuation papers again and he'd been making extra contributions for the last couple of years. This was someone who was a settled, suburban father and husband. Someone who'd turned his down-the-toilet life around in *three years*. It reminded me of someone told they had cancer, and just a year or two to live, someone who'd suddenly found the willpower and drive to change who they were.

And the evidence was there in front of me. He'd done it. For whatever reason, and it must've been a big one, he'd pulled it all together.

Maybe it was the kid. Stranger things had happened. Becoming a father made people behave in life-changing ways. Why not Andy? I sat, frowning, picking at a cuticle while I thought about it, narrowing down the bad vibes until I got to the one that really niggled.

The house.

I pulled out the mortgage folder and checked. He'd bought it three years ago with a $50,000 deposit. That was a suspiciously big lump of cash. I counted back, trying to pinpoint when he'd come to beg me for money. It'd been late summer, the end of daylight saving, and I'd been sitting out on my Melbourne back steps, enjoying the warm sun. I'd just finished packing up for my move to Candlebark. So, yes, it was at least five years ago, probably six. He'd pleaded with me for $5,000, said he'd take $3,000 if I had it, but he was desperate. 'It's my life we're talking about, Judi,' he'd said. 'Please.'

I thought he'd meant he needed the money for drugs again, or maybe he owed somebody for a deal. I felt sick, trapped, and I'd said *No*, then lain sleepless for nights afterwards, convincing myself I'd done the right thing. Perhaps he'd wanted to buy in on a big deal and make a profit, and the profit had later paid the house deposit. Yes, that made sense. It would've been well before Leigh became pregnant, and when they'd found out, the time was right to buy, the motivation – I was sort of happy with it. Until I remembered that Andy had been murdered. Had the deal come back to bite him?

But Hotshot said he was no longer using. It'd take a mammoth amount of willpower to stay in the game and not use after you'd been an addict for years, never mind the inevitable criminal element. I couldn't see it.

I picked up the envelope with the will in it with two fingers, wondering if it was illegal to open it without the solicitor present. Too bad. If I was going to arrange a funeral, I needed to know now if Andy had left instructions or wishes. I slid my finger under the flap, eased it up and pulled out a wad of pages. At first I couldn't read a word, skimming over all the legal bullshit, then I concentrated on the bequests.

My breathing grew loud and fast, echoing roughly in the silence, and when the pages fluttered, I dropped them. The bequests didn't make sense. He'd left money and his super to Leigh, but he'd left the house to me. That would make Leigh and the kid homeless.

I picked the will up, read the bequests again. 'What the hell are you playing at, Andy?' I turned the page, hoping there was an explanation. Instead, the last clause hit me between the eyes like a crow-bar. The headache that had been looming for the past hour speared through my temple. Andy had stipulated that I was to have guardianship of Mia. Not Leigh. With shaking hands, I checked the date on the will – maybe he'd made it out years ago before we stopped talking. No, it was signed three weeks ago.

I read it twice more. It couldn't be legal! The father couldn't say the mother had no rights and give their kid to his sister. No court in the land would uphold that.

Unless the mother was dead.

I sat perfectly still for a few moments, staring at a whorled knot in the floorboard next to me, trying to sort it all through in my head. Refusing to take it in wasn't going to help. It was there in black and white.

A will dated three weeks ago implied planning, and a sense that something might go wrong. Andy couldn't have known he was going to be killed, surely, but he'd obviously thought it was a possibility. And by putting me down as Mia's guardian, he must've figured Leigh could die, too. Yet he'd left her most of his money, as if they'd planned that she'd make a run for it. The will seemed to suggest it.

I badly needed to pee. I needed to do something to make this all go away, but first I needed to pee. I struggled to my feet, limped to the bathroom and sat on the toilet, head in hands, while water gushed from me. It felt like all of my blood was leaving my body and I'd stay sitting there forever, a dry husk.

I wiped, I stood, I pulled up my clothes, I flushed, I washed my hands. The routine stopped me from smashing the bathroom mirror into a thousand pieces. *How could Andy have done this to me?* I'd finished fighting life, I'd found a lovely little place in the country to hole up in, made sure the locals left me alone and didn't want me to join anything. Connor was a good friend, but I'd trained him not to get too close. I spent my days in peace and quiet, digging in my garden, growing things. I wasn't madly happy, but I wasn't self-destructive or even stressed out either. It was enough.

Until this.

I totally did not want a kid, not even Andy's. I did not want to be responsible for anyone else, of any age or size. I wasn't capable. How could he *ever* have assumed I would say yes? Leigh had to still be alive. She'd left Mia with her friend and run away, but eventually she'd come back. Then we'd sort this out and I'd be shot of it all. I felt claustrophobic in the small bathroom, went back to the lounge, but even that felt like a prison, and the photo of Leigh and Mia on the wall glared at me.

Late afternoon sunlight streamed in through the French doors and lit up the little paved courtyard. I rushed over to open the doors and step outside, raising my face to the warmth and brightness. The garden was long and narrow, with lots of low flowering natives and shrubs with vari-coloured leaves. At the far end, a park bench had been placed under a leafy gum tree. I wandered down the path, mentally naming the plants, and sat on the bench, stretching my legs out in front of me. I would not think about my brother, I would focus on... peace. The low buzz of city traffic, faint shouts and laughter from kids over the back somewhere, birds in the trees.

'Hello, love. Enjoying the sun?'

I jerked upright, squinting out from the shade into the glare. Above the side fence, a small, wrinkled face under a cloud of white curls beamed at me. 'Hello,' I said cautiously.

'Are you family then?'

'Yes.' Just what I needed – a nosy neighbour.

'Such a shame. Just wanted to offer my sympathy, dear.' She blinked hard. 'Well, that sounds like a Hallmark card, doesn't it? But I am really sorry. Andy was a lovely young bloke.'

'Did you know him well?' Maybe here was someone who could shed some light on the suburban, domestic Andy.

'We were friends. He helped me out in my garden, always brought little Mia with him.' She wiped her eyes with a lace hanky. 'I still remembered him from when he was a little lad.'

'You did?' That meant I should remember her too, from Nana's time, but my mind drew a blank.

'Yes, sometimes I'd be here visiting my mum when Andy and his sister visited Beryl.' Now it was her turn to stare at me. 'You – you're the older sister, aren't you?'

'Judi.'

'I thought so! You used to have long blonde hair. It suits you short, dear, and you look so much like your brother, even now.' Her eyes slid around to the house. 'Has Andy's wife come back yet? It's just that I've been collecting the mail – she asked me to – and I'm not sure if I should continue or not.'

'She what?'

'I thought they were going away.' A tear trickled down her rouged cheek. 'And then I read the paper and... I don't understand what happened.'

'Me neither,' I said grimly. 'I'm sorry, I don't remember your name.'

'Margaret Jones now. I used to be Margaret Simpson in those days.'

'Yes, of course.' I had a brief flash of a smiling middle-aged woman with dark curling hair and a smart suit, dropping in on her way home from work. 'Look, I'll take the mail, if you like. I should check for bills and things. Leigh won't be back for a little while yet.'

'Is she staying with family?'

I shrugged. 'I think so. This has all been a bit of a shock for me and I'm not sure of a lot of things right now.' I had no idea if Leigh had family in Melbourne, but surely Heath would've said something?

'Are you staying in the house?' she asked.

She was asking a lot of questions, and the last thing I needed was to be spied on. 'Yes, for a day or two.'

'Oh good. I won't worry then if I hear someone moving around.' She used an exaggerated whisper. 'The police were very noisy, you know, and they'd sit out here a lot and smoke.'

'Oh.' I wondered if Leigh had sneaked back at some point. 'You haven't heard anyone else in the house since then?'

'There was another man, quite good-looking, dark hair and a very nice suit. Drove a big grey car. He came a couple of times. Gave me palpitations the first time I heard him – silly me. I thought it was Andy.' She tried to smile but it was an effort.

'I know who you mean. He's a cop, too.'

'Thought he must've been.' She hesitated. 'I did think I heard someone a couple of nights ago. They were very quiet, but there's a squeaky board by the front door, and my bedroom is against that wall. Maybe I was imagining it.'

'All of this must have been very upsetting for you,' I said. God, I hoped she was imagining it. I didn't need burglars along with everything else.

'At my age, dear, it seems like someone passes away on a regular basis. But you don't expect it to be someone so young. You will tell me when the funeral is going to be, won't you?'

'Er, yes. I haven't made any arrangements yet.' I stood and moved towards the back door, hoping that would give her the hint. She looked disappointed but said goodbye and dropped from sight behind the fence while I continued inside, locking the French doors behind me.

The will lay on the floor where I'd tossed it, and I shoved it back into the envelope out of sight, but the words wouldn't disappear that easily. They bounced around inside my brain. Guardianship. The house was mine. The kid was mine.

If Leigh wasn't dead, it was weird that no one could find her. Maybe I'd ask Heath to look harder. Surely someone knew where she was. I'd find her if it was the last thing I did – I was *not* taking on the kid.

5

I searched the house again, this time for something alcoholic. Gin, wine... I'd even settle for a beer, but there was nothing. Another sign Andy had been clean. Nothing that might get you off your face and out of control, on the downward slope again.

I hadn't thought about staying in the house until Mrs Jones from next door had asked, but it'd save me finding a cheap motel, and I was hoping Leigh would turn up or at least call. I couldn't help regarding her as the rat leaving the sinking ship, even though it probably wasn't fair. Mainly what I wanted was to sort out this thing about the kid, to make sure Leigh collected Mia from wherever she'd dumped her, and get the will sorted out with the solicitor. Then I could escape.

Despite all the things I'd discovered, I still thought I'd missed something, but I couldn't figure out what it might be. It'd hardly be a clue to Andy's murder. The will had introduced some new twists, and now nothing added up. Shit, I was starting to sound like Hotshot.

Daylight saving had finished and dusk came quickly, the sun dropping like a lead weight. I took two painkillers and found a recycled shopping bag, then headed for the local shopping strip, ambling along to give my legs a stretch. Warmth radiated from the concrete under my feet but there was a chill in the long darkening shadows. The supermarket was full of people buying instant meals and milk and bread on their way home from work; I stocked up on muesli, decent bread and coffee, a roast chicken, and salad stuff. The bottle shop next door supplied me nicely with two bottles of Sauv Blanc.

The bag was heavy so I carried tomatoes and lettuce separately, my purse slung over my shoulder, glad when I saw Andy's gate ahead of me. I was just opening the front door, bags balanced on shoulders and in one hand, when I heard someone behind me unlatch the front gate. I spun around, dropping the tomatoes with a splat on the concrete.

'Damn it!'

'It's usually the crooks who are so unhappy to see me,' Hotshot said. He bent to pick up my tomatoes. 'The one on the bottom is history.'

'Yeah, thanks.' I pushed the door open with my free hand and hitched up my purse again.

'Give me something to carry,' he said, holding out a hand.

I gave him the recycled green bag, hoping the wine bottles wouldn't clink, and then thought, *Who cares?* If I want a drink, I'll bloody have one. And if I'd been feeling the need for a drink before, now I was gasping.

He followed me into the house and put the bag on the table, looking around. 'Nice house, isn't it?'

'Yes.' I put one bottle of wine into the freezer and the rest of the groceries in the fridge and cupboards. 'It used to be our nana's house, a long time ago.'

'I thought your brother bought it.'

'He did.' So they'd investigated his finances. 'He must've seen it go on the market and snapped it up. Lucky it hadn't been torn down for units already.' I folded my arms and leaned back against the sink, eyeing him warily. 'I take it you've got some news?'

'Yes, a bit more of the story, too, if you want to call it that.' He laughed but his face was pink and he was pulling at his collar again. He appeared to have shaved very recently, and his shirt looked freshly ironed. Maybe he was on his way out for the evening.

It looked like this was going to take a while, and I needed some sustenance. 'Do you want a drink? I've only got wine.'

'That'd be good.'

I pulled the wine out of the freezer again, found two glasses with Winnie the Pooh and Tigger on them – perfect – and twisted the cap off the bottle. He'd wandered over to the French doors and was staring out into the shadowed garden, his dark-suited back like a wall. I poured myself a glass, drank a couple of mouthfuls and then filled both glasses to the top. For some reason, he was making me nervous.

'Here you are,' I said, walking into the lounge room area and putting his glass on the coffee table. I sat on one of the low armchairs and he slouched on to the square, red couch, sticking his legs straight out and lifting his glass.

'Cheers,' he said.

'Mmm.' *Make yourself at home, why don't you?*

I didn't do polite conversation very well. At least he was OK to look at, now he'd stopped snarling. Nice square face, cool hazel eyes, although they held that hard expression all older police seemed to have, plus long, almost elegant fingers. Just because I'd passed forty didn't mean I'd stopped looking.

Long seconds of uncomfortable silence stretched out like thick rubber bands. He inspected Winnie the Pooh on his glass and I focused on my shoes. Why the hell wasn't he saying anything?

'Did you arrest someone?' I asked, unable to bear it any longer.

'Yeah, Tran, the guy I told you about.'

'And? Do I have to force it out of you?'

'No, I think it's OK to tell you.' He scratched the side of his face and sipped more wine. 'He said Andy rang him the day before, wanting to make a big buy. Ten thousand dollars. Tran said he couldn't do it, but Andy insisted, and Tran got suspicious. He said Andy hadn't been in the game for years, so he thought it was a set-up.' 'Was it?'

'Tran thought so. He went down to the river to meet Andy and tell him he couldn't get hold of the stuff.'

'If he didn't have it, why did he kill Andy?'

'He said Andy was really upset. Told him he was in deep shit with some underworld guys and needed to do a quick deal to make big dollars. Then he could pay off the guys who were after him.' Hotshot's eyes rested on me, as if evaluating my reaction.

'Underworld? You mean mafia?' I scoffed. 'That's just media bullshit.' I drank more wine but it didn't quench the anger that simmered inside me again. Surely they weren't going to blame Andy's death on this rubbish?

'Don't you read the papers? We had a gangland war going on here for ten years or more, with at least twenty people killed. Mules, little bosses, hitmen – going down like flies.'

'And the big bosses got away scot-free?'

'Not any more. Some of them are inside now. Or dead.'

'Congratulations.' He glared at me; I shifted uneasily on the arm-chair and tried to sound less sarcastic. 'So if they're all gone, why was Andy supposedly paying some of them off?'

'I don't know. I checked around. Andy wasn't working as an informant for anyone, not even the drug squad or guys in the Purana task force. There's always new gangs, but no one knows anything about him owing money, not even a faint rumour. Maybe it was a deal gone wrong, or someone was threatening him.' He stood up and went back to the window, peering out as if he expected there to be someone watching us.

My scalp prickled. 'You told me he'd been clean for three years.'

'Exactly.' He tested the door handle to make sure the doors were locked, then turned. 'What did your brother want the money for? When he came to see you a few years ago, I mean?'

'I assumed it was for drugs.' I wasn't going to admit that I'd had more thoughts about that very question.

'How long have you been living up in Candlebark?'

'Nearly six years.'

'It's pretty small. Doesn't even have its own footy team.'

My turn to glare at him. 'Have you been checking up on me?'

'It's my job.'

'It's not your job to sit here and drink my wine and ask stupid questions, is it?'

'I happen to be off duty,' he said. 'And it's not like you got out the best crystal.' The corner of his mouth twitched.

'Oh.' My face burned. I needed another wine, and tried to get up, but it was one of those badly designed, low armchairs and I fell sideways. He grabbed my arm and helped me up, his fingers warm on my skin. Heat flared out from the spot, all the way through me, and I quickly stepped away from him.

'You didn't finish the story,' I said.

'Not much more to tell. Tran said Andy was behaving strangely, weaving around, talking too much. Tran thought he was on something, but –'

'You said he was clean.'

'Exactly. Tran said Andy pulled a knife on him when he told him he had no drugs. Flashed it around and then tried to stab him.'

'But...' I shook my head. 'I still stick by what I'd said this morning – Andy wouldn't attack someone.'

'Tran's saying he had to shoot Andy. It was self-defence. He tried to shoot him in the arm or leg but he panicked and the bullet went into Andy's chest. Tran's very upset about it. Says Andy was his friend.'

'Some friend.'

'He seems genuinely upset and remorseful, which isn't often the case in drug-related cases.'

'What's the point of telling me all this?'

'I thought you wanted to know,' he said in a hard voice. 'Tran has been charged with murder, in case you thought we were going to let him off for good intentions.'

Someone in the house next door turned on their bedroom light and then drew the curtains. I caught a glimpse above the fence of an elaborate light shade and a Monet print on the wall before the window became a dimly glowing rectangle.

That's someone else's life. And in here, my brother's death. I suddenly saw Andy dancing in the dark, a knife flashing, a spurt of gunfire and him falling to the ground. The blood pooled out, as dark as oil. My heart was racing, and I found I was holding my breath. I tried to let it out slowly, and my head swam.

'It still doesn't add up, though,' Hotshot continued, pulling me out of my haze and back into the kitchen. 'Tran can't tell us where the gun is, even though he's confessed. He can't even tell us where he got it from.'

'Do you believe what he says about the drug deal?'

'Not really. He's not a known dealer, or a drug user. Why would Andy think he could supply $10,000 worth? Besides, your brother didn't have the money on him, and there's no record of him taking it out of his bank account.'

My brain calmer at last, I tried to remember how much was in the account – nowhere near $10,000. 'He could've borrowed it from someone.' Even I didn't believe that. It didn't make sense. 'Maybe he thought Tran would lend it to him, or had the connections.'

'Like a loan shark? Not as far as I can tell. Tran didn't say anything about that.' He rinsed his Pooh glass under the tap, filled it with water and drank some. 'I'm going to keep asking questions, follow this gangland lead, if you can call it that. The Purana detectives might help, or they might tell me to butt out. Worth a go, all the same.'

'Do you give all of your cases this much attention?'

'A lot are pretty cut and dried. This one looks like it is, but it's bugging me.' He hesitated. 'The mortuary says you haven't done anything about a funeral place yet.'

'First thing in the morning.' I didn't want to look at his handsome face, didn't want to see anything like pity.

'I've got all the details of your niece here. Where the family friend lives. She called again today. You'll need to – well, I guess I shouldn't tell you what you should or shouldn't be doing.'

Damn right.

He held out a piece of paper and I took it, then pushed it under my handbag. 'Thanks.'

'You, um, so...'

I frowned. 'Have you got more questions?'

'Not really, I was going to ask you about your grandmother and this house.'

I glanced around. The gloomy dusk was filling the room; I shivered and reached to turn on a light. 'Why are you interested?'

'Er... just making conversation.'

He had to be kidding. 'After the day I've had?'

'Well...' He smiled. 'I can talk about stuff other than police business, you know.'

'What? Like football and cricket and how gorgeous the girl on *NCIS: Los Angeles* is?' He wasn't to know those were Connor's favourite topics.

'No, I can talk about other things.'

'Like?'

'Like motorbikes and V8s and how cute the girl is on *CSI*.'

'Yeah, right.' I grinned back in spite of myself. Smart prick.

He hesitated, eyebrows slightly raised as if he'd just realised something, and then placed his empty Pooh glass carefully on the bench. 'You're right, it's been a long day. I'd better be off.' In a few moments, he was gone, and I was left feeling vaguely pissed off and disappointed and not willing to think about why. And when I crawled into bed in the guest room later on, I lay there for some time wondering exactly what he wanted from me.

6

The house in the back streets of Glenroy looked like an everyday suburban box – cream brick, double-fronted, a front garden with scraggly hebe bushes and a few beaten-up toys strewn around. I knew I had the right place by the kiddy squeals and shouts echoing from the backyard, and I cowered behind my car. It sounded like there were about twenty of them leaping around, killing each other. After Hotshot had pointedly left me the address, I thought I'd better front up and see what was going on, hoping this 'family friend' had heard from Leigh.

I walked up the cracked concrete path to the front door, aware I was clutching my big shoulder bag in front of me like a shield, and pushed the doorbell. It sounded somewhere in the house, a ghastly trill of bells, and in a few seconds the door opened and a curious face peered at me through the security screen.

'Hi. Are you Kayla?'

'Yes.'

'I'm Judi Westerholme, Andy's sister.'

The face beamed. 'I'm so glad you're here. Come on in.' She unlocked the security door then relocked it behind me. Her large body was a series of rolls, covered in a long pink T-shirt and black leggings. I followed her down a passageway crammed to overflowing with books on shelves and in piles on the floor. A quick scan told me most of them were those thick, wordy fantasy things that went on and on. The rest were battered kids' books.

'Want a tea or coffee?' she asked.

'I'm fine, thanks.' I trailed her into a large open-plan kitchen and dining area, with sliding glass doors that opened out on to a wooden deck. On the lawn, a teenage girl sprawled in a deck chair, spraying a hose on to three little kids who danced around in the sunshine, all totally naked. None of them looked to be under three years old, but I was guessing. I had no idea how big kids were at what age.

'Are they all yours?' I asked.

'God, no. I'm a foster mum, and I do family daycare sometimes, too.'

'You must have a lot of patience.' Or be insane.

'They're pretty good when they're little. I don't take kids over eight.' She followed my gaze. 'Mia's not out there. Why don't you have a coffee or something? I didn't know what time you were coming, and Mia's asleep. It took me ages to get her to go down, so I'd hate to wake her. She...'

I waited.

'She's been very unsettled. Can't blame her really. She's too little to understand. But she'll be happy to see her aunty.'

'Mmm.' I had no idea what to say and I wasn't sure if Kayla was having a go at me.

'I'll put the kettle on.' She bustled around behind the breakfast bar, getting out mugs and instant coffee and milk. I wanted to refuse when I saw the huge bulk tin but I thought I'd better not.

'Sit down.' Kayla pointed to the large wooden dining table and I did as I was told. I could see why she was a good foster mum – she had that tone in her voice that you didn't dare disobey. She checked the group outside and then resumed the coffee-making.

I carefully avoided putting my arms on the table that was smeared with something red and sticky. 'How long has Mia been here?'

'Nearly a week. Leigh sounded a bit frantic when she rang me, but I thought it would only be for a day or two. Do you know where she's gone?'

'No. Wish I did.' I cleared my throat. 'You know my brother, Andy, is dead, I suppose?'

'Yeah, I was sorry to hear about that. He was one of the good guys.' She brought two steaming mugs over and placed one in front of me. The liquid was a grey-brown colour, not a good sign.

'Did Leigh say anything when she dropped Mia off? Any hint at all?'

'She said she had to work, actually. She was being sent on a training course.' She pursed her lips. 'Course, I know now that's a fib. Pissed me off, that did. She's a friend. She didn't have to lie to me.'

'But you didn't think at the time she was lying?'

'No, why would I? Then I saw about Andy in the papers, and when she didn't come back, I rang the cops. I was worried. How come you're asking all these questions?'

Because I'm more desperate to find her than the cops are. I tried to keep my face blank. 'I was hoping she'd contacted you in the last couple of days.'

Kayla shook her head, her frizzy curls bouncing. 'Nup, not a word. Are you –'

The glass door slid open with a bang and the teenage girl rushed in, followed by three small, dripping bodies. 'Who's ready for a warm bath?' she said.

'Me, me!' they all screamed, pushing and shoving each other.

'Getting a bit cold out there,' the girl said to Kayla.

'That's fine. Don't leave them in the bath too long though. And keep the noise down. You'll wake Mia.'

'Right. Now, ssshhhh everybody.' She put her finger to her lips and the kids all made big ssshhhh noises too as they tiptoed along to the bathroom. They sounded like a herd of baby elephants to me.

Kayla turned back to me. 'Are you taking Mia today?'

I imagined Mia screaming, and cringed inside. 'No, I can't.'

'Why not?' Her tone was belligerent.

Heath had better not have told her I was coming to collect the kid. 'Look, up until yesterday I didn't know Mia existed. I hadn't seen

Andy for a few years. This is all news to me.' It was true, but I still felt like I was faking it.

'I can't keep her here indefinitely,' Kayla said. 'I've got my foster kids to look after, and it's tricky legally.'

'Well, I don't want –' I snapped my mouth shut before I said the unforgiveable, but she guessed anyway.

'You can't just abandon her!' Kayla's face flushed a deep red with indignation and I cringed. Anti-motherhood sentiment was worse than serial murder in this house.

'Look, I simply want Leigh to come back and claim her. I don't want custody.'

'You wouldn't get it.'

That's what you think, lady. You don't know the whole story. I took a big gulp of the coffee and wished I hadn't. It was like muddy dishwater. 'I'm sorry. This is a very difficult situation for everyone. I'm having to deal with everything on my own.'

Her face softened. 'Was Andy your only brother then? Mia cries for him all the time.'

'What about her mother?'

'Once or twice, but it's mostly Daddy she wants. She's a real daddy's girl.'

A knife twisted in my guts. I would've loved to have seen Andy being a dad. I took a deep breath. 'I imagine so.'

'How come you didn't know about Mia?'

'Andy and I hadn't seen each other for quite a while. One of those family things, that's all. Andy and Leigh were addicts back then, before Mia came along, and I'd had a gutful of the whole thing.' Her questions annoyed me but I needed to stay on her good side so she'd keep the kid for a while longer.

'Leigh had been clean since she got pregnant, you know. She was doing well.'

'I gathered that.'

'Terrible the way these family things blow up, isn't it?' She patted my hand and I tried hard not to flinch. 'No way to make it up to your brother now, except through Mia.'

I jumped up. 'Don't lay that guilt crap on me, please. It's the last thing I need right now.' I tried to lower my voice, but it was too late. A loud wail came from a nearby room.

'That's Mia,' Kayla said, scowling at me and getting up. 'It won't kill you to stay and say hello, will it?'

I nearly walked out then, until I heard Mia crying, 'Daddy, Daddy,' and my feet stuck to the floor. One part of my brain said *Get the hell out of here* but the other part said *Don't you want to see if she really does look like Andy?* Before I could decide either way, Kayla emerged from the bedroom, carrying a tiny blonde child who was beating her free hand against Kayla's chest while the other hand clutched at her T-shirt like she'd never let go. Tears and snot streaked the kid's face and Kayla reached for a tissue to gently wipe it off.

'There you go', she said soothingly. 'Look who's here. Your Aunty Judi.'

The kid looked at me and another tear rolled down her face.

'Hello, Mia,' I said, trying to sound friendly but not succeeding. She turned her head away from me and laid it on Kayla's shoulder. Her rejection jolted me, and I scolded myself. *What did you expect?*

'Want a bikkie, love?' Kayla asked, and got a tiny nod in reply. After a healthy-looking home-made Anzac biscuit had been scooped out of a jar, Kayla sat down at the table again with Mia on her lap nibbling at the food. I wanted to leave, but in the end I sat down, too.

'What's going to happen to her – if Leigh doesn't come back?' Kayla whispered over the kid's head.

Suddenly, Kayla had jumped from defending Leigh to the possibility she'd disappeared for good. 'I'm not sure. I live out in the country, two hours away. I'm not set up to have a child. I wouldn't know how to look after one.'

'You'd soon learn.' She sniffed. 'I can't force you to take her, but they won't let me keep her here much longer. She'll have to go into state care, be ruled by Human Services, and truly you don't want that. Once she's in the system...'

'I understand that, but...' I clenched and unclenched my hands. 'Are you sure you don't know where Leigh went?'

As if on cue, the three kids rushed in from the bathroom, faces pink and hair damp and standing on end. They clamoured for Anzac biscuits, banging their hands against the cupboard door, and I wanted to knock their heads together. The teenager followed them in, gave them all a biscuit each and herded them towards the TV in the lounge room next door. 'Is Mia coming to watch telly?' she asked.

'Not right now. Mia's aunt is visiting.'

It was like a secret code. The teenager gave me a sour look and disappeared. Maybe if Kayla had said 'Aunty Judi is here' I might have been granted a smile. Not that I cared either way.

Kayla smoothed Mia's hair back off her face. 'What about Mia's granny? I heard she was a bit senile.'

Instead of being offended, I laughed. 'Yeah, has been for about forty years. I can just imagine ringing her and asking if she wants a two-year-old. You might as well offer her a monkey from the zoo.'

Kayla frowned. 'Ohhh-kay, just so we're straight here. You're not taking Mia with you today.'

'No, I'm sorry. I can't.'

'But you realise that if Leigh doesn't come back very shortly, I'll have to let the police know, and then Human Services.' The set of her mouth told me she would do it in a second. She'd had enough.

I bit my lip, and then tried to look positive. 'Yes, but I'm sure things will work out.' If I said it often enough, it might come true.

Mia looked up from her biscuit and stared at me with Andy's big blue eyes. 'Daddy,' she said with great deliberation.

Kayla nodded. 'You do look a lot like him, you know.'

'It's the short hair.'

'No, it's more than that. She can see it too.'

'But I'm not Andy. She'd be worse off with me than any foster home, you know. I never was the mothering kind.'

Mia held her biscuit out to me and smiled. 'Bikkie.'

'She wants you to have a bite,' Kayla said.

'You're kidding.' The biscuit had spit all over it from where the kid had licked it. 'Isn't that a bit – unhygienic?'

Kayla roared with laughter, her double chin wobbling, and my face burned. I grabbed the biscuit, took a small bite, trying not to gag, and handed it back. Mia promptly stuck it back in her mouth.

'Very nice, thank you,' I said, and was rewarded with a smile around the disgusting biscuit.

Kayla opened her mouth to say something then closed it again, and I decided it was time to go before she tried to persuade me to take the kid after all. I stood up, and she did too, stepping around the table and handing Mia to me. 'I need to get a cloth to wash her face. Back in a tick.'

In surprise, I clutched the kid like a shopping bag, hoping she wouldn't start screaming, but instead she reached up and patted my face, and my breath caught in my throat. She was heavy on my hip, heavier than I expected, and I adjusted my grip. I began to feel manipulated, stuck in the middle of the room, not knowing whether to put her down and run, or wait for Kayla to come back.

Mia's big eyes were so like Andy's that I couldn't stop looking at her, fighting a memory of him and me sitting on the sand at the beach when we were little. One of the first things I could remember. I shook my head. I didn't want the responsibility of a small child; I couldn't take care of her properly, and it would show. The kid would soon work out she wasn't wanted, and I didn't need the aggravation or the guilt trip.

Kayla returned with the cloth and I immediately placed Mia in her arms, saying, 'I have to go. I have an appointment with the funeral director about Andy.' Which was a small, guilty lie, but it got me instant sympathy, and I made my hasty escape.

7

Wilson Brothers Funeral Directors were stuck in a back street in Footscray behind a second-hand furniture shop and a florist, but they'd carved out a nice-sized carpark, probably by knocking down half a dozen houses.

I eased the Benz into a shady space under a tree and immediately a huge splatter of bird shit landed on the windscreen. Great. The carpark was deserted so it seemed that lunchtime wasn't a popular time for burials these days. I'd stopped off for something to eat after I'd left Kayla's, and been tempted by an egg and mayonnaise sandwich that I now regretted as my stomach twisted into an oily knot.

I'd sat in the café for nearly an hour, staring out, unseeing, at people strolling past the windows, while I thought about my childhood years, and my funny, cute brother, and how badly we grew up. And wrestled with the possibility that I might be condemning Mia to a similar upbringing, no matter what I did. I was possibly a worse option than Leigh, but maybe I was judging her with no real evidence. My gut feeling of distrust and dislike was based on twenty minutes nearly six years ago.

On the other hand, if I decided Leigh was OK and ignored Andy's will, I could be doing it just to get out of the responsibility. I had no answers, and I couldn't stand thinking about it anymore, so I went to the next item on my 'don't want to' list. The funeral.

I forced myself to push open the stained glass front door and a bell pinged faintly, a delicate sound not at all like a death knell. The foyer was huge, carpeted in royal blue with a cream rose border, with cream walls and tastefully bland paintings of flowers. A gigantic bouquet of lilies, roses and apricot gerberas stood on a table in the middle. The scent in the air, however, was fake, maybe an oil burner somewhere, and my stomach churned again.

A door opened on my right and a short, plump woman with fluffy white-blonde hair peered out, smiling brightly when she saw me. 'Good afternoon,' she said. 'Can I help you?' She emerged fully from the room, still smiling.

I stepped backwards, quailing. 'You're probably busy. I can come back tomorrow.' I couldn't do this.

'We're never too busy,' she said, 'and we're always open.' Obviously the look on my face was disbelieving. 'Truly. We're always on call. People need us when they need us, not at our convenience.'

'Right.'

She seemed completely unfazed by my behaviour. Probably dealt with it every day. 'I'm Alicia Stevens.' She shook my hand firmly. 'Come this way, dear.'

She ushered me into a side room that held a couch, two armchairs, a low table and a huge box of tissues. Another door on the opposite side of the room was labelled *Display*. I didn't want to think about what kind of display.

She picked up a clipboard from a table in the corner and waited while I chose where to sit. I picked an armchair. I didn't want her cosying up to me sympathetically on the couch, offering handfuls of tissues. She sat in the other armchair and waited. I stayed silent, not knowing how to start, unable to form any words. Besides, I was terrified that I might cry. Finally, she said, 'Could you tell me your name?'

Well, yes, of course, and my address, and from there it was all pretty straightforward. Focusing on concrete details and arrangements let me breathe easier and stay in control. She didn't blink when I told her where Andy's body was, just said it would be no problem to collect him. I liked how she said *him*, not *it*. I decided on cremation, and a service at their own chapel. Nothing religious.

'Yes, a lot of people choose our chapel,' she said. 'Would you like to see it?'

I edged back in my armchair. 'No, thanks. I'm sure it'll be fine.'

That made her blink a bit. 'We also put the death and funeral notices in the newspapers for you, if you wish.'

My turn to blink. 'Notices? What for?'

'If your loved one has family members or workmates or friends who might want to attend, it lets them know when the service is. It's also very handy for anyone you might not be able to contact.' She waited.

My scalp prickled. *Like Leigh?* No. Work, friends – of course. Just because I didn't know them, didn't mean they wouldn't want to come to his funeral. 'Yes, OK,' I said.

'Are you going to have refreshments at your home?'

'Er...' My horror at the idea must have filled my face; her eyes widened.

'We can do them here,' she said quickly. 'At a very reasonable cost.'

'Great. Yes. Please.'

Her tone changed to soft. 'Now, the last thing is the casket.'

I clutched at my bag like it was a lifebuoy, my knuckles white. 'Casket? But he's being cremated.'

'Yes, but he needs to be... contained.'

The egg sandwich was a foul taste in the back of my throat. 'Oh. Right.' My hands ached and I convinced them to loosen their grip.

'We have a display next door, if you'd like to choose something?'

'Right.' I couldn't stop saying it, and every time I did, I wanted to smack myself. Like a robot, I stood up. 'Let's have a look, then.'

It was the most ghastly room I've ever been in. I stopped just inside the door, my legs rigid, refusing to take me any further. Two rows of shiny coffins – so shiny they reminded me of lacquered wooden toilet seats – with silver or gold handles. There was no way I was going to examine silk or satin linings, or think about engraved name plaques. Her explanations were a static buzz in my ears. I pointed at the plainest one at the end of the row, a sturdy box with no carvings and six solid handles. 'That one.' And in case she thought I was cheap, I added, 'Andy didn't like fancy stuff.'

I backed out of the room, breathing fast, and pulled out a tissue I didn't need while I steeled myself to finish the rest of the details. We settled on a date and time, three days hence, and I got out of there as fast as I could. More birds had shat on my car but I was so desperate to get back to Andy's house and have a drink that I didn't even turn on the wipers and window sprayer, just drove as fast as I dared, peering around the splatters. I scribbled a note to tell Mrs Jones about the funeral and shoved it in her letterbox; after a calming glass of wine, I went back out with a bucket of soapy water and a sponge and cleaned the crap off, then gave the window a quick rinse with the hose. My heart rate had settled and my brain felt clear again.

Three days. Should I stay in Melbourne or go home? I so wanted to get back to my garden, my small stone house, my oasis of peace and quiet. With all the mulch, nothing would need watering just yet, but I yearned for a spade and the feel of digging into the earth.

But this business with Andy felt unfinished, as if I still had to follow it through to some kind of resolution. Heath had the killer in custody, even if his story didn't make much sense. That was a police problem. The solicitor could deal with the will. But I couldn't ignore the obligation Andy had dumped on me – the kid. I needed to find Leigh, to make sure she was all right and able to care for Mia. Andy had put Mia in his will, three weeks ago, and if she was so important to him, I had to sort it out. But it wasn't only that. Something else was niggling at me.

I tidied up the lounge and kitchen, swept the floors, wiped cupboards down, but the mindless housework didn't let the answer float into my head so I went to sit outside. I stayed near the back door, under the pergola, so Mrs Jones next door couldn't see me. I needed silence. After some more thinking, I fetched a pad and pen and made a list of all the things I'd found out since I'd been here, then marked which ones made me the most uneasy when I considered them.

Funnily enough, the one that still made my guts tighten and twist the most was the $50,000 deposit on Nana's house.

Because it came out of nowhere. There was no record of saving it in an ordinary bank account. *Not like the old bastard would have.* It was like a sharp slap. Dad's face sprang into stark detail in my mind. Short, grey moustache clipped into a dead straight line. Bald head with six strands combed over. Big hands. Grey eyes that could freeze you in an instant. No running away. Just the interminable wait while he decided whether you deserved the leather strap or not. There weren't many times that Andy escaped it, especially after he start-ed getting defiant. He would've been about ten the first time he answered Dad back. I shivered at the memory of his screams. They were like an indelible, searing soundtrack in my brain.

I'd been luckier, being a girl and being more of a grovelling coward. Often, instead of the strap, I'd get one of those big hands across my head. Whack! Once I'd gone deaf for a couple of days, and thought he'd busted my eardrum, but it must've been shock or something because I eventually recovered. Just in time for the next round.

When Dad died ten years ago, it was like Andy and I suddenly relaxed, shedding the hard shells we'd built up since we were kids, and it left us both vulnerable. Him to his drugs, going on a spree that cost him everything, and me to my then husband, Max. The old bastard had left us both $100,000, God only knows why. Probably duty. And a hundred grand was a pittance compared to what he was worth. Mum got everything, and I hope she choked on it.

I didn't want to touch my money, considered giving it to some charity, but Max kept on at me. He'd been talking for ages about buying a pub, and one he liked had come on the market in North Fitzroy. 'Come on,' he'd coaxed, 'it's a sure thing. An old place that can be renovated cheaply and then we'll cash in on the boom – that old suburb is the hot new place to live.' I'd worked in hospitality for years, a lot of them in managerial positions, and I knew the ropes. In the end, I gave in, even though the thought of touching the money made me sick.

Andy had been good at real estate, clever and canny, quick to analyse and take action, good with people and their needs. He'd worked long hours and played hard every night, drinking and taking what he called 'party poppers'. I didn't want to know what he meant by that. In his twenties, he'd had a different girl every time I saw him, but when I first started going out with Max, Andy took a dislike to him. 'He's not good enough for you. He's a sleaze, a con man.'

I'd travelled a fair bit, met a few men, figured I knew what I was doing. But hindsight told me all I'd been looking for was The Man Least Like My Father, and that was Max. Good-looking, lazy, a hater of rules, a spendthrift and a womaniser. Persuading me to use Dad's bequest to buy the pub had led to the worst time in my life. I should've known the money would be cursed in some way.

The memories were like blunt axes, chopping at me, hacking apart my hard-won peace. 'Stop thinking about that crap!' I said out loud, and sat up. I'd sealed off that part of my life, pushed it all to the back of my brain. That was the whole point of living in Candlebark. I'd moved on from it all, physically and mentally. I was determined to keep it that way.

But the $50,000 kept bugging me. Heath had mentioned gang-land wars, but I couldn't see how Andy could possibly be connected. Like everyone else, I'd read about it back then, but it was unreal, like an Aussie version of *The Sopranos*. I could check in the newspaper archives, but surely old history wouldn't tell me anything about what was happening now. And it wasn't my job. Leave it to the cops.

Which reminded me that I should call Connor and ask him to keep an eye on my cottage for a bit longer. And right then, I needed to hear a friendly, familiar voice. He answered on the second ring.

'Do you want me to come down for the funeral?' he asked, after I'd given him the rundown on everything that had happened. I left out the bit about guardianship of Mia – that made it too complicated. And I didn't want to have to explain why I was refusing to look after the kid. Next thing I knew, Connor would be offering to organise child care!

'No, thanks. The service will only take twenty minutes.'

He was silent for a few seconds, and it suddenly occurred to me that he might be hurt at my curt refusal. Then he said, 'Has that detective told you anything about the suspect, or what actually happened?'

I told him what Heath had said, and the things that didn't add up to him. 'I kind of agree, but I don't know what I'm supposed to do about it.'

'Nothing! You stay out of it,' he replied. 'But you could ask for the autopsy report, and if there'll be a coroner's inquest.'

'I'm not sure I want to talk to Detective Hotshot again.'

'Hotshot?' He chuckled. 'He can't be that bad.'

'You were the one who told me to watch out for him.'

'That's because I didn't want you to get the run-around, or get pushed into anything you didn't want to do. What's this Hotshot done?'

'Nothing, really. He took me to a café, and gave me some of Andy's things. Then he came around last night – to talk about the case.'

'Yeah, right. Sounds like he was hitting on you.'

My face flamed. 'Don't be so bloody stupid! He's being helpful, that's all. Besides, he's younger than me.'

'So? Nothing wrong with his eyes, then. Now, has Uncle Connor ever been wrong about these things?'

'Yes. You're the one whose girlfriend moved to Perth.' Oops. That was a bit mean.

'She got a great job she couldn't turn down, that's all.' He sounded hurt this time.

'Sorry, I didn't mean to re-open old wounds.' I changed the subject. 'How much do you know about this gangland stuff in Melbourne?'

'What I read, and the police reports I got. It's mostly old history now, although it rears its ugly head now and then. Our big problem is ice, and the illegal tobacco crowd.' He sighed heavily. 'Ice is like a bloody cancer in country towns.'

I hunched over the handset, unwilling to let the topic slide. 'There's been a bit of talk about maybe a gangland connection to Andy's death.'

His voice sharpened. 'Why would they say that? What have they found out?'

'Nothing really. The guy they arrested is Vietnamese – no connection at all. I think Hotshot Heath was just showing off what a great cop he is.'

'I can take some leave and come down, if you want me to.'

The last thing I needed was Connor rushing down to Melbourne to act as my bodyguard, thinking the mafia were moving in on me. As if. I resolved to keep quiet about the $50,000. 'No, I'm fine. I'll be home after the funeral, don't worry.'

I hung up a few seconds later and sank back in the couch. Connor had been a great friend over the past few years, but I was always conscious that he was a lonely guy, and it wouldn't take much encouragement from me to make him think we could become a couple – as in romance, or at least sex. Sex with Connor was the last thing I wanted. Ugh. Far better to stay friends. So much less complicated.

Gangland. Underworld. Saying it out loud had given me a nasty feeling in my guts again. Dusk had fallen while I was talking to Connor, and now the big windows were black, reflecting me like dark mirrors. Woman Thinking With Furrowed Brow. *Why was Andy killed?*

I couldn't see outside, and it unnerved me. Time to draw the curtains.

At the back, I briskly let Roman blinds unfold down the French doors. A blueish-white light flickered behind Mrs Next-Door's net curtains – she was settled in front of her TV for the night. She'd said she heard someone creeping around in here, late at night. I'd assumed it was Heath, coming back for another look on his own. Now I wasn't so sure. It could've been anyone. Someone could be out there now. Silence, then a scraping, scrabbling sound at the side of the house. My heart leapt and crashed, bouncing against my ribs. A yowl, some hissing. Bloody cats!

I wrapped my arms tightly around myself, took three shuddering breaths. *Peace and calm, peace and calm. It was only a cat.* My heart slowed, and I let my arms drop. Once everything was locked up, I'd feel better.

As I drew each span of curtains, I double-checked door and window locks until my edginess settled down to manageable levels, then I turned on Andy's TV and sat on the red couch, sipping wine, trying to think about what I wanted to eat. On the screen, two men in hand-knitted jumpers were pointing ecstatically at broken pots in holes they'd dug in the ground somewhere in England.

The phone rang beside me and I jumped, spilling wine down my chin that trickled into my cleavage and soaked the front of my shirt. Bloody Connor. Surely he wouldn't insist on coming down. I snatched the phone up and pressed the Talk button.

'Just forget I mentioned that gangland rubbish,' I said.

'Why, what have you heard?'

'Who is this?' I snapped, peering down at the stain on my shirt.

'Detective Sergeant Heath.'

Oh. Hotshot. Heat rushed up my neck and into my face. 'Sorry. I thought you were someone else.'

'Who?'

'A friend. Forget it.' I wiped my sweaty hands on my T-shirt, one by one. 'I was talking to someone about Andy's funeral.'

'Good, you've organised it then.'

'More or less.' I waited, still feeling clammy. What did he want? Did he have more news?

'So...' He cleared his throat. 'I had some updates on your brother's case to discuss with you.'

'Discuss away.'

'I thought it would be easier to meet. I have a couple of things to give you.'

I tried to analyse his voice and he sounded both edgy and uncertain. Weird for a cop. 'Is one of them the autopsy report?'

'Just the prelim. If you want it. I haven't had dinner yet and I thought...'

Connor's words came back to me. *He's hitting on you*. I thought of those eyes, across the table, and couldn't think what to say.

'Never mind,' Heath said. 'I'll pick up some takeaway on the way home.'

Connor is an idiot. But my mouth opened and the words rushed out. 'Bring it here, if you want. I can always offer you a glass of wine.'

His voice brightened. 'Great, you're on. I'll be there in about half an hour, OK?'

'OK,' I said feebly, and hung up. The front of my shirt clung to me and I smelled like a backyard still. I'd have to change my top but all I'd brought with me was a black business suit and a couple of tatty T-shirts and tracksuit pants. I'd come prepared for funerals and cleaning house, not entertaining.

Skinny Leigh wouldn't have left me anything remotely large enough to wear. I rummaged around in Andy's wardrobe, looking for something I didn't have to iron, and found a pale green Hawaiian shirt with parrots on it that was a size M. Not too garish, thank God. I put it on and realigned all the suits and shirts, then straightened the ties on the rack. Andy had always had good taste in clothes, unlike me, and the parrot shirt was probably a present.

The doorbell rang and I slammed the wardrobe shut, trying to avoid the sight of myself in the wall mirror. I hadn't even had time to put on more makeup or brush my hair. I shook my head. A green parrot shirt and messy hair were irrelevant; I had a preliminary autopsy report to read.

8

I opened the front door. Heath had changed out of his suit into jeans and a blue striped polo shirt, and I immediately regretted the parrots.

He eyed my shirt, his eyebrows raised. 'Good look. Reminds me of Fiji.'

'Your last holiday?'

'No, a job. I was seconded there last year to help with a murder investigation.'

'Don't they have their own police detectives?'

'They suspected it was a policeman who did it, and they were right. Bit sensitive all round.'

We were still at the door and I stepped back to let him in. As he passed me, I smelled aftershave and spicy food of some kind. I inhaled, and my mouth watered; I shut the door harder than I intended, my face warm. He was here on business, and I needed to get a grip.

He put down the paper bag he'd had tucked under his arm, then unzipped a carry bag and laid out several plastic containers on the kitchen table. 'I got enough for both of us, if you're hungry.'

I was starving. Eating with him wouldn't kill me, so I fetched plates and cutlery. He found the Tigger and Pooh glasses and poured the wine, tactfully not commenting on how little was left in the bottle. I got the Pooh glass this time.

'Has something gone wrong? What did you want to tell me?'

He handed me a serving spoon. 'Let's eat first.'

That aggravated the hell out of me. It was like he was playing some kind of game with me. I like to get bad news over with, not pussy-foot around and pretend nothing is wrong. I drank my wine, told myself I was being cranky for no reason; he dished out the food on to his plate and sat down.

'Get it while it's hot,' he said. 'It's Himalayan, not Indian. Have you had goat curry before?'

The aroma was getting to me and my stomach grumbled so I sat and examined the pile of meat chunks and rice on my plate. 'What does goat taste like?'

'Great. It's got more flavour than lamb.'

He was eating steadily, not waiting for me, so I tried a mouthful and discovered the goat was very tasty. Maybe I'd ask questions after we'd eaten. We finished off everything in the containers and plenty of the wine as well. I was glad the parrot shirt was roomy.

I leaned back and said, 'So, what have you got to tell me?'

'Tran has been charged,' he said. 'His solicitor only turned up this afternoon, so Tran'll front court tomorrow. He'll probably be remanded. He's admitted to it so he won't get bail.'

'That's all good, isn't it?'

He cocked his head. 'Theoretically, yes. We always like it when someone confesses, but...' He rubbed at a spot on his glass. 'I don't think he's telling the whole truth.'

'He either shot Andy or he didn't,' I said irritably. 'Why would he lie about that?'

'I don't know.' He glanced at me and then away again, as if expecting me to harangue him. Maybe victims' families got angry and upset all the time. It was probably natural. I didn't feel natural. I un-clenched my teeth and drank more wine.

He was the investigating cop, he'd charged someone, but he still didn't seem to know what was what. I didn't want to be having this pointless conversation. I stood up and opened the French doors; the autumn warmth still hung in the air and I strode away from him, down to the wooden seat in the arbour.

He ambled down the path and plonked himself down next to me. His arm was warm against mine, and I wanted to edge away but there was no room on the seat. We sat in silence, staring up at the evening star. Sweat formed on the back of my neck and chilled immediately; I concentrated on breathing normally, but it was an effort.

'What star sign are you?' he said.

I nearly choked. 'What?'

He stuck his chin out. 'I like horoscopes. I always start the day by looking at mine.'

'And that tells you how many crooks you're going to catch, does it?'

'Hardly. It's just a bit of fun. Lighten up, will you?'

I bristled. I was not in the mood for jokes and fun right now. Then I let out a long breath, and looked at the rising moon and the garden, the houses with lights on and faint music playing somewhere, Andy's house with welcoming doors wide open, and tears stung my eyes. I pinched the bridge of my nose, hard.

'My brother went from coke for fun to being a heroin addict. I still believe being with Leigh made him worse. Every time I saw him, he was desperate, unable to keep himself together for more than a few days or weeks at a time. I never saw any sign that would change, or could change.'

Heath nodded. 'People do get off it. Maybe having a kid was his big turning point.'

'Maybe. But how come he begged me for a loan, then not long afterwards he buys this place? With a $50,000 deposit. Where did that come from?'

'Left over from your father's bequest?'

'No, Andy took great delight in spending the lot on drugs and partying years ago.'

'Did you get left a hundred grand, too?'

'None of your business.'

He folded his arms. 'True.'

'I couldn't find anything to indicate Andy was in financial trouble. Not even an extra loan. He was making mortgage payments fortnightly, and he had a job that paid quite well. He really had turned himself around.'

Heath stood up and paced slowly up and down the garden path, head down, thinking out loud. 'I saw the same thing. He was very neat, very detailed with his paperwork. Everything filed and in order. Normal family man, suburban life. So why did he need a lot of money all of a sudden? Why did he act so weirdly and get himself killed? Why did he ask someone to supply him who had no real access to drugs?'

I sighed, sagging against the carved seat back, feeling it dig into my spine. I couldn't answer him. I wanted this to be simple, to know it was a deal gone wrong, that Andy had been predictable to the end. I hated feeling so twisted around, as if at any moment I was about to lose my footing and crash to the ground. I liked things stable and steady. 'Wouldn't you rather send Tran to gaol and close the case?'

He grimaced. 'When things don't add up, I know there's usually a nasty surprise waiting for me around the next corner.'

'Like a mafia hit man.' I couldn't help it – a snorty little laugh escaped and I blamed it on the wine.

He stopped pacing. 'You want me to describe the two guys who got shot-gunned in front of their kids at a Saturday footy clinic? Or the guy half-burned and stuffed in a wheelie bin in Sunshine? Or the big boss gunned down at his club in Sydney Road? Christ, even the hand grenade thrown at a house more recently.'

I jerked upright. 'Don't snarl at me. That has nothing to do with Andy,' I said.

'Don't be too bloody sure.'

'Stop trying to frighten me. Or do you still think there's something I'm not telling you?'

'Is there?' His face was hard, his eyes arrowing in on me.

'No! I'm completely in the dark on all of this. I didn't know any of it – the house, the kid, or the money.' I stood up and headed back to the house, brushing past him on the path. 'I'm tired. I need an early night.' I sensed his eyes on my back and then he followed me, lock-ing the French doors behind him and closing the blinds.

'The lock on these doors is a bit flimsy,' he said, his tone conciliatory. 'You might want to add bolts top and bottom.'

'Is this a high-crime area?' I could be nice, too.

'No. I'm just not keen on French doors,' he said. 'Anyway, time I hit the road. Make sure you lock up properly, all right? Windows *and* doors.'

He was speaking to me like I was about ten years old, but I bit back my snarky reply and nodded. The way he kept scanning the curtained windows made me jumpy. I shut the front door behind him, double-locked it and put the chain on. His shadow loomed behind the stippled glass; he was standing on the step, listening to make sure I did it.

I was tempted to go back out into the garden and have another glass of wine, stay there as long as I wanted, but my heart was beating in the base of my throat like a panicked moth. I tried to convince myself he was being a control freak, then double-checked all the window and door locks, as instructed.

Later, lying in bed, running everything through my mind yet again, a slippery mix of irritation and uneasiness bubbled up. Andy had always been quick-witted and funny, but Dad turned him into someone manipulative who thought he could talk his way out of any-thing. Rat cunning, Dad called it, after Andy had lied to him and got out of a beating. Andy had worked out that it was better to outsmart them than fight them, but it didn't always work.

Maybe he'd borrowed from the wrong person. A loan shark. His death was the result of an elaborate scheme that had gone wrong. Hard to talk your way out of a gun in your face. I saw him lying in the pool of blood again and rubbed my eyes to try and dispel the picture.

The nerve up to my hip felt like a red-hot wire; I turned over again to try and ease it but stretching too far would cause cramp in my foot. Shit. Maybe I'd made a mistake staying in Melbourne. My leg didn't like it at all. I was too close to North Fitzroy; although I hadn't had many nightmares about the accident in the past year, I knew I'd have one tonight. A good reason not to go to sleep, except I was worn out. I pulled two pillows under the covers and made a bolster to rest my leg against, which helped.

The other thing keeping me awake was the kid. Kayla wouldn't put up with Mia much longer, and I didn't want to be forced into taking her. But the alternative was state care. Leigh shouldn't have left her behind. Surely it was better to take your kid with you, even if you were bolting interstate. Had she known about Andy's will and assumed I'd take over? She certainly didn't know me, so it was possible.

I didn't want to consider Leigh might be dead. The fact that she'd organised Kayla to care for Mia for a while told me she was hiding out somewhere. And that she had cared enough about Mia to leave her somewhere safe.

As for Hotshot – he acted all friendly then sneaked in little, tricky questions. Hitting on me? That was Connor being ridiculous. I hoped it wasn't a sign that he was getting over-protective again.

I turned again and cursed. Bloody leg. I'd have to take some more painkillers or I'd be Attila the Hun tomorrow. I struggled out of bed without bothering to turn the lights on – all I had to do was find my bag and I was pretty sure it was in the dining area, hooked over the back of a chair. LED appliance lights let out a faint glow as I felt my way through the door, along the wall and around the far side of the table. As I groped inside my bag for the pill bottle, I heard a scratching at the French doors. Mrs Jones's cat again.

It was followed by a grating crack and a sudden breeze ruffled the blinds then swirled around my legs. I crouched down, hardly daring to breathe, and scuttled forward to the armchair, trying to scrunch in behind it. My heart boomed in my ears, a warning drum. In the gloom I saw two men push through the gap, aiming a thin torch beam at their feet. They weren't tiptoeing but they weren't crashing in either. Who the hell were they?

The torch beam angled ahead, into the kitchen area, then around the walls, stopping at the bedroom door.

'In there,' one of them whispered.

They moved towards the doorway and, as they passed, I saw one of them carrying a short-barrelled shotgun. If they both went into the bedroom, I could get out the French doors and climb the fence. Too bad I was only wearing a long T-shirt and undies. I'd manage. I took a quiet breath and got ready to move, easing my leg out, gripping the chair to stop my hands shaking as I watched the two dark shapes at the other end of the room.

One moved into the bedroom, but the other stayed in the doorway. 'Give her a nudge,' he said.

'It's pillows,' the other one said, not bothering to keep his voice down. 'Check the bathroom.'

'Chill out. We'll get her.'

They knew their way around, and were moving faster than I'd expected. I hunched down further, straining to hear. More footsteps –into the bathroom and then Mia's room. The other pair of feet stayed still. The floorboard by the front door creaked. 'All locked here.'

The chain. They knew I was inside. Panic ripped through me like a fish-gutting blade. I bit the inside of my mouth, trying and failing to stay calm. I had to get out!

But my leg had locked up from crouching for so long – there was no way I'd be able to make a run for it now. I closed my eyes, praying they'd have a quick look around and then leave. My armpits were soaked with sweat and my leg trembled with the strain, but I dared not move a millimeter. If I stayed still and silent, I had a miniscule chance of getting out of this in one piece.

A click and the kitchen was flooded with light; a couple of seconds later and the lounge room lit up too. A tall black-haired man in camouflage pants and a black T-shirt stood by the coffee table, scanning the room. He turned slowly and his eyes caught mine; I felt like I was choking.

He grinned and it wasn't a pleasant sight. 'Well, bugger me, look at this.'

The other man with the shotgun came and peered down at me, shaking his shaved head. 'That's not Leigh. She's too fucken old.'

'I know that. Who is she then?'

'Fucked if I know,' Baldie said. 'Get up,' he said to me.

I tried but my leg wouldn't cooperate, trembling with the strain. He grabbed me by the arm and yanked me upright; I clutched at the armchair for support, trying to gently straighten at the knee, wincing at the needling pain.

'Where's Leigh?' Baldie asked.

'I have no idea,' I said. *They don't want me.* Relief washed through me.

'Who are you?'

'The housekeeper.'

He backhanded the side of my head – whack! The room went hazy for a few seconds, my ear burned and I had a sudden vision of my father's meaty hand swinging past my eyes before it connected.

'I don't like smart bitches. What's your name?'

I held my hand against my ear, feeling the heat, the stinging. There was no point in lying. 'Judi Westerholme.'

'Are you Westie's mother?'

'Sister.'

'What are ya doing here?' the tall one asked.

'My brother's dead and Leigh is missing. Why do you think I'm here?'

Baldie's hand swung up again and I ducked before it got close. The tall one said, 'Let's get outta here.'

Yes, please, just go.

'We'll go when I'm ready.' Baldie hefted the shotgun a couple of times while he stared at me and I prayed his finger wasn't on the trigger. The two holes at the ends of the barrels looked as big as cannons.

'Where's Leigh?' he barked.

I swallowed. 'I don't know. Even the cops can't find her.'

'Where's Westie's goody box then?'

'Pardon?' I had a gun pointed at me and he was asking about a goody box? Then I realised what he was referring to. Too late, I tried to keep my face blank.

He stepped closer and poked me hard in the side with the gun. 'Don't fuck with me!' he yelled. 'I can tell by your face you know what I'm talking about. Where is it?'

Goody box. That's what Andy called the heavy steel toolbox he'd bought with his pocket money when he was about twelve. He put a combination lock on it and, short of blowing it up or smashing it with a sledgehammer, Dad didn't have a hope of finding out what Andy kept in it, and it drove Dad crazy. Perfect, Andy said, and most of the time he left it empty.

'I haven't seen that box in more than twenty years,' I said. 'I didn't know he still had it.'

The tall one had been roaming around, pushing things off shelves and opening cupboards. He spotted my bag and upended it onto the table. Among the items that fell out was the envelope of Andy's pos-sessions that Heath had given me. It clunked as it hit the wooden surface. 'Check that out, Spaz,' Baldie said.

Spaz opened it and tipped out the contents. 'Two keys.'

'Bring them here.' Baldie took them and held them in front of my face. 'What are these off?'

'Black one is a car key,' I said. 'I don't know what the number 20 one is.'

'Westie was your brother. You must know.'

Here we go again. I gripped my hands together to try and stop them shaking. 'I don't. I hadn't seen him for years.'

'Bullshit.'

'Ask the cops. They'll tell you.' I was trying to sound assertive but maybe I should grovel.

'Yeah, right.'

He jabbed me with the gun again and my stomach lurched. Did shotguns have safeties on them? My sweat-soaked T-shirt had turned clammy and cold.

'Why would we talk to cops? You been spilling your guts?'

'Andy was murdered. Of course I've had to talk to the cops.'

'That was last week.'

'I'm organising the funeral.' God, all these questions. Why couldn't they take what they wanted and piss off?

'We been here too long,' Spaz said. 'Let's go, man.'

'We'll go when I'm good and fucken ready. She knows where the box is.'

'Make her tell you then,' Spaz said. He looked at me, his eyes like flat black stones, and smiled, but it was just his lips curving. His eyes were empty, and my throat closed up so tight I struggled to draw a breath.

'I'm not going to shoot her in the foot, dickhead.'

'Too noisy,' Spaz said. He looked around. 'Is there a meat cleaver in the kitchen?'

I sagged on to the arm of the chair, my legs like a rag doll's, and Baldie jerked the gun up at my face. 'How ya going to stop her screaming?'

'Stick a tea towel in her mouth. Jeez, do I hafta think of everything?' He opened drawers in the kitchen, rattling the cutlery, and took out a small, black-handled peeling knife with a thin blade, the kind I use for potatoes. Baldie pulled me up and shoved me towards the table, forcing me to sit, then rested the barrels against my neck. I clenched my teeth and wrapped my arms around myself.

Spaz had found a tea towel and sat next to me, knife in one hand, towel in the other. 'Back off,' he told Baldie. He pushed the point of the knife into the side of my neck and I closed my eyes. If this guy had any idea where my jugular was, I was dead. The room echoed around me as if I was in a cave; Spaz's loud breathing sounded wheezy in my ear. 'Open your mouth.'

I refused, not because I wanted to die but because I couldn't make my jaws work. The knife clattered on to the table and his fingers fastened around my chin. They smelled of cigarettes and car oil, and he squeezed so tightly I thought my teeth would break. My mouth opened and he thrust the towel in, making me gag.

'Don't throw up, you stupid cow, or you'll choke.'

And that would be better than? I opened my eyes and stared at Baldie, who stood across from me now, watching. There was no pity in his face, only faint curiosity. No help there. My stomach convulsed. *Don't vomit, don't vomit*! I focused every atom of me on the painting of a stormy bay on the wall opposite me. Two men on the beach. One has a top hat on. Waves are roaring. I'm going to die. Nothing seemed real except the rough cotton wad and taste of soap in my mouth.

Spaz grabbed my right hand and flattened it on the table, spreading my fingers wide. 'Where's the box?' He took the knife away from my neck and it hovered over my hand. I watched it as if it was a snake about to bite me.

I shrugged and shook my head, unable to speak but it didn't make any difference. I couldn't answer his question. My hand looked tanned, the fingernails cut short and straight, no rings or polish. A steady hand, usually. Right now it was trembling, and I kept the other one tucked tightly in my lap. My eyes hurt and I blinked, making them water, and blinked harder. I couldn't stop looking at my hand. I knew he was going to put the knife into it, I just didn't know how.

'Where's the box?'

I couldn't even shake my head this time. I tried to pull my hand back but his grip was like a vice, and when I tried to take a breath to scream, I nearly choked again. *Breathe, breathe!* The tip of the knife pricked my hand then lifted. The blade flashed in the light and came down in a swift, sharp curve. It grated briefly against bone then went through my palm into the wooden table top. For a second or two, there was no pain then it exploded in my hand like a red-hot volcano. I screamed, my throat bursting, but all that came out was a strangled squeal.

I couldn't inhale, I was choking – my free hand whipped up and pulled the towel from my mouth. Air, god, give me some air! I leant forward, gasping and sobbing, not daring to move my pinioned hand a single millimeter. Blood pooled around the blade and leaked across my hand. The pain was so consuming that I could barely whimper against its onslaught.

Faint red and blue lights flickered around the room, everything started to go black, and Spaz let go of my hand, jumping up from his chair. He said something, Baldie moved behind me and I heard a sickening crunch inside my head. Lights out.

9

I woke up on the floor, with some guy in a dark blue uniform kneeling over me, shining a light in my eyes.

'Concussion, I'd say, maybe a fracture. X-ray will show if there is.' He touched the side of my head and it felt like he was prodding it with a big stick. I tried to get my arm up to push him away but my hand flopped back on the lino.

'Stay still, Judi,' someone said, and then Hotshot's face loomed over me. What was he doing here? I was shivering with cold and a faint voice inside my head told me it was because I only had on a T-shirt and undies, and probably I needed to put more clothes on, but I couldn't quite get it together enough. Spears of pain lanced through my head, and my hand throbbed and burned; if they were competing, the head was winning. Just.

Then I remembered the knife, and Spaz stabbing my hand, pinning it to the table, and vomit surged up my throat.

'Roll her over, quick.' Hands grabbed me and pushed me onto my side, and I threw up on the floor. Goat curry was disgusting the second time around. They eased me back when I'd stopped retching, and the paramedic wiped my mouth. 'Her eyes are open and focused. Judi, do you know where you are?'

'On the floor,' I whispered.

'Do you know what day it is?'

I tried to think. Was it a trick question? 'Tuesday?'

'Who was in the house?' Heath asked.

'Santa Claus,' I said.

'Definitely confused,' a female paramedic said.

Heath smiled briefly. 'With her, that could've been a reasonable answer.'

They put a neck brace on me then checked my good hand and feet before wrapping a temporary bandage around my hand. It'd stopped bleeding but was already swollen and puffy. Using a plastic board, they lifted me on to the trolley and, just as well, no one stared at my legs and undies. The male paramedic layered a couple of blankets over me and I finally started to warm up.

'Is she going to be OK?' Heath asked. I wanted to know the answer to that too, but they were wheeling the trolley out and the vibrations drumming into my skull wiped everything else out. I held back a scream; it wouldn't help.

The ambulance rig swayed and the suspension made every bump in the road feel like an explosion inside my head. At one point, I begged for painkillers but the guy in the back with me said, 'Sorry, I can't give you anything yet. Not until the doctor's checked you over.'

After about a million years, we arrived at the hospital, where they crashed and banged my trolley into the emergency area, and then more people poked me and took blood pressure readings and asked me the same endless questions.

A woman doctor gently examined the mess at the back of my head, and a nurse just as gently washed the half-dried blood off, and I was eternally grateful to both of them. I veered between wanting to close my eyes and obliterate everything, and getting off the bed and walking out, but I doubted I'd get very far.

'We're taking you up for an X-ray,' the doctor said. 'I don't think your skull is fractured, but we'd better make sure. If it's all OK,' she told the nurse, 'they can stitch the wound.'

'What about her hand?' the nurse asked. 'A cut, is it? Take that dressing off and we'll have a look.' The nurse fumbled with my hand and the throbbing increased. Tears filled my eyes and trickled down the sides of my face. This was like my leg all over again. So much pain and helplessness; relying on others to fix me, even if it was only physical repair. I'd been stupid enough to think this would never happen to me again.

'Lot of swelling and bruising,' the doctor said. 'That's not a cut.' She bent her face close to mine. 'What happened? Can you tell me?'

'Stabbed with a veggie knife,' I whispered. 'Went right through. Bloody hurts.'

'I'll bet it does. Tell them to X-ray that, too. Hopefully it hasn't damaged a tendon. You're lucky it didn't hit a big vein.' She scribbled more notes on my chart and hung it on the end of the bed. 'They'll take good care of you,' she said, and left. I wanted to beg her to come back but some drunk guy was shouting down the other end of the corridor and a nurse said, 'Call security again,' so I kept quiet.

Some time later, way after midnight, I'd been X-rayed, given merciful painkillers, sewn up and bandaged, then left in peace to sleep. A Chinese nurse with the smallest hands I'd ever seen had tucked me in and checked everything, then turned the light out. Faint snoring echoed nearby, and I relaxed, finally drifting off to sleep. The curtains rustled and I managed to open my eyes again. It was Heath.

'You again,' I said.

'How are you feeling?' he murmured, coming close to the bed.

'Like shit.'

He smiled then turned serious again. 'Do you remember who attacked you? Or what happened?'

Sleep was like a huge piece of creamy chocolate, just out of my reach. My brain swooped, floated, focused for a few moments. 'Two guys. One bald. One tall and dark. The bald guy called him Spaz.' Their faces faded in and out and the knife arcing down took over. I shuddered.

'Did they say what they wanted?'

'Leigh... at first.'

'Later?'

'Andy...'

'Didn't they know he was dead?'

'Yes. Wanted his box.'

'What box?'

God, I wished he'd go away and stop annoying me. What was so bloody urgent about this? The guys were long gone. I closed my eyes for a second or two. 'Toolbox. Andy's had it for years.'

'We never found any kind of toolbox in the house. Where is it?'

I tried to shake my head and the pain expanded into hot thumping at the back of my skull; I breathed shallowly and must have gone white. Heath held my good hand in his, and the warmth from his skin soothed me.

'Hey, don't sweat it. I can come back tomorrow, er, today. You get some rest. I've rung a locksmith and the house will be fixed first thing. And I've cleaned up for you.'

I managed a 'Mmm' and fell at last into the dark, deep hole that was waiting for me. A couple of times, nurses woke me to check I was still alive, but I got enough sleep to help my head recover a little. Another dose of painkillers helped, too. They let me have toast and tea for breakfast, and by 9am I was climbing the walls. All the things I'd hated before about hospitals were back in spades – constant checks, questions, nurses bustling around, other people moaning and complaining.

I was in the day ward, along with everyone else that they couldn't give an actual bed to. Curtains separated us from each other, which meant I could hear half a dozen different life dramas going on around me. A woman in the next cubicle had been in a car accident and was ringing everyone in the universe on her mobile phone. I heard the same story about flipping the car and her broken elbow and sore knee about forty times.

By 10am, I was demanding to be let out and, as they were always short of beds and I was being obnoxious, by 11.30am I'd achieved it. I hadn't had general anaesthetic so I didn't need to be driven home, and they believed my lie that Mrs Jones Next Door would be looking after me. A kind aide found me a pair of donated tracksuit pants in the charity box and wheeled me down to my taxi. The cool, fresh air outside was like a tonic.

I'd forgotten that I had no keys or money, and the taxi driver heaved an annoyed sigh, but when I knocked on her door, dear old Mrs Jones tottered out to save me.

'There you are, Judi,' she said. 'That nice policeman gave me your new keys.' She held them out to me and I nearly hugged her.

'Thanks.' I told the taxi driver I'd go inside and get some money for him.

'Meter's still running,' he snapped.

'But the sympathy switched off last year,' I muttered. My bag was on the kitchen bench, wallet inside, and I hurried back to pay the driver. He roared off in a cloud of oily smoke.

'With a bit of luck, his engine will blow up before the end of the day,' I said.

Mrs Jones laughed. 'No such thing as courtesy these days.' Her watery eyes scanned me from top to bottom. 'You don't look well at all, you know. They shouldn't have let you out.'

'I'm not a good patient,' I said. 'My head will mend. It's pretty thick.'

'And your hand! You didn't punch one of them, did you?'

'I wish.' I wanted to get inside and lie down, but I couldn't find it in me to be rude right then.

'I'm so glad I rang the police when I did. Some people would call me an old busybody, but I knew something wasn't right.'

'You rang the cops?' Heath hadn't told me that bit. I vaguely remembered blue and red lights before Baldie smacked me in the head, which meant Mrs Jones had probably saved me from worse injuries than a knife through my hand.

'I knew you'd gone to bed, dear, and then I heard a funny noise, and a man shouting. I knew you didn't have your telly on, and there was some crashing around. It seemed better to be safe than sorry.'

Right then, my dislike of nosy neighbours seemed antagonistic and boring. She really was a life saver. 'I totally agree,' I said, 'and I can't tell you how much I appreciate it.'

'You're very welcome,' she said warmly, and gave me a small hug that, for once, I didn't pull away from.

I dangled the keys and counted them. 'Four? Did they change all of the locks?'

'And added one. The lock man said French doors are notorious for being easy to break in through, so he's put bolts top and bottom.' She beamed. 'He said my house was very secure, which was a great relief, I can tell you.'

'I'm sure it is.' A wave of dizziness swept over me and I staggered against the fence. 'I think I need to lie down.'

'You've gone as white as a sheet,' she said, and helped me to the front door, opening it for me and adding, 'I've left some dinner in the fridge for you. A chicken casserole. Just bang on the wall if you need me, dear.'

'Thanks for everything. I'll be OK now, as soon as I've had a rest.'

She finally left. Even the best neighbour in the world would drive me nuts after ten minutes, I thought. I was grateful she hadn't asked me a million questions about Baldie and Spaz. I didn't want to re-live it yet again, and if I told her everything, I'd probably frighten her witless. I made it to the bedroom and collapsed on to the bed, diving into blessed sleep like an Olympian at the deep end.

Five minutes later, a loud banging on the front door pulled me up from blissful darkness, and whoever it was was determined to be let in. I staggered out, cursing loudly and holding my head in both hands so it wouldn't fall off my shoulders. Just as I was about to unlock the front door and pull it open, caution or residual fear or both jumped in. 'Who is it?' I yelled, and flinched as my shout rebounded inside my head like a sharp rock.

'It's Ben.'

Who? Oh, Heath. I'd got used to his surname. I opened the door and stared at him blearily. 'What?'

'Why aren't you still in the hospital?' he demanded, his face haggard.

'I needed to rest. If you know anything about hospitals, you'd know that's not an option there. And I can't rest with you banging on the bloody door.'

I had to lie down again. But first I needed some more painkillers, and found the bottle in my bag, swallowing two with some water. The hospital had given me a prescription for more, thank God. The last ones had worn off quickly. Then I saw the clock above the stove: 6.15pm. I'd been asleep for more than five hours. I still needed to lie down, so I made a beeline for the bed. Heath followed me around like a tail on a kite, watching everything I did without comment.

In the bedroom, he perched on the side of the bed. 'Can I get you anything? Food?'

'Sleep would be good.'

He frowned. 'You've got concussion. Didn't the hospital tell you that sleeping all the time isn't a good sign?'

'No.'

I did already know that. I was monitoring my own health, and I didn't need a nanny.

'Maybe you should stay awake for a while and see how you feel.'

'I feel like crap. Do you want to ask more questions?'

'It's not urgent.' He sat there, looking stubborn, and I sighed.

'All right, I'll stay awake for a while and you can watch me. Will that make you happy?' I arranged the pillows behind me and leaned back. The pills weren't working as fast as I wanted them to, and it made me tetchy.

Instead of quizzing me about the attack, he rubbed the side of his face and said, 'Do you want to have a shower and change your clothes?'

I looked down at my T-shirt, with garish blood stains that had dried hard and didn't even pretend to be a flower pattern, and my donated worn trackies. I had a bandage around my head, and one on my hand. 'I'd better not get the dressings wet.'

'Have a bath then. You'll feel better.'

Had we gone from Detective Heath to Doctor Heath? 'What's going on? Why are you acting like this?'

He flushed. 'Why do you have to be so bloody stubborn? I'm trying to help, for Christ's sake.'

I had a flashback of him checking the locks. 'Why? Because you knew they'd come and have a go at me and you didn't stop it in time?'

'I didn't know. I just...' He flexed his hands and shook his head slightly. 'I thought it was a faint possibility.'

Pig's bum, it was faint! He'd been twitchy all night about locking up. Anger simmered under my skin. 'So you know who they are.'

'Not yet. Your descriptions were a bit general.'

'But you have a good idea.' He wasn't getting off the hook that easy.

'I told you, no.' His mouth tightened. 'I want you to come and look at photos at the station and make a statement.'

'Not tonight, I hope.'

'No.'

'Thank God.' I sighed. The whole damn thing could wait. 'I need a cup of tea.'

'You aren't having a bath?'

Not while you're here. 'Later. I do need to change this shirt though. It pongs a bit.'

'I'll put the kettle on.'

He left the room and I tried to pull the T-shirt over my head without dislodging the dressing and bandage but I got stuck, and then caught my sore hand as well. Pain speared through then it began throbbing again. 'Shit!'

He came running. 'What's the matter?'

'I'm stuck, damn it.' I couldn't move; my hand thrust out of harm's way.

'Hang on.' He stood behind me, lifting the T-shirt carefully, pulling the neck band out and over the bandage, easing the whole thing over my head. As the shirt came off, I felt his warm breath on the back of my neck and shivered, crossing my arms over my bare breasts. I veered wildly between wanting to put on a suit of armour and wanting to turn around. My face felt like a furnace.

'I'm not looking, don't worry,' he said lightly. 'Where's a clean top?'

'I only have the parrot shirt.' *Glamour Girl strikes again.*

He fetched it from the hanger on the back of the door and helped me into it, one sleeve at a time, staying behind me. His fingers brushed the scar on my upper arm. 'What's this from?'

'Long story.' I tried to breathe normally as I buttoned the shirt with trembling fingers. 'Thanks.'

'Kettle's boiled. I'll make the tea.'

'I'd rather a gin and tonic.' A huge one.

'You've got no hope.'

'Tea it is, then.' Tea and questions. I trailed him into the kitchen.

10

While he found teabags and mugs, I tipped out my bag and sorted through the contents, trying to remember what had been in there. Nothing was missing that I could see, not even the two hundred dollars in my wallet, or the credit card. Everything was in the envelope except the key on the 20 fob.

Heath poured the water, dunked the bags and added milk. Mugs in hand, he said, 'You mightn't want to sit at the table.'

'Why not?' I glanced at the wooden top. 'You mean the hole the knife made.'

'It's only small, but it's noticeable.'

'I have to sit at the table sometime.' I pulled out a chair and sat down, leaning forward to inspect the hole. It was small, but quite deep, and still dark with blood. My blood. My hand throbbed. At least I still had all of my fingers. A cleaver... I took a quick sip of tea, then another one.

Heath sat opposite me with a pen and notebook. 'Can we go through it now?'

I nodded. He asked the same questions. Who were they? Could I describe them? What did they say? At least this time I could give more detailed answers, including the fob key being taken, and what the gun looked like. He asked about the toolbox.

'I haven't seen that box for years. How would they know about it?'

'We didn't find it in the house or the shed.' He looked towards the back door, then at me. 'Well, we searched, but a toolbox...'

'Would've seemed ordinary.'

He jumped up and went to search the shed. I drank my tea in small, steamy sips and tried not to look at the hole. If he went away soon, I could have a glass of wine. His face said it all when he came back. 'Nothing. I searched the whole back garden, in case he hid it under the house or behind something.'

'Was it in his car?'

'I'll check that too.' He frowned. 'I'll make sure the box isn't anywhere we've already looked. I mean, we were looking for the gun or the drugs, but I think we would've checked inside a toolbox. What's more important right now is when are you going back to Candlebark?'

'Do you think they'll come back here?' I scanned his face and saw the answer, and an ice-chill gripped me, along with a sudden urge to get up and run. 'I'd go now if I could. The funeral is Friday, but I...' I couldn't look at the picture of Mia.

'You shouldn't be driving with a head injury like that.' He'd moved from nurse up to doctor now, from empathy to bossy.

'My head's not the problem. It's Leigh being missing, and the kid.' I wrapped my fingers around the mug, trying to draw comfort from its warmth, and failing. 'Did you know that Andy made me the kid's guardian in his will? Is that legal?'

'Easily contestable. Leigh could take you to court and would probably win.'

'No contest. I wouldn't fight her.' I sagged back in my chair. It was all so complicated, but no point whingeing about it. Just get it over with, and go home. I hadn't seen a weather forecast for rain this week. I'd hate to get back to my garden and find things keeling over from lack of water.

I watched Heath checking the windows and doors, and making sure all the new fancy bits on the French doors were bolted. A realisation hit me, and I reeled. 'You *do* think they'll be back, don't you?'

'No! They'd be mad to come back here, especially after they nearly got caught.'

My fingers found the hole in the table and I closed my eyes for a moment, trying to force the fear back into a little box but it wasn't working. It crawled all over me like cold slimy snakes. 'I want a gun.'

'That's silly. A gun will get you into more trouble, not save you.' He put his hand on my shoulder but I shrugged him off.

'It'd be better than sitting around waiting for them to try again.' I had a .22 and a licence in my cupboard back in Candlebark. I'd bought the rifle for shooting foxes after losing my second lot of chooks. I wished I'd brought it with me. I could already feel it, solid in my hands, imagine the kick against my shoulder as I put a bullet into Spaz.

'I could hang around if you're worried. Or sit outside in the car for a while.'

'Bit uncomfortable. And a waste of your time.'

He reddened. 'I've done it before. Surveillance is part of the job.'

'There's enough locks on this place now to make the prime minister feel safe.'

He glanced around and nodded. 'You're right. You should be fine.'

He wasn't convincing me, but I'd keep the .22 idea to myself. I was determined to stop acting like a frightened wuss. I stood up and gathered the mugs, taking them to the sink to wash. That way, my back was to him and he couldn't see my face as I thought about putting a bullet in Baldie as well.

The phone rang and I jumped. It was probably Connor again, or some mate of Andy's who hadn't heard the news. I didn't want to talk to anyone.

'Aren't you going to answer it?' Heath asked then picked up the receiver for me. 'Hello. Yes, she's here.' He handed it over.

'Hello?'

'Hi. It's Kayla.' Huffy breathing. 'Look, can you come over to my place? Now?'

'What for?'

'It's Mia. She's been crying all day.' She spat out the words like she'd been chewing on them for hours. 'I've got another kid with the flu and I can't cope anymore.'

Dread rose in me in a thick wave. 'I'm sorry, but... she doesn't know me. I'd probably make her worse.'

'You couldn't possibly do that. Kids don't often get like this but... she wants her dad.'

'He's dead.' Stark words that suddenly filled my eyes with tears.

'Yes, but you look like him. And I know you didn't think so, but Mia can sense the connection. I'm desperate here, and you've got to help. Or at least try.' A child's howls in the background grew louder and I imagined Kayla holding the phone out to make sure I could hear. My heart plummeted.

Heath raised his eyebrows at me. 'Is it about Mia?'

I put my hand over the mouthpiece. 'Kayla thinks I can stop her crying. I don't think I'd have a hope, but she's insisting.'

'I'll drive you over there, if you like.'

I gaped at him. 'You're kidding. You think I can do something?'

He shrugged. 'I can hear the kid from here. Sounds like anything's worth a try.'

The crying went on and on. I'd probably still hear it even if I hung up. 'All right,' I snapped. 'We'll be there soon.'

'Great.' Kayla immediately disconnected in my ear.

'I'll have to go like this. The kid will freak out when she sees the bandage around my head.'

Heath was already checking the French doors again and jangling the car keys in his hand. 'Don't worry, she probably won't even notice.'

My head was pounding; I made sure the bottle of painkillers was in my bag and followed him out to the car. Before he turned the key, he said, 'Will you be OK? Bandages are fine but collapsing on the floor mightn't be so good.'

'I'm not made of porcelain,' I said. 'Let's go.'

I wasn't going to tell him that the street lights looked fuzzy and the car in front of us was wobbling. If I leaned back and closed my eyes, I'd feel better in a minute. I must've dropped off because a few seconds later we were pulling up outside Kayla's house. Heath wisely didn't say anything, but came around and helped me out of the car. We heard Mia screaming straight away, and glanced at each other. I was sure I looked terrified – I felt it. His mouth was a thin line. Before we reached the front door, it opened and a pale, skinny man in striped pyjamas said, 'Are you the aunty? Thank God you're here.'

You won't be saying that shortly, I thought, and followed him through to the kitchen. The room was dark apart from one lamp in the corner where Kayla sat in a rocking chair, holding Mia and patting her back as she cried. The door to the TV room was closed but the sound of canned laughter was clear. The kids probably had it turned up high to drown Mia out.

The screaming abated into exhausted, hiccupping cries, which I took as a good sign until Kayla said, 'She'll start up again in a minute. It's like she's gathering more energy, but God knows where from.'

I stood in the centre of the room, and found everyone was watching me. 'What?' I said. 'I don't know what to do. I've never had a kid, or even looked after one.'

Kayla heaved herself to her feet. 'You can't do any worse than me. Here. I need to go to the toilet.'

She passed Mia over to me and, just as I expected, the sobs didn't magically stop. The kid's top was soaked, presumably with tears, and I wondered where they all came from – so many tears and so much sadness. She lifted her head, stared at me, then laid her head on my shoulder and took a deep breath. 'Uh oh,' said the man. 'She's winding up for another round.'

I tensed, waiting for the scream in my ear, but she just kept crying softly and hiccupping, her little body full of misery, her hands clutching my shirt. After a couple of minutes, I heard her say something that sounded like 'Birdies', then the sobs gradually diminished until, after a couple of sighs, she was quiet.

'Oh,' I said.

'What?' said the man.

I knew what they were thinking. I'd worked a miracle, I was the kid's saviour, the kid belonged with me. *Look how wonderful you are with her, look how she's taken to you.* Whereas I knew that I'd accidentally happened to be stuck with her when she'd reached final exhaustion and fallen asleep. Coincidence. Nothing to do with me. A little part of me wished it was, before a trapped feeling crept over me. 'Now she's asleep, I can go, can't I?' I said, determined to sneak out.

Kayla had come back from her wee. She gave me that look of hers, scornful. 'Yeah, sure, why not?'

The man objected. 'What if she wakes up and starts again? I've got to work tomorrow.'

'We'll see how she goes then.' Kayla took Mia out of my arms and, as soon as the kid felt herself changing hands, she woke up. The scream that came out her mouth could've peeled paint off the walls. She twisted in Kayla's grip, spotted me and reached out. 'Birdies.'

'It's the shirt.' That was Heath's vital contribution to the occasion.

I glared at him. 'It's Andy's shirt, not me at all. I'll take it off and give it to you.'

Kayla wasn't buying it. 'It's the shirt *and* you.' She passed Mia back to me and the kid promptly clutched at the shirt and put her head down on my shoulder. My head ached and now my hand was throbbing; nausea rose up my throat. It could've been the kid causing it but I had to admit it was probably the concussion.

Heath peered at me. 'You look wiped out.' He explained to Kayla. 'She was attacked last night. Head wound. Maybe Judi and Mia could stay here.'

That was a very stupid idea.

Kayla sniffed, obviously thinking Heath was making it up. 'There's no spare beds.'

My eyelids drooped and I swayed on my feet. 'I need to go home and lie down in a proper bed.'

'Bit of a stalemate,' said the man.

'Look, we'll take Mia with us,' Heath said.

'What?' I glowered at him. Where the hell did he get off, taking over like that?

'There's no point leaving her here if she's going to scream non-stop.' He lowered his voice. 'Kayla doesn't legally have to look after her. You do. I'll help.'

Now he quotes the law at me. 'You? Help with a kid?' God, he was a dickhead. It was me who'd have to cope with her, and I could hardly take care of myself at the moment.

Kayla looked reluctant – suddenly we weren't such saviours after all – but her partner said, 'That'll do me. Kayla, get Mia's stuff, will you?' In two minutes, he'd bustled us out the door, hauling Mia's bag of clothes and other stuff and loading it into the car. I was still holding Mia, my legs like rubber. She weighed a tonne, or maybe I'd reached the end of my strength, what I had left.

'You sit in the back with her,' Heath said. 'I don't have a child's car seat.'

I was way past worrying about road rules. I would've put the kid to bed, firmly but nicely, given her the parrot shirt to cuddle up to, and run away. Now I would have her full-time, and I had no idea where to start. Mothering was definitely not in my DNA. I didn't even know how to put a nappy on!

I needed more painkillers and bed. Heath was responsible for this ludicrous idea, so he would have to look after the kid on his own tonight. Then tomorrow she was going straight back to Kayla's. For her own good.

11

Back at Andy's house, Heath made me wait in the car while he checked inside. Good – he was being a cop for a change. I didn't need any more sermons about 'doing the right thing'.

The kid was sprawled across my lap, her head lolling on my arm. Even with the bandage, I could tell my hand was still swollen to twice its size, and it was throbbing again. When Heath came back, I told him to carry Mia inside and put her to bed.

'What if she wakes up?'

'She won't.' She probably felt as exhausted as me.

He tucked her in and put a couple of teddy bears next to her, discarding the beaten-up one. I added it again, just in case it was her favourite. Might keep her quiet. He brought the bag in and pulled out a packet of disposable nappies.

'Isn't she a bit old for these?' he asked.

'You expect me to know?'

'No.' He sighed.

'You're not going to get pathetic about this, are you? Because you'd be wasting your time.' I shook out two painkillers on to my hand and swallowed them with some water. *Bed. God, please, let me sleep.* 'I'm going to bed. You're on babysitting duty.'

'Me?'

'It was your idea to bring her back here. I'm not capable, remember?' I wanted to laugh at the stunned look on his face but thought better of it. 'If I don't get some sleep, I'm going to fall over. Sorry, but it's up to you now.'

I headed for bed and oblivion. Sometime during the night, I vaguely heard crying but I put a pillow over my head and blocked it out. In the morning, my head was much clearer and the nausea had gone. But there was a lump in the bed beside me. Mia.

'How did you get here?' No answer. She was still asleep, one hand clutching the one-eyed teddy that stared at me suspiciously. Maybe she woke up and wandered in here on her own.

What day was it? For one horrible moment, I thought it was funeral day, then I worked out that was tomorrow. I'd decided on 10 am for the service, so once we'd done the cup of tea thing, I could be on the road out of Melbourne by one o'clock. The blonde woman was organising the catering so I could relax a bit. Through a gap in the curtains I could see a muddy grey sky above next door's roof and the air was cool.

I eased out of the bed and rummaged in my overnight bag – one last pair of clean undies and jeans. Nothing else was wearable. I found a T-shirt in a drawer that fitted me and it didn't have parrots on it. Instead it said *I'm with Stupid* with an arrow pointing to the left. I'd make sure I stood on Heath's right as often as possible.

My skin felt sticky and I could smell myself. Ugh. I found a shower cap in the en suite bathroom to put over my bandaged head, and managed a lovely, hot shower with my bandaged hand sticking out past the glass door. It only got slightly wet. Clean body, clean clothes – a great start to the day. Now I needed to get Heath's arse into gear. He had to find Leigh – never mind anything else. It was crucial that she came back and got her kid.

He was already up. Freshly brewed filter coffee steamed on the bench, cereal plates and boxes arranged neatly on the table with cutlery, along with a row of jams and marmalade. Very domestic. He was pacing out in the garden, talking on his mobile and waving one arm around like a wind turbine. He shoved the phone into his pocket, looking very unhappy, and came inside.

'Good morning,' he said. 'I had to make a decent caffeine hit.'

'Couch not too comfortable?' Guilt flickered in the back of my mind and I pushed it away.

'Mia woke up and cried again, and I couldn't get her calmed down. Must've walked about ten kilometres around the house. I ended up having to put her in bed with you.'

'So I noticed.'

'It worked.' He sat down and helped himself to Weet-Bix, five slabs of it. Then piled sugar on top. I averted my eyes and focused on a small pile of cornflakes. He poured coffee, I kept eating. His phone rang and he checked the screen then ignored it.

'Don't you want –'

He cut in. 'It's the boss. I'll go in when I'm ready.'

'I don't want to get you into trouble. And if you go to work, you can start looking for Leigh.'

'We've been looking.' He spooned sugar into his mug and stirred.

'What if she's dead?' I said, an edge in my voice.

'We've had an alert out on her since your brother was killed.' He glared. 'We're not sitting on our hands, you know.'

'She needs to come and get Mia.' I stuck my chin out, angling for a fight again.

He sought an escape in his mug. 'Were you planning on taking Mia back to Kayla's?'

'Absolutely.'

'You can't. Kayla rang earlier. She said she's going away and don't bother trying to contact her.' He shrugged apologetically.

'What? She can't do that!' The cornflakes had turned into sharp wood chips in my stomach.

'You're the blood relative, and at this point the will gives you guardianship. She was just doing Leigh a favour, and she reckons the favour is over.'

'Great. So I've been landed with the kid, but you still think those two guys are after me, or the box, and I can't go home yet because the funeral is tomorrow.' I slapped my hand on the table before I remembered it was injured. The bandage didn't stop the impact arcing pain into my palm and out through the fingers. It was worse than an electric shock. I gasped then pulled it in close to my body, and gradually the pain faded down to barely tolerable again.

Heath eyed me. 'You're supposed to come into the station this morning with me and make that statement, maybe ID the guys in the books.' His phone beeped and he opened it to read the text message. 'Bugger. It's urgent. We'll have to do the statement and ID later.' He spooned in the last of his cereal and took his plate and mug over to the sink to rinse them. I stopped eating, my throat thick with unease.

He gathered up his keys and mobile, checked around for anything else he might have left, and said, 'I'll call you. We might be able to organise that ID and statement for after lunch.'

'Uh huh.' Now he was leaving, tendrils of fear climbed around my guts like ivy, strangling me. I wanted to beg him to stay, but I was too stubborn.

'That box – are you sure you don't know where it might be?' he said.

'Why don't you ask my mother?' I suggested.

'Might be easier if you did.'

'For who? There's not enough money in the world to bribe me to ask her anything.'

'Whatever.' He glanced around and up. 'If you feel up to it, you could search this place again. You never know. If it does turn up, I'd appreciate a call.'

'Sure.' *Can I call you anyway?*

'And make sure you lock up when I've gone.'

I nodded. Great. My paranoia shot up two hundred per cent, and in response, my head and hand throbbed again. As the front door closed, Mia started crying. Shit. I wanted to climb into the Benz and drive away as fast as I could, leave all this behind in a second, but I knew I couldn't. I went to the bedroom doorway and, as soon as the kid saw me, she stopped, a hopeful look on her face. 'Daddy?'

Should I say 'Daddy's dead'? Nup. Not a good strategy. 'Daddy's not here right now, kiddo. Want some breakfast?'

She scrambled out of the bed and toddled over to me, grabbing my leg and holding on like a limpet. I wasn't going to pick her up in case my head fell off my shoulders, so I took her by the hand and led her to the table. She was too little to sit in a chair but a search revealed a fold-up high chair thing in the broom cupboard. It opened up with-out too much drama and I helped her into it.

'What do kids eat for breakfast?' I asked her, not expecting an answer.

'Bix,' she said. 'Spoon.'

OK, I could do mushed-up Weet-Bix. I handed her the spoon and let her work it out for herself. That's what God invented mops and kitchen lino for. She didn't do too bad a job of it – most of it went in her mouth – but I helped her with the orange juice. Maybe I could point her at the fridge and say, 'Help yourself'.

A second cup of coffee and some pills, my headache eased and the world started to look a bit more cheery. Apart from the fact that the kid watched my every move with big round eyes, and followed me around the house. We conquered a bath, a nappy change, a clean set of clothes and an enthusiastic attempt at teeth brushing that splattered toothpaste everywhere, and then I sat her down in front of the TV. The place felt untidy to me, so I dusted and straightened, washed some of my clothes, and cleaned the kitchen. On my dusting spree, I found a baby how-to book on the shelves and put it aside for studying later. I needed all the help I could get.

I was getting twitchy. The garden was tempting but it was more the whole thing of feeling trapped in the house. I was used to being out in my garden or going for long walks around Candlebark or in the bush. Pacing the lounge room didn't have the same effect of calming me down. Heath had asked me to search the house again, which I did, but there was nothing. I even carried a ladder in from the shed and checked the ceiling space. Then Mia tried to climb the ladder behind me, I shouted and frightened her, and it took biscuits to calm both of us down.

If the box was that important, Andy wouldn't have kept it in the house with Mia around. Not with guys like Spaz after it. A toolbox full of drugs would have to be worth several million dollars on the streets. Or maybe it was full of money. Where else would he hide it? At work. That made sense. A toolbox in a car yard wouldn't be out of place, but there wouldn't be anywhere secure for it either. Bit risky, perhaps.

I was certain the box wouldn't be at Mum's house. I couldn't imagine Andy going anywhere near the old cow. Surely he'd hated her as much as I did. No doubt she was still in that huge, soulless house in Brighton, all show and no warmth inside. Just like her. Andy's and my bedrooms were small rooms at the back, narrow boxes. I always reckoned they were the original servants' bedrooms, with small, high windows and only enough room for a single bed and wardrobe.

Dad and Mum had the main bedroom at the front, with glass doors and a balcony they never used, and the other two large bedrooms were for guests, decorated in chintz and pastel carpets. Far too nice for grotty children.

I felt a tug on my jeans and found Mia clinging to me again. 'Daddy?' God, I wished she'd stop asking, but how was she to know? I needed to distract her. Books. We unearthed a pile in her room and sat on the couch to read half a dozen of them. I'd loved Winnie the Pooh as a kid, so that one got a really resounding read-aloud, with me doing the voices of Pooh and Tigger and her giggling so much she got the hiccups. Then she started to grizzle. Food didn't work; it was too early for a nap.

Maybe she was going as stir crazy as me, stuck in the house. We needed an outing, a trip to the supermarket and bottle shop in the autumn sunshine. We'd be out in broad daylight, with people all around us. I found a stroller and a car seat that looked like an astronaut's chair and took me a little while to install, strapped her in the back and set off for the shops.

We whizzed around the supermarket, then to a bottle shop and, with the car loaded with food and drink, we made for home.

I parked right in front of the house and unbuckled her first, then put her on the tiny lawn just inside the gate with a banana to play with while I hauled the groceries out of the boot. As I turned with both arms loaded with bags, a hand shoved me hard from behind, sending me sprawling across the nature strip. I fell on two of the bags, squashing bread and smashing eggs, yelling as my knee twisted painfully.

Mia screamed and, as I struggled to get up and go to her, a knee caught me in the back, crushing me face-down on the prickly grass. I was like a pinned bug, arms and legs waving. Mia kept screaming and I forced my head up. Spaz leaned over the gate and picked her up by one arm, dangling her in mid-air.

Rage roared through me, and I fought to get the knee off me, twisting and thrashing. 'Put her down, you bastard!' I shouted.

'Shut up, bitch,' Baldie said in my ear. 'Gonna tell us where the fucken box is now, are ya?'

'I don't know, you stupid prick.' I gasped for breath, his weight crushing me; I felt so useless but I couldn't budge him, no matter how I struggled. Mia's screams sent jags of fear through me. 'Get off me!' The words were eaten up by the grass.

'Right, we're taking the kid then,' Baldie said. 'We'll be in touch. You'd better find that box fucken fast, or the kid'll get it.'

My brain raced. I had to stop them. 'Stop! Tell me what Andy said!'

The pressure lifted off my back and I sucked in air then staggered upright. It was too late. Their car, a big red sedan, roared off down the street, turning the corner, too far away for me to get a number plate.

'Fuck!' Angry tears dripped down my face and I rubbed them away with shaking hands. I had no idea what to do. If I hopped in the Benz, could I catch them? Unlikely.

A tremulous voice interrupted my agonising. 'I've called the police, dear.'

Mrs Jones stood at her gate, her hands trembling on the top rail. Poor woman. She was doing her best but having a neighbour like me must be scaring the hell out of her.

'Thanks, but it's too late now.' I brushed down my shirt and jeans roughly, wanting to burst into tears right there on the footpath, but it would probably finish Mrs Jones off. 'Excuse me. I need to sit down for a minute,' I said, and went inside where I could vent all the four-letter words I wanted. It didn't help.

Mia's screams echoed in my head. I should've kept her safe. I was bloody useless. I knew I would be. Mia should've stayed at Kayla's.

Andy had given me one last thing to do and I'd stuffed it up.

12

I sat for a minute, shaking, cursing myself, then grabbed the phone and Heath's card and called his mobile, praying he wasn't out of range.

'Heath.'

For a moment, I couldn't speak, tears burning my eyes. 'It's me.'

'What's the matter?'

'They've taken Mia.' I squeezed the plastic phone and heard it crack. 'I'm sorry. They grabbed me – held me down. I couldn't stop them!'

He wasn't interested in apologies. 'Same two guys?'

'Yes.'

'Shit. The fingerprints came back – nothing clear enough to get a match.'

I sagged against the kitchen bench, and slid down to the floor. 'You mean you have no idea who they are?'

'Not yet. Have you called the police?'

'I'm calling you!'

Voices in the background, computer keys tapping. 'It's been called in. Mrs Jones next door. Top priority.'

'Thank you,' I whispered.

'You need to come and look at the photo books straight away, even if you're not feeling up to it.'

'I am up to it, trust me.'

'Right. Did they say anything to you?'

I tried to speak calmly, repeating verbatim what Baldie had told me.

'That box again. We've got to find it. I'll be there in fifteen.' He hung up in my ear, and I let out a little sob of relief. Heath might be a pain in the neck, but I desperately hoped he knew how to do his job.

I struggled to my feet, wiping away tears, gritting my teeth. I'd fucked up, badly, and I needed to start fixing it. I went next door to see how poor Mrs Jones was, and to thank her. Her pale tear-stained face said it all.

The local cops arrived; I answered their questions and one was busily writing in his notebook when Heath arrived. I'd completely forgotten about the groceries and the still-open car boot so, while Heath talked to the constables, I locked the Benz and took the groceries inside.

Heath followed me in. 'I've brought the local boys up to speed about the other attack on you, so they know we're looking for the same guys. When we get an ID on them, I'll pass it along.'

'Do you think I'll find them in the books?' I said.

'If you can't, we'll get you to work with the artist on some drawings.' He ran both hands through his hair, making it spike up in tufts. 'But it's pretty likely you'll find them. Guys who do things like this don't just start out of nowhere. They'll have been around the block before, sure to have other assaults or thefts against them. And if there is an underworld connection, that'll seal it.'

'Mia must be frightened out of her wits.' My voice cracked, and I had to swallow a couple of times to ease the ache in my throat. 'How could they do that to a little kid?'

Heath met my eyes, his gaze hard. 'It's about what's in that box. It can't be drugs – your brother wouldn't have been trying to buy more. It must be money. Lots of it. I can't see they'd go to all this trouble otherwise.'

'Andy must've known something was going to happen to him. He hid the box, and then he got killed, and Leigh took off. But why did she leave Mia with Kayla?'

'Maybe Leigh thought she'd be safer there.'

'A lot safer than with me,' I said bitterly. 'Bloody woman. If she'd kept Mia, this wouldn't have happened.'

'I think they knew about Mia all along,' Heath said. 'Which means they knew Andy or knew a lot about him. They've probably been watching this house.'

I felt like one of those caged bears, miserable and despairing, and I hated it. 'Let's do the ID thing. That's more productive than standing around here all day.'

In the car on the way to the Homicide offices, I could feel Heath glancing at me every now and then, as if checking I was coping OK. I stared out the window at the apartment complexes built where the old cattle sales yards in Kensington used to be. Fancy boxes, cheaply made, a balcony overlooking a busy, fume-filled three-lane road.

I yearned for my garden, my potato digging and mulching, my new green peas and the bulbs I needed to plant for spring. I'd planned on going home tomorrow – but I couldn't leave now, with Mia missing. The ache in my throat grew.

'I let him down again,' I said abruptly. 'Mia getting taken was my fault. He trusted me to look after her and I did a crap job of it.'

Heath shook his head. 'Blaming yourself won't help.'

'Maybe not, but it's true. I've always let him down.' My fingers twisted together, in and out, in and out. 'Dad would be in one of his moods and I'd hide, let Andy take the belting instead of me. He was smaller than me. Why didn't I stick up for him more? Why didn't I stop it?' The ache spread down into my chest and I could barely breathe, the pain spreading like hair-thin cracks across the ice.

'Sticking up for him against your father would have got him a bigger belting,' Heath said.

'You're an expert, are you?'

He laughed, but not like it was funny. 'I've dealt with wife bashers, pedophiles, child abusers. Doesn't matter whether people are rich or poor, they always take it out on those who can't fight back. And those who try to defend themselves usually get it worse next time.'

'I still could've done better. He didn't deserve what Dad did to him.' More new houses flew past – did they hold dozens of happy families? Or did every house hide family secrets and violence of some kind? I couldn't shake off the thought.

'No kid deserves abuse.' He paused, flicked on the indicator. 'What was Andy like as a kid?'

The words surged out of me. 'Dad called him a weak pussy once. Andy was only ten, but he knew what it meant and it made him really mad. He was braver than I was, most of the time. He bought that toolbox when he was twelve, but it was the last big thing he did to try and beat Dad. Once he started high school, he seemed to decide it was easier just to endure the beltings and try to stay out of Dad's way.'

'He never ran away? Or fought back?'

'Dad was a big man. I think Andy found an outlet at school. He had a ton of mates, and was a bit of a class clown. Smoked like a train since he was about thirteen, and I think he got caught shoplifting a couple of times, but he talked his way out of it.'

'Your mother...'

'Never did a thing. Hid in her bedroom.' I blew my nose. 'I thought about telling Nana. He was her son. How did he... never mind. I didn't want to upset her. I don't think she had any idea.'

We parked in a bay in the street and I undid my seat belt, put my hand on the door, ready to get out.

'Hang on,' Heath said. 'Did your brother do drugs back then? Smoke dope?'

'I don't think so. Mind you, he was at uni in the late 90s so I wouldn't be surprised.' I frowned, remembering. 'Dad made him do Law but he didn't last. He always talked about being a psychologist or teacher, and next thing I knew, he did a course and went into real estate. Was really good at it.'

'Proving something?'

I shrugged. 'Maybe. But to who? Dad? Why would you be trying to prove yourself to an old bastard you hated?'

'That's what males do, I suppose,' Heath said. ' So when did the whole full-on drugs thing start?'

'When Dad died.' It was one of my clearest memories – the phone call from Mum. Her voice dry and disembodied, like she was the undertaker. *Your father has passed away.* At first I was numb – I couldn't believe it – and when it started to sink in, all I wanted to do was drink champagne until I passed out. I managed three glasses before Andy turned up, already drunk, and proceeded to stagger around my lounge room, shouting and waving his arms, skolling from a bottle of rum until he collapsed on my fake Persian rug.

I stuck my finger down his throat in desperation and got him to vomit as much of it up as I could, then I dragged him on to the couch and watched over him all night, too scared to sleep.

'Just like that?' Heath said, jolting me out of my memories.

'Probably not. But it was like whatever was blocking the drain was gone and he had free rein to do what he wanted. So he took the money, blew the lot. I think that's when he met Leigh. They started on heroin. The beginning of the end.'

Heath shifted in his seat and rubbed his chin. 'What about you?'

The fake garden strip near the police building was filled with half-dead pittosporum, the fallback position of the unimaginative landscaper. Heath waited, and finally I answered. 'I made all the same mistakes, only Version Two. Got married to someone who I thought was the opposite of my father... do you really need to know all this?' 'I guess not,' he said, staring at the same pittosporums. 'I'm interested, that's all. Helps to background things. The marriage didn't work out?

This guy was like a terrier with his teeth into my leg. 'No. It proved what a bad judge of character I was.   I've learned my lesson the hard way. He turned out to be a coke freak and sex addict and drank like a fish.'

'Good catch.' He flinched when I glared at him. 'Sorry. What was his name?'

'Why do you want to know?'

'You said coke freak. How do you know he wasn't connected to your brother at some point?'

My irritation flared into anger. Talking about my ex-husband was like spraying petrol on a fire. 'Andy and Max hated each other. Andy tried to tell me what a sleaze Max was and I didn't believe him. Max used to hang shit on Andy for being a druggie. Happy days.'

'Max's other name?'

'Heywood, with an E. Come on, let's move. I thought you were in a hurry for me to ID these guys.'

'Settle down. I told you, I don't like dangling threads in a case, and there're just too many in this one. Every bit of information might lead to something useful.'

Now I was curious. 'How did you end up in the police?' He heaved a big sigh – he didn't like being questioned about his life any more than I did. 'My sister was murdered when I was at uni, and I got to know the detectives on the case. They were great, totally focused on finding out who did it and arresting the bastard. It was her boyfriend – she'd broken up with him and he came back and stabbed her.'

He'd wiped the smile off my face and I wasn't sure what to say. 'I'm sorry,' I said feebly.

'Hey, that's OK. You're in the same place now, and I wouldn't wish that on anyone.' He seemed lost in memories for a few long seconds, his face dark and thoughtful, and then he said, 'Anyway, I was the go-between for a while – Mum and Dad couldn't cope with talking to the police. These two coppers explained everything, kept me up to speed. It made all the difference to me.'

'Did they convince you to join up?'

'Nah.' He laughed. 'They probably would've tried to talk me out of it. But after the guy was arrested, I decided to join up. End of story.'

He pulled the keys out of the ignition and checked for his phone, then opened his door, all abrupt movements, like he wanted to get away from the conversation. I didn't blame him. Maybe he'd told me more than he'd meant to. That one event had turned him into a cop who wanted to fix the world rather than blow it up. Whereas the years of beltings Andy and I had endured had created thick, shiny armour that we'd carefully polished and worn like second skins. Until it'd fallen apart and left us floundering.

Now I wanted to get right away from my own sorry story. *Enough.* I slammed the car door and pushed through the swing door behind Heath, following him to the lifts. My hand ached but I tried to ignore it, not wanting it to distract me.

'Are you OK?' Heath asked.

I straightened, shoulders back. 'Fine.'

On the Homicide floor, we passed a large room that had way too many desks jammed into it, most of them unoccupied. Heath showed me into a small room where a young detective took down all the physical details I could remember of the two men and then entered them into the computer. It was like magic – first for Spaz and then Baldie, a whole range of faces appeared with similar hair and features, and I'd picked out both of them in no time. It felt almost too fast, but despite Baldie's head being covered in a bleached-blond fuzz, I knew it was him.

Spaz was obvious – even in the photo his flat, dark eyes had a cruel, hard expression, and I saw the knife arcing down again. The thought of them hurting Mia sent jabs of panic through me again, and I had to fold my hands under my arms and take some deep breaths.

After I'd identified them both, Heath said, 'Spiros Castella and Joseph Sands. I don't know them. I'm going to get on to a couple of task force guys and see what they say.' Outside the small room, other detectives came and went, some eyeing me curiously and some in a hurry, jabbering on mobiles and making scribbled notes. As I watched them, I tried to avoid thinking about Mia, but it didn't work.

Were they feeding her? What if she cried and wouldn't stop? Would they hit her? God, I wanted to knock them both into next week and get her away from them, but nobody had any idea where they might be. It was maddening, being so powerless to do anything but wait and see what the police could find out. Anger rose again, like an ebb tide, mixed with shame and regret. I caught myself rocking, took deep breaths, tried to stay still and conquer the rage. Gradually, I felt some kind of control returning, and just as I was beginning to wonder if Heath had forgotten me, he came back, looking grim.

'Packer says these two are small fry, sometimes associated with a guy called Titch Santos, but on the fringes. Not regarded as being on the inside. He gave me addresses for them but said they're probably long gone.' He waved a piece of paper. 'Castella was arrested back in 2008 for small-time dealing, but it never went to court. He had a good solicitor, Paul Masson. Not a positive sign.'

'Why not?'

'Masson is well known for defending dealers and lowlifes. That's no coincidence.'

'So Andy was somehow connected to these guys. But you don't know why.' I huffed in exasperation. 'Mia is out there somewhere with them. I want to know how we're going to find her, what it will take.'

'How *I'm* going to find her.'

'Fine. Make sure you do it bloody fast.' I stood up and tucked my bag under my arm. 'I'm going to find the box.'

'But –'

'You can't do two things at once, can you?' He shrugged, as if unwilling to admit he couldn't. I went on, 'I've got more chance of hunting the damn thing down, or guessing where it might be. You're supposed to catch the arseholes who've got Mia. So go do it.'

'Stay in touch,' he warned. 'Why don't you have a mobile?'

I looked at him pityingly. 'There's virtually no reception where I live. It'd be a waste of money.'

'Get one now. A cheap pay-as-you-go job. You can buy them at the post office, or any shopping centre. Then call me with the number, all right? I need to be able to contact you 24/7.'

I cringed. 24/7 was a term I loathed. 'Yes, all right.'

'And don't go haring off on your own. These guys are not playing games.'

'Christ, you don't need to tell me that,' I snapped, pointing at my head which still had a dressing taped to the back of it. But I wasn't playing games either – I was deadly serious about getting Mia back, whatever it took. It was obvious the toolbox was the key; no matter what was hidden inside, I was going to find it.

13

Heath dropped me back at Andy's house; I put the answering machine on and drove the Benz to Highpoint Shopping Centre. The place was like a maze, and had changed a fair bit since I was last there. Nothing was in the same place, but I bought some new clothes – jeans, T-shirts, a hooded jacket – then made a quick pitstop at a café, drinking strong coffee and eating a sandwich while I made a list of possible hiding places for the box.

Andy must've known someone would be after it, someone who knew he had a kid but maybe not much else. Spaz and Baldie hadn't known he had a sister until they met me. Possibly Andy had hidden the box at Mum's, but I hoped not. It was near the bottom of my list.

Heath had been keen on the connection with my ex, Max, and now I had to consider that seriously, too. I doubted Max had any gangland mates, but anything was possible. I knew lots about Max that I'd never told anyone, information I'd collected over several weeks of eavesdropping and observation and snooping before I'd kicked him out. I'd been collecting ammunition for my divorce and to try and stave off bankruptcy with the pub, but there had been details that came to light which I hadn't expected. And which I'd decided to keep quiet about. There's such a thing as knowing more than is healthy.

Initially, I hadn't wanted the pub. Max wanted a pub but had no money. I found that I loved the business side, ordering, running my own place, negotiating good deals with suppliers – but I hated being behind the bar and having to be polite to dickheads and airheads all the time. Max excelled at it. He was Mr Hospitality. But with the trendy crowd came the drugs. I fumed and shouted, and then I'd discovered Max was joining in. He'd been shagging one of the bar-tenders for nearly a year, and had also started selling coke.

I must've had my head in a mop bucket.

The dealing was financing a gambling addiction, and when I finally got all my cannons lined up and set the lawyer onto him, the accountant discovered Max had used the pub as collateral to borrow from a lethal loan shark.

Thinking about all of this again was making my whole body tremble. I sat, unseeing, in the busy café with shoppers all around me and three different kinds of music filtering in from nearby shops. My brain felt like scrambled eggs, but I had to sort through the crap of the past and examine every possible angle if I was going to find that box.

Heath could be on the right track, connecting Andy and Max over drugs. I'd confronted Max about the coke and the gambling debts and the bartender, and he'd tried to talk his way out of it, but I'd had a gutful and screamed at him to get the hell out of the pub before I had him arrested. 'And I'd bloody testify against you as well,' I yelled.

'You wouldn't want to do that,' he said.

'Why not? You deserve it.'

'I'm one of many,' he said. 'There're more people in this than you realise.'

'Well, they can all get the fuck out of my pub, too,' I said. 'Or else.'

He stared at me for several long moments, and I couldn't help noticing his reddened nose and bleary eyes. Coke and gambling would be the death of him, I thought.

'I'm trying to warn you,' he said. 'You're making a big mistake.'

'I'm not interested in your help, Max,' I sneered. 'Get out.'

I'd believed that was the end of it. I'd get him out of the pub, off the ownership papers and trade my way out of the disaster and make a new life for myself. My lawyer was glad to hear Max had gone, but he also advised caution. 'Keep your back covered,' he said.

I should've listened. The rest of that day was a blur. I'd had to deal with staff problems, suppliers who left us without bread and cooking oil, and one of the busiest nights on record. I finally sent the last staff member home just after midnight, and locked away the takings for counting in the morning. Last job before bed was to check a barrel in the cellar that one of the barmen had said might be leaking.

I'd told everyone that I'd slipped and fallen down the stairs, too tired after a long day to watch where I was going. But even now, I could still hear that soft footstep behind me, the feel of the hand in the middle of my back, my arms wheeling as I tried to grab something to stop my headlong fall down the dark stairwell. I broke my femur, hip, three ribs and an arm. I was lucky I didn't break my neck. I lay at the bottom of those stairs in the dark for seven hours, until the cleaner found me the next morning.

The pain was horrific and I passed out several times, but in the times when I was conscious, I knew something was badly wrong below my waist. I kept telling myself that the pain meant I wouldn't be a paraplegic, but as the hours wore on, I stopped believing that. I kept picturing myself a crippled old woman, strung up in permanent traction in a bed, like I'd seen in a movie once.

My mother used to tell me I had too much imagination, and that night I agreed with her. I cried on and off, and had long bouts of violent shivering from the cold, which made the pain flare like a red-hot gas oven. In my more lucid moments, I planned the most violent revenge scenarios about Max, my rage at my own stupidity fuelling the fantasies. When the cleaner found me and called the ambulance, I was filled with such relief that I passed out again, and the poor woman thought I'd died.

I never told anyone what happened, that I'd been pushed by someone who wasn't happy about losing the pub as a place to deal. Too proud to admit I'd been so stupid. Now I had to ask myself if my hatred of Max and his drug dealing, and then my rejection of Andy's plea, had led to Andy's murder.

God, I couldn't stand it if that were so. I stared down at the notebook, drew lines between names, tried to think objectively about it all. No, I'd been extremely stupid, but those two things were not connected. Not in any kind of straight line. The past might hold clues to the box's location, but not the answers to Andy's death.

I needed to make a move, start on my search, as soon as I could. That meant a phone first – I'd noticed a shop near the café – and a phone number. Then I'd go back to the house and check the answering machine, put a new message on it with my mobile number. Baldie had said, 'We'll be in contact.' I checked my watch – five hours since they'd taken her. Surely they'd give me some time to find the box? Or maybe they wanted to force more pressure onto me, scare me more.

It was working. I had to move faster. All this thinking was wasting precious minutes now. I headed for the phone shop.

14

Fifteen minutes later, I had a cheap smartphone with a shiny screen in my hand and a spotty teenager giving me instructions on the basics of how to use it. He looked astounded that I'd never owned one before.

'You want to do texting, like, you use this button here,' he said.

'I'll figure that bit out later,' I said. 'I just want to make and receive calls.'

'OK.' He got me connected, and pointed out my new number on the packet above the barcode. 'Like, good luck.'

'Yeah, I'll need it.' I rang Heath straight away and reeled off the number, then asked, 'Have you found where those guys are yet?'

'They weren't at the addresses I was given, so I'm talking to a few more people.'

I ground my teeth. 'Great.' It sounded like he was getting nowhere.

'Where are you going now?'

'Home – I mean, Andy's house, to check the answering machine. Then I'm going to where he used to work.' I was itching to hang up and be on my way, instead of shouting into a phone.

'I want to know what you're up to.'

Bossy. 'Whatever. I'll call you if anything happens,' I said, and tapped the red button.

The answering machine at the house was silent and I cursed. I left my mobile number as an alternative on the machine greeting, jumped back in the car and drove to the car yard in Footscray. Cars of all sizes and colours lined the edge of the footpath, carrying signs that shouted *Best Deal* and *Hot Price*, and a limp strip of red flags drooped over the office. A pudgy young guy in a white shirt and black pants that made him look like a wine waiter hurried over to me.

'Good afternoon, madam. What a beautiful car. Mercedes Benz spells quality. Can I show –'

'I'm not here to buy a car, sorry. Where's the boss?'

'Are you sure? This week's special is a lovely red Toyota –'

'Did you work with Andy Westerholme?'

That stopped him midstream. His fake smiled dropped off his face. 'Yes. Are you another cop?'

'No, I'm Andy's sister. Who are you?'

'John Kovic.' He resurrected the smile but it wasn't as cheery. 'You look like Andy. He was a cool guy.'

'How long did you know him?'

'Only a couple of months. I started here in January. Didn't know that was a slow time for car selling, did I?' His mouth turned down into a sulk and I wondered if he ever sold anything to anyone. A face like that would turn me off a free Rolls Royce.

'Where's the boss? Inside?'

'Yeah, in the back office, or he might be sucking up to Lindy, the receptionist.' He shrugged and headed off to trap a passerby who had been silly enough to pause in front of a 4WD.

I walked into a room with a concrete floor covered with heavy rubber mats, and breathed in the smell of hot plastic and motor oil. A large display of dusty silk flowers sat in one corner next to two grimy plastic chairs. The receptionist's desk was bang in the middle, its chair empty. No bell to ring.

'Anyone here?' I called.

A door slammed in the back somewhere and high heels tapped towards me. The receptionist emerged from the gloomy corridor behind the desk, flicking her long black hair out of her eyes.

'Can I help you?' she asked, in a bored voice that implied help was the last thing she was interested in.

'Who's the boss here?'

Her eyebrows raised into two perfect arcs. 'Mr Johnson. Is there a problem?'

'I'd like to talk to him.'

'What about?'

I nearly told her it was none of her business but it wasn't worth it. 'It's about Andrew Westerholme – my brother.'

The eyebrows disappeared under the fringe. 'Omigod, that's awful.' Her eyes filled with tears and she crossed her hands over her chest. 'I'm so sorry. He was such a lovely guy, you know?'

'Uh huh.' I needed to move past her sympathy without sounding impatient, but I wasn't succeeding. 'Did he have an office or a locker?'

'Are you here to collect his things?'

'Yes. But I also need to speak to Mr Johnson.'

'Omigod, for sure. I'll get him.' One purple fingernail pressed a button on her intercom phone. 'Mr J, Andy's sister is here. She wants to say hi.'

Hi? Well, it was a place to start. While I waited, the girl kept sneaking looks at me until finally she asked, 'Um... what happened to you?'

'Sorry?'

'You're... injured.'

I lifted my hand – with the painkillers doing their job at last, I'd forgotten about my various dressings and bandages. 'It's fine, nothing to do with Andy.' Liar.

Mr J arrived, padding down the corridor in his leather loafers, carrying a cardboard box. He shoved out a hand from under the box to shake mine, delicately when he saw the bandage. 'So sorry about Andy, my dear. Such a shock. We really miss him.'

I could see I'd be getting the cardboard box and a brush-off, so I jumped in first. 'I need to talk to you in private for a couple of minutes, if that's OK.'

'Oh. Why?' Mr J's comb-over was slipping off his shiny scalp and one errant strand floated in the air.

I kept my voice pleasant. 'I hadn't seen Andy for some time, and I was hoping to talk to people who knew him, find out more about his life, who his friends were, you know.'

'For the eulogy?' Mr J looked doubtful.

'No, not at all. This is for me. Something I need to do.' I smiled, trying to look mournful and hopeful at the same time so he couldn't refuse.

'I suppose I could spare you a few minutes.'

The place looked like no one had bought a car here in twenty years, so I doubted Mr J's schedule was jam-packed with appointments and sales paperwork. Andy must have been a great salesman to earn good money in this joint. I followed Mr J down the corridor and into an office that overlooked the car-washing area at the back of the yard. Weeds grew along the fence line and up through the cracked concrete.

Mr J put the box on the corner of his desk and sat, bouncing in his spring-loaded vinyl chair. 'Now, how can I help?'

I sat too, the plastic chair bending under me, placing me well below Mr J so that I was staring at his stomach. 'How long did Andy work here?'

'About a year,' he replied. 'He used to work at a yard down by the river – it closed down and the guy gave Andy a reference.'

'I can't imagine him selling cars – was he any good at it?'

Mr J bristled. 'Nothing wrong with selling cars for a living.'

'I didn't mean that.' My hands felt clammy, and I had to backpedal. 'I just thought Andy might have been working in real estate again.'

'He did well here. He was a friendly bloke, got on well with people. If your customer likes you, they trust what you tell them.' His eyes slid sideways for a second, but if Mr J was feeling guilty about something, I couldn't figure out what.

'Did he have anyone who made trouble? Gave him a hard time?'

Mr J shook his head. 'No. Andy had a lot of slopes around here who knew him and passed the word. They all bought cars off him.'

'Slopes?' Irritation laced my voice.

'Asians. Sorry.' He didn't look sorry, just red in the face at being caught out.

'So Andy was never drunk on the job, or hungover or anything?'

'The cops asked me that, too,' he said. 'I told you, Andy was on the ball. He didn't even come to the pub with us. Went home on the dot of five to see his little girl – he was always showing photos of her around. Great dad.'

I couldn't think of any more questions, apart from the important one. 'Did Andy store anything here? Like a steel toolbox? In your service area maybe?'

He frowned. 'Not that I know of. We don't have a service area anyway. And I've never seen a toolbox of any kind around here. You're welcome to look, if you want.'

'Thanks, I will. Did he have his own desk or office?'

'Next door. Lindy has cleared it out, though. All the stuff is in that cardboard box.'

'I know, but if I could just have a look around...'

He sighed and stood up. 'Help yourself. But there's nothing here.'

I nodded and thanked him, but I still searched every inch of Andy's old office, even pulling out desk drawers and checking the cavity. Mr J watched me like a hawk; he was probably worried I'd steal a bottle of white-out or a pencil. The service area was an empty steel shed out the back – no one had used it for years and cobwebs hung in the corners. I wiped my hands on my jeans and grimaced. *Damn.*

As Mr J walked me out to the Benz, carrying the cardboard box, he said, 'Andy often talked about you, you know.'

I stopped abruptly and turned. 'Me?'

'We have a lot of quiet periods during the week. Chatting passes the time. He told us stories about when you were kids. Sounds like you had a happy childhood.'

It sounded to me like Andy had been making things up. 'Did he ever talk about what he did before he started selling cars?'

'Not really. Just said he'd been in sales for quite a while.'

I buttoned my lips. Selling houses fell into that category, and I guess buying and selling drugs might, too.

We stood by the Benz. 'Nice car,' Mr J said, 'and a good year. If you ever want to trade it in for a little Toyota or Suzuki, let me know. Petrol prices will never come down again.'

'I don't drive much,' I said. 'This will do me for a while yet.'

On the road, I put my foot to the floor, anxious to get back to Ascot Vale. Surely they would've called by now? I rushed into the house, straight to the answering machine, but still there was nothing, and I wanted to scream. I kept picturing Mia crying like she was at Kayla's and then I couldn't breathe. I ate some chocolate biscuits I found in a jar, and the sugar rush made me feel better. I had to keep it together! And keep looking for the box.

I tipped out the contents of the cardboard carton on to the kitchen table, hoping to see an address book, or appointment book, or something with phone numbers and names. Some kind of clue, like he used to leave me when we played detective games, always by his made-up rules. It'd be too much to hope for that the two thugs' names – Castella and Sands – would be written down anywhere, but stranger things had happened. I realised I'd been seeing a rejuvenated Andy, off the drugs, back to his old ways of planning and covering the bases.

The house, the organised files, the sheer tidiness of everything told me he'd been on the ball, even if at the end he'd made a mistake that cost him his life. I knew Andy, I knew how his brain worked, and I was convinced he wouldn't have given me the responsibility of Mia without anything else to go on. All those years at home, despite my spinelessness, he'd never once left me in the lurch. I'd always been part of his plans, and my gut was telling me this was the same situation.

Maybe I was just too bloody dumb to see what was in front of me.

I spread out the pile of detritus, eager to see what he'd left.

15

I poked through the bits and pieces of his working life, hope fading. Coffee mug, half a dozen pens and pencils, a blank notepad that I checked through, a small arrangement of moth-eaten dried flowers in a vase that the receptionist probably palmed off on him.

A framed photo of Hawthorn football team, another small framed photo of Mia in which I guessed she was about a year old, and a pile of old receipts and invoices. The photo of Mia looked lumpy in the frame so I prised the back off and found another photo behind it, one that tightened my throat with an ancient, angry ache. It was of Andy, when he was the same age as Mia, dressed in a dinky little sailor suit, being held up by our mother who simpered at the camera. I put the two photos side by side – they could've been twins. It was eerie.

I resisted the urge to grab some scissors and chop Mum out of the second one; instead, I turned it over to see if there was a date on it. Mum had always been anal about dating our photos and school projects, filing school reports and certificates and finger paintings as if one day she was going to pull them all out to prove what a wonderful mother she'd been. In her own mind.

23 July, 1981. Andy's first birthday. I would've been about five, probably jealous of all the presents he received. Below the date was more writing, not in Mum's script, possibly Andy's. It was in pencil, faint and hard to read. *You could always rely on Mum to cover up.*

Wasn't that the bitter truth? Every time Dad thrashed us, Mum hid in the bedroom with the radio turned up full volume so she couldn't hear anything, and later, if one of us complained to her, she'd say, 'You should know better than to upset your father. He works hard for you children.' When she had to take me to the doctor about my ear that Dad whacked, he'd examined me and given her a funny look, then asked, 'How did this happen? It looks inflamed and bruised to me.'

Mum calmly said, 'Judi and Andrew are like little savages, the way they run about and knock each other over. One day she might stop this silly tomboy act and grow up to behave more like a lady.'

I nearly choked but I couldn't say a word because I knew she'd tattle to Dad as soon as we got home, and although he probably wouldn't hit me again, he'd take it out on Andy instead. So I kept my mouth shut, although after that day I let her know at every opportunity how much I despised her. With Dad, it was straight-out hate.

I turned the photos face-down on the table and sorted through the bills and invoices. Mostly they were for dry-cleaning, service on his car and new clothes. His car was still with the cops, so what was Leigh driving?

One receipt was for a bouquet of flowers sent to Gentle Haven Retirement Village, and I checked the recipient's name. It was Mum. Andy had sent the old bitch flowers. My skin went cold and I sat down with a thump, jarring my hip, and cursed. She was in a retirement village, so probably the house had been sold. Was that where Andy got the deposit for this place? Sucking up to her? My stomach churned.

I couldn't bring myself to believe that he would take money off her – I'd rather he was in the mafia. An insane giggle exploded from my mouth, then I shook myself.

I'd screwed up the receipt into a tiny ball without realising, and tried to smooth it out again. It was dated in February this year, the day before the old bitch's birthday. I noted the unit number at the Village, although I had no intention of going anywhere near her.

The last four invoices were for the rental of a storage unit in Braybrook. A buzz of excitement started in my head, and increased when I saw the names on the invoices – *Andrew and Judi Westerholme*.

He'd rented it in both of our names. This must be the clue I'd been looking for, aimed right at me. Hope jolted me out of the chair.

This had to be where he'd hidden the toolbox. I could save Mia. The invoices gave the address and stated 24-hour access; I frantically grabbed my bag, phone and car keys, shoved the invoices in my pocket and ran from the house. The address was easy to find, near the railway line, and I eased the Benz down narrow alleys between the soulless blocks of storage units. There was no front office that I could see, so I parked down one end and went in through a nearby open door.

The place was like a rabbit warren, and the unit number on my invoices seemed nowhere near what was stencilled on the doors I passed. Twenty minutes later, I was still pacing up and down the corridors, getting no nearer to finding the right number and fuming; one day someone would come along and find my dried-out skeleton.

Finally I spotted someone, a real person, a guy in overalls and a cap pushing a red trolley. 'Excuse me,' I called, 'can you help me out here?'

He waited until I reached him, then, when I told him what number I was looking for, pointed to the metal stairs by a pillar. 'Up there, where all the small ones are. Got your combination, have you?'

'Combination?' Of course it would be locked.

'Yeah, we don't use keys anymore. Too easy to lose them, then the locksmith charges an arm and a leg. We keep the combinations in a safe.'

'So can I get mine from you?'

He looked at me suspiciously. 'Why don't you have it?'

'My brother rented the unit and he hasn't left it for me. I've got the last invoices though.'

He grunted and shook his head like he'd heard that story a million times. 'Sorry, I can't give it to you. I don't know who you are.'

I shook the invoices at him. 'My name's on these – look. And I can show you my driver's licence.'

'You still might not be the rightful lessee. We take security very seriously here, you know.'

'But...' I didn't want to play the death card but I had no choice. 'My brother died a couple of weeks ago. That's why I don't have the combination. I've only just found out about this place.'

'Why's your name on the invoices then?'

This guy was in full paranoid ASIO mode. I wanted to strangle him. 'My brother left something in the unit for me, but he died suddenly, before he could give me all the details. I really need to get into that unit. Please.' Or a little kid might get badly hurt. Give me the fucking combination!

'Sorry. No can do.'

It took every last ounce of self-control to step back from going berserk. I took a breath. 'Right. Will it help if the cops tell you to give it to me?'

He smirked. 'It might. I'll be in the building next door, in the office. Just let me know when the cops get here.' He pushed his cap back on his head and parked the trolley by the stairs, then sauntered away, obviously thinking he'd got the better of me.

Half an hour later, I took the greatest pleasure in wiping the grin off his face when Heath turned up in response to my call and flashed his badge.

'This is a murder investigation, mate,' he said. 'We need that combination.'

'Well, yeah, sorry,' the guy blustered, 'but she never said nothing about that.'

'Yeah, yeah. Combination?' Heath held out his hand and the guy wrote the numbers on a sticky note and passed it over. 'Thanks.'

We walked up the stairs and along three corridors before we found the right unit and Heath dialled the combination that clicked the lock open. He pushed the metal door back on its frame; it sagged and creaked, scraping along the floor. My heart was pounding so loudly I was sure he could hear it. I scanned the space in an instant. 'Shit. It's not here. What the hell was Andy playing at?'

The only thing there was a shallow cardboard box with a small video camera and some cables sitting in it. They were all covered in a thin layer of dust. I stepped towards it, tempted to kick the box to bits. Heath put out an arm. 'Don't touch anything.' Then he pulled a pair of latex gloves out of his pocket, snapped them on to his hands and lifted out the metallic black camera. 'Fairly cheap model with an inbuilt mike and rechargeable battery unit. Maybe he bought it to take videos of Mia.' He opened a flap on the side. 'No memory card.'

'Why would he leave it here in a lock-up unit? And nothing else?' The air in the unit felt stifling and I edged back into the corridor. Sweat trickled down my spine and I pinched the bridge of my nose hard with thumb and finger; I was back to square one.

Heath came out with the box and gave it to me to hold while he pushed the door shut, locking it again. 'Maybe he was worried it'd be stolen.'

'You said yourself the equipment is cheap.' I looked at the camera. 'You think there's something in the internal memory?'

'Can only hope. We'll go check it out at his house then. It's closest.'

'You don't want to take it in as evidence or something?' My face burned – it wasn't my job to tell him what to do – but he nodded.

'I will later on, but I'm more interested in seeing what's on it first. I doubt there'll be any useful fingerprints. Just his.'

'OK.' I still thought he was being a bit cavalier with potential evidence but he didn't seem worried. If they turned out to be family home movies, I'd look damn silly if I pushed it.

Back at Andy's house, he used the latex gloves again to handle the camera and cables, as well as bringing two bags to put them into later. He brought in his laptop and connected the camera, then worked out how to access its files, of which there were only two. We both sat forward on the low armchairs, hunched down, focused on the screen as the file opened. The camera moved around erratically at first, but when it settled down, I recognised Altona Beach with the long pier and the heaps of seaweed. Andy seemed to be trying out the camera, zooming in and out and focusing on people and dogs at random, then talking into the microphone about being Altman or Oliver Stone and laughing. The sound of his familiar voice cut through me, and I vowed to get that camera off the cops when they'd finished with it, just so I could hear him again, and hear that laugh.

After ten minutes, the screen went blank and although Heath clicked around a bit, there was nothing else in it. 'Must have been practising,' he said, and changed files. The second one was filmed inside, and had the date stamp in one corner. 24-6-13. It was similar to the first film in that it seemed Andy was still trying out the camera, except this time it was a night-time interior, a pub bar somewhere with tables and chairs and a long wooden bar with bottles lined up behind it and fridges with glass doors.

A thin woman was serving beer behind the bar, pulling on a han-dle to fill a pot glass, and I started in my chair, my skin prickling. 'That's Leigh.' She wore tight jeans and a low-cut top, and kept glanc-ing at the camera and smiling. I examined her face, its high cheek-bones, thin chin, slightly bleary eyes, twitchy smile. Yeah, right. Then Andy moved on to three old guys sitting at the end of the bar, one of whom waved him away and muttered, 'Silly bugger, go and annoy your mates.'

The camera swung around and focused on a group of men who lounged at two tables pushed together that were covered in empty beer and wine glasses. It looked like they'd been there a while. Most of the men were in shirt sleeves, their jackets hanging on the backs of their chairs.

'Now that's interesting,' Heath said. He pointed at a thick-necked man in a white shirt and striped red tie, half-undone. 'That's

Col Stuart.' Noticing the camera, Col dipped his head and said something. 'You'd better not have that on,' someone else said close by. 'Col's not happy.' Two other men suddenly decide to ham it up, flexing their muscles and laughing.

'Who's Col Stuart?' I ask.

'A gangland heavy. Not much in the way of brains, but good backup man. Dead now.'

Andy continued to film for another couple of minutes until Col Stuart muttered to the man next to him, a thickset guy with a big moustache, who got up and signalled to Andy with a finger sliced across his throat. The screen went black.

'There's something about the way they were dressed...' Hotshot stared at the TV, his fingers rubbing at the side of his face.

I closed my eyes for a moment, visualised the last images on the screen. 'I want to see that last bit again,' I said, and he rewound it for me. I watched carefully, and a dark chill ran through me. 'Look, at the back.' I pointed to a tall, curly-haired guy who had had his back turned until a few seconds before the end. 'That's Spaz.'

'Castella, yes, you're right.' Heath frowned. 'I think they've all just been to a funeral. Col often wore a suit but the others look a bit too dressed up for a normal night at the pub. I reckon my mate in the task force could tell me who some of the others are.' He played the end of the tape again, pointing at another man. 'That's Benny Vito. He was shot a bit later, out the back of Werribee.'

I picked at the frayed edges of the dressing on my hand. 'Whose funeral have they been to? Why is Andy filming them? Was he in with all those gangland guys?'

'Not from what I've been told. But sometimes people hung around the fringes with these guys, not understanding what was really going on, or how lethal they were. It's always been an image thing, acting like they're bloody Hollywood stars. Still, Andy was taking a risk, filming them like that, even in fun.' He thought for a few moments. 'June 2013. Could have been Nicky Santos's funeral.'

'What's his connection?'

'Titch Santos's brother. Yet another payback in a long line of them. Most of the hits were either payback or getting rid of the competition.'

I shuddered. 'You talk about it like it's one of those TV police shows.'

'Sorry. It did get unreal there, you know. More than twenty killed, just gunning each other down like the OK Corral. If they sided with the wrong guy, or got too greedy, or if somebody thought they were talking... no logic to some of them.' Heath leaned forward and clicked to close the file.

'What on earth could Andy have to do with them?' I couldn't imagine Andy being anything more than small-time, caught up in drugs the way he was, but I'd been wrong about quite a few things already.

'Just because he never got caught doesn't mean he was in the minor leagues,' Heath said mildly.

I shook my head. 'Andy's boss at the car yard said Andy was good mates with a lot of the local Asians – meaning the Vietnamese, I guess – in Footscray. That's a whole different world to these gangland guys, isn't it?' I still felt stupid saying the word *gangland* but it seemed the common term. 'They don't mix?'

'Not usually.' The laptop closed down and Heath put the camera and cables into the bags. 'I'll get John to take a look at this pub one, see if he can identify anyone else. And I need to check in and see what's happening with the search for Mia. I'll call if I hear anything.'

After he'd left, I made sure all of the locks were on before I sagged back into the armchair. Whatever the significance of those videos to Heath, they were of no use to me right now. They didn't tell me where the box was, so they weren't going to help me get Mia back.

Clearly, the police had no idea where she was. I fumed at their lack of progress and checked the time – after six already – why hadn't those two deadshits rung me yet? Mia would have no idea what was going on, only that she'd been abandoned for a second time. Shit. I had to keep looking, work out where to go next.

The phone rang shrilly and I jumped. I'd been waiting for hours for this and now all I could do was stare at the damn thing. It kept ringing and I stumbled towards it, picking up the handset. *Please don't let it be Connor.* 'Hello.'

'Got the box yet?' It was Baldie.

My heart lurched, and I pressed the phone hard against my ear. *Stay calm.* 'Not yet. I'm still –'

'The kid won't last much longer. She fucken screams any more, I'll have to shut her up for good.'

'No! Don't!' I sucked in a breath. 'I'll find the box, I promise. I just need more time.'

'By tomorrow.'

'It might –'

'You want a dead kid?'

'No!'

'Tomorrow.'

Right then, Mia screamed in the background, a shrill sound that was like a knife in my guts. Someone had belted her so I could hear her cries, I was sure, and I wanted to reach down the phone and rip Baldie's head off.

'OK, I will. Don't you dare hurt her!'

'Shut up, bitch. You got a mobile?'

'Yes.' I gave him the number.

'When I call, you better have that box.'

Click.

16

I slammed the phone down. 'Fuck, fuck, fuck!' Why hadn't the cops set up one of those phone-tapping thingies so they could track the call? This could have helped them find Mia and here I was, dealing with it all on my own.

My head throbbed, reverberating like a heavy bell, and I swallowed two more painkillers with some wine, then called Heath on my mobile, my fingers trembling so much it took me three attempts to get the numbers right.

'Heath. They called.' My voice was shaking more than my hands. I told him anyway what Baldie had said. 'I have to get that box. It's the only way. Otherwise I'm stuffed. Mia's stuffed.' I felt like I was choking.

'There's no guarantee –'

'What? That I'll get her back? You watch me.' I drank more wine and stared out the window into the dark garden. 'Is this a kidnapping or not?'

'Yes,' he said carefully.

'Why didn't you put one of those things on my phone? So you could track Baldie's phone call.'

He cleared his throat. 'We, ah... the equipment is coming. They're installing it tonight.'

'Too bloody late. Thanks very much.' I shook my head. It was always the same – somebody making slow decisions in a faraway office.

'Come on, Judi, we've got eight guys working on this. It's not like we're not taking it seriously.'

'Fine then. You do your bit, and I'll do mine.'

'What does that mean?' He huffed loudly. 'You can't go charging in on your own. You already know what these guys are like. You have to let us do our job.'

Yeah, right. And aren't you making terrific progress. 'Are you look-ing for the box?'

'No, we're looking for Castella and Sands.'

'No change from this morning then. I'll keep looking for the box.'

'Jeez!' He pulled the phone away and I could hear him swearing, then he was back. 'Are you OK?'

'Fine!'

'Good. Let's –'

The phone on the wall jangled and I stopped listening to him. 'I have to answer the phone,' I finally said.

I closed my eyes and picked up the receiver, my heartbeat skitter-ing. 'Hello.'

'Hi, Judi, it's Connor. Just thought I'd see how things were going.'

Relief swamped me, and I leaned against the wall, trying to breathe properly. 'Hi, it's all fine, so far.' My voice sounded weird to me. I kept forcing the words out. 'The funeral home is doing it all.'

'That's good. Do you want me –'

'Sorry, can you hang on a moment?' I told Heath who it was and disconnected his call. 'I'm back.'

'Has Leigh turned up yet?' Connor's voice was familiar and comforting, reminding me of my cottage and my garden and sitting outside at dusk, watching for wombats. I wanted to sit down and tell Connor everything. Although so much had happened in the past few days, I hardly knew where to begin.

'No. I – I'll have to go ahead without her.'

'What about that wanker detective? Is he doing his job?'

I didn't want to have to explain that the wanker detective wasn't so bad after all. 'Things are... happening.'

'Are you OK? You sound really stressed out.'

'There have been a lot more hassles than I expected,' I said carefully. 'I'd rather be home in my garden right now, and it's a bit frustrating to have to stay here.'

He chuckled. 'Knowing you, you're probably making somebody's life hell down there.'

'Yeah, you could say that.'

'I watered your garden this morning. Used a bit of tank water – hope that's OK.'

Tears tried to leak out and I blinked hard. 'Wonderful. You're a life saver. You can have some of my potatoes when they're ready.'

'Thanks, but I didn't do it for that.'

'Yeah, I know.' I couldn't keep talking to him and lying to him as well, so I bumbled my way through a couple more pleasantries, hearing his voice growing puzzled as he sussed out that I was far from normal. Thank God he knew me well enough not to try the third degree. I hung up feeling like a huge weight had descended on me. I hated telling lies and pretending, and yet here I was doing it all over again.

My mobile rang – Heath, checking up on me again. I answered briskly. 'Yes.'

'We've got an address for Castella, in Brunswick.' His voice echoed, like he was on speaker. 'You can come along if you promise to stay in the car.'

'You're allowing me on a police operation?'

'If Mia's there, it'd be good if you were around to look after her.'

'Oh.' Hope flared up in me like a light being switched on. *Don't go there, you don't know she's there, and she might be... Don't go there, either.* 'Have they seen Mia in the house?'

'No, but they've seen him go in and out a couple of times. I'll pick you up very shortly. On the way.'

I was waiting at the front window when he arrived. It had started raining and the drops running down the window looked like tears until the red tail lights on Heath's car turned them to blood. I locked the front door, ran through the rain and slid into the passenger seat. He took off before I even got my belt fastened.

We drove in silence for a few minutes then he said, 'I've received more information on the possible funeral. Looks like it definitely was Santos's brother. He was shot over a drug deal.'

My throat went dry. 'Andy was involved?'

'Nothing says that at all. He's not mentioned in connection with any of them.'

'But Castella was in his video, with Leigh.'

'No idea yet what that was about. Coincidence?'

'As if.'

'Yeah.' He reached across and put his hand over mine; his skin was warm and dry but his touch wasn't comforting. It made my heart rate zoom up in an instant. 'Don't get your hopes up about this raid too much.'

Are you kidding? Of course I've got my bloody hopes up. 'No, OK.' I pulled my hand away.

We sped over Lynch's Bridge and past Flemington Racecourse, up towards Racecourse Road. He didn't use siren or lights, but he drove fast, passing slower cars as if they were standing still. I didn't care. I wanted him to go even faster. I didn't care if the road was slippery. I wanted to be there right now, snatching Mia from Baldie's hands.

'Surveillance says there's only one person in the house at the mo-ment,' he said, jolting me out of my thoughts. 'A woman. But Castella might turn up.'

'So no one's seen Mia.'

'They're not going to let her outside if she's there.'

I pressed my lips together, hard. I didn't want to talk anymore. I wanted to keep hoping. A few minutes later we pulled up in a quiet street, in front of a dirty white bungalow with long, scraggly grass in the front yard. Two policemen were already there, parked on the other side of the street. Heath got out and talked to them quietly, hunched into his jacket, and they pointed to a brick house further down, under a street light that was so dull it was worse than no light at all.

My hands were gripping each other so tightly that pain jabbed through my wound. *Mia, are you in there? Please be in there, please be safe.*

Another car pulled up behind me and two guys in ordinary clothes got out. It was starting to look like a mini police convention, way too obvious. If Castella arrived, he'd keep on going. They needed to move in now! The rain had eased into a misty drizzle; the cops only spoke for a few seconds, then scattered in three different directions. Heath came over to me. 'Stay in the car. It's the brick house. There're no lights on but we're going in.'

He jogged back to one of the uniformed police and they approached the heavy, screened front door together, the uniform holding a metal rammer. The other cops had disappeared down the sideway. I could see Heath pressing the doorbell, then knocking hard on the screen door.

I wanted to get out, to run to the house, to grab the rammer and smash the door in. Instead, I heard him shout, 'Police! Open up.'

17

There was no sign of movement in the brick house. No lights went on, no one bolted out of a window. I leant forward and gripped the dashboard, peering through the drizzle, holding my breath. Had they got the wrong house?

More loud knocking and shouting. Heath said something to the uniformed cop and he lifted the rammer, ready to bash the door down. The porch light went on and Heath held back the screen door with his shoulder, ready to react. The front door opened, just a dark gap. There was some brief conversation then Heath pushed the front door all the way and walked in, followed by the uniform. The hall light went on and, as the light spilled out, it showed a small dark-haired woman in a pink dressing gown leaning defeatedly against the door jamb. She pulled herself up and followed them into the house.

I heard more shouting and banging, and resisted the overwhelming urge to get out of the car and go see what was happening. No matter how much I strained, I couldn't hear a child crying.

A few minutes later, they all came out and the front door slammed shut after them. Nobody was carrying Mia. I slumped back in the seat, the hope I'd tried to keep under wraps now drifting away like smoke. The cops conferred on the footpath then the others drove away. Heath got into the car and shoved the key in the ignition, his movements jerky. He didn't look at me.

'Is that it? No one there?'

'Nup.' He banged the steering wheel and drops of rain flew off his sleeve. 'She bloody knew what we were talking about though. Clammed up. Nothing we could do, short of thumping her.'

'I'll go back and do it for you!'

He laughed harshly. 'Yeah, I bet you would, too.'

'Has Spaz even been there?'

'Not for a few days. She's lying, but Mia isn't there.'

'So where the hell are they hiding her? God!' My frustration was at boiling point.

'We'll keep looking. We've got the word out. When kids are involved, people speak up, more than they do for anything else.'

'Right.' I wanted to believe him, but why was nothing happening? 'Why can't you go to the media now? Surely it's at that point?'

'We know who they are – that's our lead. A media frenzy right now would stuff everything up, trust me.'

I bent forward, head in hands, trying to hold myself together, thinking hard. He tapped my knee, so I had to face him. 'You're not giving up, are you?'

'No way!' I grabbed my bag and pulled out my list. I'd worked out what my next step had to be, the next person on my list, but I'd been praying they'd find Mia so I could avoid it. My jaw clenched. 'Feel like going for a drive?' Heath's support was better than none at all.

'Um, sure. Where to?'

My whole face ached. I rubbed it with both hands. 'Gentle Haven Retirement Village. Prepare to meet thy doom.'

'Pardon?'

'Don't mind me.' I sighed. 'We're going to visit my mother.' My skin crawled at the thought, no matter how much I tried to be practical about it. Never mind the past – the woman had been told about her son's death and had done nothing. Andy had sent her flowers, had maybe been grovelling for money. He'd been desperate enough to go down that path. I knew I never would be.

Yet here I was, going to visit her. Except it wasn't for me, it was for Mia, and that made all the difference.

I gave Heath the address and he put it into his phone. A disembodied voice directed us around the CBD, past Brighton to Cheltenham, along the Nepean Highway. It was still busy, cars jostling for space in their lanes, and even Southland Shopping Centre appeared to be open, lights blazing everywhere. I imagined thousands of people inside, all busting to spend every last cent on something they didn't need or even really want.

Heath broke into my thoughts. 'Do you now think Andy left the box with your mother?'

'It's a long shot. Andy has been in contact with her, sent her flowers, according to a receipt I found. She might know where it is.'

He nodded. 'It's a good possibility.'

'Except the idea of him visiting her seems so bizarre. He hated her as much as I did. But I thought I should cover all the bases.' The voice told us to turn left.

He flicked on the indicator, swung the wheel, roared up the wide side street that was lined with thick-trunked trees. The gutters and nature strips were choked with layers of brown and yellow leaves, and I vaguely wondered how they got rid of them. Did people spade them up and put them in their compost heaps? Probably not.

'We're here,' Heath said, interrupting my thoughts. 'What number?'

'27A.' I pointed to a clump of little signs and arrows. 'Down that driveway, I'd say.' We parked in the visitors' area, under some curly antique-looking street lamps, and walked along a quiet path lined with flowering shrubs and little solar-powered garden lights. The rain had stopped altogether and the dank smell of wet earth floated around me. The second-to-last screen door in the row had 27A on it in yellow letters and a square white doorbell, which I rang. Inside the house, chimes carolled in what sounded like Handel's *Messiah*.

After the porch light beamed on and two security locks clicked, the door opened on a thick chain and two blue eyes magnified by thick glasses peered out at us. 'Who is it?' asked a quavering voice.

That was definitely not my mother. 'I'm sorry, I thought Mrs Westerholme lived here.'

'She did until three months ago. She's been moved up to the main building. The rest home section. Up there.' A wrinkled finger came through the gap and pointed back behind us.

'Is she ill?' Heath asked.

'No, just dotty.' The door closed, leaving us to look at each other.

'I cannot imagine my mother as dotty,' I said. 'Stark, raving mad, yes. Dotty, no.'

'We'll soon see.'

As we returned along the path, Heath said, 'You looked like you were standing on the edge of a cliff when you rang that doorbell.'

'Yeah, well...' I folded my arms tightly and kept walking.

The receptionist in the front office apparently doubled as the night nurse, judging by her white uniform and white shoes. 'It's past visiting hours,' she said before we could get a word out.

Heath flashed his police badge. 'We need to talk to Mrs Westerholme.'

That badge was quite useful at times.

'Robbed a bank, did she?' The nurse chortled at her own joke. 'You won't get much joy out of talking to her.'

'Is she...' I didn't dare use the word dotty.

'Alzheimer's. A few of them have it in this section. They need extra care, can't be trusted to look after themselves anymore.' She gazed at me. 'You're the daughter.'

'Er... yes. How did you know?'

'She's got photos of you and your brother, and he visits. You look a lot like him.'

'So I believe.' He *visits*?

'She's this way.'

She led us down a corridor with a shiny lino floor and rows of closed doors on either side, and stopped in front of one that needed her key to open it.

'Is she locked in all of the time?' I asked as politely as possible.

'Yes, she has to be now. Getting into too much trouble.'

'How do you mean?' I was trying to imagine my prim and proper mother causing an old people's riot, or climbing trees.

'Your brother didn't tell you? No, well, it's not easy to talk about...' She kept her hand on the door but didn't open it. 'Alzheimer's strikes people in different ways. Some it makes bad-tempered and prone to rages, others it turns into shells with nothing left inside, not even memories at the end. Your mother is one of the odd ones.'

'She would be,' I muttered.

'She has uncontrollable sexual urges.'

'Pardon?' I wanted to laugh hysterically but the nurse's stern face stopped me.

'We don't really know why it affects some people like that. She makes advances to the men all the time, what few are here now, and tries to get into their beds at night. So we have to lock her in at bed-time, and keep a strict eye on her during the day.'

'My God, who'd have thought,' I said, biting hard on the inside of my cheek.

The nurse gave me a sharp look and then opened the door. 'Hello, Evie, look who's here to visit. Just as well you're still up, isn't it?'

She went in, but I couldn't follow. I stood there, unable to step forward, dreading what I might see. It was like standing in front of the Gorgon's cave. Heath nudged me.

'Come on, she's a batty little old lady. She can't hurt you now.'

Don't you believe it.

The *batty* word earned him a frown from the nurse, but her eyes swivelled back to me, waiting. I shuffled forward, eyes down, and then caught a glimpse of myself in the dressing table mirror. Pathetic. I looked about twelve years old again, waiting for a hiding from Dad. Straightening up with a snap, I focused on the woman in the bed.

Small, wrinkled, fumbling for her glasses, wispy grey hair sticking out from the sides of her head. Her dowager's hump made her look like a dwarf, and the lacy, apricot nightgown added a weird splash of colour to the caricature.

This was my mother?

She didn't even glance at me; her beady stare latched on to Heath and she licked her lips. 'George, I knew you'd come and visit. Couldn't stay away, could you?'

Heath mouthed 'Husband?' at me and I shook my head. I had no idea who George was.

Mum scooted over and slipped out of bed, and the nurse was too slow to stop her, grabbing futilely at her nightie. Before Heath could move out of range, Mum was right up next to him, holding his hand and caressing it, laying her head on his chest. 'We were meant to be together. I've been waiting for you.'

The nurse took her by the shoulders. 'Come back to bed, Evie. This isn't George, it's...' She didn't know Heath's name so she said, 'It's your daughter's husband, dear.'

'Who? What daughter?'

This was more like it. Dotty or not, Mum always knew how to put the knife in. The nurse helped her to sit up and then tucked the covers tightly across her hips.

I wanted to say, 'Me, Mum, I'm your daughter.' But I wouldn't, couldn't. I didn't want to be the old bitch's daughter, especially not now. Even seeing her like this wasn't justice enough.

'Check out the photos.' Heath pointed to a row of frames on the windowsill. There was one of her and Dad's wedding, an old family studio photo of Andy and me where I looked like a nun in train-ing, and two photos side by side in one frame – Andy and Mia. Both taken in the last year by my estimate. Andy looked happy and fit, although still thin. I wanted to snatch the photo off Mum and keep it for myself. She didn't need it. I did.

Heath went over to the bed, standing far enough away that her grasping hand couldn't reach him. 'Mrs Westerholme –'

'Evie. Call me Evie.' Mum tried to purr sexily but it sounded hoarse and ridiculous.

'Evie. Is that your son in the photo?'

Mum stared at the picture of Andy like she'd never seen it before. 'I don't know. Is it?'

'Of course it is,' the nurse said brightly. 'You remember. He comes to visit you sometimes.'

'How often?' I said.

Mum leaned forward, her hand snaking out and she rubbed Heath's leg. He leapt back as if he'd been burned. 'Are you feeling shy?' Mum said, and winked.

I'd never seen anyone go that shade of puce before, and I hoped Heath didn't suffer from high blood pressure. I was horrified myself, but hysterical giggling wasn't too far below the surface. I glanced at Andy's and Mia's photos to steady myself. *I'm doing this for you.*

'Mum, do you know me?' I asked.

She looked at me carefully. 'I don't think so, dear. Who are you?'

'I'm your daughter, Judi.'

She clamped her lips shut and shook her head a couple of times. 'I had a daughter once. I think she's dead now.'

My heart gave an enormous thump and I stiffened, taking an involuntary step back. *Let me out of here.* But I had no choice – I had to forget the daughter thing and focus on Andy. *Focus.*

'When did Andy come to visit you? Was it recently?'

'Andy?'

'Andrew, your son.' The nurse picked up the photo and gave it to Mum. 'This Andrew. He came a couple of weeks ago, didn't he?'

'He might've, dear. I don't remember, do you?'

'Yes, I think so. After dinner one night. He was still here when I came on duty.'

I still couldn't believe Andy would have visited at all, but if the nurse said he was there, she had no reason to lie. 'Did he bring you anything? Any presents?'

Mum shook her head again.

'Give you anything to look after?'

'I look after all the family things, dear, like I said I would. No one else wants them.'

That nearly made me choke and I couldn't speak for a few minutes. Heath filled in for me.

'Did Andrew leave a box with you? His toolbox?'

'A box of chocolates?' She was really starting to lose it now and turned to the nurse. 'Is my show on yet? These people are stopping me from watching my show!' Her voice rose and her hands plucked at the covers. 'I want to go to the TV room. Make them go away.'

The nurse soothed her. 'It's your bedtime, Evie. You've already seen your favourite show. Would you like a cup of tea?'

'And a biscuit?'

'I think we can manage that.'

Mum turned away from us, staring out of the dark window as if wishing we would disappear. I wanted to grab her scrawny neck and strangle the answers out of her. When Heath took my arm, I jumped. We followed the nurse into the corridor and waited while she locked the door.

'It's an important question,' Heath said. 'We do need to know if her son left anything here at all, even something small.'

'I doubt it,' she said. 'There's so little room here, no storage. It's one of the things they find so hard, having to give up most of their furniture and possessions.'

'Can I go back and look in her room?' he asked.

'There's no point. I do the tidy-up every night, before they go to bed. I'm sure I would have noticed anything new, especially a tool-box. I mean, why would he leave that here?'

'It might not be the box itself,' I said. 'It could be a package or something small.'

'No, nothing like that,' she said. 'I would've noticed. The only new thing for ages has been the photos Andrew brought.'

'Right, thanks anyway.'

We trudged out to the car, Heath deep in thought and me floundering around in my memories. The woman I'd just seen was an echo of my mother. I saw bits and pieces of Mum, fragments that fanned the old hatred like wind on a smouldering bushfire, but the way she was now was... pitiful. And undignified. I grinned, remembering Hotshot's face when she rubbed his leg. The trip had been worth it for that.

'Another dead end,' Heath said in the car.

'I've got no options left now if I can't find Leigh. She's the most likely person to have the box, but God knows where she is. And if, by some chance, Andy left it with one of his Asian mates, I wouldn't know where to start looking.'

'If we're trying every possibility, no matter how tenuous, there are a couple more possible leads.'

'Like what?'

He pulled at his collar. 'Like your ex-husband.'

'Jesus, isn't my crackpot mother enough torture for one night?' My hand strayed to the door; maybe I could walk home.

'I ran a check on Max Heywood this morning.'

'My luck has changed and he's dead.'

'Not yet,' he said, laughing. 'But the connections are interesting.'

'Don't tell me, he's become a church minister and runs a homeless shelter.'

'The opposite actually. Heywood's noted as an associate of Graeme Nash, and before you ask, Gnasher is not a typical gangland boss. He's got his own set-up, a nasty bunch of boys who are into armed robbery and drugs.'

All around us, old people were turning off their lights and TVs and going to bed. 'What about that is *not* gangland stuff? You mean none of his crew got knocked off in the wars?'

'Two or three got done along the way, don't worry.'

'Part of that "eliminating the competition" thing.'

He shook his head, his jaw working. 'Heywood has been seen having meetings with Gnasher, probably doing small favours and deals, not enough to arrest him on. He's one of those we watch and wait on.'

'So Max has moved from running a pub with me to dealing coke to gangland crims. Nice.'

He started the car and turned out of the parking area, heading back towards the bright lights. 'I've got an address for Max. He should be there now.'

'Please tell me you're not serious.'

'He's a lead I can't ignore. He might know Castella and Sands, where they hang out. He might've seen your brother in the weeks before he died.' He glanced at me. 'I won't let him harass you.'

'You've got it the wrong way around – you might have to stop me thumping him.'

We drove in silence to South Carlton, parking in Queensberry Street; Heath made me sit while he watched the street and checked out the foot traffic. On the other side of the street, a small neon sign that said *Maxie's* glowed red and green above an ornate steel door that was opened back against the brick wall.

'Quiet night,' Heath said, and gestured for me to get out. We crossed the street and I scanned the building in front of me.

'Fancy door.'

'Stainless steel. You see a lot of them in Hong Kong. Ornate but almost impossible to get through when locked.'

'Is this a restaurant or a prison?'

'Restaurant, I believe. Licensed, of course. He's a co-owner with the chef, a woman called Lacey Green.' He glanced up and down the street again before ushering me down a short, gloomy corridor and pulling open a wooden door. It was heavy, varnished almost black with a wrought-iron handle, and a security camera blinked high up in the corner above it. My mouth twisted.

'Not very inviting, is it?'

'Business is good, all the same. Mind you, he's got a regular clientele of crooks and their mates. That's why the entrance here looks like the gateway into a fortress. Easy place to lock down if you have to.' He put his arm around me and gave me a small squeeze. 'Most respectable people who stumble in here only come once.'

Any other time I would've shaken his arm off, but the thought of facing Max, now I was there, was scaring me shitless. I tried not to think about it, and focused on Heath instead; I could smell a mix of sweat and his aftershave, and I breathed it in, sighing. *I wonder what he's like in bed.*

The thought was gone in a flash but it threw me off balance and I stumbled slightly.

'Are you OK? We don't really have to do this.'

'I'm fine.'

Heath tensed and I looked up. A thickset guy with one eyebrow and a scar across his chin had materialised in front of us, like a dark mirage in the murk, and I squinted. Surely this wasn't Max?

18

Heath stared down Mr Monobrow. 'Is the boss in?'

'Not to you.'

I steeled myself and stepped forward. 'How about to me?'

'You neither.' He sniggered. 'You're not wearing a short enough skirt.'

'Tell Maxie,' I said, clearly and slowly as if I was talking to a moron, which I probably was, 'that his ex-wife is here. And that he should talk to me, if he knows what's good for him.'

'No need,' Max said, coming through another black door I'd barely noticed in the dimness. 'How are you doing, Judi?' His smile was oily but I could see wariness in his eyes. He didn't like seeing me any more than I did him, and it gave me some small satisfaction. Maybe I could unsettle him even more.

'I'm fine, Max.' I looked around the dark reception area with a suitable sneer on my face. 'Not up to three hats yet?'

'Nah, that reviewing crap isn't worth the hassle.' He turned and walked towards the black door, speaking over his shoulder, like he was pretending he wasn't bothered. 'Come and have a drink, and bring your cop friend if you like.'

I raised my eyebrows at Heath who nodded. We followed Max through the door into the restaurant area and I stared around, interested to see what it was like, how it compared with the pub we'd had. Dark red carpet – that'd be a pain to keep clean, for a start. Velvet chairs and booths – Max had always liked plush furniture, even if it did stick to your clothes. Tasteless paintings of Italian scenes on the wall and two young waitresses in tight black trousers and low-cut black T-shirts. Nice to know Max was sticking to his usual form. The place was almost empty of customers.

We sat at a round booth and one of the waitresses brought us two glasses of wine without waiting for us to order. Max smirked – it was one of his little control tricks with women, one I wasn't about to tolerate. I sipped my wine. 'A Yarra Valley Sauv Blanc – at least your wine list is decent.'

The smirk disappeared. 'What do you want?'

I was on a roll with the insults. 'I'm a restaurant reviewer for the *Age* these days. I thought we'd eat here and I could write a review.'

'Crap. He's a cop.' Max pointed at Heath.

'He's a reviewer too, for *Police Life*.'

Heath tried unsuccessfully to stifle a laugh.

'Stop with the bullshit,' Max snapped, but I had him rattled. His face tightened in a weird kind of way and I wondered if he'd had a facelift, or... 'Have you had Botox injections?' It popped out before I could stop myself.

'None of your fucking business.' He was drinking what looked like vodka and ice, and he swallowed a large gulp of it. 'What the fuck do you want? Tell me or get out.'

'Sorry, Max.' I wasn't sorry at all. I was enjoying getting the better of him for a change, and feeling like a black crow on my shoulder was about to take flight. I looked him in the eye. 'It's about Andy. My brother, remember?'

'Yeah, I heard about that. I'm sorry.'

'The detective here thinks you might know something about it. Why Andy was murdered, I mean.' Was the twitch in his eyelid caused by me, or was he feeling guilty about something?

'Me? Andy was killed by the Asians, wasn't he? Nothing to do with me.'

Heath stepped in. 'It's not the murder I want to know about. It's Andy's drug connections, going back a few years. Who he was dealing for, that kind of thing.'

'What's that got to do with now?' Max looked mystified, but I wasn't fooled. Drugs were always connected to other drugs.

'More than you think,' Heath said. 'You're an associate of people in the know. I thought you might want to help out.'

'Andy had a wife and kid,' I said. 'His murder didn't end anything. I want to know what was going on, what you got him into.'

'Nothing! Jesus, you want to blame me for everything.' Max got up from his seat, making out he was going to walk away from me. I'd follow him if I had to.

'You knew Andy when he was a junkie, and I'm bloody sure you supplied him somewhere along the way. You like being Mr Clean but I know damn well you're not. Who was Andy hanging around with back then? It wasn't Asians – they're more recent friends – so it must've been your mafia mates.'

Heath was poking me in the ribs but I ignored him, staring at Max like I wanted to throw him into a pot of boiling oil. His face had paled and when I said 'mafia mates', the twitch turned into a jerk along his jaw.

'Hey, don't you connect me with those gangland guys. I don't want to end up in the morgue.' He lowered his voice and bent over to me. 'I stay out of that crap. I don't need you mouthing off.'

'So tell me who Andy was hanging around with. Titch Santos?'

'That crazy bastard?' Max's eyes wobbled in their sockets. 'Christ, you wanna stay out of his way. Look, you're talking more than six years ago. Your brother was a cunning little shit back then who liked to fuck around with the big boys, but half the time he was so high they wouldn't give him the time of day.'

I wasn't going to let him off the hook. 'What about the rest of the time?'

'All right, so he dealt a bit to keep himself supplied. Got into some trouble, and then it all went away. He probably got a beating for being a smartarse, and sucked it up. That's what you have to – had to do. It's old history.'

'So Andy didn't come to you recently to buy again?'

'No! I don't deal. Lacey would have my balls for breakfast if I did.' He glanced over his shoulder, probably checking his co-owner wasn't spying on him.

'Do you know two thugs called Castella and Sands?' Heath asked.

'No, never heard of them.' For a change, he almost sounded like he was being honest. He sniffed loudly. 'Now I think it's time you fucked off.'

'You mean we're not invited for dinner?'

'Not unless you want arsenic in your salad dressing.' He strode off, shouting at a waitress on the way, and disappeared through a swing door into the kitchen.

Out on the footpath, I felt ten kilos lighter. 'That went well.'

'It doesn't help us to find Mia,' Heath said.

My satisfaction at facing Max and rattling him faded in a blink.

'I think we can rule him out for having the box,' Heath said, 'but he knows more about Andy than he's letting on. I got the feeling he could've been talking about Nash.'

'But is it relevant?'

'I'll get someone to lean on him harder about Castella and Sands. That's our priority.' Heath sighed. 'It's late. I should get you home.'

We walked up Lygon Street to the car and headed back to Ascot Vale. We were both silent and I glanced across at him. He looked haggard, bags under his eyes and in need of a shave.

'Are you going home now?'

'No, I'll go back to the office. Mia's abduction is too important. I'll sleep later.'

'Nobody waiting up for you then.' It came out as snide but I hadn't meant it to.

He snorted. 'No. Women tend to get very impatient with me rushing off in the middle of dinner because I've been called in on a murder.'

'You must meet lots of women in your line of work, though – cops, nurses, lawyers.'

'Oh yes, I love going out with lawyers – not.' We waited at the traffic lights, his fingers tapping on the steering wheel as he stared at two young women weaving across the pedestrian crossing. 'Any woman with brains knows to steer clear of a detective. We've got signs printed on our foreheads that say *Avoid this man*. We're never around, when we are we drink too much and won't talk about our work, and we're often not very nice to our nearest and dearest.'

'So you're doomed to a lonely life.'

'Pretty much.' he said. The light turned green. 'Have I managed to put you off?'

'Off what?'

'Nothing. Forget it.' His eyes glinted and I wasn't sure what was going on in his head. 'Right now, we need to get Mia back and solve your brother's murder.'

Just hearing her name shocked me back to the reality of the situation. My hands were sweaty and I wiped them on my jeans. After a few seconds of heavy silence, I said, 'You're handling the murder. I'm getting desperate about Mia.'

'You think they'll hurt her.'

'God, parents kill their *own* kids when they won't stop crying. Look at Kayla – she couldn't wait to get rid of Mia. What do you think those two lunatics might do to her?'

'Calm down,' he said. 'I know you're worried but...'

'They've got my mobile number. I want them to call. I don't want them to call. I just... I can't find the box, you can't find Mia – it's like one of those bad TV shows with the clock ticking, and it makes me want to scream. Why can't you do something?'

The silence this time was leaden. I was already regretting shouting at Heath, but my heart was still hammering, and I couldn't figure out how to apologise. He drove, stony-faced, and flicked his indicator on for my street hard enough I thought it might snap off the steering column.

As we pulled up in front of my house, I said quietly, 'I apologise for shouting at you. I'm just... panicking, I guess.'

'It's OK,' he said tiredly. 'You've got good reason.' He shifted in his seat and looked at his watch. 'I thought I'd come to the funeral tomorrow.'

'Why?' I'd forgotten about that; it almost seemed ludicrous in the circumstances.

'We find it useful to see who turns up at these things. Obviously some of your brother's Asian friends might, but as to the others... the underworld are big on funerals, paying respects. You never know who might come out of the woodwork.'

'The funeral's going to take up half of my day. I'm not going to have much time to look for that box.' I scrabbled in my bag for my list and couldn't find it, but I already knew I'd crossed off all the possibilities. 'Not that I have any options left.'

'Whoever turns up tomorrow, especially his mates, are worth asking. Grab them and ask on the quiet – one of them might just have the box stashed in their garage.' He looked at me. 'I'll stay out of the way, don't worry. I don't want to put anyone off talking to you.'

Something occurred to me. 'What about the guy you've got in custody? Did you ask him about the box?'

'Yep. He said he didn't know where it was, although he knew what I was talking about. He said Andy kept the toolbox in his car, with tools in it. The last time he'd seen it was a few months ago.'

'Did he... did he say why he killed Andy?'

'Only what I told you before. His lame story about Andy acting weird and trying to stab him.'

'Was the box stolen out of the boot then? After Andy was killed?'

'Maybe, but by who? Tran didn't take it, and who else would've been around, or knew where the car was?' He got out and came around to open my door and help me out, still talking. 'If it's got something that important in it, I doubt Andy would've left it in the car, for just that reason – too easily stolen.'

'Back to square one then.'

'Yeah. Tran did say Andy was paranoid about it. Kept it locked with a special combination chain thing – one of those ones you need a cutting torch to get through.'

'Yes, that chain drove Dad nuts.' I opened my front gate and stood just inside, wondering if Heath was coming in or going home. I wanted him to come in, and told myself it was so he could check the house was safe.

'Think of the funeral as a great way to find some new leads on the box.' His face abruptly flushed dark red. 'Sorry, that was tactless. It's your brother. I'm a hard bastard, I know. Should learn when to keep my mouth shut.'

'It's fine. I'm not looking forward to it at all. Talking to people about that box will help me get through it with some sense of purpose, instead of having to be polite for two hours.'

'Let me check the house for you before you go in, eh?' He took the keys from me and opened the front door. 'Wait there.' In a couple of minutes, he'd been through and given me the thumbs up. 'The answering machine's not blinking, by the way.'

Disappointment sheared through me, followed immediately by relief. I couldn't bear another stream of threats that I had no way of answering. 'Oh.'

'I reckon they'll know we paid Castella's house a visit tonight. They'll keep their heads down, regroup, call you tomorrow.'

I nodded. It was after eleven. Hopefully Mia was quietly, peacefully asleep somewhere safe. Hopefully. 'See you tomorrow then.'

'Stay on full alert, all right? Don't go out again, and do ring me straight away if you get another call from Castella or Sands. Don't go haring off on your own.'

'No, sir.'

'I'm not kidding,' he said sternly. 'Keep your ears and eyes open at the funeral, and I'll watch your back. Make sure everyone signs the condolences book too – that might come in handy. Are you good at remembering names?'

'Not bad. But if they sign the book, I won't have to.'

'It all helps, especially if someone makes you suspicious. I'll be there for the service, but I might not hang around after, in case my presence makes them nervous.'

I was determined to ignore how much I wanted to ask him to stay for a drink or another coffee. That was plain stupid. *Have I put you off yet?*

'Fine,' I said briskly. 'Good night then. And thanks.'

'Keep in touch.' His car roared away, its tail lights like bright red accusing eyes. I was about to slam the front door, for no reason other than to let off steam, when I remembered Mrs Jones and latched it quietly, making sure all the locks were turned.

I paced the house, wanting to kick myself. What the hell was the matter with me? It wasn't just the sick worry in my guts about Mia, it was Heath and – now I was being honest – the flash of heat I'd felt in the car when he looked at me. God, I was behaving like some love-starved romantic, for no good reason. Time I pulled myself together and ignored that crap. Seeing Max again had dispelled a dark shadow, but it should also have reminded me why I was permanently off men. *You learned your lesson. Don't make me tell you again.*

I shuddered. That was Dad's voice, killing any tingles of desire stone dead. And just as well.

After a night of tossing and turning, I'd convinced myself by morning that I was back on track. The funeral loomed and I had a job to do.

19

I'd thrown my only decent black pants suit into my overnight bag, but I couldn't bear to wear the black silk shirt I'd brought to go with it. All I'd need was a white tie and I'd look like something out of *The Sopranos*. Before my shower, I peeled the dressing off the back of my head and found a mirror that showed me I had a bizarre short patch of hair and a row of stitches underneath.

I was at the doors of Highpoint Shopping Centre at one minute to nine, and into Target at ten seconds after. I bought a tailored white shirt with narrow red pinstripes and a black cloche-style hat that covered my bald spot nicely. Now I felt more ready to face the unknown.

Parking under the same tree at the funeral parlour, I muttered, 'Crap away, birds, you couldn't make things any worse.'

The blonde woman was there ready to show me everything from the sandwiches to the coffin. 'Do you want to see him?' she asked. 'We can open the casket.'

I shook my head. I'd seen him at the morgue and that was enough. He still wouldn't look like the Andy I knew.

'He's in the chapel if you want to sit with him for a while.'

Since I was early and I liked that idea, I went in and looked at the coffin; it had a small arrangement of white roses and lilies on top of it but when I checked, they were standard funeral home flowers. No secret cards or messages there. I sat on the cushioned pew. The soothing ambience of the chapel surprised me – maybe I'd been expecting something functional or dismal – and it felt good to sit there for a while with Andy and remember some of our life together.

Even though he was younger, there was a period from when I was about ten to thirteen where we played together all the time, and he was great at inventing games. Some of them were acting games, but we didn't just put on a play, we were Hollywood actors in a film, with servants to run after us and film directors begging us to be their stars.

We lived near the beach and Mum never cared if we went off on our own, especially in the summer holidays when she couldn't face trying to entertain us for weeks on end. We could both swim well, so we were unlikely to drown, and we knew all about the Beaumont children and how to avoid strangers.

I smiled, thinking of Andy's skinny little body and his determination to conquer the art of bodysurfing, getting tipped and rolled by the small waves time after time until he finally got the hang of it. Once we caught the train to Portsea in search of bigger waves, and he bodysurfed them as well, leaping out of the water, arms held high in victory. He never thought of giving up.

His favourite game was 'Private Detectives' – by the time that one started, I was at high school and starting to think I was too *mature* to play with my little brother. But he sucked me into it all the same.

He'd put clues around the house and garden, elaborate clues he'd spend days making up and hiding, then he'd play Watson to my Holmes. I was supposed to put my superior brain to the puzzle and solve the mystery, but often I n eeded p rodding, o r h elp w ith his clues. He'd get annoyed with me and say, 'I thought you were the brainy one,' in a sarcastic voice.

Was that what he'd done this time? Left m e c lues s o I could find out what trouble he'd got into and solve it for him? This time the clues were way too obscure for me. I'd only managed to get his daughter taken. But what if he *had* wanted me to find the toolbox and what was in it, and I was missing something obvious? I jumped up and stood next to the coffin; the surface was so shiny I could see my face in it.

'Listen, little brother,' I said, tapping on the top. 'You know I was never very good at that game. And you're not here to help me out. What on earth were you playing at?'

Something that got too big for him. Something that went way beyond his control and planning. Something that killed him.

My knees buckled and I had to lean on the coffin – he must've known it was likely he'd die. Why else would he set it all up? Had he really left clues for me that no one else would understand or was I concocting that out of a few receipts? Yet what I kept coming back to was the toolbox – I was forced to, because of Mia. But that didn't explain Tran's part in it all.

My last meeting with Andy was still engraved on my brain, his pleading face, his shaking hands. The guilt was like a huge rock, crushing me.

'Jude, please, I'll never ask you for anything again. Ever.'

'You're still using. I can see it in your face, never mind anything else.' His nose had been red and raw, and it'd reminded me of Max, which just made me angrier. 'And who's the girl? Another junkie?' She sat hunched in the passenger seat, hair lank and greasy and her face gaunt.

'I don't want the money for drugs, trust me. I have to pay some-one what I owe them then Leigh and I are both going into rehab. But if I don't pay this guy...'

'I suppose he's a dealer.' I thought I was doing the right thing, being really hard on him, but the truth was, I didn't want to listen or help.

'Yeah, but I've never had this problem before. He's threatened me, and... if I can just get out from under him, I'll be right. I know I can kick this now. It's the right time.'

'Andy, I'm not giving you money to pay off a dealer. I can't. And I won't.'

'All right. Sorry I asked.' That was the point at which Leigh had burst out of the car and started yelling abuse at me. He tried to shush her but she was almost incoherent, staggering, and eventually he half-carried her back to her side and shoved her in.

He climbed back into his beat-up old Nissan and drove away with Leigh shaking a fist at me, and I never saw him alive again.

Now he was asking for something again, and I owed it to him. Last time, I'd bailed out, and I had a horrible feeling that the guy he'd owed was somehow connected to what was happening now.

And if I was honest, the main reason I'd said no back then was because of the drugs. I linked Andy's drug addiction to Max and his coke, and I believed that the coke was the reason Max had wrecked the pub and the life we had together. Now I knew it wasn't that at all. Max was a prick, plain and simple, and I'd been too stupid to realise it, always looking for another reason to explain my big mistake. Because of that, I'd shut out my only brother. I closed my eyes, but Andy's face loomed up, clearer than ever.

Andy had entrusted me with his child, and that meant following the clues and solving his 'problem' for him after he could no longer do it himself. The two were inextricably entwined and it was up to me to unravel it, impossible though it may seem.

Look at what you've caused. Stop avoiding it. I opened my eyes, straightened my shoulders. 'Listen, brother.' I polished the silver plate etched with his name, then laid my hand where I thought his heart would be. 'You're gone now, but your daughter is still alive, and I'll do everything I can to get her back. You'd better have made some of those clues a bit easier than you used to, or I'll be out in the back garden again, on my hands and knees under Mum's rose bushes.'

'Excuse me, Ms Westerholme, the first people have arrived.' The blonde woman had crept up behind me, but I guess it was her job to be quiet.

'Thanks. I'll be right there.'

I took a deep breath and followed her out to the foyer where Mr J from the car yard and his black-haired receptionist stood, looking like waiters at a party. I greeted them and asked them to sign the condolence book, then moved on to greet other people, all strangers, who arrived in dribs and drabs. I had to introduce myself over and over, but most people seemed to know Andy had had a sister, and were happy to sign the book. As Heath predicted, a dozen or more Asians turned up, and I discovered they were all Vietnamese, like Tran. Most of them were older, quiet and reserved in their condolences.

One man said, 'He was a good man, trustworthy. I wish I knew how this terrible thing happened.'

The tightness in my face loosened a little. 'So do I,' I said.

The next time I turned around to greet someone else, Heath was standing in a corner next to a painting of pink begonias, trying to be invisible. It didn't work. A group of four young Vietnamese men spotted him and whispered to each other, but they didn't leave. I'd already greeted them and one of them told me he'd bought his first car from Andy. I ignored Heath and kept chatting quietly with people, including Mrs Jones who gave me a hug that I almost welcomed.

Then the door opened and three men entered, all in dark suits and dark shirts and ties. It was as if the real undertakers had arrived. They sent out a vibe that made everyone edge away from them without realising they were doing it, creating a circle of space. I forced myself to approach the three, wiping my hands on my pants, glad I'd taken off the bandage and replaced it with a plain plaster. That and the hat made me feel less vulnerable.

'Thank you for coming,' I said, hand extended to the middle guy. 'I'm Judi Westerholme, Andrew's sister.'

He shook my hand, his palm dry and warm. His face was square, like a block of wood with features carved out of it, but his eyes were sharp and intelligent. 'I was sorry to hear about Andrew. My condolences.'

'Did you know him long?' I asked. 'Quite a few years.'
'I don't know much about his recent friends,' I said, 'but I do appreciate those who have come along today. Or were you a business colleague?'

He smiled briefly. 'A bit of both.'

'I didn't catch your name.'

'I didn't give it.' He stared at me impassively then nodded slightly. 'Graeme Nash.'

Jesus. This was Gnasher. I fought the urge to look over at Heath, and managed a smile. 'Would you like to sign the condolence book, Mr Nash? And please do stay for refreshments afterwards.'

I glanced at his two henchmen, who stood like nightclub bouncers with their hands folded in front of them, and they looked back at me without blinking. Creepy. One of them had a hairless skull that I reckoned he polished with Mr Sheen; the other's curly red hair looked out of place with his suit. I spotted the blonde woman over Gnasher's shoulder, heading my way, and I guessed it was time to start. Sitting in that front pew was going to be harder than I thought. I wanted to sit up the back so I could watch everyone.

Instead I was going to be the sole occupant in the stalls, but there was no way I'd be the stage show as well. I could shed my tears later.

20

The blonde woman murmured in my ear, 'Are you ready to start? Would you like to go in first?'

No, I'd rather run off to the bush, screaming like a banshee. But I said, 'Of course, thank you,' and led the procession into the chapel. No one joined me in the front row, so I sat quietly, listening to the music I'd chosen – Annie Lennox singing 'A Whiter Shade of Pale'. The back of my neck prickled; everyone was probably watching me. I wondered if Gnasher was going to stay for a cup of tea. And where Heath had chosen to sit. Probably in the very back row, so he could do my watching for me.

No doubt Gnasher and his boys would recognise Heath as a cop, but probably they were used to seeing police at funerals. If Heath left straight after, like he said he was going to, I'd be alone with Gnasher. I could cope, but I needed to come up with some scintillating conversation.

The celebrant, an elderly man with woolly white hair, sat beside me for a moment, showing me the order of the service then he stood up at the podium. When the music died away, he started with the usual welcome to family and friends. Should I have brought Mum along? God, no. She'd have no idea whose funeral it was, or if she did twig, she might be disruptive. Or make a pass at the celebrant. I suppressed a smile and focused on his words.

He did a great job, considering he didn't know Andy at all. I must've given the blonde woman more information than I thought, enough for the celebrant to plant it amongst the standard prayers and ritual sentences. He asked if anyone wanted to say a few words, looking directly at me first, but I shook my head. I wasn't surprised when nobody else volunteered either.

As he finished speaking, another song began – I'd chosen the Divinyls, one of Andy's favourite bands, remembering he'd always had a thing for Chrissy Amphlett. It had been a close decision but I'd gone with 'Good Die Young', even though he'd really loved 'Pleasure and Pain', because the lyrics seemed more suitable. The celebrant didn't seem bothered by my choice. No doubt he'd heard worse, like the Collingwood football club song.

I watched the coffin disappear behind a revolving door apparatus, on its way to cremation, and listened to the song, tears sliding down my face. We'd had some happy times when we were kids, just the two of us, and some bloody awful times. I cried for our lost future, for the chance I'd never have to make it up to him, for the fact we'd never grow old together. Then I wiped my face and stood, ready for the next installment of 'who's got the toolbox'.

Handing around a plate of sandwiches, I approached the Vietnamese people first, because I was a chicken and they'd be the easiest to talk to. The older man I'd spoken to earlier said again how much they liked Andy. 'He came to my daughter's wedding in January,' he said. 'His little girl is very beautiful.'

'She is,' I said. 'She looks just like Andy did at that age.' I bit my lip. *Mia*.

'She is not here... with her mother?'

I wasn't sure what he was getting at. 'They're away, interstate. It's a difficult time.'

'Ah.' He didn't look like he thought that was a good enough reason not to attend your husband's funeral, and he was right. But Leigh probably hadn't seen the funeral notice in the newspaper.

I asked the million dollar question. 'Did Andy ever leave anything with you? A metal box of some kind?'

They glanced at each other but all I could discern was puzzlement. 'No, sorry.'

'Is there anyone else you know that he might've trusted with something?' I knew I was sounding vague but I didn't know how else to ask, and I didn't want to say the word toolbox in case someone else was listening. Like Gnasher.

'No, I'm sorry, only... Tran, but...' He held his hands up helplessly, and I saw deep embarrassment in his face. His wife hissed something in Vietnamese and his mouth tightened; it was time I moved along and left them alone.

'Thank you anyway.' Next in line was Mr J, still trying to sell me a car, and it took me a few moments to extricate myself. Another group of strangers was next, two men and a woman, who turned out to be friends of Leigh's and worked in the pub with her.

One guy with snake tattoos on his arms winding out from under his T-shirt sleeves said, 'We couldn't believe it when we heard. We're really sorry.'

'Who told you?' I asked.

'Leigh did.' The young woman's nose stud went well with her bleached-blonde hair and black roots. 'She came into work and said he'd been killed. It was awful. She looked like shit.'

'Bloody slopes,' the second man muttered, his glance sliding over to the Vietnamese and back again. He was dressed in Blundstone boots and jeans, and looked like he'd come straight from a building site. Maybe he had. Not many people could afford to take a whole day off for a funeral.

I gritted my teeth and ignored the racial slur, and asked about Leigh. 'Have you seen her since then?'

They shuffled their feet. 'No,' the woman said. 'The cops asked me the same things. She actually borrowed some money off me, said she couldn't get into their bank account. The police had frozen it or some such crap. I was hoping she'd pay me back soon. She not here?'

'No, sorry, we don't know where she is. I was hoping you might know.'

'Ooh, no,' the woman wailed. 'She's not dead too, is she?'

'Shut up, Lou,' the tattooed man said. 'She'll be fine.'

How did he know that? 'Do you know where she's gone?' I asked him.

'Nah, not really. She used to talk a lot about going bush, ya know?' He sniffed. 'Not serious, like, more that thing of wanting to get out of the city.'

'She did say...' The Blundstone guy trailed off.

'Yes?' I tried to keep a patient look on my face.

'She said once that she had a mate with a shack up near Maryborough, but she mighta been bullshitting. She was good at stringing you along.'

'Right. Thanks.' I hesitated. 'She didn't leave anything with you to look after for her?'

They shook their heads together, like clowns in the sideshow game, and I said thanks anyway and moved on. Time to steel myself and talk to Gnasher. But when I turned around, the room was nearly empty and Gnasher and his boys had left. A girl in black skirt and top was clearing away all the dirty cups and plates, and the last guests were heading out the door. It was over.

I sagged, my shoulders slumping, and put the plate down quickly. I hadn't realised how much the tension had been holding me upright.

I thanked the blonde woman for everything, wrote out a cheque to cover the invoice she'd given me discreetly in a thick white envelope, and headed for the Benz. Out in the sunshine, birds cheeped in the trees and I could hear kids playing nearby, shouting and laugh-ing. A jumbo jet flew high overhead, its engines a distant howl. All around me was normal and peaceful. Apart from some bloody shrill phone ringing somewhere close by.

I finally realised it was my new mobile phone and scrabbled to get it out of my bag, in a panic that it would be Spaz and Baldie. 'Hello.'

It was Heath. 'Did you talk to Gnasher again?' No hello, how are you.

'No, he left.'

'Pity.'

'He wasn't the talkative type, from what I could see.'

'OK. Are you going home, I mean to your brother's house?'

'I suppose so.'

'Good. I'll pick you up there in ten minutes. I want you to come and talk to Tran.'

'Tran? Why?' The breeze had chilled and I shivered.

'He's stopped talking to me. I want you to ask him again about the box.'

I sensed he wasn't being completely straight with me. 'And what else?'

'I'll tell you when I see you.' Click. No goodbye either.

I knew he was focused on doing his job, but he made me angry with his 'do this, go here' orders. What was he doing to find Mia? Here we were, running all over Melbourne after that bloody toolbox, and they couldn't find a child who must be screaming loud enough to make someone notice.

The Benz's tyres squealed as I wheeled out of the parking area; I made it back to Ascot Vale before him, racing into the house to check the answering machine. Nothing. I dialled the number with my mobile and it rang, so the phone was definitely working. I needed Castella and Sands to call me, to let me know Mia was OK, but the threats that would be part of the call made me sick with fear.

I'd left the front door open and barely heard Heath's knock, jumping when he loomed behind me. 'Are you all right?' he asked.

'Fine.' I wasn't – I'd just cremated my brother, and I still couldn't find his kid. 'Have you got any leads on Mia?' He shook his head. They were getting nowhere. Great. 'Let's go.'

In the car, I asked, 'What's this about? Why do I have to talk to him?'

He glanced at me, hesitating. 'Look, this is a bit tricky. I had to get special permission for you to visit, and even though Tran said yes, he's still requested his solicitor. We'll need to play this carefully.'

'Does Tran know that Mia's been kidnapped?'

'No. I'm not sure you should tell him.'

'Why not? He was Andy's friend.'

'Who killed him.' He sucked in a long breath. 'No, who *confessed* to killing him.'

'You still don't think he did it. Why not?'

We stopped at the lights on Arden Street and he tapped the steering wheel as he ticked off the points, his voice clipped. 'One, he denied it when we arrested him. Wouldn't say why he was there with Andy. Clammed up. Two, when his solicitor turned up the next morning and got in his ear, he turned around and confessed. Told that story about Andy being on drugs and acting like he wanted to stab Tran. Autopsy showed no drugs in Andy's system.'

'He might've been very upset or scared.'

'Three, there was no knife at the scene, no gun either, and Tran can't tell us what he did with the gun.'

'If he was confessing, wouldn't he know where he threw the gun?'

'Exactly my point.'

'But he's saying he did it.'

'Insisting he did it. The evidence doesn't back him up.'

I huffed out a breath. 'So who did do it?'

We parked in Jeffcott Street, right near the plain red brick Assessment Prison. If Heath hadn't told me, I would've thought it was an office block.

'No idea.' He leaned forward, searching for the parking meter. 'But I think he might open up to you a bit more. And you can question him about the toolbox.'

I craned my neck to look up at the centre through the leafy tree we were parked under. The first stop on your road to hell, especially if you were innocent and nobody believed you. Or, like Tran, you had confessed for some reason.

I hadn't had another call from Baldie and it was making my nerve endings fizz. If Tran had anything to tell me, I'd do whatever it took to prise it out of him. I had no other options right now.

A surly male guard signed me in and checked ID, barely glancing either at me or Heath. I went through a scanner and then a female guard ran a metal detector over me.

'You'll have to leave your bag here,' she said.

I handed it over reluctantly, wanting to ask them to answer my phone if it rang.

Heath deposited me in an interview room and went to find out where Tran was. The room was overheated, the chairs felt sticky and covered in old sweat, and it smelled strangely of burnt toast. I sat, trying not to touch anything. Eventually Heath returned, followed by two Asian men; the younger one was obviously Tran, glancing nervously at me before his eyes went back to his feet. The older man wore a light grey three-piece suit and the shiniest shoes I'd ever seen.

'We were waiting for Mr Nguyen to arrive,' Heath said. He shut the door and joined me on our side of the workhorse table. Tran and Mr Nguyen sat close together on their side.

'What is the purpose of this conversation?' asked Mr Nguyen, sounding like a school principal. 'Are we being recorded? If not, why not?'

I jumped in first, before Heath could get all officious. 'Andy was my brother. I was hoping Mr Tran could tell me what happened. I'd like to hear his version.'

'There is only one version,' Mr Nguyen said. 'The correct one, which Mr Tran has told many times already.'

'I hadn't seen my brother for a long time. I know Mr Tran was a good friend. I was hoping he could tell me what my brother was like, what he has been doing for the last few years.'

'He is pleading guilty to the murder of your brother,' Mr Nguyen said. 'How can this help?'

I was going to be lucky to get one word out of Tran at this rate. I leaned forward and focused on Tran, stretching my mouth into the most sympathetic smile I could manage. 'Mr Tran, did you know my brother well? Did you know his family, his little girl?'

Tran's eyes angled towards his solicitor, then back down at his hands. 'Yes, I know them.'

'Did you know Andy when he was still an addict?'

'Yes. He used to come to my father's restaurant. Very cheap food, very good. He was sick back then, and we tried to help him. Then he went into the rehab place.'

Mr Nguyen's mouth was a thin line, but he hadn't shut Tran up yet.

'So he was fine after that?' Tran nodded. 'Did he go into rehab because Leigh was pregnant?'

'No, that was later. He said he had had a "wake-up call".'

'Did he explain what he meant?'

A head shake. I laced my fingers together, kept them in my lap.

'Did he buy drugs from people you knew?'

'No, never. Always from the ones he called "the boys". For the first time, Tran looked directly at me, his eyes swimming. 'He said they weren't happy when he stopped.'

'What did he mean?'

Tran shrugged. 'I think someone threatened him, but Andy said he had a plan, and it all worked out. After that it was OK.'

So even back then, Andy had started to put things in place, work out how to stay safe and start again. That sounded like him. He'd been good at thinking ahead, much better than me. I kept the smile plastered on my face.

'Did you ever see him with an old steel toolbox in his car?'

'Yes. I have told the police about this already.' I studied his face and he seemed genuinely puzzled.

'I really need to find it,' I said. 'Do you have any idea where it could be? Who might be looking after it for him?'

'No. Isn't it in his car?'

'No.'

'Does Leigh have it?'

'She's missing.'

'She's dead too?' He turned to his solicitor and whispered frantically in his ear. Droplets of sweat rolled down the side of his face and neck, soaking his collar. Mr Nguyen said, 'Is she dead or not?'

Heath spoke up. 'She's alive, as far as we know. We think she's hiding.'

The relief in Tran's face was like a light switching on. On my side of the table, I suddenly felt the world teetering on the edge of an abyss. Tran assumed Mia was with Leigh. I laced my fingers tighter to stop them shaking. I was going to tell him the truth.

'She left Mia behind,' I said. 'And now Mia has been kidnapped.'

Tran stared at me, the whites of his eyes filled with tiny red blood stars. He whispered two short words in Mr Nguyen's ear; the solicitor said, 'He thinks you are lying.'

'I wish I was. I need to find that toolbox. What's in it?' I leaned forward, as close as I could get to Tran across the table, wanting to shake him. 'Do you know? Did Andy ever say one single thing to you about his plan? About what was in the box? Please, you have to help me.'

Tran hesitated, rubbing his hands over his face and then on his pants legs. 'He – your brother was in danger. I know that.'

Mr Nguyen said something in his own language, short and sharp. Tran shook his head, his chin jutting. 'Andy refused to let any of us help. He said he had the upper hand, that he had what they wanted but they weren't getting it. It would keep his family all safe.'

I heard a faint snort from Heath and ignored it. 'Did he say it was drugs or money? Why did he want to buy drugs from you? He'd stopped using. You said so.'

Mr Nguyen grabbed Tran's arm, but it didn't stop him. 'It wasn't anything like that. I don't know. I wish I did.'

'Who was threatening him then? Did he mention any names?'

'No. He used to talk about underworld people, say they were stupid.'

Mr Nguyen jumped to his feet and grabbed Tran's arm again, this time dragging him out of his seat. 'No more questions!' he shouted. 'No more!'

I jumped up too, following them to the door. 'Are you sure Andy didn't leave the toolbox with someone in your family?'

Tran looked at me over his shoulder, his eyes wild. 'No! Nobody. Not us.'

I couldn't stand the thought of staying in that hot, smelly room for one more minute. 'Let's go. Now.'

On the way out, I snatched my bag out of the guard's hands and kept walking so fast that my hip twanged and sent a jab of pain into my lower back. I didn't stop until I reached the footpath. 'He didn't do it,' I said. 'No way.'

'He's confessed,' Heath said.

'Bullshit. You know it's bullshit.' I rubbed both temples and squeezed them to relieve the pressure before my brain exploded. 'But still no box. Fuck!'

We got into the car but he didn't start the engine, just sat staring straight ahead. His phone pinged to say there was a message but he ignored it. 'You need to do a bit more thinking,' he said.

'Me? This all happened when I was up the bush. What do I need to think about?'

'How your brother might've set this all up. Tran said Andy thought he had the upper hand. Why would he say that?'

I sighed. 'Andy was a planner, and he liked to think he could out-manoeuvre people.'

'He stuffed up this time then.'

I ferreted in my bag for a tissue and blew my nose. Bloody Melbourne pollution made me sneeze. 'I reckon Tran was set up somehow. Maybe somebody paid him to get Andy there and he's feeling guilty. Or tricked him.'

'Either way, he's confessed so he's stuck in there for the foreseeable future.' He paused. 'The boss is hassling me to work on my other cases.'

'What about getting Mia back? What's more important than a little kid being kidnapped?' My voice filled the car and banged around my head.

'I've got two murders, for a start,' he barked. 'I'm Homicide, in case you've forgotten. There's a whole team working on the abduction.'

'What about going to the media? Isn't that supposed to get everyone looking for her?'

'We know who's got her. The team thinks the media will make things worse right now.'

'You won't be making bloody excuses if they kill her.'

'Jesus!' He bowed his head for a few seconds and then said quietly, 'You're angry, I'm sorry. Let me check something.' He used his mobile for a short, cryptic conversation with someone, while I waited and fumed, and then tapped the screen. 'Nothing yet. Or should

I say, a fair bit of useless info that went nowhere. Look, I'll drop you home and then call you later. I'm going into the office and I'll keep on it, don't worry.'

'Yeah, righto.' He was abandoning us. A hollow opened up inside me, and I folded my arms, suddenly cold. It probably wasn't his fault, but... I sat in silence all the way back to Ascot Vale, words and images spinning around in my brain. Something had to happen, surely. Spaz must ring, or the cops must find them. I imagined my rifle in my hands, me out on the streets, hunting them down, but that was a stupid fantasy. I had no more idea where to find them than the cops did.

As we stopped outside Andy's house, Heath said, 'The phone-tapping equipment is on the way. Castella and Sands are supposed to ring today or tonight. What are you going to say?'

'What can I say? I haven't got the box, and I don't know where it is. Full stop. I could lie, say it's in Swan Hill and it'll take me a couple of days to fetch it.'

'No, they'll know you're lying.' He tugged at his collar and undid another button. 'You'll have to stall them somehow. Give it a bit of thought so you're ready.'

Oh, for Christ's sake. What did he think I'd been doing for the last two days? I got out of the car and slammed the door, but he pushed the button and the window slid down. 'Ring me as soon as you hear anything.'

I stared at him coldly. 'Yes, of course.'

He flushed and looked away, checked his watch. His phone rang; he answered briefly and hung up. 'Possible new lead on Sands. If we find him or Castella, we'll find Mia. We can do this, all right?'

All I could do was nod.

As he sped off, my legs went to water and I leaned against the fence. Time was spinning out of control, and the police had achieved nothing. I knew they were working hard, but the reality was they were no closer to Mia than I was.

Finally making it inside the house, I locked everything and double-checked it and gave myself a talking-to about letting the police do their job. It didn't help. I hadn't been able to eat at the funeral, and my stomach was rumbling so I made some lunch. A picture of Andy's shiny coffin rose up before me and I nearly choked on my tomato sandwich. Andy was gone, really gone now, and my body suddenly felt boneless, with the spaces left filling rapidly with pain so sharp and raw and hot that I cried out. It consumed me like a mon-ster, with its burning breath on my skin.

I pushed my plate aside and laid my head on my arms, sobbing and coughing. I couldn't seem to get the tears out fast enough, as if a dam was breaking slowly, letting water out but the wall hadn't completely collapsed yet. Was I so hard and heartless now that I couldn't even cry properly?

Slowly the crying jag stopped, and I wiped my face and blew my nose a couple of times. *That was a waste of energy, wasn't it?* I laughed a wobbly laugh. If only Andy could see me now. His tough sister, dribbling and carrying on. There wasn't time for this. I had to be ready for their call. I had to get my shit together.

I gave up very quickly on making up lies about the box and trying them out loud – they all sounded fake. The solution was the box. Time to go back to the beginning, back to the paperwork and see what else Andy had left me in the way of clues or hints. I pulled out every piece of paper from the files and the drawers above, this time reading everything and slotting the parts of his life together like a jigsaw. Two interesting items stood out – Andy had power of attorney for Mum, had taken over responsibility for her house, renting it out after she went into her unit at the retirement home and acting as the landlord. The rental money went straight into Mum's bank account to pay the home, so no funny business there.

The second thing was his level of preparation – not only the will, but also a trust account for Mia that so far had only a few thousand in it, documents neatly labelled for super and house insurance, and a life insurance policy for three hundred grand with Mia as the beneficiary. All this at thirty-nine. I didn't know anyone of that age who felt mortal enough to go to those lengths.

Nothing in Leigh's name at all. Not even a joint bank account. Either he didn't trust her or he didn't expect her to survive. Well, he'd made me Mia's guardian. That said a lot. Everything was dated at least three months ago, if not more. My bet was she knew nothing about all of this, but I couldn't ask either of them.

I put it all back neatly, and scoured the rest of the house again, even Mia's room, looking for paper, even down to scribbled notes. Nothing. And not a single hint about the box. Christ, what if they did ring tonight? Or in the next thirty seconds? What was I going to say?

The phone rang, shrilling through the room, and I nearly leapt out of my skin. It was them. I wasn't ready. I should've practised one of those lies a bit more. My heart pounded in my ears and I desperately wanted a big glass of wine. I picked up the phone.

'Hello?'

'Who's that?' A woman's voice, grating.

'It's Judi Westerholme. Who's this?'

'Judi, thank God, I was hoping you'd be there, that no one else...'

It was Leigh.

21

I gripped the phone tightly and asked Leigh the obvious question. 'Where the hell are you?'

'Away,' she said defensively.

'I know that. Where?'

'I can't tell you.'

I wanted to reach down the phone and strangle her. My old instinctive dislike of her bubbled up and I took a breath. 'Why did you run away and leave Mia?'

'She's all right with Kayla, isn't she?'

'No, she's not with Kayla. Kayla got sick of the whole situation. Mia's been with me.' Talk about dodging questions. Now I was doing it. And where was the phone tap when I needed it?

'Can I talk to her?'

'Not at the moment.'

'What do you mean?' Suspicion coloured her voice. 'Where is she?'

'I don't think that's your concern now.'

'For fuck's sake, stop playing games. I want to talk to her. What's going on?'

'Where's Andy's toolbox?'

'What? I dunno. In the car, I suppose.'

'Your car?'

'Yeah.'

I started to shake with relief and hope, and couldn't talk for a few moments.

'You still there?' she snapped. 'Where's Mia? Put her on the phone. Tell her it's Mummy.'

'Never mind Mia. I need that toolbox.'

'Why?'

'Because I think Andy was killed for what's in it.'

Her voice rose, panicky. 'Then they'll be after me, too.'

'Not if I get the box and sort it out.' I put some steel into my tone. 'You have to tell me where you are so I can come and get it. I promise I won't tell anyone.'

'They might follow you!' she screeched.

'They won't. Trust me, on a country road you can tell quite easily.'

'How did you know I was in the country?'

'I guessed.' I hadn't told Heath that bit, I realised. Maybe it was better that the phone-tapping person hadn't arrived yet. Finally I could do something tangible.

She sniffed. 'All right.' She gave me directions to a tiny place near Maryborough, a miner's cottage down a gravel road. Strangely enough, it wasn't that far from Candlebark as the crow flies.

'I'll be there in a couple of hours. Don't open the box.' I knew she would, but I couldn't stop myself saying it. I hung up and raced around, gathering car keys and bag and a warm jumper. My mobile phone rang. Don't say she'd opened the box and was going to have a screaming fit about whatever was in it?

I picked up the phone and jabbed at the button. 'What's the problem?'

'You're the one with the problem. Where's the box?'

It was Baldie. Of course. Leigh didn't have this number. I closed my eyes and tried to stay calm, to focus on his voice. 'I'm on my way to get it.'

'Good. Then you can come and give it to us.'

'It might take a while.' I didn't want to say I was going bush in case they followed me. Despite what I'd said to Leigh, I'd have no hope of getting rid of them.

'No, it won't. I want it now. Like in an hour. Or the kid will come to a very unhappy end.'

'I can't do it in an hour.'

'Really? Listen to this.' I heard rustling and thumping in the background, then Mia, crying softly at first then she burst into a loud scream, as if someone had hit her. Jesus, what were they doing to her?

My brain spun like a manic tumble drier. I had to stop Mia crying, I had to do what they wanted. I had to get her back. Now. How?

'All right, I'll get it. An hour. Where?' I was acting crazy. It was impossible. I had to try something, anything. I pressed the phone to my ear so hard that it burned.

'There's a park in Cranwell Street, in Braybrook. You know it?'

'I can read a map book.'

'Good. There's a parking area runs along the front. Not there. Go down Lacy Street to the end and wait by the gate. What kind of car are you driving?'

'An old blue Benz.'

'Number plate?'

I told him. 'Are you going to bring Mia?'

'Yeah, but I want the box first otherwise you don't get her.'

'Straight swap, at the same time,' I said.

'Fuck off. We're supposed to trust you?'

I sucked in a breath. 'I just want my niece back.'

'You'll bring the cops.'

'The cops are bloody useless. I'm doing this on my own. I don't give a shit about the box or the drugs in it.'

Something in my voice must've convinced him. He laughed, and said, 'OK, swap it is then. One hour.'

He hung up and I sagged against the wall. What had I done? I didn't have the box. I should ring Heath and get the cops to grab them, but I couldn't bring myself to do it. I knew Spaz; I knew he would kill Mia in a heartbeat, just because I'd lied. Like he'd stabbed my hand without even thinking twice about it.

Baldie had laughed when I said drugs, so that's probably not what was in the box, but I couldn't have cared less. I had to find a way out of the huge mess I'd created, and I had to do it in a hurry. No box. But I knew what it looked like. I'd have to find another one, and a combination lock. Just like the one he used to have, that drove Dad nuts. I'd lock the box up with it, and by the time they got it open, I'd be gone.

It was the stupidest plan I'd ever come up with. Nothing like Andy's elaborate schemes, but it was all I had. And I had to move fast. I found a hammer and some cheap-looking tools in Andy's shed, threw them in the Benz and sped to the big warehouse-style hardware joint down the road. There was an old red toolbox in the Benz's boot, but I had a feeling these two bozos knew what Andy's box looked like so it wasn't worth the risk. I jammed the brakes on in the parking lot, jumped out and headed inside. A woman in an apron directed me to the back, behind the garden stuff, and there were the boxes, all shapes and sizes.

Too many. How big had Andy's been? I couldn't remember exactly, but it had fitted under his bed. Plain steel, not dimpled or painted. I grabbed one that looked about right, and hefted it in my hands. Yes, this was as close as I'd get. In the security section, they sold combination locks and chains that couldn't be cut with bolt cutters (so the label said) so I grabbed the plainest one and paid at the checkout.

Out in the parking lot, in the deepening dusk, I put the box on the ground, and proceeded to belt the crap out of it with the hammer. Anything to make it look less than new. There was some oil in the boot of the Benz, so I smeared some of that over it too, and gave it a few more bashes, ignoring a man who was staring suspiciously at me.

Finally, I threw in the old tools wrapped in a raggy towel for some ballast, snapped the catches closed and wrapped the chain around and through the handle, clicking the lock and spinning the dials. Done. Box in the boot and I was on my way to the park, checking my watch and the map book as I drove. As I turned off Ballarat Road, I wondered why it looked so familiar, then realised this was where VicRoads used to be, years ago. Everything was either covered in graffiti or tightly locked up with steel roller doors and barred windows.

The park was bordered by three streets, but the end of Lacy Street ran down the hill to the river. It wasn't very well treed and the dried shrubs around the parking area looked ghostly in my headlights. No one else was there. I parked and waited, goosebumps prickling my arms. I was being stupid beyond belief, just by being here. For a moment, I was strongly tempted to ring Heath, but I could imagine the shouting from his end of the phone and I couldn't bear it. I kept hearing Mia screaming and, like an echo, Andy crying and begging as Dad gave him a thrashing. Tears burned in my eyes. How could those shitty memories still be so clear? Hadn't I pushed them way down, out of range? I was tougher than that. I'd proved it, and I'd prove it again.

I debated getting out of the car. No, let them come to me. The place was deserted, just one dull street light, behind me was a huge warehouse all locked up, and the nearest houselights looked a kilometre or more away across the gully. A pair of headlights arced over the rise and came down the street towards me.

Show time.

I forced myself to stay in the Benz, my window half-down, while they parked about ten metres from me, on the wide warehouse forecourt. They kept their headlights on full so I was half-blinded. Only one man got out, but despite the glare it was clearly Baldie with his squat frame and jutting chin. If Spaz was in the car with Mia, I hoped he'd stay there. I didn't want to cope with two of them at once, and I absolutely didn't want to look into Spaz's dead eyes again. I gripped the steering wheel with both hands. *You can do this.*

Baldie walked over and stopped a few metres from the Benz. 'Where's the box?'

'In the boot.'

'Get the fucken thing out then. I haven't got all night.' He kept glancing around as if he was expecting me to have backup or several cops hiding behind the fence. If only.

No, it was better this way. If it worked the way I planned. Baldie assumed I was the dumb sister, who'd already been beaten up and scared shitless by them once, so I'd keep him thinking like that. I opened the boot and lifted the box out pretending to grunt with the effort then put it on the ground where he could see it.

'Take the chain and lock off,' he said.

I put a whine in my voice. 'I can't. Andy had the combination and he never told anyone what it was. You'll have to sort that out for yourself.'

'You got bolt cutters in your boot?'

'No. Where's Mia?' My words wobbled, but that probably made me sound weak, whereas I was steeling myself for the next move.

He jerked his head back. 'In the car. Asleep.' He hesitated.

He knows! I tried to breathe normally and look both pissed off and scared. 'Come on, give me the kid. Take the damn box.'

'How do I know it's the right one?'

'It's the only one he had, for Christ's sake. He's had it since we were kids.'

'Where was it?'

I had to think fast. For sure they would've searched Andy's house and probably his workplace somehow. Use the truth and twist it. 'In a storage place. He left me a receipt. Took me a while to get them to open it.' Was I talking too much now?

'What else was there?'

What was this – twenty questions? Use a bit more of the truth then. 'Just a video camera and some stuff to go with it. Why?'

'No reason.' He turned and walked back to his car, a black 4WD, opened the rear door and pulled out a small, limp body. Mia looked dead, lying in his arms like a sack of potatoes.

Panic flooded through my veins. 'What have you done to her?' I cried. 'Is she dead?'

'Shut your face, you stupid bitch. She's asleep, I told you.'

'No, she's not. There's something wrong with her.'

'For fuck's sake, we put some rum in her milk, that's all. Had to shut her up somehow.' He thrust her at me and I seized the little body, holding her close, feeling that she was still warm and breathing. Relief rushed through me, followed by an overwhelming urge to run. *Don't run. Get in the car. Now.*

I didn't wait to see him pick up the box. I opened the rear door of the Benz, laid Mia gently on the seat, then jumped in the front and started the engine. As I backed the car on to the street and put it in gear, I saw Baldie shove the box into the back of his 4WD and someone pull it further in. I couldn't see if it was Spaz or not, and I didn't care.

I had to get the hell out of there. But I couldn't take Mia home.

22

I floored the accelerator on the Benz and the engine roared, the car fishtailing slightly as I rounded the corner and sped towards Ballarat Road. Hopefully there wouldn't be too much traffic and I could get across and disappear down another side street. It would take them a while to get the box open, but I didn't want Baldie to take it into his head to follow me, just in case. I had no experience at losing a tail, but I did know how to drive like a maniac and I figured that would do in the meantime.

The way out of Melbourne was the Western Ring Road, or straight down Ballarat Road and keep going, but first I wound through as many back streets as I could, circling around Sunshine and somehow into Ardeer. I was completely lost by then, surprised when I came out on Ballarat Road again over the other side of Ardeer, but sure no one was following me. I checked the highway, waited, checked again before I turned towards Ballarat – it'd be monumental bad luck for them to be going the same way as me but I wasn't going to chance it.

At Caroline Springs, I pulled into a service station with a shop, filled up with petrol and went inside to pay, gathering up cartons of flavoured milk and yoghurt, baby food, muesli bars and chocolate, plus two big bottles of water. I wanted to give Mia something decent to eat when she woke up, in case she had a hangover from the rum. Bastards!

Back at the car, I checked her over carefully, using my glove-box torch. She was still fast asleep, but her colour was good and she stirred when I shone the light on her eyelids. I figured that was a good sign, too. I should have put her in the car seat but it was too difficult with my hip aching badly now, so I left her on the back seat, tucked a blanket around her and the lap seat belt. There would be no more driving like a lunatic.

On the road again, I checked my mirrors every few seconds and pulled over again near Rockbank, waiting and watching for anyone suspicious, especially a black 4WD, but there was nothing. In front of me, the road to Ballarat stretched into the darkness, and the map book told me I had to turn off later on the road to Creswick. I settled into a steady ninety kilometres an hour and relaxed a little.

I'd done it! A grin spread across my face and I knew I must look like a Cheshire cat. Andy would've been proud of me! Me – a rescuer of small children. How weird was that? I turned on the radio and sang along to a bunch of crappy songs, tapping my fingers on the wheel. I couldn't stop grinning for a while, then a rap song came on and I decided I'd had enough of the radio, but there was nothing else to listen to.

Except the mix tape of songs Andy had made for me. I still had it in my bag. No doubt they'd all be golden oldies, the kind that everyone trundles out at over-40s parties these days, but they'd be better than nothing. It'd be fun to hear what he'd picked for me. I scrabbled in my bag and found the cassette, thinking how he'd naturally assumed I'd be a techno-dinosaur with nothing like a CD or MP3 setup. I slid the tape into the player and waited.

First song – 'I Will Survive' – was the Gloria Gaynor version. Cool. I sang along with that, it finished and the next one started as I slowed for the off-ramp, heading now for Creswick and Maryborough. Little River Band, 'Help Is On Its Way'. Strange choice. Neither of us had been an LRB fan.

Suddenly the music cut out, there was a few seconds of silence, and just as I reached for the Eject button, thinking the tape had jammed, Andy's voice resonated from the speakers, freezing my hand in mid-air. The car swerved and I clutched at the steering wheel, slowing, correcting, looking for a place to stop. I jabbed at the Stop button – I needed to hear all of this, and not while I was driving.

Around the corner was a small primary school and church, with a parking area at the front. I pulled in and stopped, turned the engine off and then the key on again so the player would work. I pressed Rewind for a couple of seconds, then Play, my fingers shaking, my throat as dry as cardboard.

Ah, big sis, I knew you'd find this sooner or later. Hope it's not too much later. So I have no idea whether it's been a month since I taped this, or ten years. Whatever.

I'm sitting here hoping and praying that all the planning I've done works. If something happens to Mia because of me, well, that would break my heart. But if you're listening to this, there's a bloody good chance I'm dead, so...

I don't know where you're at right now, so I'm going to give you the bare bones. It might help, it might not. In your hands now, sis.

I have something that quite a few people want to get their hands on. It's a video. I filmed it secretly because I knew that sooner or later the guys involved would try to shaft me, and I needed leverage. The way it's turned out, it could spark another gangland war. You've probably read about all these gangland guys killing each other off. Tit for tat. Been going on for years, and has settled down now. But what I've got could start it all again, maybe worse.

To cut a long story short, I was a dickhead. You know me, I've always thought I was one step ahead, but the drugs knew better. I let myself get sucked into the hard stuff, and it's a long way back. I owed a guy a lot of money and I couldn't pay it. So he said if I went and pulled off this big deal for him, he'd let me off what I owed.

I shook my head, guts churning. That was the money he'd asked for. Why the hell hadn't I given it to him?

I went along, thinking it was sweet, one job and I'd be out from under. Only the deal wasn't a deal, it was a setup for a hit. Why did I video it? Dunno. I just had a gut feeling that something wasn't right, that maybe I was in line for a beating, or a one-way trip out the back of

Werribee. I think maybe I thought if I taped it, I'd have something over this guy and he'd never come back to me for the money. Yeah, I guess I never really believed him from the start.

We arranged it for a carpark hidden behind a pub, early morning before the cleaners turned up, and I went down and set up the camera the night before, after the pub closed. I bought one that had a remote but I was shitting myself that it might not work.

So I turned up for the deal with a backup guy, who I thought was there to make sure I didn't take off with the money. I had a look in the bag and I reckon there was more than a couple of hundred thousand dollars in there. I was supposed to pay this other guy and come back with a pile of coke. I said I needed a piss, so I went behind the dumpster and turned on the camera with the remote.

So the other guy turns up with his backup mate, and it's Titch Santos's brother, Nicky, who I knew a little bit. We're joking around and I get my guy to bring the money out of our car, and instead he brings this gun and shoots both of them. Bam, bam. I nearly shit myself for real then. My guy just grins, grabs the coke and pushes me into the car and drives off. Leaves them there on the concrete.

'Oh God, Andy.' The tape whirred and for a moment I thought it was jamming but it kept playing.

At first I was in shock, you know, and I screamed at this guy, 'Let me out!', and he tells me to stop being a fucking girl but I keep shouting at him, so in the end he lets me out. I just stood on the side of the road for a while, then thank God my brain started working and I hailed a cab. I went back to the pub, not too close so the cabbie wouldn't get suspicious, and I sneaked back to the carpark.

I managed to get the camera and make a run for it, before the cops arrived. Five more minutes and it would've been too late. I went home and just sat in the lounge room like a zombie for most of the day, waiting for someone to either come and arrest me or kill me. But nothing happened. The guy who organised it, he rang me that night, said 'Good job' like I'd fixed his toilet or something, and said we were square. And he said I'd better keep my mouth shut because if Titch ever found out it was me, I'd be mincemeat in someone's sausage machine.

I'd already had a scare – Leigh OD'd and nearly died. But this really was my wake-up call. I told her we were both going into rehab and that was it. No more junkie life, we were going to try and live a normal life with jobs and stuff. She didn't believe me at first, but in the end I told her it was me or the drugs. Make a choice.

Funny thing was, after the hit went down, fifty grand turned up. My guy paid me off, said it was worth it to get the coke and keep the money, too. I wasn't going to say no. Nana's house had just come up for sale and it seemed like an omen to me. Buy the house, maybe turn back the clock. I got a crap job selling cars, Leigh was working in a café, and then she got pregnant. What could be better?

Mia is just the angel in my life, sis. The most amazing thing that's ever happened to me. She's so beautiful...

I roughly brushed away the tears on my face. Too late to cry now.

But Leigh's had trouble staying clean. I guess I haven't helped. I hit the grog quite a bit, then I lay off it for a while, but Leigh – I've caught her a couple of times doing lines, and even though she says it's just the once, that's the road to hell again. I've tried to set things up for Mia so if the worst happens, if Leigh sinks into it again, and I think she might if I'm not there... Mia will have you. I know you, sis, I know you won't let me down.

And yet I had. Many times.

Leigh's not strong, not like you and me. She... I told her about the video, when I was drunk one night. That was my big mistake. She doesn't know where it is, but she knows what's on it. And she blabbed to her cousin, who's a dangerous arsehole and should've been one of the ones taken care of before.

Well, it's all gone to shit now, hasn't it? My sins coming back to haunt me. It's true, isn't it? You can never get away from this shit. I wish

I was tough, like you. I wish all those years with the old bastard made me into a warrior, not a wimp, but I can't change that. All I can do is leave you this and the other bits of information and trust you to work it out. I can't leave it all clear and simple, where the video is, I mean, because if Leigh knew, I think she'd... I'm pretty sure she'd try and sell it, and it'd get her and Mia killed, for sure. I think the best thing now is to destroy it.

I'm not lying about any of this, sis. Trust me, I wish I was. Give Mia a big cuddle and kiss for me. Make sure she knows I was a good guy, some of the time at least. Can you do that for me?

The tape went silent for a few long moments, then the Little River Band blared out again and I ejected the tape, looking down at it like it was a snake about to bite me. Tears spilled down my face and soaked the front of my shirt. I shivered violently and reached for my jumper. Every bone in my body ached as if I'd been thrown to the ground and beaten and kicked.

He'd sounded so lonely and sad, as if he'd tried everything he could to look after Mia and knew at the end that he'd failed. How bloody senseless and futile. Here I was, just a few days later, in the same predicament, and pleading ignorant had done nothing to help me. At least I knew now what was in the box, what I was looking for, and what it was worth.

I vowed right then that if anyone tried to take Mia away from me again, I'd kill them. Then I remembered where I was going – to see Leigh, who would undoubtedly want Mia back, and I didn't trust Leigh as far as I could kick her.

I needed to do some thinking before I drove any further. To persuade Leigh to let Mia stay with me meant I had to find something to pressure her with. I certainly couldn't tell her that Mia had been kidnapped. Although maybe Leigh in hiding was a better alternative right now than me with Baldie and Spaz looking for me. And they would be.

Andy said Leigh knew about the video. Shit, and I'd more or less told her that it was in the toolbox in her car! But surely it would have the combination lock on it, and I thought I could guess the numbers I'd need to open it. I checked Mia, who was still fast asleep, started the car and continued on, the Benz steadily chewing up the kilometres while thoughts of Andy and the guy murdered in front of him rolled around in my head. Maryborough at ten o'clock at night was nearly dead, but I kept to the speed limit all the same. Just my luck for a cop to be hiding around a corner somewhere.

I had to get the box off Leigh and take it back to Melbourne. If she fought me over it, I'd have to get vicious. I could do that. If I gave the tape to Heath, would that keep Mia safe? Andy had said lots of people were after the tape. I had to hope Leigh's cousin hadn't opened his own big mouth and spread the word.

Surely not. Andy hadn't seemed to be panicking enough to have a multitude of gangsters after him. My gut told me it was just Baldie and Spaz. Andy hadn't said the shooter was Castella, so maybe I could destroy the tape. No, they wouldn't believe me, like they'd never believed I didn't know where it was.

My brain was starting to blow a fuse. Maybe I should wait and see what condition Leigh was in, what she had to say for herself. I wanted to know whether she knew what Andy was up to, what he'd planned. And how Tran was involved. Something about Andy's murder still didn't add up. And I wanted to know who her cousin was, although I already had my suspicions.

Twenty minutes later, I found the small side road, mostly by accident. A large kangaroo, hit earlier in the evening, was still half on the highway, and I'd slowed as soon as I saw it, driving around its shattered body. The sign for Pitt Road glowed in my headlights and I turned down the rutted gravel track, bouncing along between a rickety fence and some dead ghost gums. After a couple of twists and turns, the miner's cottage appeared ahead of me, surrounded by feathery peppercorn trees. One light was on in the front room but, when I parked behind an old Corolla that I guessed was Leigh's, no one came out to check who I was.

She should be taking precautions and hiding around the back of the house until I showed myself. That'd be the sensible thing to do. That's what I'd do. Somehow I doubted Leigh would even think of it. Maybe she was asleep. I shrugged, and turned off the engine and headlights. In the deep, dark silence that engulfed me, all I could hear was my own heartbeat in my ears and the engine clicking as it cooled.

Mia still hadn't stirred, and I checked she was breathing OK before I got out of the car and did a few stretches to ease my aching bones. Still no sign of life. I closed the car door quietly and crept towards the house, coming in sideways and edging along the wall until I could see in the window, feeling like a very pathetic spy. The ragged net curtains had a couple of large holes in them and I could see into the small room; it held a TV on a side table, a low table and two worn tapestry couches. The carpet was threadbare but the walls looked like someone had given them a coat of pale blue paint not long ago.

On one of the couches, Leigh lay, head back, mouth half-open, fast asleep. The TV was still on, the volume low. I walked around the house, glad of a nearly full moon that lit my way, and checked what else was there. A decrepit shed full of old windows and fencing wire and timber, and a wood shed. The back door was locked, so I went around to the front and knocked.

After a few moments, she opened it without asking who was there, rubbing her eyes and yawning. 'Oh, you're here.' The blonde dye job had grown out and a couple of centimetres of greasy dark brown hair showed underneath. Two red pimples flared on her chin in contrast to her pasty face.

'You're not exactly on high alert here, are you?' I said.

'I knew it would be you.'

'Are you sure? It could've been your cousin.' I was still standing on the doorstep, sizing her up.

She humped her shoulders. 'Why would he be here?'

'Depends what you've been telling him.'

'Dunno what you mean.'

I opened my mouth to tell her about Andy's video and shut it again. She didn't need to know I knew. She just needed to give me the box. 'I've got your daughter in the car. Don't you want to see her?'

'Sure, bring her in.' She fell back on the couch and used the remote to turn up the volume.

The hackles rose on my neck and I wanted to shake her. I went back to the car and gathered Mia off the back seat into my arms. She stirred, whimpering, batting at my chest but her eyes barely opened, as if she couldn't quite wake up enough. I carried her inside. 'Where shall I put her?' I asked.

'There's a little bedroom next to the kitchen,' she said, waving in that direction. Finally, she got off the couch and came over to me, peering down at Mia. 'Fast asleep. She always was a heavy sleeper.'

I wasn't in the mood to tell her the truth.

I put Mia into a small bed with a lumpy mattress and musty blankets, tucking her in and eyeing the other bed with a grimace. That was going to do my hip no good at all, but now the adrenaline of the escape had totally worn off, I felt about a hundred years old and ready for any kind of sleep. Leigh lounged in the doorway.

'Can you get Mia's stuff from the car, please?' I said. 'I need to go to the loo.'

'It's in there,' she said, pointing at another small room next door before ambling out to the Benz. I scooted into the main bedroom and had a quick look through the drawers and cupboards, rushing and knowing I could miss something important with only the light from the lounge room to help me, but wanting to satisfy my suspicions. In the top drawer next to the bed, I found it – a syringe and a packet of white powder.

Leigh was using again.

23

I raced down to the bathroom, did a quick wee and washed my face and hands in the chilly water, and returned to the lounge room. Leigh was sprawled on the couch with Mia's teddy under one hand. My bag and the plastic bag from the convenience store were on the floor by the door. 'This is all there was,' she said. 'Where's Mia's clothes and nappies?'

'Um...' I hadn't thought about that. I'd been so intent on getting a fake box and tricking Baldie into handing Mia over that ordinary stuff like clothes had never occurred to me. 'I was in a hurry. I forgot them.'

She rolled her eyes and I itched to slap her. My earlier feelings hadn't changed – I really didn't want to leave Mia here, but I had no choice. In the morning, I was going to have to tackle Leigh about the drugs. But first things first. I sat on the other couch.

'Mia will be pretty grumpy when she wakes up,' I said.

'Why?'

'She's been given rum, to make her sleep, probably too much of it.'

She sat up, gripping the teddy bear tightly in one hand. 'What did you do that for? You could've made her really sick.'

'I didn't do it,' I snapped. 'The guys who kidnapped her did.'

'What?' Her screech hurt my ears. 'Which guys?'

'Your cousin, Castella, and his mate.' I was guessing but the look on her face confirmed it for me.

'Bullshit. They wouldn't take Mia.' She threw down the bear and crossed her arms, tucking her hands under her armpits like she was trying to physically hold herself together.

'They did. I only got her back tonight by tricking them. They'll be after me again, and maybe you.'

That made her smirk. 'They wouldn't hurt me.'

'No? So why are you hiding up here then? Having a nice country holiday?'

'Nah, I'm not,' she said. 'Bloody boring here. I'm going nuts. Andy told me I had to come here and stay out of sight for a few weeks.'

She was lying, I was sure. 'I doubt he said anything of the kind. What did he really tell you? And don't lie, because he left me some information about this whole situation.'

'He said Mia and me had to be ready to get out of Melbourne, maybe permanently. He was gonna tell me when it was OK to come back.' Tears filled her eyes and they looked genuine. 'Then he got killed and I panicked. Kayla said she'd look after Mia for a couple of days, and I came here.'

'A couple of days? You've been gone for over a week. Kayla duck-shoved Mia on to me.'

'And you got her kidnapped? Nice going,' she sneered.

'I don't think you've got anything to feel superior about,' I said. 'Where's Andy's toolbox?'

'In the boot of my car. There's nothin' in it. I looked already.'

Her words hit me like a hammer. 'How did you get the combination lock open?'

'There wasn't one. Go and look if you don't believe me.' She turned away and hiked up the volume on the TV. I stood and went outside, going straight to the boot of her car. It was locked but I found her keys in the ignition and opened it, glad the interior light was still working. Straight away, I saw it was the wrong toolbox. This one was small and had one hasp. I opened it anyway, not surprised to see a few spanners and a shifter and nothing else, but I felt like a huge deep pit had opened up under my feet.

Baldie and Spaz wanted the video, and they'd want payback now as well. I'd made fools out of them. Spaz's flat stony gaze haunted me. I leaned my head against the boot lid. How the hell was I going to get out of this? To bluff and win, you had to hold a secret hand. I'd shown my cards already and I had nothing left and no money either. Well, that wasn't strictly true – I could probably scrape up enough to pay them off if I had to. I could sell Andy's house, if all else failed. Four hundred thousand should make anybody back off and leave me alone.

But I didn't want to give the bastards one single cent. Not one. I straightened and slammed the boot lid down. And I bloody wouldn't either. They could rot in hell before they got one more thing out of me. Except for the video. If I ever found the vile thing, they could have that in a flash.

I threw Leigh's keys back on the front seat and went inside. She was asleep again and I shook her awake, a bit more roughly than I needed to.

'Whaaat? Leave me alone.'

'Sit up, you stupid girl.' When she was upright, scowling like a five-year-old but paying attention, I said, 'That's not the right tool-box. I want Andy's old grey steel one, the one he'd had since he was a kid. Where is it?'

'I dunno. I haven't seen it for ages.' She stared at me suspiciously. 'Why do you want it? Why do you keep going on about toolboxes?'

'Andy said you told your cousin about the video he'd made.' Her face fell, and I went on, glad I had something on her that I could use. 'That's what started all the trouble, that's what got Andy killed.'

'Did not! You're bullshitting, trying to freak me out.' She huddled back in the corner of the couch.

'Your cousin and his mate are still after that video. They killed him to get it. You can't deny it.'

'It wasn't my fault. Andy thought he was too smart for them, but he wasn't. He shoulda given it to them when they offered him the money.'

'Maybe he should, but that doesn't alter the fact that if your cousin hadn't heard about the video from you, he would never have wanted it in the first place.'

'Oh, whatever. Jeez,' she said, shaking her head.

'What do they want it for?' I asked.

'Money. It's worth heaps. A quarter mill, maybe more.'

'Who on earth would pay that?'

She smiled slyly, and for the hundredth time I wondered what Andy had ever seen in her. 'They were gonna auction it. See who wanted it the most.'

'So you know what's on it then?' I asked, watching her closely.

'Nah, Andy never told me. But Spiros was gonna give me a cut.'

The blood rushed up my neck to my face in a wave. 'What? You'd better not be telling me you sold Andy out, or I'll fucking kill you myself.'

'I didn't!' She was like a disgusting white crab, scuttling further back into the couch. 'He was talking about the auction, after Andy sold it to them.'

'Andy had no intention of selling it.'

'Well, he should've, shouldn't he?'

I couldn't stand to listen to her crap any longer. 'I need to find the toolbox. I think the video is in it.' I tried my final bullet. 'You and Mia and I – none of us will be safe until I find it.'

'We're fine,' she said. 'Spiros won't hurt us.' It was like she'd turned off a tap. She stood up and turned the TV off. 'I'm going to bed.'

I sat alone, trying to control the rage surging inside me. I wanted to do the girl some kind of injury, but I knew it wouldn't help. And in the back of my mind, I had already decided to stay on speaking terms with her so I could keep an eye on Mia. I doubted Andy's will would stand up in court, and I wasn't going to test it out – not yet, anyway. Although I thought she was a useless piece of trash,

I couldn't believe she'd sold Andy out to Baldie and Spaz. She would've seemed guiltier for a start, and also they would have the video by now.

The fact that she didn't know where it was either had probably saved her life. It didn't help me at all. In the tiny kitchen, built out of second-hand cupboards and more scrappy carpet, I put my food and water in the bar fridge and made myself a sandwich and a coffee. It looked like Leigh had been living on bread and coffee – there was nothing in the fridge except milk and margarine. The bed in Mia's room was as awful as I suspected, the mattress an old kapok and horsehair type that was at least forty years old. It smelled of mildew and dust, and the pillow was a slab of foam rubber, but I slept for about six hours straight without any effort at all.

Mia woke me just after six, grizzling and grumpy. She sat up, bleary-eyed, crying big tears and pulling at her hair; she probably had a headache and a hangover, and I felt her misery. I waited a few moments for Leigh to come in to her, but when there was no movement from the other room, I struggled out of bed and picked Mia up.

'Yes, you're stuck with me again, kid.' I poured some chocolate milk into a chipped mug and helped her drink from it, with tears still dribbling down her face. In the bathroom, I was relieved to find hot water and a small hip bath behind the shower curtain. When I undressed Mia, I discovered a sopping nappy that had soaked through into her tracksuit pants. And I had nothing to replace it with. 'Leigh,' I called loudly, but there was no response. A trip to the nearest shop was definitely in order.

After her bath that seemed to make her feel better, I wrapped Mia's bottom half in a towel and sat her on a kitchen chair, then made a honey sandwich that she ate while I drank black coffee. 'Time for your mother to take over,' I said.

Leigh was still fast asleep, the doona humped over her, and the bedroom stunk of stale sweat and urine. Surely she couldn't have peed the bed? I nudged her but she didn't stir, so I pulled back the covers and leant down. 'Leigh! Wake up!'

Drool covered the side of her face, her skin was a dusky grey and her mouth looked blue. My guts crawled and I jerked back. She wasn't asleep, she was... dead. Shit. How long had she been like this? I felt for a pulse on her wrist, then her neck, not sure if I was doing it right. Nothing. But she was still warm. I checked on the other side of the bed and saw the strap and syringe on the floor. She'd OD'd. What the hell was I going to do now? CPR wouldn't help.

I ran into the lounge, searching for my phone in my bag. The battery was flat, probably had been for hours. There was no landline in the house either. I had to find her phone. It was in the bed with her, half under her arm. My brain zinged from one possible move to the next. I had to make a decision – fast.

Call the ambulance. Put her in the car, drive until I met them. Maybe, just maybe, it wasn't too late. I had to try. The nearest ambulance would be Maryborough. Come on, woman, move!

000.

'Police, fire or ambulance?'

'Ambulance.'

A calm voice on the other end listened to my garbled explanation and asked questions. 'Are you sure it's an overdose?'

'Not a hundred per cent, but it's pretty likely. There was a syringe. I'll get her in the car and meet you halfway to save time.'

The voice assured me that the ambulance was on its way, and confirmed I was driving a pale blue Benz. I hung up and got moving.

I dragged Leigh off the bed, struggling with her dead weight, pulling her arm over my shoulder and heaving her out of the house and across to the car. As I tried to get the rear door open, I almost lost my grip on her, falling sideways against the car and grunting at the pain in my hip. I pushed her half into the car, ran around the other side and pulled her the rest of the way. She didn't look comfortable but that was the least of her worries.

A cry from the house – Mia. Christ. I nearly forgot her. I raced back inside, picked her up, towel and all, and discovered she was wet. Another towel, my bag and phone, running, running. Mia in the front seat, the seat belt no use but I put it on anyway. She was crying again and I spotted a chocolate bar half-under the seat as I backed the car around. I ripped off the top half of the covering and shoved it into her hand.

Roaring down the potholed road, I had to hold Mia on the seat with one hand, wrestling the wheel with the other. Thank God for Mercedes suspensions. Out on the highway, I made sure the phone was handy and floored the accelerator. This early in the morning, no one else was on the road. Just as well.

Eight minutes later, I spotted the ambulance in the distance and, when it was closer, flashed my headlights at it and pulled off on the verge. I got out to wave them down just in case, but they saw me and stopped just past me. The two paramedics jumped out, one going to the back, the other coming straight to me.

'Where is she?'

'On the back seat.' I opened the door and he climbed in, hovering over Leigh, checking her eyes and looking for a pulse. Mia put her head over the seat, her face smeared in chocolate.

'Sit down, Mia,' I said, trying to keep my voice firm, not sharp.

'No pulse, not breathing,' the paramedic said. 'How long has she been like this?'

'I found her like that, in her bed.' I checked my watch. 'That was about twenty minutes ago.' It felt like about three hours.

Mia had decided something was wrong, and started shrieking, so I went around and lifted her out of the car, keeping the towel wrapped around her legs in the cool air. 'Hey, kiddo, it's OK, hey, there.' I held her close, away from Leigh, and hoped that kids her age didn't remember shit like this. She kept crying on and off but I suspected she was still feeling the after effects of the rum. Poor kid.

When I turned back, the paramedic had climbed out. 'I'm really sorry,' he said, shaking his head. 'She must've been dead when you found her. It's too late to help her now.'

'Oh God.' I had known that in the logical part of my brain, but now it started to sink in properly. My chin quivered and I had to bite my lip hard to stop myself losing it.

He eyed me sympathetically. 'Is she your sister?'

'Sister-in-law.' Even if they'd never married, I was sure Andy would want me to say that, to claim her somehow. 'She was an addict, quite a while ago. I thought she'd kicked it.'

He shrugged. 'Some of them never do. This was probably accidental. The heroin being sold at the moment is pretty good quality.'

Mia was quiet again, for which I was grateful right then. 'This is her daughter. I have no idea what to do now.'

'We'll put your sister-in-law in the ambulance and take her back to the hospital.' He looked apologetic. The other paramedic came up behind him and they murmured together, then he said. 'She'll have to go to the morgue. And we have to inform the police, unless you've already done that.'

I shook my head. 'No time. I suppose they'll want to ask me what happened.'

'Yes.' They brought the trolley and carefully lifted Leigh out of the Benz and onto the stretcher, then covered her with a sheet. Thankfully, Mia was more interested in the magpies warbling in the nearby gum trees.

'Do you want to follow us back?' the paramedic said.

'Yes, but – I need to find a shop and buy Mia some nappies and food. We left the house without anything.'

'The supermarket is just down the street from the hospital. I'll direct you when we get there, if you like.'

I thanked him and put Mia in the car, in the car seat this time. The thought that I'd have to leave it there permanently flashed through my mind but I let it go. It didn't seem too important at that moment. The ambulance turned around in a driveway and headed back to Maryborough, no lights or siren, and I shivered again. It was only a few days since I'd been in one of those myself, and I still had the on-off headache as a souvenir.

The drive into town was sedate, and I stayed in my car while they unloaded Leigh and took her inside. At the sight of her covered face, I closed my eyes, guilt like a lump in my stomach. Could I have saved her if I hadn't been so angry and unsympathetic? But I had no idea how many times she'd used the stuff before I got there. She could have died two or three days ago, and no one would have known where she was. Whoever owned the house would have found a decaying corpse, for God's sake. I let out a long, slow breath. No, surely this one at least wasn't on me.

When the paramedic came out, he told me how to get to the supermarket. 'They've rung the police, so if anyone turns up before you get back, I'll tell them to wait.' He raised his eyebrows, as if waiting for me to promise I'd return.

'Yes, right. I should only be ten minutes.'

And I was. At that hour the supermarket was quiet, and I quickly found toddler nappies, yoghurt, milk and snack foods like cheese sticks and pizza rolls, Mia perched in the front of the trolley. They even had kiddies' tracksuit pants. At the checkout, another young woman with a little boy struggled to keep him next to her as she paid for her groceries. As he tried to run off yet again, she grabbed him by the jumper and hauled him backwards, which made him scream at a volume usually assigned to aeroplane engines.

Mia watched him with great interest, and I avoided the woman's eyes. The checkout girl grinned at Mia. 'You're a nice, quiet girl today, aren't you?'

Mia pointed to a pile of small soft toys in a box next to the cash register. 'Foggie.'

'That's right,' said the girl. 'It's a tree frog.' She smiled at me. 'Environment group in town makes them to raise funds.'

I looked closer and saw frogs, snails, wombats and other assorted animals I couldn't identify. Definitely handmade. I picked up the frog and held it out to Mia.

'Foggie,' she said, and took it, holding it up and waving it.

'She knows that word,' said the girl. 'My little niece can only say Mum and Dad so far, and dog. Does your littlie talk much yet?'

I stared at Mia, thinking. 'No, not much.' I had no idea when kids started talking, but I'd heard others talk about toddlers who were real chatterboxes. Not this kid. It could well be that all the upset and change in her life was causing her to retreat. I knew that feeling.

I paid for the groceries and the frog and, on the way back to the car, spotted a takeaway shop open. After wrestling a disposable nappy onto Mia, I bought a hot, strong coffee and three steaming delicious potato cakes that I shared, breaking hers up and blowing on the pieces to cool before giving them to her. 'Yep, this is a food group, kid,' I said. 'I can guarantee it's a staple.'

With potato cake in one hand and frog in the other, she looked like she couldn't care less. I didn't either really at that point. I kept seeing Leigh huddled under the doona, and her eyes half-closed, mouth open. Andy knew she was back on it. That's why he couldn't trust her.

Still, if I'd said something to her, maybe... I shrugged it off. Right in front of me was the perfect reason not to go back to the old ways, stuffing potato cake into her mouth. I'd brought Mia up here and Leigh's response was to OD. I knew that underneath the addiction was usually a feeling, loving person, but it was impossible for me to see that right now. The destruction she'd caused overwhelmed me.

But at some point I would need to really try to see her just as Mia's mother, and nothing more. Poison could work both ways.

We arrived back at the hospital just as a police car pulled up and parked a few metres away. I climbed out and left Mia sitting with her food, hailing the two cops before they headed into the hospital. 'I think you're looking for me.'

The younger, curly-headed one smiled and came over straight away. The other guy, short and stocky with a buzz cut out of the Navy Seals, looked me up and down and sauntered over. He had it written all over him: I was just the druggie's mate. So I spoke to the younger one, giving him my name and Candlebark address, explaining that I'd been looking after Mia and had brought her up to her mum.

'So the deceased is your?'

'Sister-in-law. De facto, I guess. Mia is my niece.'

'Was your sister-in-law all right last night?'

'Yes. It's possible she'd used heroin before I arrived, but I didn't think so at the time. She must have taken it after I went to bed.'

'Didn't share it, then?' the stocky cop said with a smirk.

I stared at him for a few long moments but he didn't look away. 'I don't take drugs. She was an addict up to a few years ago. It obviously got the better of her again.'

The younger cop scribbled in his notebook. 'Did you see any heroin or other drugs around the house?'

'Yes, there was some with a syringe. That's what made me think she'd OD'd.' Would I be in trouble for not taking it off her?

'We'll have to go to the house and collect the gear, and carry out a search,' the stocky cop said. 'You'll have to come, too. Give us permission so we don't have to waste any time.'

'All right.' I could do my own search of the place in case the video was there and I'd missed it, but I'd have to wait until they'd finished. And I'd have to pack up Leigh's stuff and take it... where? I could

go back to Candlebark from here, avoid Melbourne altogether.
'Pardon?' The young cop was talking to me.

'Are you OK to go back? Now?' He smiled, ignoring the other
guy's scowl. Helping the public didn't seem to be on his agenda.

'Of course.'

'And... er... there'll have to be an autopsy,' the younger cop said.
'Who's her next of kin?'

Spaz? Surely not. 'Um... I'm not sure. Sorry, I didn't know her
that well. I hadn't seen much of my brother or her in the last few
years.'

'What about your brother?'

'He's dead.'

The stocky cop grunted. 'Recent, was it?'

'About a week ago. He was murdered.' I gave them Heath's name
as a contact.

They glanced at each other. 'Was she depressed?'

'It didn't seem like it, but as I said, I didn't know her. I don't
think it was suicide, if that's what you're getting at.'

'That'll be up to the coroner,' the stocky cop said. 'Not you.'

'Shall we go then?' The young cop snapped his notebook shut
and jangled his car keys.

Mia was standing on the back seat of the Benz, bouncing her frog
along the top, and it took me a few minutes to persuade her into the
car seat, but finally we were ready. We made an orderly procession
out of town, and I stayed well within the limit as I cruised back to the
cottage. It was a relief to have them come with me and take away the
drug gear. I didn't want to touch it. My mind went back to the question of where I'd go after this – Candlebark or Melbourne? My small
stone house at Candlebark beckoned temptingly, as did the rifle in
the cupboard, but I couldn't stand the thought of Baldie and Spaz
tracking me down there. It was my last remaining haven, far too precious to risk. I couldn't kid myself. I'd got Mia away from them, but

they wouldn't give up. The only way to end this was to either make a run for it interstate or find that bloody video.

I'd run once. Away from Max, Andy's drug problem, my vile mother, the disaster that the pub had turned into – it had worked for a while. Candlebark had been perfect for a practising recluse. But things had changed. I'd changed. I'd licked my wounds, but they'd only healed on the surface. Underneath, there was still plenty of raw flesh, suppurating nicely. I was getting sick of patching it over. And deeper still, I'd discovered there was still a core of steel that I thought I'd lost. I was pleased about that.

Anger had got me a long way in the past few years. It had protected me from feeling anything else. I'd kept my anger bubbling while I hid behind the wall I'd created to keep everyone out. Even Connor, if I was honest. The one person I could truly call a friend, but even he had no idea of my past, other than surface comments I'd made, mostly as jokes. I'd let Heath inside the walls more than Connor.

The realisation was a shock. But I didn't have to pretend with Heath. He knew the worst about me, had seen the worst of me, and it didn't matter to him. I huffed out a laugh. I was probably small fry compared to some he'd encountered. He was tough and experienced, but I still wasn't sure he could protect Mia and me. I needed to do that myself. I had to do it myself, to be sure.

One way or another, I would get Baldie and Spaz out of my life. Whatever it took.

Ahead was the sign for the side road; I put my blinker on, slowed and turned, taking it easy along the rutted track. I parked under the peppercorns, next to Leigh's car. I had no way of getting it back to Melbourne so it would have to stay here for now.

Inside the house, the smell of death seemed to linger and I opened the front and back door to let some air in, then put Mia down on the lounge room floor with her frog. She grizzled so I turned the TV on and found a kids' show for her to watch and gave her a cheese stick, hoping both would keep her quiet. The two cops had followed me in and were searching Leigh's bedroom, taking photos and muttering to each other. Curly came out with a plastic bag that he held up to show me. Syringe, belt, packet of white stuff. I nodded and went to turn the kettle on and offered them both a hot drink.

Their search didn't take long. As they were drinking their coffee, Curly said, 'What are you going to do with the little girl?'

'She'll have to stay with me,' I said.

'The mother's family might want her,' the stocky cop said. 'What'll you do then?'

'I have a document that gives me legal guardianship. If anyone wants her, they'll have a fight on their hands.' The words had just popped out, but it was true. I'd already decided I was keeping Mia, no matter how much the idea scared me – I'd be doing what Andy had wanted me to. Mia and I had been through a lot together already, and I hadn't done a good job of looking after her, but now I was totally ready to step up. Mia was my family, all I was ever likely to have. I wouldn't give that up lightly again.

The cops left and the house fell into a country hum. The peppercorn trees rustled, birds sang, in the distance a tractor rumbled across a paddock. I gave Mia some of the yoghurt I'd bought and tackled cleaning up the house, stripping Leigh's bed and shoving the sheet, doona cover and her clothes into garbage bags to take home and wash. In the wardrobe was an overnight bag that the cops had been through – it only held clean underwear and a pair of runners. I shoved in her personal items and left everything else, such as soap and a shower cap, for the next tenant.

Mia fell asleep on the couch, clutching her frog, so after putting a pillow under her head I spent the next hour searching the house and sheds again. All I found were termites, redback spiders, a blue tongue lizard and lots of dust and junk. There was no sign of anything recently buried, and I doubted that Andy had even been here. This had been Leigh's bolt hole, somebody's weekender, hardly used. Whoever owned it, it hadn't been anyone known to Baldie or Spaz, or they would've been up here by now.

Still, maybe I shouldn't hang around.

I bent over Mia with a blanket, ready to gather her up and put her in the car. God, she looked so much like Andy; I swallowed hard. This wasn't the time or the place to get sentimental. I had to stay hard and determined, right to the bitter end. She whimpered as I picked her up, then settled once the blanket wrapped around and soothed her. I laid her into the car seat, closed the strap clasps over her and gathered up all my bits and pieces. I'd already filled the boot with the bags of Leigh's belongings.

I spent the trip back to Melbourne working on a plan of attack. There was paperwork and a will to sort out with the solicitor, a house to rent or sell, stuff to pack up. I'd turn Andy's house into a bunker if I had to, but Baldie and Spaz would know the police were after them. They'd hardly risk breaking in again.

The biggest challenge ahead was to somehow find that video.

24

My mobile phone rang as soon as it had picked up enough power from the charger at the house.

'Where the hell have you been? Why weren't you answering your phone? Shit, I've been going nuts here!' Heath sounded furious, which made my head spin. I felt like I'd been on another planet for the last 24 hours.

'You've been calling me?' I had no idea where to start, how to explain what I'd been doing, so I played dumb for a few minutes.

'Of course I've been bloody calling you! There's two pricks out there with a little kid, for a start. Anything could've happened. Have they rung you?'

I took a deep breath. Time to face more yelling. 'They did, yes. And I have Mia back. She's safe.'

'What?' he shouted. 'How did that happen? Did you find the... Where have...'

I could hear him breathing heavily on the other end, as if he'd worked himself up into such a state that he couldn't talk properly.

'Look, I'm sorry about the phone. The battery went flat and I forgot to take the charger.' He sucked in air, ready to bombard me, so I cut him off. 'I can't explain it all over the phone. Can you drop around?'

'Not right now. I'm about to interview someone. I'll be at your brother's house about six – I presume that's where you are now?'

'Yes. Thanks.'

He hung up without another word. On my end, I put the phone down gently and watched Mia, who was sitting on the floor, introducing her new frog to her old bear. They kissed half a dozen times, then she was satisfied they'd get on all right and hugged them against her as she focused on the cartoons.

I checked all the doors and window locks again, made sure the curtains were all pulled tight to the corners, and settled down with a novel from the shelf, but I couldn't concentrate. Instead, I rang the solicitor on his mobile number that was listed on his office stationery. He was a bit annoyed, since it was Saturday, but agreed I could see him early Monday before his first meeting. 'We have been trying to contact you,' he said.

Good for him. I wished it was Monday already.

One thing on my list done. I checked the street and then pulled the garbage bags out of the boot, dragging them inside and locking the door again. Everything went in the washing machine, and two loads later, I was rotating things through the drier and hanging the sheets outside under the pergola. I felt a bit silly, checking in every direction whenever I went out the door, but it was necessary. No point hoping they'd given up.

A few minutes after six, Heath knocked at the front door and I checked it was him before opening it and letting him in. His face was drawn, two lines etched either side of his mouth. As I explained everything that had happened, he groaned several times and shook his head. When I described snatching Mia, he stared at me as if I were crazy.

'Why the hell didn't you call me? You promised! Anything could've happened!'

'Yes, but...' I remembered how scared I'd been, how I'd wanted to call him more than anything, how I'd felt in my gut that doing it my way was my only option. He wouldn't accept any of that, so I ploughed on with my account of driving to Maryborough.

After I'd told him about Leigh, I said, 'But after all that, I know what's in the toolbox, and why they want it so badly. Andy left me a tape to tell me.'

'What? Where?'

He insisted on listening to the tape in my car while I fed Mia some soup, and I served up more for both of us. We ate in silence, Heath's face furrowed and thoughtful, and I let Mia have a go at feeding herself some yoghurt from a plate.

'It's a voice from the grave,' he said. 'And it explains the video camera in the storage unit. Trouble is, he doesn't tell us what we need to know – who's on the footage with him and who set up the hit.'

'I might never have found the cassette at all, or played it. Leigh might have, though, and he wouldn't risk putting that information on it, just in case. He was right not to trust her.' I buttered another piece of bread and took a bite. 'Andy loved laying clues. He used to drive me nuts with that stupid detective game, but these ones are a bit too obscure for me. I keep feeling really dumb, like I'm missing something obvious. But he used to do that, too – make them really hard, and then feel all superior when I couldn't solve it.'

'How badly do you think he wants you to solve this one? Or maybe he doesn't?'

I shrugged. 'Mia's safety is at stake. Surely he wouldn't make the clues too impossible?' A thought struck me. 'Do you reckon Spaz and Baldie know who's on that video? Who the killer was?'

'Who are they?'

'My names for Castella and Sands.'

He rubbed his face with both hands, as if trying to get rid of cobwebs. 'Shit, I don't know. I'd say not. Sounds like they knew the *what* but he never told anyone the *who*. But if word got out the video existed, those who knew about the hit could work it out.'

'So... Castella and Sands are the only ones on the scene right now, which says they haven't told anyone else what they're after. But they would once they got their hands on it. Leigh said they were going to auction it to the highest bidder.'

'What? Christ!' Heath stood up and paced to the back door, checked outside, paced back again. 'Talk about the perfect recipe to start another chapter of the gangland war. Old kingpins are still being taken out, even in gaol. I've got to get hold of that video before they do, before any of those pricks do. Have you had any more ideas of where it might be?'

'No,' I said. 'But if no one knows where it is, if I can't find it either, couldn't we say it's gone forever? Tell them it's been destroyed? Couldn't you lie and say the police have it?'

'They won't believe it. Not after all that's happened. They'll think you're lying, or I'm lying to protect you. Besides...' He glanced at Mia, who had yoghurt in her hair and all over the high chair and now had her fingers in the bowl. 'You tricked them.'

'They'll want payback,' I said flatly.

'I think so.'

I already knew it, but it was like an electric shock to hear him agree. 'So I'm stuffed either way.'

'We're back to square one. Find the footage. If they think they'll get big bucks for it, they might accept it in return for your and Mia's safety. They're greedy bastards, both been around for a while, wanting to get in with the big guys. They're not as dumb as they look, or Sands isn't anyway. The video would give them kudos as well as money.'

I stared at him. 'Are you saying you'd let me give it to them, if I found it? And start another war?'

'Yes! No! I don't know!'

Mia jumped when he shouted, her face crinkled up and she burst into tears.

'Oh shit, I'm sorry,' he said. 'I've frightened her.'

I wiped her face and hands with a paper towel. 'Time for a bath and bed for her I think.' I lifted her out of the chair and sat her on my lap, which calmed her down a bit. 'She's all right. I'm just relieved to have her back.'

'You took a big risk, doing that,' he said, and suddenly grinned. 'Worked a bloody treat, didn't it? Bet they were really pissed off.'

His smile warmed me. 'I was nearly wetting myself, never mind them.'

'If you're worried about Mia, maybe Kayla would take her for a few days again.'

I raised my eyebrows. 'Are you telling me to hand her over to someone else?'

'Well, you were talking about it at one point.' As Mia settled against me, he said, 'But I guess not any more.'

'No. It freaks me out totally, to take on a kid for the next how-ever-long – years and years. But now Leigh's dead... things have changed.' In more ways than one. I sighed. 'I have a few things to sort out here, like the solicitor and the will, and I'll have to decide what to do with this house.'

'You're not staying in Melbourne?'

I grimaced. 'Not my favourite place. The thing is, I keep waiting for those two to make a move on me again.'

'I'd like to say we'll give you 24-hour protection, but I can't promise, I can only ask.'

I debated for a moment. 'Maybe I should go back to my house.'

'Bit isolated, isn't it? You wouldn't get help arriving in five minutes.'

'Would I get that here?'

'Probably.' He pulled his tie loose and then took it off, undoing the knot and folding it up. 'Look, I could stay here tonight, if you want. Keep an eye on the place.'

I nearly dropped Mia. 'You?'

'Yeah, me. I've got to go back to the office for half an hour and explain to the boss how you got Mia back. Once I let them know, they pulled most of the team off the abduction.' He let out a heavy sigh. 'The escalation in ice-related murders at the moment is stretching us to the limit. You're going to have to make a statement, too.'

'But...'

'The abduction was reported, and we put a lot of men on to it. You can't just say, don't worry, it's fixed.'

'It's not fixed though, is it?' I said softly. 'When will I have to do it?'

'Probably tomorrow.' He stood, glancing around. 'I won't be long. Keep the place locked up tight.'

While he was gone, I ran a shallow bath and put Mia in it, washing her all over with a sponge and then letting her play for a while with some rubber toys while I sat on the toilet seat and kept an eye on her. This was how it was going to be, for as far ahead as I could imagine – never out of my sight, dependent on me for every single thing. I couldn't give her back when I was tired or angry or I'd had enough. I was gradually coming to terms with it, but one part of me still cringed at the idea.

Stop being a wimp. You can do it.

After Mia was dried, nappied and in her pyjamas, I was about to find a story to read when my mobile rang. Maybe Heath was running late.

'Home again, are you, you smart bitch?'

Oh Jesus, it was Baldie. I couldn't answer.

'Thought you were being fucken clever, eh?'

'Not really,' I squeaked. Where the hell was Heath?

'We want that box or you're both dead. I'm sick of fucking around, and I'm ready to fix you right up.'

I closed my eyes and summoned every ounce of strength I could find. 'I've told you a hundred times – I don't know where the box is. I've looked in every possible place. Leigh didn't have it either.'

'Where's Leigh? She must know where it is,' he snarled.

'She's in the morgue.'

'Whaddya mean?'

'She died this morning – OD'd.'

I heard muffled talking, as if Baldie had his hand over the phone. Probably giving Cousin Spaz the good news. He came back. 'Listen, you cunt, your stupid fucken brother wouldn't've got rid of the video, so you have to try harder to find it.'

'I told you –'

'No, I'm telling you. *Find it*. You've got two days. And this'll tell you how fucken serious we are.'

He hung up in my ear and I slammed the phone down at my end, sitting down fast on the floor before my legs gave way. Mia came out of her bedroom with the frog and came over to me, holding it out. 'Foggie.'

'Thanks, kid, I need a frog right now.' What I needed was a bottle of gin, and bugger the tonic. As I leant forward to take the frog, I heard a sharp crack and glass breaking then the picture on the opposite wall fell to the floor and broke.

I grabbed Mia and lay on the floor, my breath stopped in my throat, my body rigid. Listening. For several long minutes. Waiting. Mia squirmed and grizzled in my arms. 'Ssshhhh, kid, stay here.' But she wouldn't. The grizzle escalated to a wail and I released my too-tight grip.

'OK, let's get you out of sight right now.' Her room was in the middle, with only one small window covered by wrought iron bars, and her bed was in the corner. It was the safest room in the house for her. I made a game of it, crawling along the floor, avoiding the broken picture, into her bedroom. My voice was squeaky but I managed to read her a story, then left the night light on and crawled out again, hoping she'd go straight to sleep.

As I reached the hallway, someone knocked at the front door, and my heart lurched. I stopped, listened, waited. Another knock, sharper this time. 'Judi?'

It was Heath. I scrambled up, edging along the wall, and opened the door. He took one look at me and said, 'What's happened?'

'He rang. Threatened me. And then –' I gulped, coughed, caught my breath. 'I think they bloody shot at me. Through the window. Bastards. They could've killed either of us.'

'Which window?'

'One of the back ones, I think. I'm not sure.' I gestured at the broken picture. 'It hit that.'

'Fuck. That's all we need.' He pulled out his mobile and punched in a number that wasn't 000. 'Lou – it's Heath. Sands and Castella are on the move. Just took a shot at our victim again.'

Victim? God, I hated that word. It made me sound useless and pathetic. Heath walked around the room, talking, inspecting the hole through the window and curtain, and then the wall behind where the picture had been. 'Could be a .22. Went through the window but not too far after that.' He turned the picture over. 'It's stuck in a picture that was on the wall. Yep, OK.' He closed his phone. 'Someone will be here shortly.'

'In five minutes?'

'No, but soon.' He sat me down in a kitchen chair and poured me a glass of wine. 'You're shaking. Drink this. Slowly.' I picked up the glass and let my other hand rest on the table; he took it in his. Warm, dry skin. Strong hand. Long fingers. Bitten nails. It made me feel better. I didn't want him to let go.

'Mia in bed?' he said quietly.

'Yes. She didn't have a clue what happened. Nice to be too little to understand.'

'Mmm.'

We sat in silence. I drank more wine. He held my hand. I was warm all over, and the trembling had stopped. I liked the calm protective silence.

Knocking. The boys in blue had arrived. Heath let them in and I stayed at the table, dreading the questions, the futile searching, the feeling that I was trapped like a mouse on one of those red plastic wheels, getting nowhere fast. A tall sandy-haired guy in a dark blue suit and red and white tie strolled in, followed by a younger guy in a long-sleeved black shirt who went straight to the window, pulling the curtains aside.

'You shouldn't –' No, let Baldie take a shot at them if he wanted. They might catch him then.

Sandy Hair shook my hand. 'Detective Senior Sergeant Kidd. That's Detective Constable Wrightson over there.' The black-shirted cop gave me a wave and said, 'I was here the other day. You probably don't remember.'

No, I'd been bashed and stabbed then, so probably not.

'You were here alone?' Kidd asked.

'With my niece. She's in bed now, asleep. She's two.'

'No good asking her for a witness statement then.' Kidd smiled, and I liked him a little better. 'What happened?'

'I had a phone call. Sands again. Threatening me.'

Kidd glanced at Heath. 'This connected to the assault?'

Heath nodded. 'And then the niece who was abducted. Ms Westerholme managed to get her back last night. I've just found out about it.'

Kidd sat down heavily and opened his notebook. 'Right. A bit more to this than I thought. Let's do tonight's action first.' He scribbled as I talked – it didn't take long. Just as I finished, another man arrived to do the crime scene stuff. He, too, had apparently attended after my assault and was familiar with the house. It was like old home week.

'You'll have to come in and make a full statement tomorrow,' Kidd said. 'About everything.' He got up and jerked his head at Heath, who followed him over to the window where they muttered to each other for a couple of minutes. Kidd was frowning a lot and wagged his finger at Heath a couple of times, leaning into his face. I had a feeling they didn't like each other very much. Was Heath stepping on Kidd's toes by being here?

Kidd came back to the table. 'Detective Sergeant Heath says he'll bring you in tomorrow, so you can make that statement. We'll have more questions, no doubt. If I were you, I wouldn't stay here tonight.'

'But I –'

'I'll find her a safe place to stay,' Heath said, warning me with his eyes. 'Thanks, Harry.' He turned to the crime scene guy. 'Was it a .22?'

'Yep. Just as well. Something bigger would've done a lot more damage.' He finished taking photos and put his camera away.

As the two detectives left, Kidd said, 'Make sure we can contact you if we need to. You got a mobile?' I gave him the number and let Heath show them out and lock the door.

I didn't care about the picture but now they'd finished, I picked it up and looked at it. A Klimt print, with a ragged hole in the middle of the woman's stomach. The glass on the floor was in pieces; I collected it up and wrapped it in newspaper, then swept up the frag-ments. The small job gave me time to run a few things through my head. *Safe house*. Not Candlebark. I wasn't leading Baldie and Spaz up there. Where could I go? Kayla's? No way. I had no other friends in Melbourne, none that I could just land on and perhaps put them in danger. Maybe Heath was going to hide me at his place. As if.

The house was quiet again, and I could faintly hear Mrs Jones's TV next door. She must have it up loud; she was probably half-deaf.

'Right,' Heath said, fidgeting with his keys, making me nervous. Maybe I was right – maybe he was taking me back to his place. A giggle bubbled up and it was hard to force down, but his face was set in a hard mask. He wasn't in the mood for a laugh.

25

I waited for Heath to say what was on his mind, but he didn't continue.

'What's the problem?' I asked. 'I can go to a hotel – that's the easiest solution, isn't it?'

'Yes, it is.'

'And?'

His face flushed. 'I was, ah, thinking about putting you up at my place, but... nah, you're right. A hotel. No point in complicating things.'

'Conflict of interest, I guess.'

'Yeah, I've already...' He jingled his keys again and his eyes scanned the room. 'There's a place in the city, not too expensive. I know the security guy. He'll look after you. It's big enough that you'll blend in with the tourists. No point in a motel – you'd be too easy to follow and spot.'

'Right. Let's go then.' I gathered up my bag, and stopped. I might be able to pack up and leave in a few seconds, but it wasn't just me anymore. 'Oh, hang on. I need to pack for Mia. Sorry. It's hard to get used to lugging along another person's gear.'

I wanted to get out of the house now that the other cops had gone. I felt like one of those tin ducks in a shooting alley, popping up above the parapet and getting my head shot off. But if I was going to be stuck in a hotel, I'd better plan ahead a bit better this time. I grabbed everything that looked useful, from nappies to teddy bear to clothes to hair brushes. Heath wrapped Mia up in a blanket, tucked her frog in with her, and carried her out to his car.

'We'll leave the Benz here,' he said, 'and leave the lounge room light on.' He hesitated over the child seat for Mia but in the end we decided it was safer for us both to stay down low.

I didn't like being stranded without my car but I had little choice. I lay in the back seat with Mia, knowing it was sensible even though it felt silly. We drove into the city, taking the extra-long route through back streets, stopping for a few minutes here and there while he checked we weren't being followed. In the city centre, we turned left a couple of times, and went down a small back street into an underground carpark. Heath had been on his mobile and his mate met us at the boom gate then took us up in the lift to a large room on the eleventh floor.

Heath and the security guy muttered together by the door, while I put Mia into one of the two double beds, right in the middle, hoping she wouldn't roll out. The window overlooked the Yarra River and Southbank. At this time of night, all the lights sparkled on the river's surface.

'Judi?'

I turned.

'This is Martin – sorry I didn't introduce you before,' Heath said.

'Hi.' I shook his hand. He was an older guy, his grey hair in a short spiky cut, and he wore a smart suit and pale blue shirt.

'Hello. I'll give you my mobile number – you can call me anytime. I live in the hotel so even if I'm not on duty, I'll still be around.' He smiled. 'You're registered under a false name, Mrs Gayle Ingliss. My wife's name, actually.'

'Thanks. I really appreciate it.' He gave off an air of calm and control that made something inside me suddenly loosen and relax. I hadn't realised until then how tense and rigid my whole body had become. My neck felt like it had bricks packed around it. I ached to get under a hot shower and stand there until the hotel's entire supply of hot water ran out.

Heath hovered after Martin left, looking like he was planning on staying for a while. Three hours ago, that would've made me happy, but now I needed time alone, time to wind down the corkscrew feeling that had gripped me. 'We'll be fine,' I said. 'Truly. Don't feel you need to babysit.'

'Oh. OK.' He checked the bathroom again. 'I'll see you in the morning then. Is your mobile charged up?'

'Yes, boss.' I walked to the door and opened it for him.

'You should've checked through the spyhole first,' he said.

'Yes, boss. Goodnight, boss.'

Finally, he went, and as soon as the door closed behind him, I wanted to fling it open and beg him to come back. And I didn't want to think about why that urge was so strong, but it had everything to do with suddenly remembering the touch of his warm hands. I was perfectly safe now and having him there wouldn't make me any safer, but... a hot shower was definitely in order. Maybe even a cold one.

In the end, I kept it to ten minutes, soaking up the hot, sharp needles on my skin, and washing my hair with the tiny hotel bottles of shampoo and conditioner. The towels were thick and fluffy, and it wasn't until I searched through the bag of clothes that I realised I had brought nothing to sleep in but a T-shirt. It'd have to do. I checked Mia was still in the middle of her bed, put a pillow either side of her and crashed into the other bed, falling asleep in a few seconds.

Mia woke about 4am, grizzling, and I took her into my bed where she went to sleep again, sucking her thumb. By 7am we were both up and dressed and ready for a solid breakfast. The hotel information brochures told me there was a buffet from six to nine, and I figured it was pretty unlikely anyone who knew us would walk in. We were both desperate for a decent meal, and for me that meant eggs and bacon and strong coffee. Mia started with a plate of chopped-up fruit and soon moved on to an apricot Danish she chose herself.

Heath arrived and moved the chairs so he was facing the entrance, then sat without speaking while the waitress poured his coffee and fussed around the table. 'Do you want anything from the buffet?' she asked.

'I'm fine, thanks,' he said, without smiling. She took the hint and moved away.

I examined him while he checked out the dining room and what he could see of the lobby. He did look like a cop – the suit and tie gave it away somewhat, but it was more his manner, watchful and hard-edged, never smiling unless it suited him. If not for that, any woman would've agreed he was damn good-looking.

Just as well I wasn't interested in men like that.

He laid his mobile on the table and stirred sugar into his cup, not meeting my eyes. I wasn't surprised when he said, 'I've made a call this morning, but I'm not sure you're going to agree with what I've arranged.'

'What's that?' The tone in his voice was enough to make me grit my teeth.

'Kayla has agreed to look after Mia again for a couple of days.'

My knife clattered onto my plate. 'What? I thought she couldn't wait to see the back of us.'

'I made it an official request. After I told her that Leigh was dead.'

'Was she upset?'

'Yeah, quite a bit. They'd been mates since school, apparently.' He drank some coffee, flicked a glance at me. 'That OK with you? She's only met Castella once, a few years ago. Says he'd have no reason to think Mia was with her.'

'I don't like it. What if she's lying? What if she hands Mia over five minutes after I leave?' Leigh had been so good at lying and Kayla was her friend. I looked at Mia who was tucking into a croissant, crumbs flying everywhere. 'No. She's staying with me.'

He hmphed. 'Mia would be a lot safer there. And it would be easier for you.'

'That may be true, but... I'll cope.'

He nodded. 'All right. What are you going to do today? Stay here?'

'No. I have to keep looking for that bloody box.' I grimaced. 'I've got an appointment to see Andy's solicitor on Monday. It's just down St Kilda Road so I can catch a tram.'

'Maybe Andy left the video with him?'

'Surely if it's that important and the solicitor had it, he'd have told me. All Andy's done is leave me red herrings, or vague clues that mean nothing to me. The storage place, Mum's rest home, the car yard, Leigh's car – they were all possibilities that went nowhere. If I were Castella and Sands, I'd be totally flummoxed by now. But I'm his sister, and I'm totally out of ideas. Even the audio tape was no help.'

'He's been pretty clever.' His mobile chirped and he ignored it.

'Or bloody dumb. He was like that. Sometimes he'd have such brilliant ideas that it left me gobsmacked, but then he'd do something incredibly dumb. One of his plans to make money, when we were kids, was to sell raffle tickets, door-to-door. He told all the neighbours it was for Save the Children, and conned me into selling them too.'

'Why would they buy a ticket for nothing?' he asked.

'Oh, there was a prize. Dad's new lawnmower. Andy was going to unlock the garden shed and make a mess, and tell Dad it must've been stolen. He was hoping the prize winner would live the furthest away from us. Less likely Dad would find out, he thought.'

Heath grinned. 'Not a bad plan, for a kid.'

'You're not supposed to praise a budding criminal!' I smiled, too. 'Anyway, it fell apart. Andy drew the winning ticket out and it was the man next door. If Dad had seen him with the mower, he would've accused him of stealing it.'

'Why didn't Andy rig the raffle so someone else won?'

I shrugged. 'He said the neighbour won fair and square, so he couldn't lie about it. He went around and gave everyone back their money.'

'Andy must've thought through this whole thing pretty thoroughly.' Heath picked up the salt and pepper, and a spoon, like he was going to act out a breakfast implements scenario about the tape, then he sighed and put them down again. 'What are we missing?'

'The problem is me. I was never any good at his detective game, and I've tried to remember all the times we played it in case there was something from back then that he's using, but my brain is coming up empty.'

'Maybe...' He tapped the spoon on the table. 'Maybe there are more clues, and we haven't found them yet. Maybe you should be looking for clues, not for the box.'

I stared at him, biting my lip. Was he right? How many clues would Andy give me? As few as possible, at first, then he'd get frustrated when I was so dense, and feed me more, one at a time. 'So where do I find more clues?'

'Possibly at the solicitor's. But also look at what you've been given already and try to think of what they might lead you to, if it's not the box.'

Great. I could see how far I was going to get with that strategy – nowhere. But I kept my face blank and said, 'OK, it's worth a try. Are you going to help?'

'No, I can't.' His mouth twisted and I wished he'd smile occasionally – every time he looked so depressed, it made me feel worse. 'I'm in a bit of strife at work. I've let some of my other cases go and the boss has put his foot down. I'll be catching up on paperwork and spending hours on the computer today.'

'What about Castella and Sands? Did Kidd find anything last night?'

'Not that I've heard.'

'Wouldn't he let you know?'

'He wouldn't go out of his way, no.' He focused on Mia and her frog, avoiding my eyes again.

'You don't get on with him?'

'It's a bit obvious, is it?'

'Just a bit. What's the story? If I have to deal with him, I'd like to know.'

He pulled at his shirt collar and I recognised that signal from before, like he was being strangled. 'I used to be married to his sister.'

I sat, stunned for a few seconds, and then I said carefully, 'I guess it didn't work out.'

'I was thirty, she was twenty-two. It lasted just over a year. Harry is her older brother, a bit over-protective, that's all.' His tone said the subject was closed, which was fine by me. I didn't want to hear about other people's train wrecks, especially not his.

The waitress came back to clear the table and bent to tickle Mia under her chin. She squirmed and giggled and held up her frog. 'Foggie.'

'What a lovely frog,' the waitress cooed. To me, she said, 'She's gorgeous. Is she your only one?'

'Er... yes.' That caught me by surprise, as much as Heath had. Two tongue-ties in one morning. I was slipping.

'She's quiet, isn't she? My sister's got twins, about this one's age. They chatter like parrots, drive us nuts.'

I smiled and didn't reply. When she'd gone, I said, 'I have no idea if she's quiet or not. How would I know what normal is?'

He leaned over the table to Mia and pointed at me. 'Mia, who's this? Who's this person here?'

Mia looked at me, solemn-eyed, but didn't speak.

'This is Judi,' he persisted. 'Can you say Judi?'

She glanced at him, then back at me. 'Daddy.'

'Close, but no prize for the kid in the red T-shirt,' I said. 'Come on, let's go.' I gathered up our things while Heath took Mia out of the chair and carried her across the restaurant. Was I disappointed she couldn't say my name? Hardly. It wasn't like I'd been training a budgie, was it?

As Heath was about to leave, I said, 'If I need more clues, I'm going to have to visit my mother again.'

'Are you sure?'

'Yes. They might be with her, seeing as how he kept in contact. Did you know he was renting out her house for her? Paying money into her account?'

'Yes. Nothing wrong with that, is there?'

'Only if you knew how much Andy hated her and Dad.'

'Maybe he'd found a way to move on, you know. Get on with his own life.' He gave me a strange look.

I bristled. 'You think I haven't done that?'

'I didn't say that. But if you're feeling negative about your mum before you go there, you mightn't get what you want. You mightn't see the obvious.'

I didn't bother to answer. She'd always be 'the old bitch' to me, no matter what Andy had or hadn't done for her. When Heath had left, I asked the guy at the hotel reception about the best way to get to my mother's. Since I needed a car seat and I had never set up something called Uber, it would have to be a taxi.

We zoomed through the city and down Dandenong Road, avoiding the tunnel and the toll, and I checked to see if anyone was following me, but after all Heath's security and secret hotel stuff, it was unlikely.

Outside the rest home, I asked the driver to wait and unbuckled Mia from the seat, trying to psych myself up to go inside. It was stupid, incredibly stupid. I'd seen the old vulture and she was harmless, batty with Alzheimer's. What could she do to me now? Maybe

Heath was right – I was doing it to myself. But it was as if Andy's death had brought back all the hate and vile memories more vividly, instead of lancing them like boils. I couldn't seem to get rid of my anger, no matter how much I told myself it was all past and done. Maybe facing her again and talking to her would help. Yes, I believed that like I believed aliens landed in the outback and had sex with people.

Still, I knew one thing that was bugging me. There had to be a reason Andy had looked after her. I wanted to know what it was.

26

I forced myself to walk into the rest home with a halfway pleasant smile on my face, but she wasn't in her room, and the smile dropped, leaving my face tight. Mia pulled on my hand, wanting to climb on the comfy armchair by the window. A plump Indian nurse walked past and said, 'She'll be in the Green Room, dear. It's cards day.' She directed us down the corridor and I found the Green Room really was green, with a garden mural painted on one wall. Something I think they call trompe l'oeil, where it's made to look three-dimensional. Half of the residents were grouped around tables, chattering and playing card games, while others watched TV or stared into space. I spotted my mother in a corner, hunched in a tapestry arm-chair, a magazine open on her lap while she gazed out the window.

Taking a deep breath, I walked over and sat down in the armchair next to her, and persuaded Mia to sit on my lap. 'Hello, Mum.'

Her head swivelled around and she looked at me as if I were a stranger. 'Hello, dear.' She smiled at Mia. 'Ah, you brought Andrew. How nice.'

This was going to be as rough as I expected. 'This is Mia. Do you know who I am?'

'You're Doris, my next-door neighbour.'

If only I was. 'No, Mum, I'm your daughter, Judi.'

'Oh.' She sounded suspicious, and looked away from Mia, to the doorway. 'Where's Andrew?'

'He's not here today, Mum.' I couldn't bring myself to say *He's dead*.

'He promised to bring me some chocolate ginger.' Her fingers picked at her skirt and the magazine slid to the floor. I caught a flash of Angelina Jolie's big smile before the page flipped over. 'He's late. He's usually here by now. Who are you?'

'Judi. How often does Andrew visit you?'

'All the time! What are you doing here? Who said you could visit me? You should know better.' Her voice rose and I could hear the old Mum behind the querulousness, her absolute belief that Andy and I were devil's spawn, nothing that could have come from her body, and her husband was the only person who could keep us under control.

My hands clenched, and I wanted simply to knock her into next week. Mia squirmed, feeling my tension, and tried to get down. 'Hang on, kiddo,' I muttered.

I stood up abruptly, Mia at my side, ready to run.

'Is everything all right?' It was the Indian nurse. 'Would you like a cup of tea?'

'Arsenic might help,' I said.

She giggled. 'Don't worry, lots of family members feel like that, and then feel guilty. It's very frustrating to visit and not be recognised.' Her sing-song voice soothed me a little. Mum had gone back to picking at something on her skirt and the nurse patted her hand. 'Mrs Westerholme, I'll get you some tea and a biscuit, all right? And some for you?' She glanced at us.

I wasn't tempted for a moment. 'No thanks. I actually need to talk to the manager. Sort some financial stuff out. Where's the office?'

She showed me where to go and, as soon as I mentioned money to the receptionist, I was shown in to see the manager, a balding guy in rimless glasses and thick, bushy eyebrows. 'Is there a problem?' he asked.

'Probably not. I understand my brother, Andrew, was handling my mother's affairs and paying her fees here?'

'That's right. It was a monthly transfer from your mother's bank account.' His eyebrows twitched. 'I wasn't aware that Mrs Westerholme had a daughter.' He frowned at Mia, who had gone to investigate his fake rubber plant, and I wondered how many little kids ever came into this place.

'Yes, not by choice.' I took a breath. 'I suppose I'll have to be the contact person now, so I need to give you my address and phone number. The bank stuff can stay as it is, as far as I'm concerned.'

'Your brother is no longer able to administrate your mother's affairs?'

'My brother is dead.'

'Oh dear, I am sorry.' His whole head turned pink.

'Nobody contacted you?'

'No.'

'I need information though, especially about my mother's possessions, where they're stored, and anything else you think I should know.'

'I can certainly show you the accounts, and give you copies of things.' He stood and went to a bank of filing cabinets, pulling out a drawer and extracting a large file. 'Your mother started off in the units, and was transferred to the nursing home section about...' He flicked through the papers. 'Three months ago. She's doing well, considering.'

'Considering what?'

'Well, she's been diagnosed with Alzheimer's, but she's quite healthy for her age.'

She hasn't rotted from the inside out then. 'That's all fine. What happened to her things when she moved?'

He frowned at Mia again, who had moved on to checking out a strange pink vase with feathers in it. 'They came with her. Nothing was thrown out. Your brother may have taken some of the excess furniture away, I think.'

I found it hard to believe that Mum had managed to whittle down a whole house full of stuff to what was in that one room. On the other hand, maybe the house was rented with the furniture still in it. I'd have to check that out.

'I need to look through her room, if that's OK.' Even if he wasn't happy, I was still going to do it, but it was better to keep on his good side.

'Oh. Why?'

'I'm not checking up on you,' I assured him. 'There's something my brother may have left with her that I need to find. A family... heirloom.'

He didn't have a problem with that so I went to Mum's room and started searching, giving Mia a small hand mirror to play with. Keeping her happy with stuff to play with was a full-time job. I tried not to sneeze with the old-lady lavender musty smell that permeated everything. Every drawer and cupboard was crammed with clothing and underwear, neatly folded or hung in plastic bags. It looked like most of it was never worn, only kept for special occasions – there wouldn't be many of them in here. I even tipped up all of her shoes and got down on my hands and knees to inspect under the bed and dressing table. Nothing.

The last items were the photos in frames, arranged along the window sill and dressing table surface. One by one, I prised the backs off and checked for notes or pieces of paper. Under the last photo, one of Andy as a little boy of about six, I found a second photo. It was the two of us, in Nana's front yard, Nana kneeling with her arms around us. We were all laughing into the camera and I felt a sudden ache in my throat for those happy times with her. I couldn't remember the photo being taken – did Dad take it? He was the only one who I remembered owning a camera.

I turned the photo over and there, in pencil in Andy's handwriting were the words – *Who took this?* That was a question I couldn't answer, neither could I work out why Andy would give this photo to Mum. It would've been as precious to him as it was to me. But he hadn't given it to her – he'd hidden it behind the other one, which was why I put it into my bag.

Maybe he'd left it for me and it was another clue. If so, it was no help. I had no idea who took the photo, but I was pretty sure it wasn't Mum or Dad. I was the only person now who was likely to know. Mum was too gaga to get a sensible answer out of, that's for sure.

Damn you, Andy. If you were here right now, I'd give you a thick ear. But you had your reasons for doing this and I need to try harder, I guess.

Time to leave before Mum came back from the Green Room for a nap or whatever old people did after lunch. I couldn't cope with the whole 'Who are you?' routine again.

Back in the city, after paying an exorbitant taxi fare, Mia and I wandered into Melbourne Central. The last time I'd been here, the Japanese department store had consumed most of the shopping space but now it was gone, replaced by dozens of small outlets. Everyone was out to spend money, milling around, and most of the young ones were outside mobile phone shops, peering in the windows and pointing at various models and prices. It reminded me to check mine was on and functioning. If Heath rang and left a message, I wasn't sure I could work out how to retrieve it, but it didn't look like anything was waiting for me.

I found a café with an empty table near the back, and ordered a toasted pide for lunch with ham and cheese, whatever the hell a pide was. I was turning into one of those grumpy women on the TV show. From the bain-marie I chose macaroni cheese for Mia, figuring it was sticky enough that she could feed herself.

While I was waiting, I pulled out my notebook and pen and listed the clues Andy had left – invoice for the storage unit, audio tape, two cryptic notes on the back of photos. At least I knew what I was looking for now – a video that may or may not still be in the toolbox. Heath had told me it was likely to be a small plastic memory card. Strange to put something that small in a toolbox, but it was the security chain around it that was the important bit. I thought about the envelope of items that they'd found on his body – it was still jammed in the bottom of my bag, so I found it and spread the contents out on the table. Keys for his car – police had searched that at least twice. I doubted Andy would have taken the card to the river anyway, not if he was expecting trouble. Otherwise why go to all this trouble to hide it?

If Baldie and Spaz had killed Andy, he must have told them it was in the toolbox. Or something. I was guessing.

Baldie had taken the key with number 20 on the fob, but I was sure he didn't know what it was for either. I went through Andy's wallet again but there was nothing in it of use, nothing with another cryptic note on the back. Heath said the USB only had photos of Mia on it. As for Dad's watch, I thought probably Mum had given it to him. Knowing Andy, he'd been wearing it as an everyday watch simply because it was worth so much.

The video of Altona beach didn't tell me anything. And I was sure there was nothing in his papers at the house either. I ate the pide without tasting it while I helped Mia with her macaroni cheese, and then ordered another long black, but it didn't help my brain power much, just made me feel more wired up. My hip and leg were aching again, so I found a chemist and bought the strongest painkillers that didn't need a prescription, dry-swallowing a couple straight away.

It was late afternoon, already getting dark, and a light drizzle turned gradually into a downpour as we walked slowly back to the hotel. I tried to carry Mia a couple of times but it made my hip feel on fire. Toddler speed it was then. On the way, I saw a kids' toy shop and we wasted some time exploring all kinds of stuff I'd never seen before, and came out with a highly recommended shape sorter that the assistant assured me was 'very educational and fun'. I restrained myself from pointing out that 'very fun' was ungrammatical.

We made it back to the hotel just after five and I headed for the bar, sitting in a banquette in the back corner where the lights were low and Mia could play with her toys. A couple of glasses of wine later, the pain in my hip had subsided and my head was light and fluffy, but I'd got no further with my notes and heavy-duty thinking. We ate in the dining room and then upstairs in our room, I cleaned my teeth and crawled into bed with Mia, putting the TV on and finding a kids' channel. By the time the talking puppet show had finished, we were both asleep.

At first, I thought the knocking was in my dream then gradually I came to and heard it for real. Either the hotel was on fire or it was Heath at the door. Best to put my jeans on before opening the door. Through the spyhole, I saw his face moving, checking up and down the corridor; I undid the safety lock and opened the door.

He grinned at me. 'We got one of them!'

'Which one?'

'Castella.'

Spaz of the flat, evil eyes. 'Thank God for that.' I let him shut the door – I had to sit down. 'Don't wake Mia up. How did you find him?'

'He wasn't being very bright,' he said softly, but his glee was evident. 'He was drunk in a nightclub in Brunswick and harassed a girl who complained to the manager. When he confronted Castella, he threw a punch so they called the police, who nabbed our boy as he was leaving. They're bringing him down from the station up there shortly.' He sat on the empty bed and bounced a couple of times, fizzing with energy. 'About time we had a breakthrough on this. We had a reported sighting of Sands last night in King Street, but nothing came of it.'

I frowned. 'That's only a couple of blocks from here.'

'Coincidence. It's the nightclub area of the city – lots of people hang out there. No one knows you're in this hotel.'

'Apart from you, and Martin, and how many people in your department?' I didn't want anyone to know where I was, not even other cops.

'Only my boss.' He pulled at his earlobe. 'Well, it's in the report that I wrote today, but that goes straight to him.'

'Uh-huh.' On paper. On a computer. For anyone to see. I tried to shrug it off. 'So you think Castella will tell you where Sands is?'

'Probably not. But Sands won't continue this on his own. And I'll make sure Castella doesn't get bail.' He slapped his head. 'Bugger! You were supposed to see Kidd today and make that statement. He'll be breaking my balls about it.'

'I'll go tomorrow after I've seen Andy's solicitor.'

'How did you go with your mum? Any luck?'

I shook my head. 'Just this.' I showed him the photo and the note on the back.

'Who took this photo?' He raised his eyebrows at me.

'No idea. I don't even remember it being taken.' I stood up and went over to the window, pulling the curtains open and staring out across the city to the Westgate and Bolte Bridges. The blue light around the Bolte was eerie, and this time on a Sunday night the traffic seemed light. The rain had tapered off to nothing and I wondered briefly if any had fallen at Candlebark. I hadn't rung Connor for several days. Was he ringing me at Andy's house and wondering what had happened? I'd call him tomorrow if I could.

Heath came to stand behind me, his hands on my shoulders. 'I could say it's a jungle out there, but I think that one's been done to death.'

'Yeah. At least one of them's out of the way.' I turned, forcing him to drop his hands but he didn't move away. 'Are you going in to see Castella?' He was close enough that I could feel the heat emanating from his body. To get away from him I'd have to climb over the bed.

My breathing had gone a bit funny which made me cross for some reason.

'Yes, I want to question him, see if he'll cough up anything useful.'

'He might confess.'

Heath laughed. 'Yes, and I just saw a pig fly past the window.' He put a hand up to my hair and I flinched. 'Sorry, is your head still sore?'

'No, it's fine. Just a reflex action, you know...' I couldn't look at his face so I concentrated on the buttons on his shirt, but that led me to think about what was underneath. *For Christ's sake, get a grip, woman!*

'Judi, I...' His hand came up again, touched the side of my face.

My breath stopped for a few moments and it was as if there were a dozen hands inside me, all reaching out for him. 'This... um... probably isn't a good idea,' I said, knowing I sounded lame.

'No.' He stepped back. 'I should head for the office. See what's happening.'

Disappointment crashed through me. I folded my arms tightly. *Hold it together.* 'Mmm.' I steeled myself to look at him now he was at a safe distance. He seemed tense, taking a moment to button up his jacket then unbutton it again.

'Look, this is something –' He stared at me intently, as if coming to some kind of decision. About me? My breath stopped. All he said was, 'I'll call you when I know anything useful. Keep your phone on.'

He left in a rush, as if he couldn't stand to be in the same room with me. Was that a good sign or not? I was so bloody hopeless at this stuff. One minute I wanted to push him as far away as possible, the next I was imagining ripping his clothes off and jumping into bed with him. This was my version of lunacy. He'd said *something.* Nothing I could stand to think about right now.

I took off my jeans and crawled back into bed, my brain working overtime again while Mia slept peacefully. The TV was still on, the volume low, and I gave my full attention to a very bad comedy movie with an idiotic blonde, determined to focus on silliness for however long it took for me to fall asleep again. As if that was going to happen easily. The movie morphed into news and another bad movie, and finally at 12.30am my mobile rang. I snatched it from the side table.

No hello. 'Castella's dead.' He sounded rushed.

I jerked upright. 'Is that a good thing?'

'No. They were bringing him in the side entrance and he was shot getting out of the car. There'll be an internal investigation.'

'You mean one of your lot shot him?'

'No! Of course not.' Heavy breathing. 'Two guys were on the footpath, drunk and fighting. We think now they were a diversion. Our guys were getting Castella out of the divvy van and they got distracted and someone else came out from behind a car and shot Castella, then bolted.'

A movement caught my eye. It was my reflection in the window. I looked like a black-eyed ghost. 'What does that all mean?'

'Someone wanted to shut Castella up.' Heath's voice had lowered, as if someone at his end was too close. 'Before he went inside where they couldn't get at him anymore.'

'Did anyone manage to question him before this happened?'

'No. The guys at Brunswick didn't know why we wanted him.' A flurry of noise in the background. 'I'm going to be here all night.'

'Seems a bit convenient, doesn't it?'

'What do you mean?' he snapped.

'Who knew they'd be bringing him in? You said before that he was arrested for causing trouble in that nightclub.'

'Are you suggesting... what? A leak? Here?'

'Somewhere. Maybe.'

'That's highly unlikely.'

'This whole business with the video and these two nutcases is un-likely. But the one thing I have learned so far is that there are no coincidences.' I hesitated. 'Should I move to another hotel?'

'No! Damn it! Maybe.' He sounded mad at me now, but it wasn't my problem, even though the tone of his voice made my guts churn. 'Go back to sleep. I'll ring you as soon as I know anything.'

I hung up, checked the door locks again, and pulled the curtains shut, but then the room felt like a tomb so I opened them again, and climbed back under the covers. I lay, huddled against the spare pillow, eyes wide open.

Go back to sleep? As if.

27

My mobile phone rang again at 6.12am and I nearly threw the bloody thing down the toilet. I'd finally got to sleep about 4.30am and my head felt like a monumental ball of cotton wool. 'Yeah, what?' I mumbled.

'Sorry to wake you.' He didn't sound sorry, he sounded exhausted.

'Wassup?' I struggled to sit up and concentrate. Mia sat up next to me, so bright-eyed it exhausted me even more.

'Sands is dead.'

'You said Castella was dead.' I rubbed my face. 'Did you get the wrong guy?'

'They're both dead. We found Sands an hour ago, in a car in Heidelberg, shot in the head.'

'Oh.' The familiar feeling of dark dread crawled through my stomach. 'Is someone trying to tell us something?'

'You haven't found the video yet, have you?'

'I think I would've mentioned it.' It wasn't too early for sarcasm.

'Right.' He paused. 'There's information come in that Castella and Sands were dealing ice. That this is about a deal gone wrong.'

'So it's not about the video.'

'No.' But he didn't sound convinced.

'If it is, then someone else is also after it.' I was wide awake now, my mind flipping through the possibilities. 'Someone else knows about it.'

'We've seen no evidence of that. It's all been these two guys.'

'But then why would he leave me clues?'

'Maybe they weren't clues. Maybe we just thought they were.'

We were going around in circles.

Heath went on. 'Look, the two guys who were after you are both dead. If no one else knows about the video, you're off the hook.'

'What if they do? Are you giving up on me?' I couldn't afford to feel any relief at his words. My brain was struggling with what felt like Heath leaving me in the lurch.

'No, of course not. But right now, I have to focus on these two murders and find out who did it. That might tell us where the video is.'

The bloody thing is still hidden wherever Andy left it, you idiot. I definitely needed coffee, and some headspace to think, which meant pushing him away. He could hunt for the killers all he wanted, but I was convinced more than ever that he was on the wrong track. Andy wouldn't have gone to all that trouble for nothing. 'Yeah, all right. You'd better go then, I guess.'

I punched the red button and lay back. Spaz and Baldie dead. Really dead. Could we go home now? Really home to Candlebark? I could stop looking for the video, clues or no clues. It no longer mattered.

All I can do is leave you this and other bits of information and trust you to work it out...

And I'd been getting nowhere. But Heath had said they wanted to find out *who* killed Spaz and Baldie. What about the *why*? They didn't have the video, but maybe one of them had opened his big mouth, hinted at the auction Leigh mentioned.

Fuck. I was worse off now than I was before.

Or perhaps I was over-reacting. Seeing bogie men where there were none. Heath had said it was an ice deal gone wrong. That was just as likely. Mia was grizzling and I guessed she was hungry, so we showered together, dressed and went downstairs for breakfast, then I ordered another taxi. The solicitor was down past the US embassy and the driver found the office building easily with the map thing on his screen. Mia and I went up in the lift to an office on the fifth floor.

Peter Thompson was nothing like I expected. I'd had a picture of a dark, stocky guy with a twirling moustache, but he was tall and gangling, with receding blond hair and an infectious smile. He shook my hand and showed me into his office.

'Don't mind the mess,' he said. 'We're moving up one floor this week so things are being sorted and packed up.' Piles of binders and bound reports and law books sat on the floor in rows, and half the bookcases were empty and dusty. His desk, however, was tidy and clean, with only one file and a padded envelope lined up in the middle. Tina Arena played softly on a CD unit on a shelf. 'Tea?'

'No, thanks,' I said. I set Mia up on the floor with her shape sorter and sat down in the padded chair. On the solicitor's desk, the file said *Westerholme, Andrew* on the front, and the room suddenly seemed darker. I swallowed. 'I'd better tell you some news first. Leigh – Andy's partner – died on Saturday.'

'Oh. Goodness me.' He sat down abruptly, grimacing. 'That's terrible. I'm so sorry. You must feel like everything has come down on you at once.'

'Yes, a bit.' I pointed at the file. 'I've read Andy's will, and saw that he made me guardian of Mia. I was going to question the legality of that, but if Leigh is dead, it'll change things.'

'It will mean she can't contest it, of course.' He steepled his hands.

'Obviously. But...'

'You sound like the guardianship was a surprise.'

'It was. I hadn't been in contact with my brother for quite a while. I didn't even know Mia existed.' I gripped the arms of the chair. I wasn't sure what to say, in case I caused trouble with the will. 'I mean, I'm happy about it, but I wondered if he was actually allowed to do that.'

'It would be more about whether anyone would contest it. He believed that Leigh would not – he told me she had agreed to it. He hinted that she had something like cancer, without saying the word.'

Not cancer, drugs. I didn't want to go down that path and complicate things. 'So we'll leave it as it is then?'

'Unless Leigh's family want to contest it. Have you heard from them?'

'I don't know her family at all, whether she has any. Do you?'

He shook his head. 'Andrew didn't mention anyone.' He pushed the padded envelope towards me. 'He left that for you to collect.'

'But...' I thought back to the neatly labelled files, the will, the preparations. 'Did he tell you he thought he was going to die? Is it usual for someone his age to go to all this trouble?'

'No, not really.' His lips pursed. 'He was very particular and exact about everything. And anxious. I thought it was because of his partner, but then... he was killed. I did wonder. But it's not my job to speculate.'

'You're not a criminal lawyer,' I said. But he was still keeping it all at arm's length, sidestepping anything that wasn't directly his job.

'Oh no, property and probate mainly. That kind of thing.'

I tried to think of what else I needed to ask him. 'The house in Ascot Vale still has a sizeable mortgage on it?'

'Yes. It's your brother's main asset. He didn't have much in the bank. On the other hand, he did have a life insurance policy with Mia as the beneficiary.'

'When did he take that out?'

'About three months ago.'

That would've been around the time Leigh blabbed to her cousin, perhaps.

He went on. 'If his death had been a suicide, the policy would've been void, but someone doesn't go out and get themselves murdered on purpose, do they?'

'No.' *But you could still have a fair idea it was coming.*

'You haven't asked how much the policy is worth,' he said, smiling slightly. 'Most family members ask that first.' His smile widened. 'It's $300,000.'

I didn't bother to tell him I already knew. 'I'm glad Mia's getting that and not me.'

He laughed out loud. I didn't think it was that funny.

'You will have to administer it for her, as her guardian.'

'Can't we put it in a trust or something?'

'Andrew had already set one up, so it can go into that.' The smile dropped from his face, as if he'd suddenly realised that maybe Andy *had* been expecting to die. 'Yes, well, you don't have to worry.' He opened the file and skimmed through the papers, avoiding my eyes. 'There are a few thousand dollars in a savings account, and a small amount of superannuation for which you're listed as beneficiary. You may have to pay tax on it. Andrew made me executor so I can finalise everything and send you the papers as they need to be signed. Your address is still in Candlebark?'

'Andy gave you my address?'

'Yes, of course.'

No matter how much I knew of Andy's preparation, each new revelation was like a slap in the face. I swallowed hard. 'What if... what if something happens to me? What about Mia then?'

'Are you ill?' A row of lines creased his forehead.

'No, but if I'm the only family member left, it's a bit of a worry.'

'She could end up as a Ward of State. You don't want that to happen. You really don't.' He shuffled the papers again. 'There is no one else listed anywhere here as a family member. Your mother is now incapacitated, I believe.'

'Yes.' I was stressing him out, a pointless exercise. 'Don't worry, I'm as strong as a horse. I was curious, that's all. Now, do I need to do anything about my mother's house and the financial arrangements there?'

'No, not unless you want to change anything.'

'I don't.' We discussed a few more chores I would need to do then I stood up and shook his hand again. 'Thank you. You'll be in touch?'

'I will.' He handed me the envelope and, after I'd picked up Mia's toys, he showed us out. I gripped Mia with one hand and the envelope with the other, all the way down in the lift, wondering if I held another audio tape. I couldn't wait until we got back to the hotel. I sat on a couch in the foyer and ripped the envelope open. Three small objects fell into my lap. One was a small brooch in the shape of a butterfly, but the other two were very odd; a plastic spade and a funny little grey-haired farmer's wife. At first I thought they were toys for Mia, the kind of thing you buy in packets – a farm, full of animals like chooks and dogs and horses, with tractors and fences and trees – but she was too little to play with these. She'd choke on them. Already she was reaching for them so I held them out of reach and emptied out her shape sorter again. That thing was worth its weight in gold.

The brooch was old-fashioned, with a pink stone in the middle and little flowers on the wings. A bit tacky and not expensive. It must've belonged to Mum, or maybe even Nana, although I didn't remember either of them wearing something like that.

I looked at the plastic toys again and muttered, 'What the hell is this supposed to tell me?' They looked new, not chewed or worn with playing; maybe he'd bought a whole farm set and picked out what he needed.

I shoved the toys and brooch back in the envelope and stared out of the plate glass windows at all the people in business clothes, carrying takeaway cups and lunch bags, most of them head down and focused on their phones. I hadn't missed my phone in Candlebark, and I knew the world had moved on without me. I didn't care much about that either. What I cared about was playing detectives and lowing these weird clues, and the internet was unlikely to help me with what had been inside Andy's head.

These toys were another clue. The farmer's wife had to be Mum, but the video wasn't in her room. Nor did I think it was under the plants at the rest home. Too risky. The gardener might have dug it up accidentally. I checked my notebook of possibilities. There it was. Mum's house. Our old house. Still owned by Mum, and rented out by Andy. That had to be the answer.

28

I was sick to death of waiting for taxis and paying out money I didn't have right now. One more paid-for ride took us to Ascot Vale, where I gratefully picked up my Benz. I put Mia in the car seat and wrestled with the straps and buckle, then sat in the front seat and looked at the toys again.

Surely I wasn't supposed to dig up the garden? But one game of detectives we'd played, he had buried something – a ring of Mum's – under the lemon tree. The same lemon tree that Dad liked to piss on in the name of fertiliser. After I'd worked out where the ring was, I'd refused to dig it up.

My pulse rate rose a notch. I was finally on to something – something only Andy and I would know. The pissy lemon tree. I'd have no trouble digging it up now. Dad's pee would be long gone.

I drove fast at first then remembered I had Mia in the back and, even though she'd dropped off to sleep, I slowed down and took it more calmly. Brighton looked much the same, with its streets full of trees and old houses with attics and high fences, and my guts tightened into knots. This would be the first time I'd been back in over twenty years – it was at least ten years since Dad died. I'd imagined Mum living in squalor, stockpiling old newspapers covered in mouse shit and keeping half a dozen mangy cats. No, that was impossible. She'd been such a stickler for perfection, right down to the vases matching the curtains matching the pictures on the walls. Cleaning was her religion, and we'd never been allowed pets.

I could still recall every room in that house, every stick of over-priced furniture, every carefully coordinated colour scheme. For years, my room had been pink and flowery with plenty of frills and not a thing out of place. I'd mess it up; she'd come in while I was at school and tidy it, then greet me with pursed lips and the silent treatment. In Year Eight I had a huge 'accident' with a bottle of ink that ended up indelibly smeared over everything. Finally, I was allowed to redecorate in navy blue and white.

But still she invaded every inch of my life, reading my diary, listening in on my phone calls, going through my drawers and wardrobe on a regular basis. I never brought friends home in high school. Sometimes I'd wake in the middle of the night and know she was in my room, watching me.

I hated her for her intrusion into every aspect of my life, and then the total withdrawal when Andy or I went up against Dad. It never made sense to me, and all I could think of was how to get out of that house and away from both of them forever. Years later, after submitting to counselling as part of my recovery from Max and my injuries, I recognised that there was something wrong with my mother, but that didn't help me forgive her.

Maybe Heath was right. Andy had moved on but I hadn't. I couldn't remember a single word of advice or help the counsellor gave me, although I know she did at the time, and I tried to listen. The thought that I might've become my own worst enemy was starting to really bother me.

I turned into my old street and gripped the steering wheel, white-knuckled. There it was, Number 57, a red brick monstrosity with white shutters. Two storeys, tiled roof, white columns on the porch. The picket fence had gone and there was now a rendered white wall about two metres high. The spiked-iron gate was closed but I could see a 4WD in the driveway. Someone was home.

Mia was still asleep but I couldn't leave her in the car. I lifted her out, ignored the grizzling and she sagged onto my shoulder. I was going to have to do some weightlifting to get used to carrying her around. 'Welcome to the house of horrors, kid,' I muttered as I opened the gate and went in.

The neat rows of roses had all gone, replaced by low shrubs and mondo grass, and the concrete driveway was now sand-coloured paving. The door knocker was the same, a lion's head that had become worn over the years and smooth to touch. I used to believe that anyone knocking on the door would give the lion a headache.

I hadn't thought about what I might say to the people living in the house, but it would probably be sensible to explain about Andy and that I was the new 'landlord'. It would at least give me an excuse to look around. I rang a doorbell that hadn't been there twenty years ago and waited. Footsteps echoed inside and the door opened to reveal a small dark-haired woman, dressed in white pants and a flowered jersey-knit top. She was perfectly made up, with not a hair out of place. I felt like a country hick in my jeans and T-shirt.

'Hello,' she said cheerily, looking more at Mia than at me.

'Hi. I'm Judi Westerholme.'

'Yes?'

'My brother was managing your rental of this house? For our mother.'

'Oh yes. You do look like him. Please come in.'

She stepped back to let me pass, then showed me into the kitchen. It was still the kitchen but looked hugely different. Someone had gutted it and extended outwards to double the size of the working area and cupboards, plus add a tiled area for a kitchen table and chairs. Beyond that, sliding doors opened out onto a terrace and the back garden. My mother's wooden cupboard doors had all been replaced by pale cream versions with metal rod handles. I could almost believe I'd never lived here.

'Wow,' I said. 'This is different.' She raised her eyebrows at me. 'It's been a long time since I've been here.'

She shrugged. 'It was like this when we moved in. Would you like some coffee? Juice for your little girl?'

'Thanks, that'd be great.' Mia had woken up properly and I put her down, keeping hold of her hand. My feet took me to the sliding doors and I gazed out at the back yard. The apricot tree was still in the corner, looking old and gnarled, but the lemon tree was gone, and so was the veggie garden. Where the lemon tree had been was now paved, so there was no hope of digging that up.

I pressed my lips together hard – I wasn't giving up yet. There was something here for me, I knew it.

The woman put a plastic glass of orange juice on the table and I sat Mia on a chair and helped her to drink some of it. 'Would she like a snack?' the woman asked.

'Sure. Thank you.' Mia tucked into the plate full of apple slices and crackers like she hadn't been fed for weeks. I'd have to start carrying a food supply with me.

After pouring our coffee, the woman said, 'Is there a problem with the rental agreement?'

'No, not at all,' I said. 'I just wanted to let you know that my brother... passed away last week.' I hated the euphemism but I didn't want to upset her. 'Nothing will change. I presume you like the house, it suits you?'

'Yes, my husband is a banker and we are here for another two years or more, so this is an excellent house for us. I have only one child, a boy.'

I nodded and drank from my cup, breathing in the aroma. 'I'm here because I wondered if my brother had left anything in the house or garage, stored any belongings of any kind?' I held my breath.

'Only some things in the garage.' She smiled. 'A couple of boxes of books and photos, he said, and some tools. He was planning to come and collect them soon.'

'I can take care of that instead.' It was close, I felt it. A buzz ran through my veins, and I focused on helping Mia drink more juice while I tried to stay calm. 'I'll take it all today, if you like. What I can fit in the car.'

'Of course.' She smiled and offered me a plate of chocolate biscuits with both hands.

I took one and bit into it, savouring the rush of sugar. What with that and the caffeine and finding Andy's stuff, I could go out right that minute and run a marathon, I was so wired up. She'd said tools. That had to mean a toolbox, surely. *Don't assume – you've been wrong before*. But I couldn't help myself.

After some chat about the weather and her son's school and a leaking tap in the laundry that I promised to ask the letting agent to fix, I said I'd better collect Andy's boxes and be on my way. She came with me to help, unlocking the side door to the garage and turning on the interior lights. The space was almost empty and very clean; I saw the boxes straight away, on a shelving unit at the back, and went closer. There was the toolbox, on the bottom shelf, exactly as I remembered it, with a security chain and combination lock around it. For a long moment, I felt as if my heart had seized up. I heard Dad's voice: 'Open that bloody box or else!' And Andy lying, saying, 'Sorry, Dad, I can't. I've had a brain snap and forgotten the combination.' I had to force myself to move. My last hopes had been pinned on this place, but now I could hardly believe I'd found the box.

There were no other tools around, and certainly no bolt cutters, so I carried it out as it was and put it into the boot of the Benz. The woman helped me carry out three cardboard boxes and stow them in the back seat and boot, we shook hands, I strapped Mia in and away we went. Knowing the toolbox was in the boot was like knowing I'd won Lotto. I couldn't think straight. After a couple of minutes of driving a bit erratically, I headed towards the beach and parked in an area where there was no one else near. There was nothing in the boot I could use to cut the chain, and I tried every combination of numbers I could think of for the lock. Andy's birthday, mine, Nana's, Mia's – nothing worked. Finally I gave up and called Heath, telling him about the box.

'Where are you?' he asked, excitement in his voice.

'Still near Brighton, down by the beach.'

'I don't have anything that will cut a security chain like that.' He paused, thinking. 'We need a decent-sized cutter. Can you come past my office and pick me up? I'll wait out the front.'

'OK. Wave when you see me in the distance.'

Twenty minutes later, he was in the passenger seat and we were on our way to North Melbourne. 'I know someone at the fire station near St Vinny's,' he said. 'I called him and he reckons he can help.'

The fire station was a vintage model, and the main building was probably under a historic covenant of some kind. A class of school kids in yellow polo shirts and black pants crowded into the museum next door, chattering excitedly as a fireman in full regalia, mask and all, came out to demonstrate the equipment and tell them all about being a fireman.

Heath found his mate out the back and he took us into an area where they stored bigger apparatus and spare hoses. Mia wanted to go and see what the kids were doing in the museum but I held onto her hand tightly. She wailed until I found a bunch of keys in my bag for her to play with. Heath's mate set up the contraption called the 'jaws of life' that worked off hydraulics and could cut through car bodies or prise metal apart. I was itching with impatience and was elated when the cutter snipped the chain like it was a piece of string. Heath thanked the guy who grinned and said, 'No body parts in there, are there?'

'Not likely,' Hotshot said. 'Maybe a few million dollars?'

He carried the box back to the Benz and put it in the boot. 'Aren't we going to have a look now?' I asked.

'Do you want to do it here?'

I looked around. Cars everywhere, no way to tell who was watching, even though I doubted anyone was. 'Yes. Right now.'

'Not a good idea. Let's go back to your hotel.'

I drove in silence, sulking even though I knew he was right. After a few minutes, he said, 'There's no going back once we have the video, you know.'

'I know.' I was lying. Actually, I hadn't thought beyond finding it and getting Spaz and Baldie off my back, although that was irrelevant now. 'What are you going to do with it?'

'I've been thinking about what you said – about destroying it.'

I knew what he was going to say. 'Your boss won't let you do that.'

He lapsed into silence again. In my hotel room, I changed Mia's nappy, trying not to be sick when it turned out to be a pile of disgusting poo, and turned on the TV for her. He put the toolbox on one bed, and we sat on the other bed and looked at it. 'I need a drink,' I said, reaching for the mini bar and opening it to find a half-bottle of white wine that I helped myself to. Heath grabbed a beer. We looked at the box some more.

'I've also been thinking about the other thing you said.' He picked at the label on the bottle. 'About there being a leak in our area.'

'You think I'm right?'

'Maybe. I went back through the unsolved files and found the murders your brother talked about. It was Santos's brother got killed, all right, and it went down as a drug deal gone wrong. No suspects. A few people interviewed, but none of them was Andy.'

'So he really was free and clear on it.'

'Yeah. Trouble is, although the other guy was a lowlife with some pretty desperate customers, the main man killed was a Santos. Titch is into payback, like most of them, and he's still around. He's got a long, obsessive memory. If this video is what Andy said it was and it gets out, it will probably start another round of killings. Christ, as if there haven't been enough.'

'It's already started,' I pointed out. 'Castella and Sands.'

'Yeah. And who knew they were involved?'

'Me. And you. And your boss, you said.'

'Mm. And a few others.' He tapped the toolbox. 'OK, let's do it.'

He reached out and undid the hasps on the box, then slowly lifted the lid. I let him do the whole thing – push the lid back, lift out a grease-stained shirt, two tattered car repair manuals and a packet of replacement wiper blades.

'Shit,' he said. 'It's not here.'

29

'What?' I said. 'It must be.'

Heath looked grim, shaking his head. I grabbed the box and shook it, checked for a false bottom, went through everything he'd taken out. 'I don't believe it. All this time I've been looking for the box and the video's not even in it.'

'A memory card is pretty small. Still, it's definitely not here.' He shook the stained shirt again. 'Maybe he did destroy it in the end. It could've been the last thing he did.' Heath finished off his beer in three long swallows, and checked his phone for missed calls and texts, tapping out replies.

I sat next to the box, seething, thinking if Andy had been there I would've strangled him. What the hell had this stupid goose chase been about then?

'How will we ever know whether the memory card even exists?' I said. 'I mean, he could've lied all along about filming those murders. He could've bought the camera and pretended he was using it. He might've thought it would be leverage, if he ever got into trouble.'

'He died, Judi. Castella and Sands either knew or believed a hundred per cent that he had it.'

'I thought he might've buried it, at our old house.' I told him about the plastic toys, and the lemon tree.

'Why did we ever think it was in the toolbox?' Heath asked.

'He said so on his audio tape... no, hang on, he didn't.' The tape was in my bag. I didn't want to have to go downstairs and use the player in the Benz to listen to it again, but I would if I had to. 'He just explained what the footage was of, and how those guys were after it.'

'So...'

'It was Baldie, when they came to the house. He kept demanding I give him the toolbox, and that's what they took in exchange for Mia.'

'And we put two and two together and got fifteen.'

'Not really.' He'd better not be trying to blame me for jumping to the wrong conclusion. 'Baldie and – I mean Sands and Castella obviously totally believed the video was in that box. Maybe Leigh told them. Or even Andy, to trick them. Maybe he *was* keeping it hidden in there at one point.'

'And then he hid it somewhere else, because he suspected she'd told them.' The furrows on his face deepened. 'Maybe it's in the local tip.'

'No. I think he really did leave it somewhere for me. That's what the audio tape was all about – explaining it. He must've known they wouldn't give up, and he sure thought it was likely he'd cop it, otherwise he wouldn't have organised his will and all that stuff with the solicitor.'

'Back to square one, then,' he said. 'I just can't help worrying that those two bastards told someone else. You really think it could be buried in your mother's old back yard?'

'Possibly. Are you going to dig it up?'

'Not me. But if I put this all together, I can persuade the task force guys to do it, as part of their gangland investigations. They've got ground-penetrating radar that can tell whether the ground's been disturbed recently, although in garden soil...' He put out his hand. 'Can I have the audio tape?'

I didn't want to give it to him – it was the only thing I had of Andy's voice. 'Are you going to give it back?'

'Of course. I'll make a copy and get it back to you as soon as I can. I should have done it before.'

'How will you find out if anyone else is after the video?'

'One of our informants might have heard something. If it's Santos, he's not known for his subtlety.' He turned the audio cassette over and over. 'Let's hope nobody else knows. I think we're fairly sure Andy didn't spread it around.'

'This all started with the money he owed back then.' Mia had stood up and was whacking her frog against the TV screen. 'Mia. There's only one green frog on telly and yours isn't it.' She turned at my voice and came over, wanting to be picked up, so I obliged. 'Maybe if I'd given him the money, none of this would've happened.' I hugged Mia, trying to dispel the guilt that clung to me like sludge.

'You're not to blame. It doesn't sound like he knew what he was doing back then. It probably wouldn't have made any difference.' He stood up and put the tape in his pocket. 'You should think about witness protection, or an interstate holiday for a couple of months, just in case.'

'No thanks. There's a big difference between choosing to live out in the sticks and being forced to run away to somewhere remote.' I looked at the toolbox sitting innocently on the bed. 'I think this is it. It's got to be over now.'

'I'm going to organise protection anyway, someone to stay with both of you for the next few days.' He mustered up a smile. 'You never know, we might find that video tomorrow and it'll really all be over.'

'Protection? What does that mean?' I imagined a weightlifter with several guns stacked under his armpits following me around.

'It means I'll have peace of mind. And you still haven't given a statement to Kidd – you'll have to do that tomorrow. Promise me.'

'Yes, I will.'

'Look, I need to take those toys you told me about, too.'

'They're in the Benz.'

'They'll help me explain it.' He half-shrugged.

'Otherwise the boys in blue will laugh and tell you about Thomas the Tank Engine?' I could see how it might all sound pretty pathetic. Kids playing detective, burying treasure...

'Sort of.' He took my keys and went down in the lift, after telling me not to open the door unless I knew it was him. I waited, and he shortly returned with the envelope. 'Your brother had a strange sense of humour,' he said, tipping the toys and brooch out and grabbing them up before Mia could get her hands on them. He peered into the envelope. 'Did you know there was a letter in here as well?'

'No.' I put her on the floor and took the envelope he offered. 'It's not a clue, is it?'

'No, it's addressed to Mia. But he says it's up to you to decide when to give it to her.'

'Oh, great.' My heart lurched. That sounded like a goodbye letter. He ruffled her hair. 'Might be a few years before she'll be old enough to read it.'

I nodded.

'Right.' His phone pinged again and he read the text. 'Constable Merrick will be here at 7am. You can't go home until she arrives, all right?'

I locked the door after him and put the toolbox in the wardrobe. After dinner I called Connor, feeling guilty that I'd left him in the dark for so long. But it still seemed impossible to tell him everything by phone and deal with all of his questions. I promised myself I'd explain it all when we got home. He was so gobsmacked that I'd be returning with a two-year-old that he barely asked about anything else.

I slept seven hours straight, and felt a million times better for it when a knock at the door woke us up. Mia sat up, rubbing her eyes. After checking the spyhole and then Merrick's badge, as instructed, I let her in.

'I'll have a shower and then we can have breakfast.'

'I've already had mine,' she said cheerfully, 'but I'll come with you.'

She was the athletic type, probably didn't need a gun with all the muscles she seemed to be packing. A shower improved my mood slightly, but it wasn't much fun climbing back into the same clothes I'd been wearing for three days. At breakfast, Merrick fed Mia some soggy cereal then let her have the spoon.

'She's getting the hang of it,' Merrick said. 'My little boy took ages.'

'You've got kids?'

'Yeah, just one.'

'We're going back to Ascot Vale today, aren't we?' I was determined to get out of the boxy hotel room.

'Yes, I'll follow you so I can see what's happening, and I can move faster if there's any trouble.'

'Right.' That should've made me feel better but it didn't. I kept feeling hemmed in, like I couldn't move a millimeter without someone checking what I was up to. That was what being stuck in a hotel room did for you. I gave Mia some toast and Vegemite and drank more coffee, making a mental list of things I needed to do today. That bloody statement for Kidd was one, and when I mentioned it to Merrick, she said, 'Kidd said to come in at 2pm, if that's OK.'

Christ, she was even managing my appointment book. I pushed the irritation down and tried to feel grateful that she was watching my back.

It seemed like weeks since I'd been in the house – Saturday night, to be exact, which meant the window was still broken. Someone, presumably a cop, had taped cardboard over it. Amazingly, no one had broken in and stripped the place clean. I rang a window company and managed to persuade them to come within two hours, and vacuumed up the last of the glass before they arrived. I didn't need Mia standing on it.

The house was tidy, but I tidied it again, vacuumed the rest of it, went through Andy's papers again, looked in his and Leigh's wardrobe, wondering what to do with the clothes. I washed and dried my and Mia's clothes, and Merrick helped me get Mia started on potty training, of all things. Mia, of course, did nothing of interest but she wanted to put the potty away in the bathroom cupboard. In her enthusiasm, she jammed her fingers in the cupboard door. Her screams nearly pierced my eardrums, and tears rolled down her face. I stood uselessly in the doorway for a few seconds, then squatted in front of Mia and gathered her into my arms. The screams dropped down into sobs, thank God.

'Hey, Mia, it's OK. Show me your hand.' She stuck her arm out like she wanted her whole hand to just disappear into outer space, and I could relate to that. The skin wasn't broken but she'd have a nice line of bruising. 'Want me to kiss it better?' I offered, thinking she'd probably say no, but she nodded and held her hand up. I gave it several gentle kisses, and the tears stopped.

Squatting was awkward; I sat on the floor and gathered her on to my lap. After a few minutes, Mia seemed happy again and wanted to get up. She wandered off to find her frog, leaving me sitting on the floor, a silly grin on my face. I'd actually managed to do something right with the kid for a change.

After lunch, I put Mia down for a nap and settled on the couch to watch TV, but I felt like ants were eating at my insides. I hated being cooped up yet again, and longed to get some dirt on my hands, even if it was just weeding. It'd calm me down.

'I might do some gardening,' I said to Merrick, and headed out to the garden shed. The back garden was simple to weed, and the front garden was even easier, with tons of mulch over everything. Merrick made sure I left the front door open, and she came out every few minutes to check on me and survey the street. Every time she did it, I grew more irritable.

The front lawn was the size of a large table, but the grass was a bit long. Andy's mower was a manual job, with sharp blades that whirred around like mad bees. I pushed it up and down the lawn and finished it in a few minutes. As I breathed in the lovely tang of fresh-cut grass, Merrick came out again. 'That's what I'd like,' she said, 'something small and easy to maintain.'

I grunted a response as I used the yard broom to sweep the path. 'I'll put the kettle on,' she said, and went back inside. Over the front fence, the nature strip was scraggly too, and there were McDonalds wrappers in the grass. How that could happen when the nearest outlet was a kilometer away was beyond me. I carefully checked the street, which was quiet with no cars passing at all, then pushed the mower across the path and got started. The blades whirred loudly and grass flew into the air, then the mower jammed on a tough weed.

I cursed and bent to pull it loose, and was grabbed. One hand over my mouth, another on my upper arm like a vice, and I was shoved head first into the back seat of a car, where someone else grabbed me and pushed me down on the floor by his feet. I tried to scream for help but the guy thumped me on the back and all that came out was a feeble croak.

I didn't have a hope.

30

I struggled hard against their hands and tried to get my head up, but they were too strong. The car accelerated, slamming me back against their legs, and I banged my hip against someone's knee. Pain knifed through me, into my back and down my leg, and I couldn't breathe, falling further down between the seats, my face on a dirty Nike runner. Where the fuck was Merrick?

But she was way behind me, back at the house, inside where I should've been. At least she had Mia, and she'd call Heath and the rest of them in a few minutes. But it'd be too late. She wouldn't have seen the car. Christ, after everything else that'd happened and I had to let myself be snatched like this. Shame and anger burned through me, and I blinked back tears. *Come on, suck it up. Don't give in.*

A man in the front seat said something and I listened but couldn't make out the words. At one point we stopped and a train went past, then after a few more stops and starts, I heard a tram. It didn't help much. We could be anywhere, but my guess was Brunswick or Carlton. I tried to move, to ease the pain in my hip, but it arced down to my knee and I groaned. The guy whose foot I was resting my head on pushed a smelly travel rug under my head, which at least was better than his non-existent Odor-Eaters.

I had to think! Had to work out what was going on, who'd grabbed me. Keep an eye out for opportunities to escape. But I wasn't in some pathetic TV movie where the brave heroine seized the moment and outsmarted the villains. My hip ached so much that I'd probably manage a fast hobble if I was lucky, and having my lower legs bent upwards didn't help. Thank God I was in jeans.

The car slowed and turned, drove down a short, steep driveway into an underground garage. Were we in a hotel? A roller door rattled behind the car and everything went dark. It went darker still when the Nike guy tied a length of cloth around my head. My guts clenched and sweat broke out under my arms. I was praying it wasn't an executioner's blindfold. I didn't want to die. I didn't want to end up dumped in the weeds like Andy. Then the guy bent down near my head and said, 'When you get out, keep your mouth shut, orright?'

I nodded and hands pulled me backwards, out of the car, until I could stand. Sort of. My knees wobbled and decided to hold me up, and I shook off the hands. Surprisingly, the two men stepped away from me, although I could smell sweat and a very rank aftershave. Probably there was nowhere to run. The blindfold was crooked and I could see underneath it. From what I could tell, the garage was under a house, big enough for three cars, and the dark blue 4WD we'd arrived in was the sole occupant. A light over the exit door in the corner provided a dim glow, enough to show me I was surrounded by four men, all bigger than me, all dark-haired. Two in leather jackets, one in a soccer shirt, one in a dirty sweatshirt with *Bite Me* on the front of it. I couldn't see their faces.

Two of them took me by the upper arms and hustled me towards the door, following Mr Bite Me who pressed a button on an intercom on the wall and said, 'Yeah, we've got her.'

'Password?' said a crackly voice.

'Fuck.' He turned to the others. 'Stupid fucken password. Who the fuck else would it be?'

'Shuddup,' said one of the guys holding me. 'Just tell him Frosty, for fuck's sake.'

'Frosty,' Bite Me said, and a buzzer sounded with a lock clicking open. With the door wide open, they hustled me through it and one of them helped me up the stairs. Every time I tripped, the pain jabbed again. In the hallway, the carpet was a dirty sandy colour and didn't look like it had been vacuumed for about ten years. Someone standing in front of me held a gun down by his side. A shiny silver gun that made my guts twist.

'Where's the man?' Bite Me asked.

'He'll be here shortly. Put her in the back bedroom and tie her up good. I don't want no trouble. She been screaming?'

'When we grabbed her; not now though.'

'If she starts getting noisy, stick something in her mouth.'

'Yeah, yeah.' We trooped down the hallway and into a room where they made me lie down on a single bed with a scratchy blanket on it. I was hoping they'd tie my hands in front, but they yanked them behind my back and tightened a thin plastic strip around my wrists. 'Jesus,' I muttered, 'does it have to be so tight?'

'Shuddup.'

My fingers started swelling up and I knew they'd only get worse so I tried to push my hands closer together without much success. Maybe if I was double-jointed I'd have more luck. Another one went around my ankles then they left me alone. I tilted my head back as far as I could and saw the door had been almost closed. There was no other furniture in the room, and bars outside the window. I was well and truly stuffed.

Up until now, I'd been silently cursing myself and them and Heath, staying angry, listening for any clue as to who they were or how I might get out of this. Now, alone on the smelly bed, I sobbed quietly, hot tears soaking the cloth over my eyes. This had to be about the video and I didn't have it. Maybe the cops had it by now. It didn't make any difference. Andy hadn't had it either, but he still died, left in a pile of rubbish down by the river. It obviously hadn't mattered what he'd promised them, they killed him anyway.

After a few minutes of bawling self-pity, I stopped and took a few deep breaths, and sniffed hard, unable to blow my nose. Spaz and Baldie must have told someone and now I was in deep shit.

So who were these guys? Heath had said there were two rival gangs of thugs who were most likely to be involved, run by Santos or Nash. I wished I'd paid more attention instead of scoffing at his underworld stories.

What saliva I had left had turned gluey in my mouth and I coughed, trying not to move too much and make the ties cut in more. The room was growing darker – I'd been here a while. Was Heath looking for me? Was Merrick looking after Mia? That made me want to cry again, and I bit my lip. Fat lot of good I was to the kid. All the promises I'd made to myself about doing the right thing had evaporated. God, if I ever got to see her again, I'd do a bloody sight better job next time.

I turned slightly, trying to get more comfortable, but my arms and hands were seizing up. Plus I needed to go to the toilet. My bladder ached fiercely and no way was I going to pee my pants, lying here.

'Hey! You guys! Hey!' I shouted as loudly as I could.

Footsteps and the door swung open. 'What?'

'I need to go to the toilet. Now. I'm desperate.'

'Ah, shit. Hang on.'

'Hurry!'

He walked away and came back a few seconds later with two more of them. One of them took the cloth off my eyes. It was Bite Me. His black hair was cut close and neat, with two exactly even sideburns, and two white scars criss-crossed his chin. The second guy said, 'Why'd you do that? She can identify us.'

'She wouldn't want to try,' Bite Me said. He cocked a finger and put it to my head. 'Or she'd be sorry.'

I jerked my head away from his finger and he sniggered. The first guy opened a flick knife and cut the tie around my ankles, then Bite Me hauled me upright and dragged me down the hallway to the bathroom. The toilet was in the corner, next to the shower. 'You – watch her,' he said to the others.

'Watch me? I can't pee with you watching,' I said.

'Piss in your pants then,' Bite Me said, and walked away.

I stared at the two guys who shrugged. 'He's the boss,' one said. 'We gotta stay here while you do it.'

'I can't even get my jeans down unless you release my hands,' I said.

They whispered to each other, glancing at me. I jiggled on the spot, making it clear I needed to pee very soon. The one with the knife came over and cut the tie. The blood roared back into my hands and the pins and needles burned like acid. I held my wrists under warm water from the tap for a few minutes, waiting to see if they'd leave, but they lounged against the doorway. 'Come on,' one said. 'Have your piss. I'm missing my TV show.'

'What? *Neighbours*?'

'No, *The Simpsons*, smart bitch.'

'You could at least turn your heads,' I said, and grudgingly they did. It took a bit of effort to unbutton my jeans and get the zip down, but finally I could sit and let go. The relief made me feel dizzy for a few seconds, and I checked they were still turned away before I stood up.

Someone out in the hallway said, 'She finished yet? The man is here.'

'Yeah. Typical sheila.' He wouldn't let me wash my hands; I was pulled out of the bathroom and pushed down the hallway towards the front of the house. We passed a kitchen, benches piled high with dirty dishes and pizza boxes left open with cold slices congealing on the cardboard. The lounge room was large and gloomy, the curtains closed and a damp, grimy smell of sweat and dust made my throat close up. The cream vinyl lounge suite looked like someone had been slashing it with a knife and stuffing popped out here and there.

I was pushed down on to a dining chair and my hands pulled behind my back. It hurt like hell. 'Ow, do you have to?' I tried to lean away from them and Bite Me slapped the side of my head hard enough to make my vision blur, but at least he let my hands go.

'That's enough,' someone said behind me. 'She's not going anywhere.'

I twisted my head around to see who was talking. No one I recognised. This guy was short and had a pointy head and a little bullet nose. He was thinning on top but there was plenty of hair sprouting out of his V-neck shirt. He was mercifully free of heavy gold bling, but his clothing looked expensive and well cut. He walked around in front of me and sat on another chair, crossing his legs and lighting up a cigarette while he watched me closely. I kept my head up and stared back.

'Ms Westerholme, I believe.'

I didn't answer. He was like a fat little snake, waiting to strike.

'No need to be shy. We're all friends here.'

I blinked a couple of times.

'Your brother used to be one of my boys.'

'I doubt it.'

'Why? Because he went straight for a while? Didn't do him much good, did it?'

I tried to push my fury down to somewhere it wouldn't get me into trouble. 'That was your fault, was it?'

He held up both hands, the cigarette smoke curling upwards around his fingers. 'Hey, you can't pin that on me. Andy was trying to be too clever. Doesn't pay.'

'I guess not, when you're dealing with bozos.'

He pursed his lips. 'That's not very nice.'

'I don't have much reason to be nice.' I was glad my voice was coming out snappy and sharp, because my stomach was a writhing mess.

'I was supposed to receive an important package tonight,' he said. 'But something happened to my delivery boys. You know anything about that?'

'Castella and Sands? Only that the cops found them dead.' My brain whizzed around, working through what he said. If he didn't kill Baldie and Spaz, who did?

'The cops,' he mused. 'Good friends of yours, I hear. Looking after you... sometimes.'

I stayed silent on that one.

'So you still have my package. I have to come direct to the source. That's not convenient to me.'

Who was this guy? It had to be Titch Santos. He sounded like something out of a 50s gangster movie, a bad one. 'I don't have it.'

'I don't believe you. I am one hundred per cent certain that you know where it is.'

'The cops went out to dig it up this morning. They have it.' At least, I hoped they had it. If they didn't, I was in deep shit.

'No, they don't. They didn't find a thing under all those roses and paving stones.'

How the hell did he know about that? 'That's not my problem. If it wasn't where I said it was, well...'

'You've been given clues. So now you will tell me where they lead.' He nodded to Bite Me who, before I could register what was happening, grabbed my left hand and bent back my little finger in one swift jerk. I heard a crack and then the pain rushed in, far worse than the stabbing I'd had. This was like my hand was on fire. I clutched it to me, cradling it, cursing, crying, but nothing helped. Bite Me grabbed me by the hair and wrenched my head up. Santos leaned in towards me, his breath stinking of garlic and whiskey. 'Want to tell me yet?'

'I – don't – know, damn it.'

Bite Me hooked his arm around my neck from behind and half-lifted me off the chair, choking me. I gasped, trying to pull his arm down with my one good hand, but he was like a wrestler, immovable. A second later, he let go and dumped me back on the chair. I didn't know whether to rub my throat or protect my hand again. I went for my hand, whispering, 'Fuck you, fuck you,' under my breath.

'You've got guts, Ms Westerholme. I could've let him kill you. A quick snap around and bang – broken neck. Nice and quiet.' Santos sat back.

'Yeah, whatever,' I said, no longer willing to confront his ugly gloating face.

'I want that video, and I will have it. I have a great need to avenge my brother. So speak up, or my boys will go and get your niece again. And this time, you won't be playing any cunning little tricks to get her back.' He stood up. 'I'll let you think about it for a few minutes.'

Behind me, a mobile phone rang, singing a jangly version of 'Für Elise'. It was the guy who watched me in the bathroom who answered it. 'Yeah?'

A short, loud explosion of words on the other end.

'Right. I'll tell Mr Santos.'

'What?' said Santos.

'Vuko's been ambushed. Him and Mars are holding them off.'

'Fuck,' Santos said. 'Is it cops? I'm not getting into it if it is.'

'Nah. He reckons it's the Lebbos from Campbellfield.'

Santos hesitated, and Bite Me picked a gun up from a table by the couch. The weapon was huge and gleamed dully, like it was made out of thick plastic. These guys casually carried guns around like they were handbags. 'We gotta go,' Bite Me said.

'Yeah, yeah.' Santos wasn't happy about going, but he didn't want to let Bite Me run the show. 'Connie!' Santos bellowed.

A young guy in his late teens, white pimples peppering his oily face, came out of the kitchen, a piece of half-eaten cold pizza in his hand. 'Yeah?'

'You stay here, watch her.' Santos pointed at me. 'If she gives you trouble, belt her. Better yet, tie her up again.'

'Me?' Connie squeaked, but the others were already halfway out the door, heading down to the garage. In the silence left behind, the roller door below rumbled up and the 4WD revved a few times before roaring up to the street and away.

Connie took a bite of his pizza and chewed, mouth half-open, tomato sauce dribbling down his chin. He edged towards me as if he thought I was going to leap on him and give him a good thumping, but my hand hurt so much, I wasn't about to attack anyone.

'Oh for God's sake,' I said, 'I'm not going anywhere.'

'You might. And then Mr Santos would make sure I was very sorry I didn't do what he said.' He picked up a plastic tie from a packet on the breakfast bar.

'Can I have some pizza first? I'm starving. And I need some painkillers.'

He hesitated. 'I dunno.'

'Can I go in the kitchen and look? Please?' I used my most wheedling, pathetic voice.

'I guess so.' He went into the hallway and checked the locks while I tried to decide between extra meat and salami, and bacon and egg. Neither one was very appetising but I was hungry. I went for the meat option, one-handed, still cradling my hand. The finger was either broken or sprained, I wasn't sure which, but the pain wasn't subsiding at all. I started opening drawers and cupboard doors, hunting for a clean glass and some painkillers.

'Whaddya doing now?' Connie asked.

'I want a glass so I can have a drink, and everything on the bench looks like it's harbouring a dose of bubonic plague,' I said. I found some wineglasses in a top cupboard, and then a packet of ibuprofen in with the rubbish bags and kitchen foil. In the fridge, there was nothing but beer and cola, but I spotted a bottle of brandy in another cupboard and poured myself a liberal dose, using it to wash down four pills. Connie was still in the doorway, watching my every move.

'Hurry up, they'll be back in a minute,' he said.

'No, they won't. Besides, we'll hear the garage door, won't we?'

I wondered if I could stand to eat another slice of cold, congealed pizza. It might be the last food I'd get for a while. I reached for another piece.

'Come on!' Connie said, jiggling on the spot. 'I have to tie you up again.'

I ignored him, drinking more brandy, savouring the instant warmth in my stomach. He went up the hallway and I scanned the room for a phone, ready to risk dialling, even if I didn't get to speak, but he came back, waving a gun around. He looked awkward and amateurish, and I stepped back, wary. 'You have to go in there and sit down now.'

I heard a tremor in his voice. 'You had a broken finger recently?' I asked. 'No, thought not. There is no way you are tying my hands up again.'

'I'll b-bloody shoot you,' he said.

The doorbell rang, a loud ding-dong that made us both jump.

'See, they're back and you've got me in trouble,' he yelled. 'Get in there!' He waved the gun at the lounge room and I thought I'd better at least sit down otherwise I'd probably cop a fist as well. I lowered myself on to the chair and waited. The doorbell rang again.

'Shit. Fuck.' Connie fumbled with the locks, and only remembered the vital part at the last moment. 'What's the password?'

The door burst open, slamming back against the wall, and a tall red-haired guy in an Army jacket shoved a gun against Connie's head. 'Fucking let me in. Will that do ya?'

31

I stayed where I was, not sure what was going on. I didn't want to get involved in anyone else's fight, and it was obvious these weren't Santos's guys. Connie slid down the wall to the floor, the redhead's gun following him down. 'I'm dead, I'm fucking dead,' he wailed.

'Yeah, you will be if you don't tell me where the woman is.'

I had about two seconds to hide under the table but I had no hope of moving that fast. Another guy with a shiny shaved skull saw me hunched down on the chair. 'She's in here.'

Were these cops? Had Heath found out where I was? But these two looked familiar. Where the hell had I seen them before? Andy's funeral. Oh, shit.

'Right,' said the redhead. 'Let's get the fuck out of here.'

Mr Shiny hauled me up off the chair and I cried out, 'Watch my hand!'

He peered down at the swollen finger and whistled. 'That's gotta hurt. Come on.'

Redhead bent down and punched Connie, hooking up under his chin. The boy was lifted off the floor with the force of the blow then slumped back down, unconscious. Outside, two more men waited on the steps. When we emerged, they turned and ran down to a 4WD sitting at the kerb and leapt in. Redhead and Mr Shiny headed towards another one further back, shoving me in the back seat alongside another guy who looked about the same shape as a chest freezer. He never said a word, just pointed at my seatbelt. I lifted up my bad hand and pointed at that and he grunted, leaning across and buckling me in.

We took off down the street behind the other 4WD and lurched around the corner. I recognised the street – we were in North Carlton, heading towards the cemetery, and in a few minutes we'd reached the Eastern Freeway. The Freezer leant over and tied a large, dark green hanky around my eyes and I smelled laundry soap. At least it was clean.

Being blindfolded again seemed to allow my brain to start working. This was another crowd of guys who all carried deadly looking guns and waved them around like they'd shoot you in a heartbeat. I'd been kidnapped by Santos, and grabbed – not rescued – by another gang, who presumably also wanted the video. Bloody thing. How I wished Andy had destroyed it.

These guys belonged to Gnasher. Nobody seemed to care if I saw their faces, but they didn't want me knowing where we were going. I held my hand close to my chest, the throbbing pain like fire. We were on the freeway for a while and when we left it, I guessed we were near Blackburn. Not a suburb I knew at all well. A short while later, we slowed, turned and stopped, then reversed, probably up a driveway. My door opened and I cringed away from it, but someone helped me out, leading me inside, and I was pushed down on to a low, squashy couch.

I heard muttering and shuffling, some kind of strident rap music that was shut off pretty quickly, and then a TV in the next room went on. The painkillers were finally taking the edge off the pain. Exhaustion crept over me, heavy and thick, and I stopped trying to think ahead, work it out, come up with an escape plan. My body leaned sideways until I lay on the couch, legs tucked up, and drifted off to an uneasy sleep. A couple of times, a door slamming woke me with a start, but the room was warm and they left me alone for ages.

Suddenly, hands pulled me upright and someone adjusted the blindfold to make sure I couldn't see. Footsteps, muffled by the carpet, stopped in front of me. 'Ms Westerholme, I'm sorry it's come to this.'

I stayed silent. Was this Graeme Nash? I tried to remember his voice, but my heartbeat had speeded up so much I could hardly

breathe. I didn't like this – being allowed to sleep and then confronted so politely. A bashing was more predictable.

'I need some information from you. I hope you will cooperate.'
Yes, it was Nash.

'I don't have it,' I said flatly.

'I know. Aren't you pleased we rescued you?'

'You might turn out to be worse.'

He laughed politely and my skin crawled. This guy wasn't the
threatening, blustering kind. I kept my mouth shut.

'Your brother was playing a losing game, and now he's passed the
ball to you.'

'So you're a footy fan,' I said.

'All my life.' He coughed, and it sounded like ball bearings
rattling in a tin. 'Where is the video?'

'I don't know. I wish I did. Then I could get you guys out of my
life. Maybe the police have it.'

'No, they don't. I need for you to handball it to me. It will save
everyone a lot of trouble if you do as I ask.'

Ask. That was a joke. 'I've said it a hundred times and I'll say it
again – I don't have it. And I don't know where he hid it. I've looked
in every possible place. I think he destroyed it.'

'No, I don't think so.' His voice hardened to steel. 'I'm prepared
to torture you to get it.'

My stomach lurched and for a moment I thought I was going to
vomit. I swallowed several times, forcing it back down. 'I can't give
you what I don't have, for Christ's sake!'

He paused for a few seconds. 'All right, I believe you that you
don't have it yet. But I think you will find it, sooner or later. I want it
to be sooner.'

I groaned. Why wouldn't he listen? I'd tried everything!

'Your niece is very cute,' he said.

'Leave her out of it.'

'I will, on one condition. You keep looking for that video, and give it to me as soon as you find it. Or she'll suffer.' He laughed softly. 'Kiddie's legs break so easily at that age, don't they?'

I shook my head, my eyes burning, my brain showing me what I didn't want to see – Mia in pain, screaming, her legs twisted. Shit!

'You have such a nice little country home,' Gnasher said. 'But you won't be safe anywhere and neither will she. Am I clear?'

I nodded, because my mouth wouldn't work.

'So this is what will happen.' He was all businesslike now. 'I will give you a mobile phone number. It's not traceable so don't even think about giving it to the jacks. I'll have someone watching you. When you find the video, you'll ring that number and someone will come and collect it. If you tell the jacks, your niece will die. Do you understand?'

'Yes,' I whispered.

'My men will take you back into the city and drop you off. I will wait to hear from you.'

'The cops will want to know what happened. They'll hassle me if I don't tell them.' I couldn't face lying to Heath, that was the problem.

'You can tell them all about Santos and his men. We'll even give you the address of where you were held.' He sighed. 'You were lucky. They left the back door unlocked and you escaped. You make up a believable story. Or else. It's your niece's life at risk here, so don't you forget it.'

I was hustled out of the house into the 4WD and driven back along the freeway. I could tell it was still night time, but when they dumped me by the steps of Parliament House in Spring Street, and I finally got the blindfold off, dawn was breaking between the skyscrapers. The 4WD was nowhere in sight. I was alone. I was alive. Despite everything, I felt clean, clear joy blossom inside me. I was seeing the sunrise. I'd never take it for granted again.

In my pocket was a slip of paper with a phone number on it. I shoved it right to the bottom.

I waited for a few minutes until a taxi cruised along the other side of the street and waved – the driver spotted me and did a U-turn. As I got in the back, he sniffed the air but the brandy must've worn off and he decided I was worth the risk. He didn't know I had no money so thank goodness the pay-before-you-ride curfew had ended. When we pulled up outside Mrs Jones's house, I said, 'My grandma has my wallet. I have to go inside and get it.'

'Blutty hell,' he said. 'I am coming with you then.'

I prayed Mrs Jones was up with the birds, and she was, her small, wrinkled face filled with concern. 'Yes, of course I can lend you thirty dollars, dear,' she said. The taxi driver hmphed but went away happy.

'Can I have that spare set of keys, please?' I asked her.

'Of course,' she said. 'But what on earth happened to your hand?'

I said I'd tripped and fallen, bending the finger back when I hit the ground, which she accepted as the truth. Maybe she thought I'd been out all night partying, and had fallen over drunk. One day I might tell her what really happened.

I was desperate to get into my house and check if Mia was there, if she was safe, if Merrick was looking after her. I unlocked my front door and walked through, ready to say hello and tell my story, but the house was empty. I felt crushed and panicky at the same time. If she wasn't being looked after by the police... if they'd put her into care. Surely I could trust Heath to take care of her.

I badly wanted to lie down and sleep; the bed called me like a siren, but I had to know where Mia was. I picked up the phone and carried it over to the French doors, opening the curtains and gazing out into the tidy garden.

Gnasher's words echoed in my brain. It was crucial that I find the video, now more than ever. Next to the deadly Graeme Nash, Baldie and Spaz looked like rank amateurs. The clues trickled through my mind – the storage unit, the photos, the audio tape, the toolbox, the spade. If the police hadn't found the memory card at Mum's house, maybe it was here after all. Andy seemed to like gardening – the neat shrubs and flaxes, the mulch, the paving and the garden seat down the end all shouted green thumb. That was one thing we had in common. I hoped my potatoes hadn't grown too much or the new orbs would be turning green in the light.

I debated with myself. My finger was screaming at me, the side of my face also ached now where Bite Me had belted me, and Heath probably thought I was dead. Mia possibly hadn't noticed I was missing yet. I knew there were people waiting desperately to hear from me.

An early morning breeze ruffled the flax and the young eucalypts over the back fence swayed. My good hand flexed, I watched the plants ripple, counted how many holes I would have to dig.

The decision was tearing me in half but I had to choose. I swallowed four painkillers and went out to the garden shed, pulling out a fork, a trowel and a garden broom. I started by the decking and worked my way along, using the fork to lever up the soil and the trowel to dig down if I hit anything lumpy. A few centimetres at a time, all the way to the back, each side of the garden seat, and down the other fence. Then I swept up all the mulch and put it back on the garden.

My hopes had nosedived yet again, but I was satisfied that the video wasn't in Andy's garden. Now I could find out where Mia was.

I would have to call Heath. I steeled myself for the inevitable shouting.

32

Heath answered his mobile before the second ring. 'Heath.'

'It's Judi.'

Long, husky breath out. 'Where are you?'

'Home. Andy's house. I'm OK, apart from a possible broken finger.'

'You need to get it looked at. How did it happen?'

'I'm going to the doctor's shortly. Where's Mia?'

'What happened?' His voice was rising.

'In a minute. Where's Mia?'

'She's safe. She's with Merrick. Who, by the way, is in deep shit.'

'What for?'

'Letting you get taken.'

'Oh, for...' I cleared my throat. 'It wasn't her fault. I'll swear it on... *The Art of War.* She couldn't have stopped them and protected Mia at the same time. I shouldn't have been out the front, but they would have just broken into the house.'

He cleared his throat, breathed out. 'Yeah, maybe. Who was it?'

'Santos.' I told my story, the one I'd carefully worked out, hoping he'd accept it as it was.

'How do you know it was Santos?'

'The men called him by name.' I was trying to work out where Heath was – not in the office. At home, or in his car. 'Are you alone?'

'What do you mean?'

'Are you at work?'

'No, I'm sitting in my kitchen.'

'Right. Well, you need to know that Santos knew all about you guys digging up Mum's garden and not finding the video.'

'What?'

I held the phone away from my ear until the shouting stopped. 'He told me he had good information.'

'I can't believe it.'

'You got any more bright ideas about where the video is, you'd better keep them to yourself.' I leaned against a chair without thinking and agonising pain seared through my whole hand; I held back a moan, biting my lip, and sat on the couch, nursing my hand and blinking back tears. 'I really need to go to the doctor's.'

'What's the matter? Do you want me to come and get you? Take you to emergency? I can get you in faster.'

I smiled. That'd be right. The police probably had their own special queue. 'No thanks. It's just my finger. I'll call you when I get back. I need Merrick to bring Mia here, if that's OK.'

'Sure.' There was an awkward pause. 'I'll come around, too.'

My heart thumped alarmingly. 'You want to ask more questions?'

'No, damn it, I want to make sure you're OK.'

'Right. OK. Bye.' I hung up and sat for a few moments, a stupid grin on my face, and then I pulled myself together. I'd noticed one of those general clinics near the shopping area, so I'd try there. But first a shower and a change of clothes. Despite being as careful as I could, I still banged my hand a couple of times, which made me shriek and swear, and stand immobile for a minute until I could move again.

At the clinic, as soon as I showed the receptionist my hand, which made her shrink back and turn pale, she put me into a consulting room and a doctor came in a short while later. I lied again, told him the falling over story which made him frown but he didn't dispute it. 'I don't think it's broken,' he said. 'Probably a dislocation of the metacarpophalangeal joint. But we'll need an X-ray to be sure.'

That meant going next door and putting my hand on a plate, and then waiting while the X-ray was finished off and delivered to the doctor. While all this happened, they packed my hand in ice and gave me anti-inflammatories, which helped a fair bit. An hour later, he said, 'Yep, dislocation.' With a local anaesthetic to help, he pushed the finger back into place. No cast, just splinting to my third finger, wrapping and a sling. Wonderful. Only six weeks and it might be almost back to normal. If nothing else happened to it. I only had two hands and both of them had been in the wars now.

It was nearly lunchtime so I stopped off in the local pub on the corner, and had a double gin and tonic and a plate of hot chips to cheer myself up. The lounge bar was nearly empty but the large public bar was busy, the pool tables ignored while tradies and locals had a beer and a steak sandwich and a chat.

I called Heath on the way home and by the time I reached my front gate, he was pulling up in the Commodore with a marked police car behind him. It was Merrick in the back seat with Mia. The kid clambered out, legs and bum first, and raced down the path towards me. 'Juddy!' When she reached me, she grabbed me around both legs and held on so tight, I nearly fell over. I squatted down to her level and gave her a one-armed hug.

'Hiya, kid.' Her little arms around my neck made my throat close up. 'Good to see you're working on my name.' Merrick was standing in front of me, a sheepish look on her face.

'I'm really sorry,' she said. 'I should've been watching you, watching the street.'

I managed to stand up and held on tight to Mia's hand, but she batted at my leg and Merrick lifted her up into my arms. I gave her another hug. 'It was my fault,' I said. 'After everything that's happened, I should've known better. Should've stayed inside.' I meant what I'd said to Heath, though. If Santos's men had barged into the house, Merrick could have been badly injured or killed.

Merrick gestured at Mia. 'She missed you. I felt so awful, knowing her dad and mum were gone, and now you...' Her mouth twisted. 'I really am sorry.'

I smiled at her as Heath zeroed in on me. 'How's your hand? You look terrible.'

'Gee, thanks.' I liked the concern in his face. I held up my bandaged hand and sling. 'It's fixed now.'

He nodded. 'I've organised for the forensics boys to come back this afternoon. They should be here any minute.'

'What do you want them for?'

'I checked and we've never dug up your brother's garden, only searched the property.'

I fought to keep my face blank. 'Oh. So they're going to dig the whole place up?'

'No, no, just prod and poke and make sure the thing we're after isn't here under our noses.' He frowned. 'I set it up myself, with the boss's approval. No one else knows.'

'Except everyone who's here now,' I pointed out.

'It'll be fine,' he said frostily. 'I have it under control.'

'You go for it,' I said. *And good luck because I already know it's not there.* 'Try not to kill anything.'

He grunted. 'We need to go through what happened in detail. And this time I'll get a statement right now while I've got you in one place.'

I ducked my head, not daring an answer, gathering my thoughts for the story again. He followed me inside and got out his notebook. I had plenty to tell him about Santos and Bite Me and the house, and I'd already worked out the timing so I wouldn't leave any holes. I doubted anyone in Santos's mob would admit any of it, so they weren't likely to dispute what I said.

The phone and the piece of paper with Gnasher's phone number on it was now buried deep in a side pocket in my bag, but it was as if there were a huge neon sign above my head, shouting, *She's not telling you everything!* I had to keep my mouth shut about Gnasher, and I had to find the video, and I had to do it alone. There was a leak in Heath's area, and given that both Santos and Nash knew about the video not being found, it was even possible there were two of them. A scary thought. And another thing I couldn't tell Heath yet.

It was vital that I kept him out of the loop on Nash and forged on on my own.

The solution felt close for some reason. Maybe it was because I'd been out of action for a day and I thought I could now see things with new eyes. Or maybe my brain had had a wake-up call with the pain in my hand and had decided to work harder. Either way, I wanted to get rid of Heath and Merrick and everyone else, and just think without distractions.

'Merrick is going to stay with you,' Heath said. 'Then someone else will take over at eight.'

'I don't want anyone,' I said. 'I've had enough.'

'What if Santos comes and attacks you again?'

'You really think he'll try?' I shook my head, knowing I couldn't explain. 'I assume you guys are searching that house right now and are after them.'

'Well... yes.' Heath tapped his fingers on his notebook. 'But he won't give up, you know.'

'I'll be fine – as long as you lot do your job. Please don't waste Merrick's time by making her stay here.' I smiled at her. 'Let's face it, they had me and couldn't get what they wanted. I made it really clear that I didn't know where the video was, and it's caused them more trouble than they expected. He'll lay low for a while.'

'You don't know that,' he argued.

Yes, I do. Gnasher will take care of it. 'I'm sure enough that I don't want any more protection. Probably tomorrow, I'll pack up and go home. We'll be fine up there.'

'You're going back to Candlebark?' He seemed more upset about that than anything.

'I need to go back to my own place and chill out for a while. The past week has been... a bloody nightmare, to be honest.' I glanced over at Mia who was lying on the couch with her frog, watching TV. 'Mia and I need time alone to get to know each other. I need time to read some child-raising books!'

His mouth thinned into a grim line. 'Right then,' he said briskly, and stood up. 'I'll sort out the forensics boys and leave you alone.'

'I didn't mean you –' But he was gone, pulling out his mobile to make a call and closing the front door after him.

'Shit.' I went and sat next to Mia. She cuddled in closer to me without taking her eyes off the screen. 'The first thing we'll do is buy some more books, kid. You're getting square eyes.' I focused on the TV where something that looked like a kitchen sponge pranced around in shorts. 'And some of these characters are very weird. I'm sure they're bad for you.'

Not that I was any great role model that was for sure. Maybe Connor could help.

A couple of hours later, the garden had been carefully turned over with Heath watching like a vulture from the deck, and they'd all gone home, including Merrick, still looking apologetic despite me insisting she should go.

Even Heath had left. In a bad mood. I couldn't work out if it was because they'd come up empty-handed in the garden yet again, or whether he was mad at me for wanting to leave Melbourne. He did make me promise to call him the moment I was worried about anything, and checked the window and back-door locks twice. Finally, he said, 'There'll be someone watching the house tonight. In a car. They won't bother you, all right?'

I nodded. It wasn't worth arguing about.

When I shut the front door after him, relief rushed through me. It was like being let out of prison and even while I knew that was unfair, that he'd done his best to protect me and was still trying hard, the sense of freedom made me feel ten kilos lighter. I needed to finish this thing, and I needed to do it alone, to do it my way.

I poured a glass of wine and spread everything out on the table, then added a large sheet of wrapping paper I'd found – I was using the white side for diagramming all the links, the people involved and the clues. I'd always worked better visually, although I did love my lists, and I thought it was time to give this method a try.

An hour later, I had a lovely diagram, embellished by Mia with some colourful scribbles and lines, and no solution. There were things I wasn't sure about – did Andy have another storage space perhaps? The number 20 key that he'd had in his pocket was long gone. There was no invoice or bill anywhere that I hadn't double-checked.

I got up and stretched, took more painkillers now the anaesthetic was wearing off, and gave Mia some crackers and cheese to eat. The late afternoon sun angled in through the French doors, giving that end of the room a reddish-gold glow that was warm and comforting. I opened the doors and breathed in – someone nearby, maybe Mrs Jones, had daphne or gardenias and the scent was a rich perfume. I closed my eyes. Far off, factories and traffic hummed, and the roar of a plane overhead echoed faintly.

Next door, Mrs Jones came outside to find her cat. 'Here, Mason, here, kitty kitty. Where are you, you naughty boy?' She tapped a spoon on the side of the cat-food tin. 'Come on, Mason – kitty, kitty. Dinner's waiting.' Her footsteps moved along the fence line and she kept tapping the tin. Maybe that was why he wasn't coming out. He could tell by the tap that it was a flavour he didn't like.

'There you are, you silly boy,' she cooed. 'Get out of there. That's my favourite buddleia. Don't you scratch the trunk. Shoo!' An indignant meow – the cat was caught. 'Andy planted that for me. Don't you dare dig your business holes there.'

Several things shot through my mind at once, tumbling over each other. Jesus, was I dumb or what? I called out, 'Mrs Jones, are you still there?' and raced over to the fence, climbing up on to the crossboard to pop my head above the top. 'Hello?'

She stood near her back door, cat tucked in one arm, tin in the other. 'Oh, dear, you gave me such a start.'

'I'm sorry,' I said. 'I just – did you say Andy planted things in your garden for you?'

'Yes, dear, he often helped me. We did the gardenias here, and then a couple of months ago he put in two camellias and that beautiful purple buddleia.'

'The butterfly bush.' *Old lady, spade, butterfly.*

'Yes, that's the common name,' she said. 'Just wait while I feed Mason.' She put the cat down and spooned food into his bowl, then straightened again. 'Andy loved gardening. Well, I suppose you knew that.'

'Not really. But I enjoy it, too. Were you helping him when he put the buddleia in?'

'Oh yes. When I wasn't making him cups of tea. And Vegemite sandwiches for Mia, of course.'

I had to get down from the fence – my one-armed grip was slipping. 'Can I pop in for a few minutes? I need to ask you something.'

'Of course, dear.'

A few minutes later, we were in her back sunroom and she was making sure Mia didn't annoy Mason who was growling at the thought of having his dinner disturbed. 'This might sound strange,' I said, 'but would you mind if I checked under a couple of plants in your garden?'

'Whatever for?' she said. 'If you want to take cuttings, I can lend you some secateurs.'

'No, it's not that.' I decided to be honest with her. 'I think Andy played a little trick on me. I think he buried something here for me. He did kind of tell me about it, but not where it was. I've worked out that I think it's under your buddleia.'

'Goodness.' She smiled and all her wrinkles joined up happily. 'He was such a funny boy, wasn't he? I'll get you a trowel.'

It only took a few seconds of prodding and digging before I hit something around the back of the small tree. Trying not to disturb the tree or its roots, I excavated carefully, even though I wanted to rip the tree out and dig like a maniac. My good hand shook, and I cursed that my other one was out of action. My whole body was buzzing, like I'd struck an electric fence and voltage was zipping through me. As I cleared the soil, I could see black plastic at first, then wads of tape, and I used the trowel to lever the small package out. No way to open it without a cutting knife. Andy had made sure it was both waterproof and insect-proof. I pushed the soil back into the hole and patted it down, then got to my feet, the package in my hand. It was rectangular, the size of a cigarette packet.

I felt like screaming, 'Hallelujah!'

Then I thought about what was on that video, and how my brother had died for it, left in a puddle of blood down by the river. No one had cared about him, or Mia. They'd wanted the video for power, for money, for revenge, for how they could use it to blackmail others. I wanted to find the nearest furnace and throw it in, get rid of the evil thing forever.

But I couldn't.

I had a phone call to make.

33

Mrs Jones stared at the plastic-wrapped package in my hand. 'Goodness me,' she said. 'Is it important?'

If you only knew.

'No, it's just a little box of stuff from when we were kids,' I said, lying through my teeth. 'Toys, probably.' I remembered something else that tied in. 'Did you ever take a photo of Andy and me with Nana? In her front yard?'

Her brow furrowed into a hundred wrinkles. 'I think I did. With your nana's old box Brownie. I was on my way to work and she said it might be the last time you visited for a while, so she wanted a souvenir.'

'Yes, it probably was the last,' I said. 'We moved to the other side of town.'

She grimaced. 'Your nana said your father refused to let you see her anymore. He told her she was a bad influence.'

'She told you that?' I bristled. 'That was typical of Dad. Bastard. Nana was the only good thing Andy and I had back then. I know it sounds stupid, but she was our real family, the only one who really cared. Dad and Mum – well, I don't know why they ever had kids. They made it pretty clear we weren't wanted.'

'Yes, you were supposed to have your regulation two, and they had to be perfect,' she said. 'It doesn't seem fair, does it? Your mum and dad with kids they didn't want, and me not being able to have the ones I was desperate for.'

'I'm sorry,' I said. 'I didn't mean to –'

'Don't be sorry,' she said. 'That's the way it happens, and there wasn't a darned thing anyone could do about it. It's different now. You just make sure you bring little Mia here over to visit every now and then.'

'I will.'

Back in my house, I put the package on top of the fridge and tried to ignore it while I made dinner for Mia and myself. I needed another glass of wine and some food, and then I could look at the thing without falling apart. I knew the sooner I rang Gnasher, the sooner I could get rid of it and put this whole mess behind me. That was the sensible thing to do. Let the gangland boys work the rest of it out themselves. If there were a few more put out of action, too bad. I had no reason to care about them.

The question hanging in front of me wouldn't go away: was I going to watch the film before I handed it over?

Andy had told me what was on it, so I shouldn't need to verify it was the real thing. To see what had caused several deaths, including my brother's. Watching it wouldn't lay him to rest for me. But it was always possible the video was of something else, perhaps something worse. I didn't want to think what that might be.

I'd come a long way. Rescued Mia, stood up to Santos, worked out Andy's clues, found the video – all of those things showed I was bloody stubborn, but I'd always known that. I looked across at Mia picking up peas, one by one. I was also stronger than I'd realised. It wasn't just about thick armour for myself, it was about letting her inside my defences and then protecting her. My gut was telling me that this was still unfinished business, and I must finish it once and for all, so we were safe.

I got into the bath with Mia and a pile of bubble mix, added a few ducks and plastic balls, and had a great time playing with bubbles and laughing, even though the water was only lukewarm. After she was dry and in her pyjamas, I read her three stories and put her to bed, feeling at last like I might be getting a handle on this kid thing, for today anyway.

Alone in the lounge, I cut open the package and pulled out a cigarette packet and then a wad of rag tucked inside it, shaking it open. Sure enough, a small rectangular memory card fell out on to my lap.

Something so small and innocuous and yet it had caused so much death and destruction. I worked out how to turn on Andy's small laptop – now returned by the police – pushed the card into the media slot and then clicked on the single file before I could change my mind. The screen filled with flickering and jagged silver lines, and at first I thought the card was damaged. Then it cleared and there was the carpark Andy talked about, with two street lights casting puddles of orange on to the asphalt. Only one car was visible, a dark two-door sedan that looked like maybe a Nissan with a huge tail pipe.

I jammed my finger on the Pause button, closed my eyes, thought it through again, opened my eyes and pressed Play. Andy appeared from the left, walked over to the passenger side of the car and got in. For a few long minutes, nothing happened, and I fast-forwarded the tape until another car, a white ute, pulled into the area and stopped about ten metres away.

No one moved then finally a man opened the passenger door of the ute and got out, staying behind the vehicle. Andy emerged from his car and a conversation ensued which I couldn't hear clearly until the other guy said, 'You're full of shit.' Andy bent down to listen to what his driver was saying then he went around to the boot and opened it, pulling out a dark gym bag. There was a lot of gesticulat-ing, and the driver of the ute rolled down his window and yelled, 'Stop fucking around and get it done.'

The other guy dragged a black garbage bag out of the ute and he and Andy approached each other. As they did, the driver got out. He was a young man but overweight, his stomach bulging over his belt, his face so round that the goatee looked like the tag on the bottom of a balloon. Andy's driver suddenly appeared around the bonnet of his car, almost from nowhere. He shouted, 'He has to open the bag first.'

The fat guy gave him the fingers. 'Nothing wrong with our fuck-en money, you dumb paddy.'

Andy's driver had his back to the camera so I couldn't see who he was, but I could see the gun he was holding down by his side, behind the car. The two in the middle did the 'show and tell' thing and swapped, so Andy ended up with the garbage bag. He turned and headed back to his own car to put it in the boot.

That's when his driver opened fire. The gun was eerily quiet, just a few deadly pops. I knew it was going to happen, but I still sat with my mouth open, unable to move. It happened fast and both men dropped backwards by the ute without a sound.

Andy spun around. 'What the fuck did you do that for?' He took two steps forward then stopped as if realising he might be next.

'Orders, mate. You wanna argue?'

Andy's mouth gaped like mine. I couldn't move.

'Get your fucking arse over there and pick up the gear. Hurry. Someone might've called the cops.' When Andy didn't move, the guy pointed the gun at him. 'Move it, dickhead, or you'll join them.'

Andy staggered across and picked up the gym bag, then backed away. His driver turned to get back in the car and I jerked in my seat. It was the red-haired guy who'd grabbed me from Santos's house – Gnasher's right-hand man. He gunned the motor, shouting at Andy, who half-fell into the passenger's seat. The car accelerated out of the carpark, Andy's door swinging wide for a few moments until it slammed shut.

Silence. The two bodies lay there in black pools of blood. After a few seconds, I fast-forwarded again with shaking hands until I saw Andy run across the bottom of the screen looking demented, and then the screen went black. I sat on the couch and saw it in my head, again and again and again. I blinked hard and could still see the two men lying in pools of blood. That was the price I'd pay for being nosey.

I recalled what Andy had said. The two guys shot were Santos's brother and another mate. The killer was Gnasher's boy, under his orders to take the two out and keep both drugs and money.

Out of all the gangland murders, this was one that had never been solved. There was no motive except the drugs and money and that meant it could've been anyone. No doubt the cops suspected Nash's connection but they hadn't been able to prove it. Andy had never talked and neither would the red-headed man. Santos must've guessed this tape was of his brother and revenge for family would be top of his must-do list. Nash obviously knew that. And from what I'd seen, I thought Santos was crazy enough to order a hit on Nash as payback, even if it was the last thing he did.

It was all quiet in gangland at the moment, with so many dead and more in gaol or heading there. Organised crime and drug dealing still went on, people got beaten up, big crooks and bikie gangs stashed away millions tax-free, and it looked like a few cops were still being paid off. Or maybe just one. Still, this video wasn't going to help find out who he or she was. If I handed it over to the police, it would probably get leaked. At the very least, the police would use it to go after Nash's red-haired thug, and Mia and I would be targets for revenge. No way was I going through that again.

I had no part in any of it. I wasn't a cop, I wasn't even a piss-weak vigilante. I was a woman with a murdered brother, a batty mother and a small kid to take care of. Gnasher could have his video and choke on it. I'd bet good money that he'd destroy it.

I stood up slowly, every bone in my body feeling like I'd been run over. Time to get back to my own garden at Candlebark; to show Mia what real frogs looked and sounded like; back to my long evening walks, my books, and my quiet life.

I found Gnasher's number and dialled it.

'Yeah.' It wasn't Nash but I didn't care.

'I have the video.'

Muffled voices as someone held his hand over the phone. 'Footscray Park rowing sheds. Half an hour.'

'No.'

'You don't get to say no.' It wasn't Nash speaking but I knew he was there.

'Brewster's Hotel, Union Road, public bar. And I only hand it over to the boss.' Even now, I was careful not to let on I knew who the boss was. This would be on my terms, in a public place.

More muffled talking. 'The boss says no.'

I put venom into my voice. 'Then I'll give it to the cops.'

A long pause. Muttering. 'All right. You'd better be on your own. Any cops and the kid is dead.'

'Don't be so fucking stupid.'

That shut him up. The phone went dead.

I washed my face and hands, then went next door to ask Mrs Jones to mind Mia for me while I went to see a friend. She was more than happy to. I took off my sling, put the memory card inside its cigarette packet in my bag and headed for the pub. It was the one where I'd had a G & T just that morning. That felt like a year ago. This time of night the public bar might be quieter, but it didn't really matter. Someone would give up a table to me if I asked nicely.

I couldn't spot Heath's surveillance car – maybe he hadn't been able to organise it. That didn't really matter either. They couldn't stop me going for a solo drink. The public bar at Brewster's was quieter than I expected; half a dozen regulars sat at the bar and some young guys were playing pool. I ordered a double gin and tonic and took it over to a corner table where I could keep my back to the wall and see who was coming and going. My watch said it was twenty minutes since I called, so Gnasher was on his way.

My face felt stretched tight, like canvas over a frame, and I'd developed a twitch in one eye. The gin was a bit weak but it gave me something to do with my hands although I had to keep putting the glass down in case I spilt it. I concentrated on deep breathing twenty times until I settled down.

I didn't want to think about what I was doing. It was a means to an end. A real end to the crap I'd been holding on to without realising that it was still poisoning me. When I got rid of the card, I'd see how it felt, what it left me with, what else I needed to resolve.

A few minutes later, after a greyhound race finished on Sky TV and Bob's Your Uncle had won by a head, Gnasher entered the bar, flanked by two of his men. The red-haired guy was one of them and he towered over the other two. The hair on my arms prickled and I swallowed a huge mouthful of gin, feeling it gurgle all the way down. Gnasher stared at me then muttered to his two guys, who sat at a separate table, glaring at me.

The other patrons had sensed something going on. They sat, glancing over their shoulders occasionally, and leaning in to mutter to the barman. He polished the same glass a few dozen times and kept an eye on us. Gnasher sat opposite me and nodded. 'Ms Westerholme.'

'Mr Nash.' I was relieved to hear my voice clear and unwavering.

'Let me see the video.' He sounded calm, like he was asking to see my holiday photos.

I pulled the packet out of my bag and opened it, tipping the card and a small cigarette lighter I'd found on to the table close to me, and covered them with my bandaged hand. I didn't think he'd make a grab for the card – he was too used to having people do as he wanted.

'Is it the real thing?'

'Yes.' I wasn't going to say I'd watched it. I'd deny it anyway.

'How do I know?'

'Why would I give you a fake? You'd find out as soon as you looked at it.'

He nodded. 'Hand it over then.'

'What are you going to do with it?' I was curious to see if he'd tell me, if he'd be honest. Even though I'd already made my decision.

'What do you care?'

I shrugged.

'I'll keep it safe, in case I ever need it.'

Wrong answer, buddy.

I held the card between two fingers and flicked the lighter. I knew it worked well – I'd practised. I held it close to the memory card, and it flared and burned with the nail polish remover I'd dabbed on it. As Gnasher realised what I was doing and leaned over to grab the card, I dropped it on to the cigarette packet and watched it curl and shrivel.

Gnasher's hand swept up and took me by the throat. It was like a steel vice, squeezing the tendons and veins. 'You fucking stupid bitch. What did you do that for?'

'Oy!' the barman shouted. 'I've rung the cops. You'd better leave her alone. We don't want your sort here.'

Gnasher's hand dropped.

I rubbed my throat. 'My brother died because of that fucking video. Why should I give you a reason to kill more people?'

'I wasn't going to –'

'Of course you were. It's better that it's gone. And it is gone, totally. No copies. You saw me destroy it.'

'That could be a fake. Why should I believe you?'

I looked at him with such contempt that he visibly recoiled. 'Because I'm not like you. And I never will be.' I nodded at his two thugs, who were standing, waiting for orders. 'I'd get moving if I were you.'

I expected rage or threats or a smack around the head, but Gnasher looked at me for a long moment then said, 'If that video or a copy of it ever turns up anywhere – anywhere at all – you are dead.'

The sweat trickling down my back turned icy. 'It won't,' I said.

Then he simply stood up and left. That's why he was still the boss, running things while the others were dead or in gaol. I was pretty sure he wouldn't bother me again.

I broke the shrivelled card into tiny pieces, scooped them into the packet, finished my gin and stood up. As I left, the barman called, 'You right, love?'

'Good as gold,' I said, smiling. 'Thanks for your help.'

I drove home, senses on high alert, but I saw no one. After Mrs Jones went home, I sat on the couch, the TV on, but saw nothing as I repeated the words in my head again and again. *It's over.*

34

After checking Mia was asleep, I sat out on the back deck, rugged up against the autumn chill, and toasted myself with a glass of wine. Nana's garden – Andy's garden – stretched out before me, the wooden seat at the end just a grey shadow. Nice to keep this in the family. I wondered how much of those early years with Nana Andy had remembered – enough to want to buy her house, for sure, enough good memories to make this a special place for him.

I'd put the photo of us and Nana in a frame and it sat next to me on the deck. It belonged here, not with Mum. I doubted I'd rent this house to anyone – I couldn't stand the thought of strangers leaving marks on things, filling the rooms with tacky furniture and cooking smells. I wouldn't live here. I couldn't give up my haven in Can-dlebark. But I'd use it as a weekender, keep it for Mia. One day she might be going to uni and need a house.

I laughed. Once upon a time I'd rebelled against thinking further ahead than next week, wanting nothing more than the freedom to make daily, spontaneous choices. Now I was planning years ahead, and it felt good. Burning the card hadn't magically exorcised all of my ghosts – I'd be seeing Andy's face for a long time and no doubt having flashes of Spaz and poor dead Leigh. But when I thought of Max, I felt nothing much at all – a positive sign – and somehow my mother's Alzheimer's seemed like poetic justice, so I thought one day I could let her go, too.

Knocking at the front door interrupted my meandering thoughts and I went to answer it, knowing it'd be Heath. I hadn't wanted to call him again and give him more stress, but he deserved to know what had happened. His face was drawn and eyes red-rimmed, but he was out of his usual suit and dressed in jeans and a pale green shirt. It took me a moment to process the look; he seemed like a different person in normal clothes.

'Have you had another phone call?' he asked.

'You sound exhausted,' I said. 'You want a coffee? Or a beer?'

He shook his head. 'Neither, thanks. What's the problem?'

I led him to the kitchen table where I'd put the small pile of twisted, blackened plastic fragments. He stared at it. 'Is that... the card?'

'What's left of it.'

'That could be anything. How do you know –' He stopped and fixed his gaze on my face, his mouth tightening. 'You burnt it, didn't you?'

'Yes.'

'But – it's evidence. Of a murder, for Christ's sake! You've destroyed crucial evidence.'

I thought for a moment that he was going to explode then he gripped the back of a chair and took some deep breaths, muttering something I couldn't make out.

'If you'd had the video, you couldn't have stopped the fallout. You have a leak, remember? Anyone could've made copies.'

He opened and closed his mouth a couple of times, then finally said, 'That may be true. But now no one knows, or will believe it's destroyed, except me. That doesn't get Santos and everyone else off your back.'

'I destroyed it in front of Graeme Nash. He knows.'

'You what?' he shouted, his eyes glittering.

'Don't wake Mia!' I knew he'd be angry but this was a bit excessive. Maybe he'd been under more stress than I'd realised. 'It's finished. I finished it.'

'Jesus!' He started pacing up and down the lounge room and back to the kitchen, his mouth working; probably he was trying to find something to say to me that he wasn't going to regret.

'Look, I know you're angry but it was the best thing for me to do. I can't go on living like I have been this last week, looking over my shoulder, scared out of my wits that they'll do something to Mia. Let's face it, the police force weren't going to be able to solve this one for me, or for Andy.'

He stopped pacing, and his teeth were clenched so hard he could barely get the words out. 'You had no right.'

'I had every right to protect Mia the best way I knew how.'

He went to the back door and stood staring out into the darkness for a few long minutes. I hoped he was calming down. Finally, he spoke and his voice was quieter. 'We let Tran go this afternoon. He finally told us what really happened.'

'Oh.' My legs felt suddenly wobbly and I sat down. 'He didn't kill Andy?'

'No. Castella did. Andy asked Tran to come along and back him up. He was going to tell Castella the video wasn't for sale, that he was going to destroy it.' Heath came and sat down opposite me, pushing the plastic scraps aside. 'Castella had assumed that Andy was bringing the video – he'd already put out the word that him and Sands would have it any minute – and when Andy said no, he went berserk. He threatened Andy with a gun, and then he shot him.'

I imagined Andy facing Spaz. His fear and desperation. And tried to swallow past the lump in my throat. 'Where was Tran while all this was happening?'

'Andy had made him hide behind a wall nearby, just in case. He said he felt like a coward because he didn't help Andy. After Andy was shot, he just ran for it.'

'So why did he lie and say he did it?' I was confused.

'Sands was waiting up on the road and caught Tran as he was bolting. They got to his family – said if Tran didn't confess to the murder, they'd shoot his whole family, even his grandma.'

'I can believe that.' I shivered, remembering the knife – I could still hear the sound it'd made as it went through my hand, and see the look in Spaz's eyes.

Heath poked a finger through the bits of plastic. 'What did Gnasher do when you burned the card?'

'He grabbed me by the throat, and then he... let me go. And he went home.'

'Not very happily, I bet.' He smiled a small rueful smile, just enough to let me know I was almost forgiven.

We sat in silence for a few long moments then he said, 'So... you're heading back to Candlebark. Does that mean you're selling this house?'

'No, I'm going to hang on to it,' I said. 'It'll be handy for the occasional weekend in Melbourne.'

'Occasional.'

'I thought I might take Mia to visit my mother now and then.' I grinned. 'You could come along. She likes you.'

He laughed out loud. 'She'd make one hell of a mother-in-law.' As soon as he realised what he'd said, his neck and face flushed a brilliant red.

'I think you're safe,' I said. 'From her, at least.' And felt the blood rush to my own face.

His mobile phone shrieked and he took it out of his pocket, checking the screen. No doubt he'd be leaving in a minute. But he pushed a button and turned it off, returning it to his pocket. 'Now, where were we?' he said.

ACKNOWLEDGEMENTS

I remember my mum reading crime fiction from the sixpence borrowing library when I was very young – maybe that's where it started. Or with my high school teacher, Kay Boese, who gave me dozens of books from her shelves including plenty by Mickey Spillane, Raymond Chandler and Ed McBain. But the writing? The people I want to thank are Tracey Rolfe and Western Women Writers, my longtime writing group, and then Lucia Nardo and Demet Divaroren from Big Fish. Workshopping is only part of it – it's the support and encouragement and the 'keep going' from all of you (and the cakes). My email writing companion, Kristi Holl, has been amazing support as well. This book probably would not have seen publication without the CWA Debut Dagger Award. I'd been dreaming of entering for a few years, and then I did it, thanks to a kick up the rear end from Craig Harper. I entered initially because I was hoping for a judges' report that could help me improve the manuscript. Instead, the publicity led to people asking to read it, and here we are. Thank you, CWA!

My thanks also to members of Victoria Police who have helped me in different ways. Firstly, Detective Senior Constable Howard Beer (ret.) who endured all of my questions in the early days (and still is with vast patience), and then Senior Constable Mark Boysen and Klute at the Victoria Police Dog Squad in Attwood, Victoria; Senior Constable Shane Flynn (ret.); Senior Constable Roger Barr; Constable Simon Robertson and Ben, New Zealand Police. You may not see their fingerprints so much in this novel but you will in the next! Special thanks also to Dr Sandra Neate who answers all of my questions, no matter how gruesome. Any mistakes are about the plot, not their advice and assistance.

Thank you to the people at Verve Books – Katherine and Clare – who were so keen right from the start and provided great feedback for the last rewrite. And my agent, Brian Cook, who is probably still scratching his head over my left turn back into crime writing after all the years of writing children's books.

This looks like a major left turn, but *Trust Me, I'm Dead* has been ten years in the making, with at least eight rewrites. I'm yet to find the box that holds the little news magazine cutting that started it all. I will one day.

Thank you, Lesley and John, for always cheering me on. Finally, thank you, Brian McCabe, for putting up with the mess, the eyes glazing over as I 'disappear' yet again, and all those walks to the library to return yet another overdue book.

To be the first to hear about new books and exclusive deals
from Verve Books, sign up to our newsletters:
vervebooks.co.uk/signup

**VERVE
BOOKS**

About the Author

Sherryl Clark has been writing for children for the past 20 years while harbouring a secret vice – writing crime for adults. She lives in Melbourne, Australia where she teaches creative writing to all ages, mainly adults at Polytech, and works as a freelance editor and manuscript assessor. She believes you can never own too many books – you just need more bookshelves.

Follow Sherryl on Twitter @sherrylwriter